WAYWARD SONS

A JERRY SNYDER NOVEL

Caribbean Mystery Series
Volume 1

WAYNE STINNETT
and
STEWART MATTHEWS

Copyright © 2021
Published by DOWN ISLAND PRESS, 2021
Beaufort, SC

Copyright © 2021 by Wayne Stinnett and Stewart Matthews
Print Edition

Library of Congress cataloging-in-publication Data
Stinnett, Wayne
Matthews, Stewart
Wayward Sons/Wayne Stinnett and Stewart Matthews
p. cm. – (A Jerry Snyder novel)

ISBN: 978-1-7356231-6-0 (print)

Cover photograph by Lunamarina
Graphics and Interior Design by Aurora Publicity
Edited by The Write Touch
Final Proofreading by Donna Rich
Audiobook Narration by Nick Sullivan

This is a work of fiction. Names, characters, and incidents are either the product of the author's imagination or are used fictitiously. Any resemblance to actual persons, living or dead, businesses, companies, events, or locales is entirely coincidental. Most of the locations herein are also fictional or are used fictitiously. However, the author takes great pains to depict the location and description of the many well-known islands, locales, beaches, reefs, bars, and restaurants throughout the Florida Keys and the Caribbean to the best of his ability.

Dedicated to the voices of the voiceless.

"I am the voice of the voiceless; Through me the dumb shall speak. Till the deaf world's ears be made to hear. The wrongs of the wordless weak. And I am my brothers keeper, And I will fight his fights; And speak the words for beast and bird. Till the world shall set things right."

–Ella Wheeler Wilcox

If you'd like to receive my newsletter,
please sign up on my website:
WWW.WAYNESTINNETT.COM.
Every two weeks, I'll bring you insights into my private life and writing habits, with updates on what I'm working on, special deals I hear about, and new books by other authors that I'm reading.

FROM WAYNE STINNETT

The Charity Styles Caribbean Thriller Series
Merciless Charity
Ruthless Charity
Reckless Charity
Enduring Charity
Vigilant Charity

The Jesse McDermitt Caribbean Adventure Series
by Wayne Stinnett

Fallen Out
Fallen Palm
Fallen Hunter
Fallen Pride
Fallen Mangrove
Fallen King
Fallen Honor
Fallen Tide
Fallen Angel
Fallen Hero
Rising Storm
Rising Fury

Rising Force
Rising Charity
Rising Water
Rising Spirit
Rising Thunder
Rising Warrior
Rising Moon
Rising Tide

Coming this fall
Steady as She Goes

FROM STEWART MATTHEWS

The Detective Shannon Rourke Series

Chicago Blood
Chicago Broken
Chicago Betrayed
Chicago Lies
Chicago Creed

The Barrett Mason Series

Matador
Tyrant
Jackal
Ghosts
Wardogs
Red Star

WEBSITE: https://www.smwrites.com

THE GASPAR'S REVENGE SHIP'S STORE IS OPEN.

There, you can purchase all kinds of swag as well as Autographed copies of Wayne Stinnett's books.

WWW.GASPARS-REVENGE.COM

Visit Stewart Matthews website at

WWW.SMWRITES.COM

MAPS

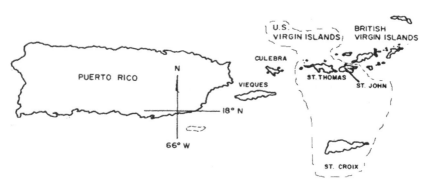

Puerto Rico and the Virgin Islands

El Caribe

PROLOGUE

Living this life, you've got to play your part. You can't bait a man, unless you let him think he set the hook. If he doesn't believe you're the ten-foot marlin he's been angling for all his life—the one he can show to his buddies when his wife is bored and looking the other way—he'll cut and run.

That's the game. It's played the other way. Ain't no such thing as a fisher*woman*. You're here to get caught, so you can't let him know you're actually the one angling him. You get too eager, he's gone. You try to take too much off him, he'll know it. But if you act like he caught you, you can slice him right, and you'll be feeding your family with chunks of him for a good long while. If you're real good, he won't even feel the knife slipping through.

Amalis Jules had learned the techniques long before she'd ever sat down at the cabana bar at the Wild Life Resort on Zoni Beach. This was a damned good fishing spot, but not one you came to on your first day out. No, you needed experience. Especially on a day like today, when the fish were out, and she needed a big catch. No baitfish, no broke boys. She wasn't in for charity. In this world, if you did something good, you didn't do it for free.

She let her line hang loose. Sipped her rum drink, listening to the waves loving the sand, then sneaking away. Soon enough, a man would come, swearing up and down he was gonna charm this beautiful black girl into bed. He was gonna tempt her with private cabanas and champagne baths, just flapping that tongue deeper onto the hook.

They'd pay for overstepping. Everybody did.

Mommy, in her own way, had warned Amalis about boys overstepping. When Amalis was a little girl back home, Mommy had told her about those Temple Yard boys smoking herb out back of the artists' stalls, stashing joints under their arms when the policemen walked by, singeing the few hairs they'd grown. Amalis grinned at the thought of how they'd tried to bait her all the time, their little hands grasping for her skinny-girl body and talking like they were all grown men, and not kids.

If Mommy knew what she did now, she would've let them. Then they'd have to repay her before she cut line and let those boys go free.

She remembered one little boy, Ras-Under. He looked older than the rest, but he must have been a year or two younger than Amalis. Had a shine in his face nobody could snatch out. Always getting into trouble, the way boys that age did.

One morning before school, when she was helping Grand-mama stock her spot in Cheapside, she saw a policeman get Ras-Under. Grabbed him by the shirt collar. Yelled at him about smoking on the street, said he was gonna scare the tourists, but everybody from Temple Yard smoked there—even Amalis, and she lived in Whitepark. Ras-Under was a skinny boy with a ball of dreads bigger than his head. He talked back. Them dreads didn't do nothing when that policeman's baton cracked him. He screamed. Blood came down his face.

All day at school, Amalis had thought on Ras-Under, his white teeth flashing against his lips, red with his own blood. She knew Grandmama saw, but she didn't speak on it. Supposing she hadn't seen it, she had to have heard it.

"Why did that policeman bust Ras-Under's head?" she'd asked Grandmama later that day, when Amalis was sitting in the hot, sticky kitchen, helping Mommy cut up Grandmama's mangoes for frying.

"He overstepped," was all Grandmama said.

But that didn't seem no answer. Yet, when Mommy spoke, her knife tapping the cutting board, she'd nodded. "He overstepped."

For ten years, Amalis peeled at Grandmama's words in her head, hoping some sense would come out.

Sense came when a white tourist boy got her pregnant. He promised her the whole world. Said she could leave Bridgetown on his pretty white sloop, and they'd be together on the seas that she loved, with their baby rocked by the waves all night and day. They'd love each other under moonlight, and they'd come back this way whenever she wanted to see Mommy and Grandmama. A month before baby Lawrence came, that white boy sailed to Miami.

Amalis's baby boy was five now, and he ain't never seen his white papa. He only ever been as far away from Bridgetown as they were today, living on Culebra.

Hard not to be mad at Lawrence's papa all the time. But when Amalis wanted to scream northward, hoping that scared boy would hear it, she remembered the two gifts he gave her.

First being Lawrence, and second, helping her understand what Grandmama meant. He overstepped.

From that lesson, she learned how the white tourist men would chase her if she looked right, if she wore her hair like a white girl, and how she could catch them for overstepping.

Before the last catch went back to San Juan, then to his job and his family in Indianapolis, Amalis got enough to feed her and Lawrence. Some rent money from the man, a finder's fee out of the pocket of a charter captain she brought her men to, and she re-sold the jewels he gave her to a Japanese couple on the street for twice what them stones was worth.

A few years back, a catch that size would've kept her and Lawrence going about a month, but she'd taught herself how to survive better than most—which she found her pride in.

On this night at the resort bar, that money would be gone in three weeks, which put Amalis out angling.

Coral eyeliner was a good lure. Caught a certain type of man's eye. Rich man. Tired of his boring wife. Man looking for a slender, big-eyed, dark-skinned black girl, filling out a bikini the way his woman never did.

Like Amalis.

And just like Ras-Under, they'd overstepped. Wanting something they never should've had.

At that resort bar in Culebra, Amalis felt one swimming up beside her. He was a cool old man, with white, thinning hair parted near the side of his head, blue eyes, dancing and sort of wild. His spine hunched near his neck, and when he reached into his pocket and slid a few bills to the bartender, his crooked fingers bent the money around his thumb.

He wore a diamond-encrusted wedding band, and he was tall,

even with his hooked spine. Flashed a handsome smile when the bartender took his money. If that man was forty years younger, she might reel him in and let him keep her company for free. But, no, all the kindness she had for strangers was gutted from her.

She was what she was. No apologizing.

"Why would anyone come to a bar alone?" His voice was like the leather on her favorite pair of sandals, the thong worked and worn soft against the insides of her toes, and the soles massaged her heels.

"For the drinks." Amalis wrapped her lips around the straw and sucked up a ball of rum and pineapple juice from her painkiller. His pupils widened as he watched her. "Ain't no other reason why."

"Oh, no," he said with a grin. The bartender slid a chilled glass of rum into his hand, the ice cubes chattering. "You can get a drink at home. You could kick your feet up on the coffee table, maybe sit in your underwear if you please—with nobody around to stop you from smoking a joint. Sounds far more relaxing than sitting at a bar if all you want is a drink."

Amalis turned her shoulders more his way, then leaned forward a touch, letting him take a look at the goods. This bikini halter top set her girls just right, made a man feel like he was getting a sneak peek before the real show.

"Suppose it's the idea of meeting someone new, then," she said. "Even if I don't, sitting out here alone is better scenery than sitting at home." She nodded to her right, away from him and toward the surf, where the water broke the reflections of the bar's lights into glimmering schools.

He smiled. He knew the game. Then, with a look, he motioned behind her. "Some scenery."

She looked over her shoulder. At a table outside the cabana, a man about twice Amalis's age, dipped in the orange glow of tiki torches, was letting it all hang out. His flabby belly touched the tops of his thighs and his chest jiggled as he used a credit card to chop out a line of coke.

The topless lady sitting across from him squealed in delight and clapped her hands, her tits like a pair of old basketballs. She bent over the table and snorted the whole damned thing.

Amalis shook her head and laughed, then took a drink.

"See what I mean?" the old man said. "It's a hell of a lot more interesting than Jimmy Fallon."

"I guess I come here for more than looking at the water."

"It's a fine place," he said. "People here aren't afraid to be honest. Unlike folks walking around most places, nobody here pretends that they've got some code, some morality, that they'll die following—when they know, and I know, and you probably know, their morality comes off like a wedding ring when it suits them."

He looked at her like he wanted an answer.

Rich man acted like he wanted to hear what a girl like Amalis had to say, but he didn't. She'd open her mouth and overstep. He'd get mad and pull himself free, and all that time she spent wouldn't get her nothing. What he really wanted was a pretty girl to be that wife he never had—the one who don't spend his money, who's sweet and rubs his feet while he talking about how hard a rich man got it.

"You right," she said in agreement. Then, took a sip. "People lying all day, every day."

"Liars, all of 'em." He took a drink from his rum and curled his lip back like a stray dog. "You shouldn't ever let some Puritan asshole tell you how to feel, Miss—"

"Amalis." She offered her hand to him. He scooped it up, then kissed her knuckles, leaving a wet spot behind.

"Jacob Sherman," he said, looking her up and down. She felt his eyes prodding her bare shoulders, her stomach, her naked thighs, the tops of her feet. "God, if you aren't the finest creature I've laid eyes on in years. Would you do me the favor of accompanying me back to my villa?"

She laughed.

"I've got a bottle of champagne being chilled as we speak. Vintage 1918—the last year of The Great War. It was liberated from Marshal Philippe Pétain's personal stock in Vichy at the end of World War II. I've been looking for someone unique to share it with."

"What about your wife?" She touched his wedding band with a look.

"What about her? After what I said, you think I'd enter a marriage where the both of us were expected to hold up some medieval idea of honor? Marriage is financial. She and I both understand and respect that."

Not that Jacob being a kept man would have stopped Amalis, anyway.

"I'm not going to your villa," she said. "But I don't want to stay here. Buy me a new drink." Her painkiller was half-finished.

"Bartender," Jacob said without breaking eye contact. "Bring my new friend a fresh drink."

"Right away, Mr. Sherman." The bartender got to work.

"I'm not doing you," Amalis said with a grin. She held Jacob's eye contact.

He wasn't shook. "There's little point in getting physical with a man my age. I've learned to get everything I need through good conversation." He finished his rum and smacked his glass on the bar.

A few minutes later, they walked onto the beach together, toward the water. Amalis held onto the pit of his elbow with one hand, her drink in the other. He didn't lean on her for support. Didn't tilt side to side like some old folks. He walked like a man about to get laid, but she didn't slap him back for it. Amalis knew that was just the way this cocky old bastard walked.

They came to a cabana topped with palm fronds; the frame draped in a linen that was tied back around each of the four posts. One of a couple dozen on the beach. Under the canopy, a bed with a few pillows, which might as well have condoms sitting on them.

Amalis fell back, her drink sloshing over the cup's rim and dribbling off the Scotchgarded fabric covering the bed. She stretched out, then propped herself up on one elbow. Jacob slumped down in the moonlight, sitting halfway on the bed, and halfway off.

Somewhere behind her a woman giggled, then moaned.

"You're younger than most of the people who come to a place like this." His eyes were hidden under shadows, but his crow's feet bunched up. "You know that, don't you?"

She shrugged. "Ain't the first time I found myself in a club like this one."

"My girlfriend is about your age."

'Course this man has a wife and a girlfriend, she thought, *and he's still out here, chasing tail.*

Overstepped.

"Oh, so you got a girlfriend now, too?" Amalis grinned at

him, teasing.

"A man has needs. Neither she nor I are deluding ourselves. What exists in our partnership is not love. She looks good on my arm when I want to make an impression, but she's not free."

"Why didn't you bring her tonight?"

"Eager to meet her?"

Amalis laughed and could tell Jacob was letting the vibe get into him. Kept stepping closer.

"She never wants to come to places like this. She's young, still has hang-ups." He scratched the side of his face, then brought his other leg onto the bed, bending his knee with his hands, now facing her. "That's what I like about you, Amalis. When I saw you at the bar, I wondered what kind of woman I was looking at—were you lost, or were you here because you wanted to be? I quickly found you were more beautiful, strong, and confident than I could have ever imagined."

When her cheeks flushed, she thanked God they were in the dark. Man had charm, wasn't no denying that.

"You got some tricks, don't you?" She tugged the short sleeves of his shirt, like she was looking for a wand and said, "Are you like this with all the girls you meet?"

"Only the ones I like."

She patted his shirt's pocket. Felt something small in there, like pebbles. She dipped her fingers in and before she pulled out a tiny plastic baggie, she knew she'd find pills.

"This your Viagra?"

"No, my sweet girl, that's something called 2C-B. Have you ever heard of it?"

"Not a catchy name." She couldn't see them, only feel they were small and round, not diamond-shaped.

"True. Some people call it Nexus, but I personally find that name to be trite. Tries too hard." He took the baggie from her, opened it up, then, against the stars behind him, she saw his palm tap his open mouth. He chased the pill with a swig of his rum. "It's a hell of a lot more fun than the name makes it sound, believe me."

"That right?"

"If you sit quietly and enjoy the trip, you'll experience beauty like you never thought possible. All the people on the beach, all the fish on the water, the stars in the sky—you'll see the whole world exhaling."

Now that was something Amalis ain't ever seen. Her adult life was spent breathing in, and in, always looking for more air, feeding the tightness beneath her ribs, holding her breath while her feet stepped back and forth across the line.

"All right. You got me." She put out her palm. "How long this stuff supposed to last?"

"That's the best part," he said, as the bag crinkled. "Only an hour or two. Then you're back on your way."

He pressed the pill onto the tip of her finger. A little thing. Smaller than it felt through the fabric of his shirt. She popped it, let it rest on her tongue. It tasted like nothing. She chased it down with her drink.

Nothing happened. Not yet. Probably took a minute to kick in.

Amalis flopped on her back and watched the stars poke through the tattered palm fronds at the edge of the cabana's roof.

"Where you find this stuff, anyhow?"

"Kingston," he answered. "My girlfriend and I attended a club her friend told her about. It was the best kind of place—

steamy in the night, full of people, the drinks hard enough to singe your nose hairs. I saw these kids on the dance floor doing that dance they do. You know, where the fella picks up the girl and spins her around like he's trying to knock the walls down with her head while he has sex with her."

"Daggerin'."

"Yes, that." He chuckled to himself. "People doing that cleared the dance floor. Except for one group of kids, standing near a corner, dancing with each other like they didn't have a care in the world. Reminded me of my younger days. I knew they were on something.

"Anyway, I went to the bathroom, and I found out what it was." He flicked the baggie. "That was a year ago, and 2C-B has been my drug of choice since then. I nearly broke my knee dancing at that club."

"So, this stuff make you hyper?"

"Not at all. It enhances your perceptions. You'll feel some euphoria, as well. It's a bit like a mixture of a low dose of LSD and Ecstasy. You'll feel the effects most acutely in an hour. We could go back to the bar while we wait for it to kick in?"

Amalis lifted her head and looked behind her, toward the bar. That woman with the basketball titties was laid across it, her naked man, and two new guys, doing body shots off her.

"No, thanks."

"I'm glad you said that." He raised himself up, his back hooked, and reached a hand to Amalis. She sat up and took it.

"Nothing matches the experience of feeling the water on your feet when the 2C-B takes effect."

He waddled her to the water's edge, where they sat in the wet sand, and the cold slapped her on the ass. She would've walked

11

most times, but she'd lose a night's work if she cut bait now. She let him snake his arm around her back and plant his hand near her butt.

"Don't be getting any closer," Amalis said.

"You should know I'm a perfect gentleman."

She raised her eyebrows, giving him a doubtful look. Not too many perfect gentlemen popped pills with girls less than half their age.

"I know what you're thinking," he said. "The drugs don't disqualify me."

They talked for a while after that. He told her all about his personal business. His wife, his girlfriend, how he made money as a banker, buying businesses in trouble, then cleaning them out for all they was worth.

He had money. All she had to do was keep jiggling her lure, make him think he charmed her—which wasn't hard to fake. Being on Zoni Beach in Culebra helped. The white sands, the warm night breeze, coqui chirping in the brush—even a talking pile of garbage couldn't mess this up.

Best of all was the night sky. Up there, Amalis saw her baby boy's eyes, lit up with light and love while he blew out the candles at his fifth birthday. The stars were clearer than she'd ever seen them, full of whites, blues, pinks, greens—things she didn't know existed out there in the vastness of God's eternity.

"You're feeling new sensations," Jacob said.

She looked at him, not scared, but surprised. Feeling like he'd walked past her cracked bedroom door and stopped to marvel at her beauty. She wasn't ashamed.

"You have tears in your eyes, darling." He reached up and wiped them away. The ends of his fingers were alight with joy, and when she looked into his face, she forgot about angling and overstepping and all that mess she'd come here to smear on him.

He was beautiful. This moment was beautiful. The closer his face came to hers, the more she wanted him to come closer still. His lips met hers, and she fell back onto the sand, each granule tingling her skin, rolling her into endless joy and love.

He started working at the knot of bikini string behind her head. Without breaking her mouth from his, she moved his fingers aside, then pulled the knot loose. His hands slid up her body, leaving pleasure in their wake.

The water caressed her feet. The tightness in Amalis had been chased out by lightness. She no longer saw a line to overstep. Here, on Zoni Beach, all those things she cared about and fought for left with the tide, out to sea.

A hand brushed her ankle. She didn't open her eyes but pulled her mouth from Jacob's.

"Tell your friend I don't get down like that," she said, as he kissed her neck.

"What?"

She sat up on her elbows, opening her eyes, seeing the rainbows swirling around the stars, the water, the beach, and Jacob, alone.

The waves came in again, and she felt the hand on the bottom of her foot. Then it flopped up onto her thigh. Her skin said it was both warm and chilly cold.

"What the hell?" She sat up fully. A billowy white thing played in the surf at her feet. A plastic bag, or… "Tell me that ain't your shirt."

No, he still had it on. She squinted and saw a man's hand, limp, and dancing in the water. A dead man.

She didn't hear herself scream.

CHAPTER ONE

A man is most dangerous when he's desperate. As a cop, I'd learned that lesson through blood and bruises and dead co-workers. I kept it in mind as we marched into Robert Beck's office.

When I was a kid, I thought I knew what desperation was—from hearing my dad's stories about businessmen and bankers coming to him with moths in their pockets, begging him to keep their doors open, or to snap up a property dragging down their books.

I didn't know a thing.

My early years were spent growing up in SoCal with the proverbial silver spoon in my mouth. My grandfather had gotten into real estate when the counties around L.A. were cheap, and Dad carried the business forward. I was next up, but by the time I hit high school, I wanted nothing more than to get away from private schools, travel soccer teams, and month-long chalet rentals in Aspen.

I enlisted in the Air Force, thinking that might clue Mom and Dad in to how I really felt. When I finished my service overseas,

Dad asked me when I was going to take over Snyder & Burkhart Holdings. I gave him his answer when I became a cop.

Now, I'm married, in my mid-thirties, and out of law enforcement—officially, at least. This new life that lay ahead of me took me to a place I'd never expected—somewhere far away from my family's hometown, Newport Beach.

I'd moved to St. Thomas and started work as an investigator for the Armstrong organization, which brought me to where I was now: facing down a desperate, dangerous man.

My partner, DJ, and I might have had Robert Beck penned into his big, leather chair, behind an even bigger walnut desk, and he might've worn a disarmingly bewildered smile, but above those charming fangs, the slick bastard had the venomous eyes of a cornered rattlesnake.

A lot of people had Beck pegged as an okay guy, but DJ and I knew better. It was our job to know better.

Beck was the director of The Cruz Bay Villages—a retirement community that came close to having more yachts than residents. He treated white-haired ladies to steak and Maine lobster dinners—not cheap in the Virgin Islands. How many grams of meth bought a filet mignon on St. John? Because Beck's salary as director wasn't paying for it. He made his *real* money slinging dope. DJ and I had figured out his small part in one of the biggest meth-smuggling operations I'd ever heard of.

My partner and I came at things from different angles, but we'd both known Beck was dirty. DJ was a former Army Ranger and approached obstacles with a "strike fast and hit hard" attitude, no easy task for a man missing a leg. Being a pararescueman and former police detective, I preferred to use methodical, legal means to an end.

Nobody could say that DJ Martin and Jerry Snyder didn't get things done. This was our second assignment together and pretty soon we'd have a 2-0 record.

"Wipe that smile off your face, Beck," I said. "You thought you'd never see our happy asses again."

Beck blinked at me, then looked over at DJ. "Mr. Snyder, Mr. Martin—good morning to the both of you. What brings you back to my office?"

"You already know. And you could at least do DJ and me the courtesy of not pretending we're busting up Mr. Rogers's neighborhood."

The man's eyes hardened, his focus sharpening. The gee-golly-shucks-church-bingo smile didn't leave his face, but it did little to dull his eyes.

"All your talk of being a family at Cruz Bay, of caring about your residents, telling their kids how good their folks have it here. That was the biggest pile of bull I ever witnessed," I said. "But stepping on old ladies to make your money? That is truly something else—and I've seen a lot."

"Yeah," DJ added, "Jerry was a cop, so he knows a thing or two about stepping on the little guy."

Beck chuckled.

I cut DJ an unamused look. No verbal snipes. Not now.

"Gentlemen," Beck began. "I'm not sure what to make of all this. Are you suggesting I'm involved in something… unscrupulous?"

"Just tell us who's supplying the meth," I said.

"Mr. Snyder—" Beck twisted his chair, as if he meant to stand up. I stepped to the left of the desk, and clapped my hand to his shoulder, keeping him planted. He got the message.

"I haven't the faintest clue what you're talking about," he said. "If you think I'm some kind of drug kingpin, I can assure you I'm quite busy keeping all of my residents active—it's a full-time job and then some, as either of my assistants will tell you. If I had extra time, I assure you it would be used toward leisure, not wasted on running some kind of drug empire."

"At least we agree in part." I bent down; my face was level with Beck's. I wanted to see that hardened edge in his eyes shatter—I wanted to take that moment in and commit it to memory. "You're not the top dog in your outfit—he wouldn't have made the mistake you did."

I looked him up and down; nice suit, gold pinky ring with seven inlaid diamonds, creased trousers, and leather loafers. I grinned. "You tried to buy yourself into the position, though. But we both know you're not all that important."

A tinge of indignation dragged the corners of Beck's lips downward, but his eyes kept their cutting gaze. "Maybe not in your estimation," he said. "But I am an important man to the people here. And I don't appreciate having my time wasted by you gentlemen."

I stood up straight, looking down my nose at him. I wanted Beck to feel small—even smaller than he was. "Maybe you are, Mr. Beck—we couldn't care less about how popular your shuffleboard nights are. But you're only a couple of kilos above a street dealer in the dope game. That's my read, anyway—because in the busts I've seen and the gangs I've staked out, the guys that have all those fancy cars and gold jewelry and caviar dinners aren't the guys at the top." I winked at DJ. "No, I think Mister-Mercedes-and-Italian-Loafers here"—I kicked the bottom of his shoe "—he knows he isn't important. That's why he's gotta try so damned hard to make others think he is."

I stepped back and looked him over again. Summing up my thoughts, I concluded with an air of finality, "You handle logistics. You're a delivery man—UPS for meth wholesalers in Haiti, Cuba, the BVI—all across the Northern Caribbean. Your link in the chain moves the drugs in small amounts from here to your distribution partners over in San Juan, and you charge bottom dollar to do it."

"Kinda sad when you put it that way," DJ chimed in, smirking.

"You aren't wrong there, partner," I said. "Taking down this maggot was barely worth getting out of bed."

"I haven't done any of the things you're accusing me of," Beck said, but the flop sweat on his forehead and his fluttering eyelids seemed to say otherwise.

DJ laughed and Beck's eyes sliced in his direction for a moment, then back to me.

"Let's see how long you hold out when the police arrive. With lies sounding that flimsy, Beck's gonna have dinner at the jail on St. Croix," I said to DJ.

"This is getting sadder, man," DJ responded, shaking his head.

Beck didn't flinch. I didn't imagine he would. Not yet, anyway. Even the worst of them clutched their lies tight as a rosary while they pleaded silently for God to bring his mighty finger down and smush the law like gnats.

When he realized that wasn't going to happen, he'd crack—whether it was here, inside a jail cell, or in an interrogation room with the macho DEA guys going chest-to-chest with him. Most of the people I'd apprehended over the years didn't admit to anything until they had their freedom taken from them, even if it was just a temporary holding cell. Especially men like Beck, who couldn't handle confinement, even for just a few days. They rolled over and cut a deal to save their own asses.

"You don't want the police thinking you've lied to them. That'll only piss them off. The best way to have this out is to tell me and DJ everything you've ever done."

Beck bristled at the idea. He was too proud to take the lifeline I threw.

"You're sure you don't want to talk to us?" I asked.

"What is there to talk about? I haven't done a thing."

"Hey, Dep?" DJ jerked his head to his left. His long goatee, stiff with sea-salt, moved with his head. He wanted a chat with me, and I already knew what about.

On the boat ride over, DJ had voiced some dissent about my arrest strategy. I waved him off, assuring him everything would go smoothly, so long as we appeared united. I hoped he'd listen to me, and forget whatever idea percolated in his head.

Now wasn't a great time for a debate.

My partner had no law-enforcement experience, and it showed. You didn't hash things out when you were the only two guys in the room with a dope smuggler. You detained the perp first and talked out a change in strategy after.

In private.

DJ cleared his throat again. He wouldn't let it go. He never let anything go. If I brushed him off now, I'd pay for it later.

I pointed at Beck. "You *can* stay still for me, can't you Mr. Beck?"

He didn't move, just glared. He was as petulant as a third grader.

"There you go," I said with a big smile. "Just like that."

I stepped three paces sideways, away from his desk. Close enough that if he were armed, my long legs could eliminate the gap and get the gun away from him before he fired. Far enough that he couldn't hear me and DJ whispering.

DJ came around the desk. Below his cargo shorts, his titanium right leg gleamed in the sunlight coming through the window overlooking Cruz Bay. When he got within whispering distance, I smelled the beer seeping from his pores. I hadn't noticed it this morning when he'd picked me up on his boat, *Reel Fun*.

I was becoming accustomed to the smell.

"I know you're not used to the way I do things yet," I whispered to DJ, "but you have to roll with me on this. Now isn't a great time to discuss the finer points of our strategy with Beck."

"Now's the only time we've got," DJ said, a little too loudly.

I grabbed him by the arm and led him another step away from Beck's desk. He rolled his eyes at me.

"We talked about this," I hissed. "The DEA can get the information we need out of him. When they find out we caught Beck dead-to-rights with his hand in the cookie jar, they're going to lean on him hard. You just show them those pictures you snapped, and they'll want to find out who his supplier is. They'll throw everything they can at him, and since he's trafficking from one U.S. island territory to another, this whole thing is federal. As soon as Uncle Sam looks him in the eye, he'll blink. Guys like him always do."

"Man, you're believing your own bullshit," DJ said. "Look, I know I agreed to do this your way, but I just had another think about the way we're going here. Beck's loaded, Jerry. And he's connected to somebody—we both know that. He'll have lawyers crawling up every orifice Uncle Sam has."

I pinched my lips together. I could've done without that imagery.

"And even if he ends up in prison," DJ continued, "it'll be a Hilton. Guys like him don't do time the way some crack-dealing bum off the street does. That ain't the way the world works."

DJ's cynicism grated on me. Ever since the day we'd started working together, I could see that his attitude didn't jibe with mine. I clenched my jaw and looked away from Beck for a second. When my eyes set back onto him, he smirked. The rift between DJ and me was too obvious to hide.

"This wannabe Scarface was sewing meth packets into old ladies' day bags," I said. "And you want to what—kick his teeth in before you ask him to sing? No way, DJ. That's not happening. The cops are taking him."

"You know that's how it has to be, Dep?" DJ's whispering became strained. "But you know what? You do what you want. Tell him about jail time and the feds and whatever other Boy Scout crap is pulling the wool over your eyes. See if he talks about who's paying him. I'm gonna stick to reality."

He turned and went back to the other side of Beck's desk. I didn't care to stop him—I didn't need to get the last word in, because I was right.

And we were doing this my way.

"Hey, Beck," DJ barked. "There a bathroom behind that door?"

He pointed at a partially open door in the wall behind and to the right of Beck's desk.

"Uh, yes, there is," Beck answered.

"Good. I'm gonna take a leak." DJ said, as he walked to the

door. With his back to me, he thumbed in my direction. "Deputy Snyder over there, is gonna take you in for questioning."

Beck looked from DJ to me, furrowing his brow, and holding back a chuckle.

I could've skinned DJ alive.

Instead, I approached Beck's desk. Before we hopped off DJ's boat, I'd shoved a pair of handcuffs in the back pocket of my jeans. I ripped them out and dangled them right at Beck's eye level.

"Are you actually a deputy?" Beck asked.

"No," I snapped back at him. "But if you don't tell us who your supplier is, these handcuffs are going on your wrists, and you're gonna meet a couple of DEA agents. Once they see what DJ and I have on you, you're going to jail for a long, long time."

Beck laughed, threw his head back, and wrapped his arms around his pot belly. Then he looked me in the eye and smiled. "You're serious?"

I held his eye contact.

"Well, Mr. Snyder, you're welcome to call the police on me, but in the long run, I think you'll be extremely disappointed. I'll admit, right here, right now—you and Mr. Martin have done a fine job of getting to the bottom of this whole thing. I am exactly what you suspect—though I'm more important to our operation than you believe.

"To be frank, I'm surprised you managed to figure it out. I assumed the two of you were nothing more than an air-head surfer-boy and a beer-soaked conch looking to squeeze a few dollars out of someone by pretending to be investigators." He smiled and interlaced his fingers, resting his hands on his stomach. "But I'm afraid this investigation goes no further. I won't give anyone up. I'm not a rat. I'll happily sit in whichever federal penitentiary I'm confined to. And I'll keep my mouth shut the entire time."

Dammit. DJ'd guessed right.

"We'll see." I stepped around the corner of his desk and slapped one of the cuffs on his right wrist. "Guys like you talk a big talk, but—"

The bathroom door suddenly swept violently inward, like it was being sucked out of an airplane at altitude. DJ leapt out on his good leg, holding his prosthetic high over his head like a sledgehammer. In one quick motion he swung it down toward Beck, who moved to shield himself with his arms.

I jerked on the handcuffs, trying to yank Beck away. But DJ was deceptively quick. All I managed to do was pull Beck's right arm out of the way of the crashing blow.

DJ's fake leg smashed into Beck's left forearm, making a popping noise—like the muffled sound of a tree branch snapping in a hurricane.

The force behind DJ's swing propelled his fake leg downward, past Beck's broken arm. The leg stopped only when it bashed into Beck's lap, sending him spilling from the chair, and ripping the other end of the handcuffs from my grip.

Beck hit the floor, face down, howling in pain.

But that wasn't good enough for DJ. He hopped closer to Beck and brought the leg up again, eager to smash him to a pulp.

I bounded over Beck, wrapping one arm around DJ as my other hand flew upward, catching his wrist and stopping him from making a bigger mess than he already had.

"Jesus, DJ!" I screamed at him. "What the hell are the police going to say?"

"Screw the damned cops!" he yelled back at me. DJ twisted around, trying to get free of me—and he almost did. But I let myself sink backward until I leaned against the door frame, which took his one leg out from under him. Without a base to stand on, he couldn't fight me.

"You're a fool, Dep!" Anger coiled up behind his face. "Laws don't work on guys like him, and you're kidding yourself if you think they do!"

I began to say something back when I saw Beck's reflection in the bathroom mirror over DJ's shoulder. He was writhing on the floor and reaching upward, trying to grab something under his desk.

With one quick motion, I shoved DJ aside, and dove on Beck. He howled like a wounded mountain cat, then bit his tongue as a snub-nosed .38 Special spilled from his right hand and thumped across the floor.

I scrambled to my feet and snatched up the revolver, then turned to face the both of them.

DJ used Beck's desk to pull himself to his foot. I stared long and hard at him. On the trip over, we'd discussed the importance of handling Beck with cool heads. We were coming into his office, and he was likely armed, which meant we were at a deadly disadvantage, and any escalation could be a bigger problem for us than it would be for Beck.

"What the hell was that?" I screamed at DJ. "Were you going to knock the poor bastard's brains out, then ask his corpse questions? You swore to me you wouldn't pull any cowboy junk!"

The man only had one leg; surely, he knew he'd get smoked in a straight-up fight. And I didn't want to call our handler to explain how DJ got hurt on my watch.

24

"You can take the cowboy out of Texas—" DJ started to say.

"You're not even from Texas," I spat back, exasperated.

He shrugged. Then, with one hand on the desk to steady himself, he hopped toward Beck and stood over him. He wielded the prosthetic like a sword, holding it by the titanium shaft above the ankle and pointing the cup down at Beck's throat.

"Mr. Beck, I think you might wanna tell us who you're smuggling that glass for."

"Go to hell," Beck hissed. "I'm not a rat! I won't give up anybody! You want to ask me a question? You have to ask my lawyer first!"

DJ chuckled. Using his prosthetic, he prodded Beck's broken arm. He only touched him lightly—barely a nudge, and on the upper arm, nowhere near where the bones had snapped. Still, Beck let out another tomcat howl.

"I don't see your lawyer in this room right now. You don't wanna give me lip, man." DJ grinned at him, his teeth looking white as fresh milk against his coffee-colored goatee. "I ain't no cop. Just a busted-up door kicker. You should see how the mujahideen interrogate—they gave a man like me a lot of interesting ideas."

When Beck didn't immediately answer, DJ crooked his elbow, pulling the leg back for a second jab.

"Bonaire!" Beck shouted.

DJ froze. He looked at me and his smile widened.

I took a deep breath through my nose, fighting back the urge to sock him. DJ and I had only worked together for a month and change, though I'd known him for a couple of years. But he already got under my skin in a way nobody else in my life ever had.

"Be specific," I said to Beck. "Name somebody."

"I don't have any names," Beck said. "I swear! But you'll find them just outside Rincón. They have a lab in the national park. It's underground."

"Now, that," DJ said, the grin still plastered across his face, "is very specific."

CHAPTER TWO

The cops picked Beck up without much trouble. The arresting officer asked about his arm and DJ told him that Beck had fallen. I stayed quiet. The officer didn't ask a second time.

It wasn't necessarily how I would've reacted, had two private investigators—if that's what DJ and I could actually call ourselves—turned over a suspect with a broken arm. As far as anyone on the outside of Armstrong was concerned, we worked for an oceanographic research company.

As I sat on the back of *Reel Fun*, DJ's Viking 48C charter fishing boat, I looked up at the bone-white condos stacked on the hills around Cruz Bay. Was this the right spot for me? Had I run from Newport Beach into the arms of even more trouble?

DJ strutted through the door from the salon, a can of Medalla Light in each hand. "For a surfer boy out on the water, you look pissed, Dep."

He stepped down into the cockpit, tastefully decked in teak, and dropped one of the beers into a cupholder in the console to my left, which divided the white vinyl couch I was seated on into two halves. I sat on the port half, and, after brushing away a crumpled pink thong, DJ plopped down on the starboard half. Or was it the other way around? I'd never been much of a boater.

While he cracked his beer open, I didn't touch the one he'd offered me. Of course, that didn't escape DJ's notice. He picked it up, opened it for me and held it out.

I kept one hand in my lap, and the other balled up against my cheek. Just as I'd been when he came out.

DJ tapped the cans into each other.

"Helluva job, DJ," he muttered to himself. He sipped from one can, looking at me with one last invitation to take the beer. When I didn't accept, he sipped from it, too.

We sat next to each other for a time, watching the other craft drift past—low, long sailboats rocking with the winds, cabin cruisers bullying through the small waves, and fishing trawlers converted into lumbering retirement rafts.

If somebody didn't say something, this whole boat was gonna sink under the weight of what we were keeping from each other.

"I respect you, DJ," I finally said. "And I want to keep working with you, but we've gotta be more careful with the way we do things. If we keep taking wild chances, someone is going to get seriously hurt." I turned to him, trying to get a feel for his reaction.

The beer can seemed frozen to his lips. He didn't move, except for what he had to do to get a sip. Somewhere past his tangled mane, I saw a pair of hooded eyes.

"Seriously hurt," he repeated, after he swallowed.

"That's right," I said. "I've seen it. Guys who think they're invincible, they bleed like everybody else."

"Seen it too." DJ rested his beer can on top of his knee. "Held my buddy, done up like a pincushion from 7.62 rounds, while he bled out in the mountains." He visibly shuddered and turned to face me.

I didn't need a lecture on the everlasting horrors of other men bleeding out in my arms. Whatever DJ had seen, I'm sure I'd been there ten times over.

"But you can't play fair with some of the people out there. South Florida, the Bahamas, the Caribbean—they're wilder and crazier than any bunch of bored housewives you had back in Orange County, flipping coke for fun."

I scoffed. Newport Beach wasn't Compton, but it had danger all the same. As a detective, most of my investigations involved spillover gang violence and drug activity from Southeast Los Angeles and Long Beach. I'd gone toe-to-toe with hardened criminals and violent gangbangers.

"A guy sewing meth into grandma's day bag ain't nothing, Dep. Not compared to some of the things I've seen people do to their fellow man. Murder and mayhem in paradise. Sometimes you don't have a choice but to kick the crap out of somebody. But you should know that already, Jerry. You remember that cult, right? The one McDermitt dealt with?"

"They tried to kill me and my wife." I clenched my fist, then relaxed it. "And I know the atmosphere in these islands is different. But my point stands; we can't go around breaking the arms of everybody we suspected did something wrong—"

"Suspected?" DJ spat back. "Look, man. You gotta get past this notion of only the courts deciding when someone broke the law. In the real world, you can know something's true. We knew Beck was dirty."

"If you make a habit out of that," I countered, "you'll have both your feet standing in deeper shit than you can wade out of. Or worse, you'll end up hurting somebody who didn't do anything at all."

DJ laughed, which pissed me off more than I'd like to admit.

"Right," he said. "It's rich that you're lecturing me about that. Like a cop never beat up or shot anybody who didn't deserve it."

I knew there were dirty cops out there, even stupid ones, but I was neither. I prided myself on being patient, on being part of a community and abiding by the rules. To have anybody question that—even somebody who knew as little about me as DJ Martin did—really put the hooks under my skin.

Instead of taking the bait, I snatched my beer—DJ's second beer—out of the cup holder and swigged it down. And when I'd finished that drink and still felt like chewing him out, I took another drink. And another. Until I had cooled off enough not to bite onto what he held out in front of me.

It was fair to say DJ and I didn't agree very often, and a handful of times I'd let him get the better of me, which only got in the way of doing our job together.

Sometimes I wondered if anything short of one of us leaving Armstrong or getting reassigned would fix the problem between DJ and me.

Almost certainly, I was the guy who'd leave first. DJ relished the chance to be the authority. A little too much for my tastes. On days like today, when he was exceptionally reckless, he was no better than a vigilante. And, by association, so was I.

Taking that a step further, Armstrong Research would be painted with whatever bloody brush its operatives used—and what gave us the right to conduct ourselves that way? What would keep us from turning into a street gang dishing out punishment for anyone who we thought did wrong on our own turf?

Sure, Armstrong busted up drug smuggling rings, shut down people spewing toxic waste into the environment, and even tracked and killed terrorists, all while maintaining the outward appearance of a legitimate oceanographic research company. But how long before somebody made a bad call? How long until Jack Armstrong, himself, steered all of us in a bad direction?

The sat phone in my pocket rang.

"Tell Alicia I said hey," DJ quipped, without taking his gaze off the water.

I ignored him. It wasn't Alicia, anyway. It was Travis Stockwell, head of security aboard Armstrong's main research vessel, *Ambrosia*. He'd taken on the role of "handler" for me and DJ, as well as a couple other operators, giving assignments and checking up on our progress.

Stockwell was a retired Army Airborne colonel, which gave him an instant bond with DJ, but as time went on, the Colonel and I came to respect each other. I appreciated his no-nonsense approach to business and the precision with which he operated—both professionally, and personally.

"This is Snyder," I said as I answered the phone.

"What happened with Beck?" Stockwell had a voice like an old diesel engine. Low, rumbling, and with a growl reminding you that you disrespected him at your own peril.

"Well, Colonel," I said, "Robert Beck is in police custody now. By this time tomorrow, they'll likely hand him off to the DEA."

"I know that, Snyder," he said. "What I don't know is, did

you get the lead? Are we going higher up the food chain or not?"

My eyes cut to DJ. He must've seen me turning a shade lighter. He tipped his head at me and hoisted his beer.

"We got it," I said. "He's buying meth from an operation on Bonaire. He said there's an underground lab outside Rincón, in the national park thereabouts. But he said he didn't know any names."

"Did you believe him?"

I glared at DJ. "My partner had just broken his arm and was about to inflict more bodily harm, but I think his information was credible. It tracks with what we found out prior."

Stockwell grunted—he'd received the message.

"DJ whacked the guy with his leg, against my recommendation."

"DJ's creative." I thought I heard a smile behind Stockwell's voice. My brain tried to picture his tanned, weathered face, the creases deepening around his mouth. But his eyes would stay hard as steel beneath his close-cut silver hair.

"Yeah, he sure is," I said.

"Is that regret I'm hearing?" Stockwell said.

"It's just not how I would've done things, sir."

"You got the job done, didn't you?" Stockwell said. "You put away the bad guy and got a lead on his supplier."

"That's what everybody tells me." I took another deep drink from my beer. I wasn't going to fall ass-backwards into an argument with Stockwell. God only knew how badly that might turn out.

"Then everybody's right," Stockwell declared. "You need to get past whatever bad blood you and DJ have between you, Snyder. Jack Armstrong put the two of you together to solve problems, not bicker like stepbrothers. Armstrong doesn't make mistakes."

"Of course not, sir," I said. "It wasn't my intent to imply he had."

"Good. Because I've got a new assignment for you two."

"A new assignment, sir?" I asked. "What about following up on the information we got out of Beck?"

"We've got someone down in the Leeward Antilles who's going to handle it," he said. "This new problem is right there in your backyard."

"All right," I said.

"You're going to talk to Detective Antoine Collat with the Puerto Rican Police Bureau—*La Uniformada*. A body turned up in Culebra this morning. Scared the daylights out of a couple pleasure seekers at one of those sex resorts."

"Sounds... interesting, sir," I said. "When does he want to meet? Tomorrow morning?"

"Now," Stockwell answered. "I'll send coordinates to your phone. Get a move on."

"Yessir."

CHAPTER THREE

The nurse slipped past the open door like a kid cutting class—eyes forward, feet moving quiet and quick as a house spider in the open. Too much momentum to stop and talk.

She must've sensed the question rumbling around Gabriela's mind.

Gabriela softened the tension in her legs—no point in getting up and running after the nurse. She'd only look a fool.

Still, who could blame her for chasing the nurse down? She could scream like a lunatic while she did it, too.

Gabriela Ramos had earned the right to desperation. She and her daughter, Flor, had been sitting in the small room with a single window sliced in half by a beige wall for at least a half an hour, waiting for Flor's doctor to stop by, so the question could be asked—a question that would kink the tube steadily dripping poison into her daughter's vein.

Forgive her for not displaying the proper level of etiquette when her little girl's future would be decided by a stranger in a lab coat, far removed from hair loss, brittle fingernails and nights spent crying over a little girl's mortality, her loss of innocence and wonder, and … whether she lived or not … all the bills that hung from this poisoned tree, which Gabriela must harvest now, and for the foreseeable future.

Gabriela looked into her little girl's deep brown eyes, sunken and dry. Flor smiled at her and reached for her mother's hand but stopped when the tube in her arm went tight.

Dragging her hard plastic chair forward, Gabriela took hold of Flor's fingers and squeezed. They were so cold.

Worrying about bills didn't make sense. Not now.

"Mama, we're gonna be in the shower for days, getting this smell out of our hair."

The hospital smell. Hand sanitizer and latex gloves. It stunk.

Whenever she and Flor made their visits to the oncology department of San Juan University Pediatric Hospital, that stench lingered in their hair for days. They both had typical Dominican woman's hair: dark, thick, and laden with tight curls. It held onto everything.

Even the strands of Flor's hair that came out after she bathed reeked of rubbing alcohol. And also, the pervasive fumes from diesel generators that ran on an endless cycle to keep the hospital going since Hurricane Maria had hit the island. They'd become well acquainted with it. At twelve years old, Flor was on her third tumor.

Li-Fraumeni Syndrome, the doctors called it. For some reason, a gene inside Flor had turned off, or had never been on, and without that gene, there was next to nothing stopping her cells from pumping out cancers.

The only action was reaction. Doctors' visits, exams, tests, results, chemo, and radiation. Then, more tests to see what worked and what didn't. More waiting. The waiting might've been the worst part. Flor said it was.

Gabriela, at twenty-eight years old, had never experienced cancer, but it must've been a special horror, knowing that at any time the thing that claimed your life might already be inside you, might be stuck on your liver while you were eating breakfast, or filling the space in your lungs when you were talking to your best friend, or ballooning in your brain until one morning, you woke up and couldn't remember your mother's name while she got you off to school. Three times Flor had been here.

Three times Gabriela had been alongside her, holding her daughter's hand while a bag of poison was drip-fed into her little body.

Gabriela could barely afford it—neither the physical and emotional cost, nor the financial.

Which was why, during one of her research sessions two months back, she'd jumped at the chance to enroll Flor in a drug trial. A chance to cure her daughter's Li-Fraumeni Syndrome.

So, when Flor's oncologist, Dr. Juan Soto, came through the door, Gabriela couldn't help but feel God's hand fanning the dense air from the room.

"Flor, how's your day?" A question so beside the point, it was cruel.

"She's had a good morning so far." Gabriela's eyes flicked toward her daughter.

"Well, she has fantastic support. We're all in this together, right, Mama?"

"All the way through." Gabriela wore her bravest face.

Dr. Soto took Flor's chart out of a pocket next to the door. He flipped through the pages as if he couldn't care one way or another about what it said. The man didn't have to put on a show for them. Not anymore.

"I have some news I'd like to discuss with you, Miss Ramos," Dr. Soto said, gesturing toward the hallway with his eyes. His flat demeanor made it impossible to tell if any news was good or bad. He spoke and left the judgment up to Gabriela, who passed it to God.

God told the hair to stand up on her arms. He told the skin on her head to go tight.

"Mama?" Flor turned her eyes away from the TV hanging from the ceiling.

The child was ignorant of the drug trial. And she didn't have a clue that Dr. Soto had helped Gabriela apply. The fear she must've felt, seeing her mother step into a private conversation with her Doctor. These secluded, secret talks always ended with Gabriela delivering bad news to Flor—increasing dosages, switching to more powerful drugs, or worst of all, more tumors. Surprise attacks from tumors always ended up necessitating doses of medicine that made Flor throw up all night, as if they were designed to induce her body to exorcise the tumors by force. Gabriela always stayed up with her. Always prayed.

She patted her daughter's cheek.

"There's nothing to worry about, little girl. Jesus has you. While I'm gone, he's sitting next to you, helping you fight." She kissed Flor's forehead. It was hot and slick. "You stay brave. I'll be right back."

The moisture clung to Gabriela's lips as she rose to her feet, following Dr. Soto out of the room. She remained a step behind him, going down the hall, past the inner reception desk to the chemotherapy suites, the impression of Flor's skin walking the entire way with her. They stopped at automated double doors.

Gabriela came alongside him as he pushed the button that made them hum open.

She tried to read him. Dr. Soto had a card shark's face, his mouth hidden by a thick moustache, and his eyes shaded and stolid. She'd have better odds guessing the emotional temperature of a smart phone.

The doors opened. Dr. Soto moved and Gabriela followed.

Past darkened rooms and overworked nurses, they turned and strode down a hall only lit with emergency lights near exit doors on either end. The staff would never admit to it, but the hospital struggled for power, the same as everybody else on the island. Anything that didn't need to suck electricity, like a half dozen lights down a hallway, wouldn't.

Dr. Soto's office was at the end of the hall, bathed in one of the patches of light. He opened the door without a word.

The big window inside was enough to keep the room from feeling dim. He glided behind his desk and mechanically folded his body into a seated position in his chair. Gabriela nearly collapsed in one of the two chairs positioned in front of the desk while he typed something into his computer.

"I received word from MRL," Dr. Soto said, referring to Markel Research Labs—the organization running the trials she wanted Flor to join. His eyes briefly darted from his computer screen to Gabriela, then back again. "Flor's participation in the trial of Anthradone has been declined."

The information was delivered so clinically, Gabriela didn't at first understand.

"What was that?" She leaned over, getting her face into his line of sight, dragging his eyes off the computer screen. "What did you say?"

Dr. Soto rubbed his eyes. Gabriela thought she saw a corner of his mouth flex downward before he covered it with his palm.

"I'm sorry, Miss Ramos, but Flor won't be part of the next round of Anthradone trials."

Her throat tightened. She'd heard what he said, but he was talking Swahili. The sounds hit the surface of her brain, but they didn't penetrate. Heat shimmered across her scalp, the words trying to burn through her skull.

"Why?" was all she managed to ask.

"I wasn't part of the deliberations. If I were, I would've lobbied on Flor's behalf."

But Flor wasn't supposed to be denied.

The door was shut years ago, but this experimental drug was the open window. Gabriela had read about Anthradone's other trials through her work. This drug was the way—the miracle they needed; it fixed Li-Fraumeni. All those papers said Anthradone turned the P53 gene back on, letting patients' bodies kill cancerous cells before they matured into knobs of agony.

Without it, Flor would die. Her baby girl would be gone. No smiles, no laughs, no jokes. No one to argue with about putting away dishes. No homework to help with. No one to listen to Gabriela tell her stories about being a pregnant girl and scrapping to get what she got.

She would be alone. The greatest piece of Gabriela would disappear.

"Miss Ramos?"

Did she hear her name?

"Miss Ramos?"

Dr. Soto tapped her shoulder.

The swarm of thoughts stopped and Gabriela saw clearly

again. He was out of his chair, in front of her. Then her eyes clouded, and hot tears flowed, salted with rage, bitter with sorrow, and begging for a chance to stop a little girl's life from being taken before she had a chance to live.

There wasn't time for crying. She ground the tears into her with the palms of her hands.

God *had* to find a way. It was His plan. Stay with Him. He knew everything, and He saw all. Whatever happened was His will.

But this was her fault.

She'd given Flor her genes. Oh, sure, they could be her father's, but blaming *him* for anything had never gotten Gabriela anywhere in the past. The man might as well have not existed at all.

Misery was inherited. Sins passed from mother to child, each new generation bearing the mistakes and the guilt of the last. A mother who ignored her babies would make daughters who sought comfort in the arms of wicked men, who in turn stole those girls from their children, and so on and so on.

But Gabriela had broken that cycle. Didn't that mean she could break this one too?

Only through the power of God.

"Apply again," Gabriela said firmly.

"Miss Ramos, that's not how this is supposed to work."

"Do it anyway." Gabriela's fingers bit into the armrest of the chair. "From what I see, a lot isn't working how it's supposed to. Little girls aren't supposed to get cancer. People aren't supposed to be able to fix what she's got. We aren't supposed to apply again, but what's the worst thing that can happen?"

Dr. Soto tapped his desk.

"This is the best hope I have to fix Flor," Gabriela said. "You understand that." Gabriela reached across the gulf between her and the doctor and tried to take his hand.

He slipped it away, so she wrapped her fingers around his wrist. "This is her cure. This drug is what she needs."

"Anthradone won't cure Flor's cancer."

"But it'll cure the thing causing all the tumors. So, if we get that stuff, and she beats the tumors she's got, that's it. No more cancer."

Dr. Soto grimaced.

"Once this treatment is available to the public, I'll do my level best to ensure that Flor receives medication from the first supply. You have my word."

He broke away from her clutch, then retreated behind his desk, as if to say his answer was final. Gabriela couldn't accept that.

"She's twelve, Dr. Soto, and she's had cancer three times already." She fought to keep from raising her voice, but God help her, how could she? "How much longer does my Florita have to suffer? Does Flor have to throw away her entire childhood in oncology wards, getting chemo dumped into her veins until she's nothing but skin and bones—not even hair? All her hair is pushed out. My girl's pretty hair…"

Despair crept out. She stopped herself from crying again.

"What else do we have?"

"Miss Ramos, I don't know what else to say." He turned his chair until he, at least, faced her. "If I didn't know better, I'd wonder if you blame me for Flor not being admitted into the Anthradone trial."

Maybe she did blame him.

But Dr. Soto had been nothing but good to Flor—he cared about her in his own way. Even in her darkest moments, how could Gabriela question that? She looked down at the four crescents her nails had pressed into her palms. All that rage that had flashed through her cooled just as quickly as it came on.

"I'm at the end. I'm sitting beside my little girl, every day, watching her slowly die."

He patted his desk, bringing her attention up. Dr. Soto's hand hung over the edge, waiting for Gabriela's.

This time, she took it. His fingers were cold, but long enough to wrap around her palm—as if to lay hands on the marks she'd made.

"There will likely be another trial for Anthradone when this one concludes," he said, as warmly as she'd ever heard him. "You have my word as a medical professional—as a man with a heart—that I'll do whatever I can to put Flor in it. They'll likely deny us, but I'll do my best." He nodded at her, his face pinching. "We aren't done."

His eyes were wet. She felt ashamed for doubting his conviction, however briefly that doubt took hold.

"Thank you."

"Your daughter is a fighter," he said, squeezing her hand tighter, then letting go. "She will make it through this. Just like last time."

"What about next time?"

"We can only focus on what we see in the here and now."

That might've been true for him, but it wasn't Gabriela's truth. And it certainly wasn't Flor's. Beating the cancer she had today meant readying Flor for the next round.

Compounding that, treatments were neither free, nor cheap.

Someone had to pay for them. And she was still making payments on Flor's second treatment from last year. Meanwhile, the bills for this treatment had begun flowing into her mailbox this week.

Somehow, she had to stem the tide. Debt collectors would start calling in a couple months, when the bills still weren't paid. Until then, she'd have to figure a way to stay afloat. A hundred dollars a month to the hospital, two hundred to a specialist, another four hundred for this month's drugs.

Then there were groceries—what was the point in all these treatments if Flor was going to starve—and rent on an apartment that lost power whenever it was least convenient for everyone. That did make utilities cheaper, though the water company had raised their rates each month for the past year. New pipes, they said.

God would find a way. If He willed it.

"Is there something else concerning you?" Dr. Soto craned his neck closer to her.

She ran her hands through her thick, dark curls, pulling her hair from the sides of her face, cooling her neck and shoulders.

"Money," she said.

"Have you spoken to the billing department?"

"They don't want to hear anything else out of me, except dates for when the checks were written."

He closed his eyes and straightened his back. "I understand."

Nothing else to say.

Billing was out of his hands. The hospital didn't want doctors hounding patients for chunks of $10,000 hospital bills, and they didn't want irate patients screaming at doctors and nurses about missed mortgage payments and overdue school lunch bills.

And, anyway, it was easier for some no-named cog hidden in

a back room, hunched over a computer, typing out five-figure invoices one after another after another. Debt-bound patients shouldn't have a face to go along with the bills.

Instead, they faced an impartial system of inscrutable costs propped up by collection agencies and insurance companies.

"Thank you for trying Dr. Soto." She stood from the chair. "I should get back to Flor."

"I'm sorry, Miss Ramos." A pair of heavy eyes settled over her.

She nodded at Dr. Soto and turned to leave.

After stumbling through the long, dark hallway, ignored by anyone she passed, Gabriela found her way back to the outpatient room.

Flor was as pale as the seashells they used to collect before all of this had happened. Her eyes were open, but seemed weighted down—heavy, dark bags, swollen with tears that would never come out of her desiccated little body.

"What did he say, Mama?" she asked. "Do I have another one?"

Her chin trembled, and Gabriela's heart hitched. Another tumor, she meant. The entire time Gabriela was back with Dr. Soto, this poor little girl had been sitting by herself, worried that she had another tumor.

Gabriela took her daughter's hand.

"No, *mi hija*. No." And Gabriela's tears trailed out, thick enough for the both of them. She leaned over, laying her head on Flor's shoulder, gingerly at first. Putting weight on Flor had to be done carefully, with a steady, slow pressure, until, finally, Gabriela was sure she wouldn't break her.

Her thin shoulder was the most comforting headrest Gabriela

had.

"Then what's wrong, Mama?" Flor asked. Her smallest finger stroked Gabriela's.

How could she answer? How could she tell Flor that a cure existed for her disease, but she would not get it?

Flor shuddered. She was crying without tears.

Gabriela sat up and turned to her, the sweet, sad girl.

"Is it the money? All my bills? I'm sorry," Flor said. She motioned towards the tube running down to her arm. "I messed things up. This is all my fault. If I wasn't here, your life would've been so much better."

The air was swept out of Gabriela's lungs.

God help this girl. She was too much like her mother for her own good. Gabriela wiped her eyes clear.

She cupped Flor's cheek, bringing her sunken eyes up.

"You have nothing to be sorry about. Understand me? Nothing at all." She forced a smile. "None of this is your fault. None of it. You work on feeling better, and I'll do the worrying."

CHAPTER FOUR

"What'd Stockwell say?" DJ asked.

"We won a trip to San Juan," I replied.

DJ stood and drained his beer. "Puerto Rico? The hell for? We're flying from there to Bonaire?"

"New assignment," I replied, heading to the rail. "Somebody else will take care of Bonaire. Stockwell wants us in San Juan like right now."

"I'll fire up the engines," DJ said, heading for the ladder to the bridge deck. "P.R. is about ninety miles—we can be there in three hours. Get the dock lines."

I did as he ordered. It was his boat, and he was the captain. I at least knew what the chain of command was on a boat.

Once out of the bay, DJ brought *Reel Fun* up to thirty knots and headed northwest, following the natural channel, to get clear of St. Thomas and Hans Lollik Island. I filled him in on everything Stockwell had said as we slipped out. After half an hour, he turned due west for Puerto Rico.

Ninety minutes later, we passed under the old Spanish ramparts at the western end of Old San Juan. DJ slowed and turned into San Juan Bay, then headed back to the east toward the marina.

"What's that?" I asked, pointing to what looked like a small platform just a few feet out of the water.

"A good chunk of some poor bastard's retirement fund, I'm guessing," DJ replied.

As we passed, I could see through the clear water to the boat's hull resting at the bottom, just before the entrance to San Antonio Canal. The only thing above water was the small roof over the boat's tuna tower, which looked a lot like the one capping *Reel Fun*.

"Maria probably sank it," he said, as we peered over the side of *Reel Fun's* flybridge into the dark blue waters. We idled slowly past, within fifteen yards, and I could see the top half of the tower's seat protruding from the water just below the roof. The roof itself had been stripped of any lights, radar, antennas, or whatever else had been attached there.

DJ radioed into San Juan Bay Marina, on the mainland side of the short bridge to Old San Juan. After the dockmaster had him change channels, DJ identified his boat, requested a slip and was given directions to it. He was also told a dockhand and U.S. Customs official would be there to help tie off.

"Why customs?" I asked. "Both St. Thomas and Puerto Rico are U.S. territories."

"I know," DJ replied. "It's weird. Americans traveling from P.R. to the U.S. Virgin Islands don't have to clear in, but coming into Puerto Rico from there, they do."

DJ steered *Reel Fun* to a double slip beside a sailboat with a jet-black hull. The name on the stern was *Dark Horse*.

I dropped fenders over the side and tied them off to the rail.

When we were close enough, I tossed a stern line to a dockhand waiting on the finger pier, who looped it around a cleat as DJ reversed the engine on the opposite side. With the line holding the stern in place on the dock side, the boat could do nothing but pivot around the end of the finger pier. Once lined up, the dockhand released the line from the cleat and DJ backed into the slip. I tossed the bow line to the guy and he tied it off as well. I could see the customs officer standing to the side.

DJ made it look so easy. My new boat was no longer than his, but it was wider. Still, I was apprehensive about our first sea trial.

The customs agent asked a few questions and checked our passports but didn't bother boarding. Once cleared, I hopped down with the bow line in hand and quickly cleated it to the dock. My knots weren't as sure as the dockhand's, but once DJ hopped off the stern and checked my work, he nodded approval.

Good to know I was making progress. My own boat, *Wayward*, waited for me in a private marina down the street from my house on St. Thomas. Alicia and I didn't have the confidence to take it out yet, but I'd promised we'd hire a skipper to show us which way to point it, and how, just as soon as we put Robert Beck away.

He was away now, I reminded myself.

When I'd made my promise to Alicia, I'd been under the impression we'd have a week or so between assignments.

Guess not.

DJ's eyes scanned the dock behind me. "Stockwell tell you where we're going to meet this detective?"

His attention settled to my left, farther from shore than where we stood, toward the sound of trop rock music and women laughing.

Always on the hunt.

"You can get their numbers later," I said. "Let's head the other way and see if someone jumps out at us."

I turned around and walked. DJ followed, his titanium leg thudding against the deck boards. Though he wore the same shoe on each foot, there was a distinct difference in the sound of each one's footfall.

We marched past every kind of pleasure craft I knew; sloop-rigged sailboats, ketches and schooners, fishing charters and fifty-foot yachts with dinghies strapped to the stern.

A figure drew my eye from the boats. A diminutive, wiry, black man in a light blue button-down shirt and gray slacks. He walked like a man with something big on his mind, his pistol bouncing in a hip holster with every step he took. Near the opposite hip, the badge clipped to his belt glinted in the crystalline sun.

"There's our detective," I said.

My legs picked up the pace, leaving DJ behind. I wanted to make a good impression on Detective Collat, at least for a few seconds, before DJ came and inevitably turned the meeting chilly by grumbling about the police.

"Mr. Snyder?" A half dozen paces from me, he extended his hand. "Detective Antoine Collat, Puerto Rican Police Force."

I met his hand with my own. He had a firm, confident grip, paired with the steely, troubled expression of a career detective who had seen too much.

"Good to meet you, Detective," I said. "This is my partner, DJ Martin."

Behind me, DJ brought up the rear as I motioned toward him, but I kept a firm hold on Collat's hand. I didn't want DJ screwing everything up by refusing to shake his hand.

"Hey, man." DJ kept his hands in his pockets.

"Is there a private place where we can have a conversation?"

Collat spoke with the slightest hint of an accent, but not Puerto Rican; Haitian maybe.

"I'm disinclined to talk out in the open." As his mouth moved, so did the rest of his face—his cheeks bobbing, his nose flattening, and his eyes coming together such that they revealed a scar running crossways from his forehead to his cheekbone.

"Of course, Detective," I said, guiding him past DJ toward *Reel Fun*.

We sat in the salon—DJ on the couch that bent around the port wall, me on a stool at the bar, and Collat sitting rigidly on the edge of the aft-most couch.

Nobody had said a word since meeting on the dock. And Armstrong's training didn't include a primer on what to do when approached by a detective for help, so I broke the silence.

"Detective," I began, "I understand that you contacted Armstrong looking for help with something."

He adjusted in his seat, trying to get comfortable. When he couldn't, he took his service weapon off his hip, still in its holster, and placed it on the white vinyl cushion to his right. He then did the same with his badge.

"Do you mind if I leave that there?" he asked me, motioning to his handgun.

"DJ?" I looked at him.

DJ shrugged. "It ain't the only weapon on board."

The scar between Collat's eyes puckered as he looked from DJ to me, then down at DJ's leg, extending off the edge of the couch like a gang plank, and then back up to his eyes.

"Are you the captain of this boat?" Collat asked.

"And owner," DJ said.

"Oh…" he trailed off, and then made an empty gesture with his hands.

He'd assumed the boat was mine. An easy mistake. DJ didn't look like he slept in the master stateroom of a forty-eight-foot yacht.

"Anyhow," Collat said, "I've heard through some of my colleagues that Jack Armstrong is more than the owner of an oceanographic research company. That he's a problem solver, and not afraid to take on things that others might… shy away from."

"You heard a lot. Who from?" DJ asked.

"Men I've worked with."

"Cops."

"I am a police officer," Collat said, narrowing his eyes, "so that would follow. Is there a problem?"

DJ scoffed, then combed his fingers through his long goatee.

"There's no problem," I answered for him. "You've got the right impression of Armstrong. What can we do to help, Detective?"

Collat took a deep, frayed breath. I knew veterans like him weren't easily bothered—my first night working as a detective with the Newport Beach PD, I shadowed a guy who conducted himself like Collat. We worked a traffic accident involving a motorcycle, where, as a funny prank, some deputy holding a trash bag walked up to me and asked if I wanted to see something cool.

Sure, I answered. But I knew something was off before I peered down.

From inside the bag, the motorcyclist's severed head gawked

up at me. The deputy laughed himself into a fit. I wasn't impressed, and neither was the detective I shadowed. He grabbed the trash bag with one hand and the collar of the deputy's shirt with another, then stuffed him into the back of our unmarked car.

As long as I shadowed him, I never saw that detective lose his cool like that again.

All of which is to say, it probably took a hell of a lot to get a guy like Collat going. Must've took even more to get him to come to a group of civilians, asking for help.

"Before you agree to anything," he began, "I want to make it perfectly clear that what I'm going to ask of you two gentlemen is strictly off the books. You aren't working for the Puerto Rican Police Force in any official capacity. You don't have any special rights or privileges that come with this badge." He tapped the shield next to him. "If I hear that two white guys are walking around dropping my name, we're going to have a conversation nobody wants to have. Understand? Both of you keep silent on this—don't do anything to get noticed."

Maybe he was small, but Collat really filled up the room when he wanted to.

I wasn't so sure about what we were getting into. I was happy to help an officer with a personal request, but the way Detective Collat talked, I doubted if I was going to like doing this favor.

"We'll do it," DJ said.

Outstanding.

Detective Collat breathed a visible sigh of relief. "Good."

Before he said anything more, his Adam's apple slipped up and down his throat. I could tell he struggled to get his words around whatever thought squirmed within his head. This was going to be far more than anyone bargained.

"A body was found on Zoni Beach over in Culebra." The words left Collat's mouth quickly, like they were dodging his teeth. "It had been picked apart by wildlife, but we were able to identify the victim, and there was enough material in the right places that the coroner said he found nylon fibers embedded in flesh near the victim's ankles. He said the fibers led him to believe this person had been tied up by a rope. There was sea water in his lungs."

The muscles in Collat's jaw rippled.

"The coroner said it was a suicide," Collat summarized, but he didn't sound convinced.

"You have some doubts about the coroner's report?" I asked, but all the pieces were being drawn toward each other in my head. This didn't stop at a flimsy coroner's report. He wouldn't go through the trouble of contacting Armstrong and meeting with us just for something as tiny as that.

Collat nodded, his eyes fixed to a spot on the floor. "He wouldn't kill himself. I know he wouldn't."

DJ and I quickly looked at each other.

"Who was he?" I asked Collat, sure to put the question forward gently.

The way Collat's gaze shot up to me, I knew. I think DJ picked up on it as well. The dead man was close to Collat. A friend. Maybe family.

"My brother-in-law."

I nodded, trying to lend as sympathetic an ear as I could.

"Luc Baptiste," Collat continued. "He is—or was—an investigative journalist. He was well-known. And despised."

My mind's eye began to open up to the meandering course of the coming investigation. "What was he working on?"

"I don't know." Collat shook his head, then pressed his fingers to his closed eyelids. "I should know, shouldn't I? Isn't that something a man in my position should know? But I don't. I just don't. Luc and I knew we both had something to gain by working together on occasion, but whatever he had this time, he kept me out of it."

He took another deep breath, then lay back, his closely buzzed hair resting on the top edge of the couch.

"You don't know nothing at all?" DJ asked.

"Luc told me someone was following him." Collat's voice fell low. "I said, 'You're crazy. No one would follow you. Why would anyone want to do something like that? You've got a voice people listen to, and anybody who would try to follow you doesn't want their name said aloud,' but by God, I was wrong."

"You have reason to believe someone was following him," I said.

Collat's eyes bored into mine. "Yeah. He's dead."

Stupid thing for me to ask. DJ rolled his eyes and silently chuckled.

"Why aren't you looking into your brother-in-law's death, then?" DJ asked. "Why you gotta have us come in?"

"I lack grounds to follow up." Collat swiped a finger across the scar over his nose, then looked DJ in the eyes. "The case didn't get assigned to me. It was assigned to another detective—a man who is three weeks from retirement and couldn't be bothered with a murder case. He's taking the coroner's ruling at face value."

"He's not gathering any evidence to prove or disprove it?" I said. I figured the procedure here was much the same as it was back in Newport Beach.

"None that I've seen."

"Big surprise," DJ muttered.

"What makes you think this other detective isn't performing due diligence?" I asked.

"I've been keeping tabs on the case file," Collat said. "Every policeman with something behind his badge knows a murder is a ticking clock; the longer you take to investigate, the lower your chances of solving the case. It's been nearly forty-eight hours since the discovery of Luc's body, and he hasn't logged a single piece of evidence, hasn't spoken to any witnesses, hasn't even contacted the family.

"My wife and her mother wouldn't have known about Luc's death if I weren't a police officer—and I wouldn't have been informed if someone in the coroner's office didn't know Luc and me from a while back." He balled his fists until his knuckles cracked. "Think about that. What kind of detective can't even be bothered to notify the next of kin after identifying a body?"

A negligent one, I thought.

"Have you tried to go through any official channels?" I asked. "Talked to the other detective's lieutenant or precinct captain, even?"

Collat waved that idea off. "No one wants to rock the boat. I've tried going to his superiors unofficially, but they've made it clear they aren't going to second-guess the work of an experienced detective and the coroner, just because the detective is nearing retirement. His lieutenant offered to have the case reassigned after this other guy retires, but after three weeks, it's too cold. It'd be pointless."

No question. A three-week-old murder was as good as dead and filed with other cold cases. If no real investigation had started by then, it was more than likely no one would ever be appre-hended. Contrary to TV shows, more than a third of all murders in the United States were never cleared and remained unsolved.

"Luc wouldn't commit suicide," Collat said. "He was tough. He was fearless. I've heard stories about how he'd stowed away on drug boats and snuck into places I wouldn't dare go unless I wanted my throat cut. Luc had a way of bonding with people. He earned their trust, their respect. Even guys who would shoot their own mother for a few bucks would invite Luc into their inner circles. And he was never afraid to accept. Does that sound like a man who would drown himself?"

No, it didn't.

But I wasn't suicidal and never had been. I would never un-derstand the pressures that pushed a man to take his own life, so I wasn't an authority on whether Luc Baptiste had killed himself or not. But the method; jumping off a boat with ropes tied around your ankles? I wondered how the M.E. could call that suicide. Unless there was a note.

Then again, grief distorted reality.

"I can see that look on your face," Collat said to me. "You think I'm not looking at this clearly."

"No," I lied. "No, it's just that this isn't the kind of thing Arm-strong normally deals in."

"Then you won't help me."

"I didn't say that." My eyes shifted to DJ. "We already prom-ised we'd help."

"Good. I'd hate to see Mr. Armstrong's record get tarnished."

Collat rose off the couch, brushed himself off, then turned around and collected his badge and his gun. He clipped them on his waistband.

"I think you should check Luc's boat first." Collat reached in his pocket. He produced a small key and held it out. I reached my hand out, accepting it. "He's got a slip at Krum Bay Marina on St. Thomas. You'll find his boat there—an American Tug 365 with a forest green hull. Name's *St. Thomas Gazette*."

CHAPTER FIVE

O nce again, *Reel Fun* carried DJ and me across the ocean, this time from San Juan, around Culebra, to the lee side of St. Thomas, and into Long Bay. The return trip took the same three hours.

DJ guided the boat to the mouth of West Gregerie Channel—between St. Thomas and Water Island, west of Charlotte Amalie. Then he swung northward, taking us into Krum Bay—a place I'd never heard of.

Alicia and I had moved to St. Thomas a few months ago. I didn't have the lay of the island memorized yet, but I knew most of the important landmarks. Places like Charlotte Amalie, the capital of the USVI, where all the big cruise ships docked for multi-day excursions into Blackbeard's Castle and Fort Christian. I'd been to Magen's Bay Park, facing the Atlantic side of the island, and Cas Cay, on the windward side, where I taught Alicia some of the basics of snorkeling and free diving.

Learning what leeward and windward meant was easy. The wind always blows from the east—windward. Sometimes the northeast or southeast, but always out of the eastern quadrant.

The east side of these islands was rugged, with rocky coasts and cliffs. The leeward sides never saw much wave activity and that was where you found the best beaches and anchorages.

I'd learned the places where locals ate and shopped and unwound, away from pesky tourists asking for the best places to get a burger, touch sea turtles, or score some weed.

As far as I could remember, nobody ever said to stop by Krum Bay.

As we motored further into the bay, I figured out why. From my spot on the settee on the flybridge, I looked toward the western shoreline and saw the island's desalination plant. Near a few rectangular steel buildings, dozens of long, white and royal blue pipes ran parallel with a concrete patch covering the ground.

No one wanted to see industry sucking up the turquoise Caribbean waters, extruding them through filter after filter, until they were scrubbed into sterility.

On the opposite shore—beyond DJ's goatee flapping in the wind, sat thick walls of deep-green trees. On the western edge of a dirt clearing was a boat ramp. There were holding tanks of some kind there, the big ten-thousand-gallon suckers. I guessed they either held water or fuel for the plant, for when the power inevitably cut off—which it often did on St. Thomas.

After passing around a sunken barge, DJ held *Reel Fun* steady. Within a few minutes, we came upon a small marina. At first glance, I guessed there were no more than two dozen vessels docked there or moored nearby.

Halfway up the nearest dock we saw Luc's boat, just where Detective Collat had said. The *St. Thomas Gazette* was a thirty-six-footer with a deep green hull. It looked like a miniature tugboat with a commercial-style bridge, but the deck was tiny—barely enough to walk around.

I tapped DJ's shoulder and pointed at the boat. He acknowledged me with a mutter lost in the light breeze, then spun the wheel in the direction of the *Gazette*.

While he maneuvered closer to an empty spot at the end of the dock, I went down the ladder to the cockpit, and got the lines and fenders out, tying the lines to the boat's cleats to be ready to tie us off.

We idled forward, the dock coming up on our starboard side. I dropped the fenders over, and then, as soon as I'd gotten a loop around a cleat, DJ cut the engines.

I hopped off *Reel Fun* and cleated the line, then went forward and grabbed the bow line before DJ could get down from the flybridge.

Confident that I'd done it right, I stepped back as DJ came slowly down the ladder. He shut the aft storage door in a way that made it clear he wasn't happy about me leaving it open. Then, he peered down at the dock lines…and grimaced.

"Sloppy work, Dep. That cleat hitch is wrong," he said with a big grin. "Tie it again."

I thought I'd done a solid job. Maybe the first time I'd been confident about my knots. But when I looked at it again, he was right. The knot wouldn't hold unless I tucked that last section of line beneath itself and cinched it down tight.

I jumped onto the boat's aft deck.

"Ain't you from a beach town, Dep?" DJ asked as I went past.

I hoisted myself onto the thin stretch of starboard deck. "I am," I said. But when I was a kid—before joining the Air Force—I didn't tie up boats. I didn't fill holds. I didn't scrub hulls or chart courses. Dad hired people to do that for us.

"Nobody's coming through here," I said as I retied the line. "The water's calm—nothing is going to shake that knot loose."

"Once we get some salt on that pretty little boat you got docked around the way, you can tie the knots as loose as you care to. I'm captain on my boat. And Captain Martin says re-tie your line, sailor."

"Aye, sir." I leaned back on my haunches, holding my hands toward the knot for DJ's inspection.

"That's ship-shape, Deputy Snyder," he said with a nod.

"Good. Now that you're satisfied, Captain, maybe we can go do the job we came here to do." I vaulted the rail amidships and dropped five feet to the dock. DJ sat on the edge of the starboard railing, swung his legs over, then used the toes of his good leg to pull the boat as close to the dock as it could get. Then, he pushed off, sliding onto his feet, standing straight on the dock. It was a pretty tricky maneuver for a guy with one leg. I wondered how many times he'd screwed it up and fallen in.

"That sounds like a fine idea," DJ said. "You might rethink jumping down like that. One rotten board and you're going into the drink."

Whatever.

I led the way down the dock. We walked past three slips—two empty, one holding a fishing trawler. The boat rocked slightly on the calm water in the bay. I assumed that meant someone was moving around inside, but I didn't want to talk to any of Luc Baptiste's neighbors yet. Not until I got a look at his boat.

The *St. Thomas Gazette* looked well-maintained on the outside. The hull was free of any hangers-on that I could see. The paint job hadn't faded in the sun, or chipped from harsh weather, which meant Luc had probably had it painted recently.

Odd thing to do for a man considering suicide.

DJ stepped onto the swim platform. "You got that key Collat gave you?"

"One second," I said. "I want to get a good look at the outside before we go in."

Could be nothing helpful on the outside, but every investigation required a methodical approach, so I walked the dock around the outside of the boat. Overlooking some small detail, due to being rushed, could be the difference between confirming the coroner's report about Luc Baptiste or finding something else. To a coroner, there were only five manners of death: homicide, suicide, accidental, natural, and unknown. The question still nagged at me. Even if there was no evidence to support homicide, why had the coroner chosen suicide over unknown?

As it turned out, the boat looked exactly as I'd expected. Everything clean. No rust stains caused by water dripping from toe rails. No cracks in the glass around the bridge. Nothing out of place.

When I came back around to the stern, DJ had let himself aboard from the swim platform.

"What's the theory? Navy SEALs climb up the side of the boat and drag Baptiste into the water?"

I dug into my pocket and pulled out the key. "Not this time."

I tossed the key to DJ and he snatched it out of the air.

"Hell, the poor son of a bitch probably *did* drown himself," DJ said, as he walked to the salon door. "I mean, look at this place. Ain't exactly the most picturesque spot in the whole Virgin Islands. I'd tie stones to my ankles and jump into the water too."

"Maybe you would," I said, as I climbed aboard. "But if you were going to do it, you'd probably do it right here where your boat is. And your body probably wouldn't have washed all the way out to the north end of the island. You'd be lucky if you ever made it out of Krum Bay."

DJ lifted an eyebrow at me. He looked impressed.

"If I want to dump a body, guess I know who I should be consulting." he said with a grin.

I shook my head at him. "Open the door, DJ."

"Hatch," he said, correcting me. "A door on a boat is called a hatch. Windows are portholes and the living room is the salon."

"Last I knew, a boat doesn't sink if you call the bathroom a bathroom," I said.

His smile broadened as he shook his head, turned the key in the lock, and pushed the door open.

Inside, the living room was trashed.

Everywhere lay everything; food, dishes, cleaning supplies, clothes, books; even the TV had been ripped off the wall to our left. Immediately on our right, the fridge hung open, and the microwave had been torn clean out of its cubby above the fridge. All the cabinet doors were ajar, one of them literally hanging by a single hinge. I tasted the stench of rotting melon in the back of my throat.

"Ain't this something curious?" DJ said, stepping through the door, and kicking a cabinet shut under the sink at the same time.

I came in behind him. The settee cushions lay in an uneven mess on top of the frame, like trees after a hurricane. They'd all been sliced open, their stuffing hanging out.

"Very curious," I said. "Safe to say somebody was looking for something."

"You ain't kidding about that." DJ was already up the trio of steps in the forward part of the living room—the salon—leading into the pilothouse. "Wonder if they found it?"

"Soon as we nab whoever killed Luc, we'll ask."

There was no longer any doubt in my mind that Luc's death wasn't a suicide. I allowed the possibility on our ride over from San Juan, or even the off chance that he'd been in an unfortunate accident. But now that I saw Luc's place, I was certain he'd been murdered.

"What do we do now?" DJ asked.

"Check around the boat. See if we notice anything out of place—anything that might give us a hint about where to go next. You start up there, I'll start down here."

"Seems to me like everything's out of place," DJ said.

"Then look for something that's where it's supposed to be. Maybe if we can find where they stopped looking, it'll tell us what they were looking for."

Over at the settee, I looked down into the storage compartments which would've normally been hidden by the cushions. I saw towels scattered, a tackle box upended, hooks, lines, and sinkers glittering up at me. In the compartment on my right, a DVD collection had been meticulously riffled through—each case opened.

There was my first hint: whatever they were after must've been small enough to fit in a DVD case.

"Keep an eye out for something compact, DJ. CD-ROMs, DVDs, thumb drives, pocket notebooks—anything that could hold Luc's notes."

"I'm on that, Dep," DJ called from the pilothouse.

"And stop calling me that. I was never a deputy."

I took the stairs up to the pilothouse. I saw DJ going through the storage bays under the seats. In front of me, against the portside wall, a second set of stairs led downward and toward the *Gazette's* bow.

"I'm going to check down there," I said, pointing in that direction.

After I took the stairs down, I found myself in the main stateroom. Straight ahead of me, the bed had been tossed and stripped of its sheets. The bare mattress leaned against the wall, a large tear nearly bisecting it, and the storage beneath looked much like the settee storage in the salon—everything pushed around and disorganized. Anything that could be dumped—like suitcases, a backpack, and a toiletry bag, was spilled out all over the floor.

Behind me, the bathroom looked like the rest of the boat. The medicine cabinet yawned open, empty pill bottles had been uncapped and dumped into the sink or the commode.

We spent the next couple of hours picking through the boat. The most prominent through-line to the ransacking seemed that the perps were after something small. Whether it was the size of a credit card, or a postage stamp, I couldn't say.

I had been searching the bedroom for at least an hour when, on my hands and knees, I noticed a small panel to the left of Luc's bed. If I didn't have my nose to it, I would've easily missed it, but this close, I saw the faux wood-grain pattern on the false panel didn't match up to the grain around it.

The panel had a little give to it, like a cabinet door held with a magnetic latch. Now opened, I found a waterproof container inside the compartment about the size of two shoeboxes pushed together. I pulled it out, sat it on the bed, and opened the latch.

Inside, next to a small, black, zip-up case, I found a bundle of documents tied together with twine. I took it out, slid them out of the twine and thumbed through one after another.

The bundle was a hodgepodge of different things like legal documents, handwritten letters, photographs, bank records, bills addressed to people other than Luc Baptiste—all of it appeared deeply personal. The kind of stuff no one wanted another soul to see.

Luc had built up a nice trove of dirt on a lot of people. Some would see it as gathering information, but it looked a lot like fodder for blackmail to me.

I pulled out one letter written in neat cursive. The letterhead came from the office of Rachel Little, Chief Executive Officer of Hildon Pharmaceuticals. It appeared to be a divorce settlement between Ms. Little and an ex-husband, citing her own infidelity, and dated over three years ago. A lot of assets seemed to change hands.

"DJ," I called out.

His hair flung down from the door to the stateroom. Took my eyes a second to find his.

"Luc Baptiste kept a whole stash of private information on people." I set the letter aside and picked up the next thing that caught my eye: a photograph of a gray-haired man with his lips locked on a much younger woman. I recognized his designer suit. Must've seen it a dozen times on a dozen different businessmen. "Blackmail."

The boat shook when DJ landed at the base of the steps. He walked over to me.

"Lotta folks knew who Luc Baptiste was," DJ said, as he took the bundle and riffled through it. "If you had money and something to lose, you didn't want him knocking on your car window and shoving a voice recorder in your face. You think this was work or pleasure?"

"Could've been both." I examined the photograph more closely.

"Oh, man," DJ said.

When I looked over, I thought I saw him hide a grin.

"You ever heard of a guy named Nick Garner?" He slipped a piece of paper from the bundle and handed it over to me.

"Should I?"

"A lot of the locals on St. Thomas do. Including Luc Baptiste. He runs that Wild Life resort."

I glanced down at the paper to see a black and white copy of the USVI seal. This was some kind of official document.

"It's a restraining order," I said. "Luc had a restraining order against this Nick Garner guy?"

"Check the date, Dep."

Last week. I looked from the paper to DJ.

"You're gonna hate this dude's guts," he said with a grin. "Wanna take a quick ride up north?"

CHAPTER SIX

Traveling west from Krum Bay, DJ and I took *Reel Fun* through the heavier boat traffic of Long Bay, then turned westward, toward Culebra. We passed Savannah Island, then covered ten miles of open water before we slipped through the channel between Culebrita and Cayo Norte.

As we came through, I noticed a dock on the eastern shore of Culebra. At this distance, I couldn't see much, except that there were more than a dozen boats tied to it.

Further to my right, a buoy with a white sign swayed on the waves, about halfway between *Reel Fun* and the dock. Writing was scrawled across it in red. I took a pair of binos from a compartment near DJ's knees.

The sign read: *Welcome to Wild Life at Zoni Beach*! in big, friendly letters, flanked by an elephant and a tiger's face with flashing eyes.

"Does Nick Garner run a wildlife preserve?" I asked DJ, as I lowered the binos. "I thought you said this place was his resort."

"This place is whatever it has to be. Whatever gets him the biggest tax break. Last I knew, he was reorganizing to make it a church." DJ had the VHF mic in his hand. He clicked the button down, identified his vessel and asked for a day slip.

I turned the binoculars toward the dock and watched people file onto a party barge. The wind shifted, and I heard music thumping from that direction. To the north of the pier, the crowd on the beach looked older than what was typical. I put the pieces together in my head.

Then I spotted an African elephant wading near the shore, spraying water from its trunk.

"He's got an elephant."

DJ snorted and shook his head. "If he's got one, he's got a half dozen. When Garner kicks off, there'll be a herd of them eating the daisies in your front yard."

"I'll invest in a good pooper scooper."

"It's not a joke," DJ said. "No wild animal should be forced to depend on a guy like Nick Garner. He'd let the tourists take a bite of one if he thought the money was better."

"So, he's a real captain of industry."

"He should be shot." DJ eased back *Reel Fun*'s throttle, slowing her down as we neared the dock.

A young man's voice cracked over the VHF, instructing him on which slip to take, and what the fees would be.

When we pulled into the dock, a couple of college kids took our lines and helped DJ fit his boat into its spot.

On land, DJ led us up a gravel path cut through the oceanside brush, which branched to the left about a hundred meters in. We passed a large in-ground pool with a swim-up bar. A sun-beaten woman lay across it, her bikini top barely holding on as an older man fondled her.

"They're enjoying retirement," I noted.

DJ said nothing, following the wrought-iron fence around the pool, hooking a corner, and taking us through a gap in adjacent buildings, where a half dozen air-conditioning units coughed and rattled. On the other side, we crossed over a roundabout positioned between seven or eight buildings like the central hub on a wheel. The roundabout encircled a small hill covered in flowering Puerto Rican hibiscus trees, and as we ducked under the branches, I got the impression that DJ knew this place better than he was letting on.

We exited the far side of the grove, slipped through another gap between the buildings, and walked a paved roadway, going up a hill.

A trio of twenty-something girls in a golf cart zipped down the hill, going the opposite way. They wore the same uniforms as the guys on the dock, except their shirts were much tighter, and each had a crown of hibiscus flowers.

"You think we should stop and ask somebody where Garner is?" I asked. "Like those girls that just went by?"

"Nah. This time of day, I know where he's at."

"You seem pretty familiar with this place, DJ."

"Not by choice."

I wasn't sure what he meant, but I knew I wouldn't get more than that out of him. I left it alone for now.

At the top of the hill, we came upon a small crowd of people. I'd guess about twenty or so, sitting on concrete bleachers dug out of the far side of the hill. Each person had their attention set on a stage with an arched covering about thirty meters ahead.

A woman in the same form-fitting T-shirt as the girls in the golf cart stood at center stage. She wore a pair of shorts that wouldn't have passed school dress code. A mic headset tamped down her blond hair like a headband.

She cradled a chimpanzee in a diaper.

I didn't hear what she said, but everyone clapped as DJ walked along the left side of the concrete stands, toward the stage. Behind it, I spotted a trailer sporting a graphic of an elephant bathing in the crystal blue Caribbean waters. The same animal I'd seen at Zoni Beach on the way in.

DJ and I came around the trailer and had a full view of the back of the stage. A wild energy seemed to bounce between the people back here. Some attended to exotic animals parked in cages, presumably getting them ready for their turn in the show. I spotted a lemur, some kind of large snake and something that looked like a guinea pig but was as big as a pit bull.

At the center of it all stood a middle-aged guy with a beer belly, buzzed hair and a gray, braided beard dripping down to his chest. He wore a top hat and matching jacket over a tropical print shirt and a pair of black shorts. He was a mix of P.T. Barnum, Tommy Bahama, and Steven Seagal.

A blond lady in tight black motorcycle leathers and matching helmet gripped the handlebars of a dirt bike. The visor of her helmet up, she planted a long kiss on the ringmaster.

While they smooched, DJ crept up behind him. I stayed back a few paces.

DJ tapped the ringmaster on the shoulder.

"DJ?" He tilted his head, then looked at me. "I didn't know you were coming by today. Where's Blunt? Or are you cutting this guy in?" He held an upturned palm in my direction, then seemed to balk at me. "Christ, DJ, you gotta check your eyes. Aside from the surfer-dude hair, this guy looks like an undercover cop."

"He's not a cop." DJ was clearly annoyed—whether it was Garner's assumption or that I was there, I couldn't tell.

"You sure about that? He's got that vaguely cop-ish way of standing, ya know?"

I crossed my arms. I'd never heard I stood like a cop— however one did that.

"Don't worry about him. He's working with me."

"Working with you? Are you striking out on your own?" Garner's brow folded. "I thought you didn't need money."

"Shut up a minute, man," DJ said. "A little bird told me a body washed up on Zoni a couple days back. You know—that piece of water out yonder that you own? What do you know about that?"

He licked his lips, his eye slow dancing between DJ and me. He shrugged.

"The police took care of it. Who knows how a body got there, anyway? My guess is some guy drank more than he could handle, fell off his boat and drowned." He shrugged, then nudged his head toward the stage. "I've got more important things to think about."

DJ didn't appear convinced by Garner's answer.

Neither was I. Any businessman would be losing his mind about a body appearing on his property, whether he ran a coffee shop, a garage, or a strip club. I'd have to think a luxury resort like this one, which depended so much on putting people in a relaxed mood to get at their wallets, would be averse to anything that might pierce the veil of paradise.

"That's your story?" DJ asked.

"Please, DJ. Don't put on a front for your buddy," Garner said, nodding my direction. "Or are you going to tell me that you suddenly care about a body being dropped?"

Quickly, DJ looked left, then right, before his hand har-pooned out and hooked the front of Garner's shirt. DJ reeled him over, marched him to the big trailer with the elephant picture, and slammed him against it.

The rattle of Garner's body smacking it was lost against the sound of a dirt bike's engine revving up to applause.

"Don't put this on me, man. I'm not like you—don't ever compare us," DJ said between his teeth, as I grabbed him by the shoulders and wrenched him off Garner.

"You're full of it!" DJ yelled as I walked him back.

"No more than you, my friend," Garner answered. I turned to get between them again, but Garner stayed with his back to the trailer, re-buttoning his shirt.

"You don't know anything about Luc Baptiste?" DJ asked, as I let him go.

Garner's fingers stopped buttoning.

"Luc Baptiste?" He took off his hat, then ran his hand over the top of his head. "That's who the cops found on the beach? The same Luc Baptiste?"

"The same guy who took out a restraining order against you last month?" DJ asked.

Garner's face darkened. "You heard about that?"

"We found the court documents on Luc's boat," I said.

"That was blown out of proportion."

"The judge who issued the order seemed to think you made a credible threat of bodily harm against him," I said. "Restraining orders don't happen without probable cause."

Garner put his hat back on and broke into a smile. "Man, DJ, he really is a cop, isn't he?"

"Don't change the subject," I said.

He sighed and turned to look toward the stage, then set his eyes back on us.

"I swear I didn't know it was Luc's body." He put his hat back on. "I get why you're talking to me. The restraining order looks bad. But I was on some… things. Did I shoot my mouth off at Luc? Yes. Was it wrong? Of course. In the heat of the moment, I made a mistake. I was out of my mind—you can't really believe anything I say when I'm… having my perceptions expanded."

In my experience, drugs had an outsized influence on murder. Generally, it was the acquisition of them that led to one person killing another. People will do just about anything to snuff out the embers of withdrawal.

That didn't fit every case, however. Once or twice, I had seen the aftermath of psychosis after a powder or a liquid tripped a primal switch deep inside the human mind. Rare, but not unheard of.

"I've never known anybody to flip out when they're on LSD," DJ said.

Garner sighed and scratched his chin. His jaw squeezed as if he had to keep himself from talking.

"You're getting into harder stuff, aren't you?" DJ asked. "I thought you were strictly a psychedelics and weed guy."

"Believe me, I am, especially after what I said to Luc."

"Which was what?" DJ asked.

"Something… regrettable."

DJ and I exchanged a glance. A powerful white guy like Nick Garner threatened by a black man with a platform like Luc Baptiste's. We both had an inkling of what was said.

"Tell us." DJ wasn't going to let him get off so easily.

"It doesn't matter now," Garner said.

"You think you're in a position to refuse us?" DJ asked, bunching his fists.

Garner slumped his shoulders and looked at the ground. "You heard about the article he wrote about me?"

I looked at DJ. "I'll tell you about it later," he said.

"After the fines his little exposé brought on me, I sued him in civil court to recoup some of the damage," he said. "The day before I called Baptiste, I got a message from my lawyer saying the judge had dismissed our case before we even had a chance to go to court. I was pissed, okay? A day later, when I decided to call him, I was still pissed. I took some stuff to mellow out, I called Baptiste with every intent to be civil, and he laid into me. Said he was going to come back for me, and that he had more on me, and all kinds of stuff that just made me madder."

He paused, holding his breath for a moment, then released it and chewed his lip.

"I lost it. I screamed at him, 'If you dig in my business again, nigger, I'll string you up.' He got it on tape. I screwed myself. I shouldn't have ever called him that, and I shouldn't have called him when I was high."

"You know, Nick, for a guy who's got a lot of people convinced about how smart he is, that was pretty dumb." DJ put it better than I could have.

"What about the drugs?" I asked. "What did you take?"

He peered around the corner of the trailer once more, then turned back to us.

"Are you worried about somebody showing up?" I asked.

"My wife, Betty," he said. "She'd be pissed at me if she heard me talk to you guys about this, but the whole thing was Tara's idea. She wanted to experiment with a combination one of the volunteers invented."

"You mean the college kids working for you," I said. "You aren't paying them?"

"They get a stipend," he said, annoyed. I took his reaction to mean this was a frequent topic of criticism. "I don't know what the kid put in the stuff he gave me, but he called it a wild ball. Named it after our resort."

DJ laughed. "Man, you gotta be kidding me. Nick Garner messing with something, and he don't know what's in it? What happened to all that self-possession, self-reliance trash you used to pedal?"

"It was a lapse in judgment," he said. "The kid named it after our place, so I felt obligated. And I didn't want Tara to think I was too scared to participate. You don't head up the group that's around here by being a pussy."

"Who's Tara? The woman on the bike?" I asked. "She doesn't strike me as the hard drug type."

"That's Songflower," Garner said.

"Is your wife aware you're kissing your girlfriend backstage?"

"Songflower's my wife."

I looked at DJ, who didn't appear the least bit fazed. "I thought you said your wife's name was Betty?"

"It is. We're also married to Songflower and Madeline."

My instincts about this resort were turning out to be more accurate than I'd imagined. "This is still U.S. soil, is it not?"

"We're married in spirit. And the government doesn't get to dictate how I live my life," Garner answered. "I moved out here years ago to get away from the tyranny that has become shockingly commonplace on the mainland. I'm not going to fall in line with government overreach."

Sure, the USVI wasn't a full-fledged state, but the U.S. federal government still had control over the island.

"Don't think too hard about it, Jerry," DJ said. "Nick Garner is a libertarian-type when it suits him. But, as you heard a minute ago, this jackass is happy to use the courts to sue people. And the wives come and go. Last time I was here, Nick had four."

"Samaya left me after Luc's article broke in *The Times*."

"As in *The New York Times*?" I asked.

"The same."

"Heard that article cost you a cool two million in fines from the EPA." A hint of a grin rolled across DJ's eyes. "I imagine that figure doesn't include all the fine folks you had to employ to clean up all that construction trash you dumped into the water."

"I didn't do that. That was a contractor. No one ever heard me tell anyone else to dump their trash into the ocean." Garner's face reddened. "Wild Life has done a lot to protect the waters around here and around Culebrita and Cayo Norte, okay? We've constructed protective barriers, put out buoys to warn private craft, and hosted fundraisers to keep the islands' natural splendor intact. I don't remember hearing about concerned citizens like DJ Martin putting up a cent from their considerable fortunes."

"DJ Martin didn't do anything to hurt no animals in the first place," DJ answered.

"I didn't hurt anything or anyone."

Having not read Luc Baptiste's article in *The New York Times*, I wasn't seeing the whole picture of how this went down.

"Did you dump chemicals?" I asked.

"I'm not getting into it," Nick said quickly.

"I will," DJ said. "This fine gentleman owns about four hundred acres on this side of Culebra. You seen those condos we walked past, right?"

"With the roundabout in the middle?"

DJ nodded. "He built those about a decade ago. Since then, he got wind that there was more money in renting out private villas. Only thing, there ain't too many private villas this way, on account of this land being a park until recently, so he's building them. Rather than dispose of his trash properly, he's let all his guys throw it wherever to save a few pennies. Most of it just followed the currents northwest and ended up along the beach. Luc Baptiste caught him."

"That was the contractors' choice, not mine," Garner said, in a way that suggested even he didn't believe his crappy argument.

"Two million is a lot of cash to lose," I said.

Garner's lips pinched together.

"I wasn't a fan of Luc Baptiste, and I'm not sad to see him gone, but if you think I killed him, let me ask you this: why would I dump his body near the beach I own? I've obviously learned which way the currents flow around here."

"Maybe you didn't do it," DJ said. "Maybe one of your volunteers is trying to impress you. Sounds to me like that kid who made the drug cocktail also wanted to impress one of your girls. Maybe that hundred bucks a week you pay him ain't enough to satisfy, so he's trying to get something on the side."

"If you have a problem with our volunteer stipend, take it up with the government. Everything we do at Wild Life on Botany Bay is legal."

"Except the weed growing," DJ said with a laugh.

Garner's face went a shade redder. He didn't seem amused.

"If you want to have a chat with the authorities about that,

DJ, be my guest. But I think you, of all people, won't want to take that up with anyone."

Behind him, the crowd roared again. Garner adjusted his hat and smiled at DJ. "If you'll excuse me, gentlemen, I have a business to run."

We watched him walk away, taking hold of a leash with a tiger on the end.

"He's not going to talk unless we have something more concrete," I said. "I want to give Luc's boat another once over."

"That's your call, Dep. You wanna go back there, we'll go back there." DJ took the first step away. I expected he wouldn't want to stay. There was a lot of baggage lying around this place, and he didn't want me picking through any of it.

CHAPTER SEVEN

We came back to the *Gazette* around sundown, after tying *Reel Fun* to the same spot on the marina as earlier.

"You feeling one way or the other about Garner?" DJ asked me, as I put the keys into the salon door and unlocked it.

"What I feel doesn't matter. What matters is what we can prove or disprove," I said, as I slipped them back into my pocket.

"All right, man. Tell me what doesn't matter."

I glanced in DJ's direction as I opened the door. The big lights over the marina cast shadows across his face, and for a moment I felt as if I were gazing into deep ocean, an Atlantean soothsayer reading the ripples, trying to guess at fate.

"What's Garner like, emotionally?" I asked.

DJ tilted his head. "I dunno, man. He's like any other prick-in-charge."

"I ask because the damage Luc did to Garner's reputation and business were already done. Garner is a creep and an asshole, but he struck me as self-serving, and mostly in control of his temper. Excusing one extreme lapse in judgment, he doesn't seem like the type to make trouble for himself. But you know him better than I do."

"Sure wish I didn't. But you read him right: he's always played cleanly, and he's almost always got his head on the way he wants it." DJ followed me inside the *Gazette*, the mess exactly as we'd left it. "What do you think about one of the kids smoking Luc to get on Garner's good side?"

I paused in the salon, giving it another visual check for anything we may have missed.

"That seems more likely to me, but that theory is the weakest kind of circumstantial. What I want to know is what Luc was working on. Did he dig up more misdeeds on Garner? If he did, we've got a compelling argument about how Garner would benefit from Luc's death, and maybe a stronger circumstance for one of our theories."

DJ nodded in agreement. "We never checked the cockpit holds. I'll get to it. After that, I'll poke around in the engine room."

"Sure," I said. "Since I found that compartment in his bedroom, I've been thinking I should check around the rest of the interior too."

The next couple of hours, DJ and I combed through every bit of the *Gazette* we could think to check—from bow to stern and radio mast to bilge. Other than a pair of handguns tucked in odd places, the bundle of papers I'd found earlier, and a baggie of either cocaine or heroin, we didn't stumble over any secret diaries or deeds to forgotten pieces of land.

Eventually, we decided our search of Luc's boat had reached the point of diminishing return. About the only thing we hadn't done was search the hull below the waterline.

DJ and I walked out to the cockpit. I turned around and put

the key into the lock on the salon door.

"Well, Luc Baptiste was on plenty of peoples' lists," I said, as I turned the key. "At least that packet of papers on *Reel Fun* tells us that. A guy like him kept a lot of dirt on a lot of powerful people."

As I turned around, I noticed DJ completely frozen. Something on the boat next to us had his full attention.

Over my left shoulder, I saw what it was. A man on the strip of dock off *Gazette's* starboard—between Luc's boat and the fishing trawler I noticed on the way in.

In the weak light, he looked like he'd just stumbled in from a trop rock festival. His hairy, tanned beer belly popped out from his open Hawaiian shirt, and his long, brown hair made him look like David Crosby coming off a 1969 world tour. Streaked with gray, his beard might be home to a hermit crab or two.

And he clutched a mean-looking sawed-off shotgun.

"That's illegal, you know," I said, motioning at the gun.

DJ kicked my ankle. "Shut up," he hissed.

"Hands up. Both of ya." The man's voice was a tar-laden grumble, like he rose from a rum bottle with a cigarette in his mouth every night when the sun went down.

Still, we put our hands up.

"Y'all were smart enough to come in the middle of the night a couple days back," he said, "when ole' Nels was sleeping off the beers. But this time, you showed up too early, and now you done pushed your luck too far."

"We aren't who you think we are," I said.

"Yeah, I'm sure you're not." He hocked a loogie and spat it on the dock. "Sure, you're cops or something, right? If you're cops, you show me y'all's badges."

"Do we look like cops? We're not cops, moron," DJ said.

"You gonna call me a moron, son?" Nels asked sarcastically. "I caught the two of y'all breaking and entering into a man's private property. According to law, I can stand my ground and I'm at liberty to shoot both your asses full of buckshot right here, right now."

"That's not actually how a stand-your-ground law works," I said. "And even if there is one in the USVI, I don't think you'll be able to argue its use when you shoot us with an NFA-restricted weapon." I nodded toward the shotgun. "Plus, we didn't break and enter. We used a key."

Nels's jaw twisted like he was chewing gristle, and his eyes burned hotter.

"Don't do the cop thing right now," DJ hissed before turning to Nels. "Look, man I understand why you're wary of the two of us," he began. "We've seen the inside of Luc's place—somebody's been there for sure. But we ain't robbing it. I mean, if we were, you're right to say we're about the two most piss-poor burglars that the Almighty ever made. I left my boat docked right there." DJ motioned at *Reel Fun*, behind Nels, but the man didn't take his eyes off us. "And neither of us is carrying a thing, which seems like bad business sense if we're a coupla thieves looking to make a profit."

"You're a pair of no-good criminals. Empty your pockets," Nels said. "Both of y'all."

"I'm not emptying my pockets," DJ grumbled.

"Just do it," I whispered back as I turned mine out. I held up my sat phone, showing it to Nels, then my wallet, and then dropped them both onto a seat cushion. I showed him my house keys. "These are mine." I held the keys high, then brought them low and dropped them on the cushion, as well. "And this is for

Luc's boat," I said as I held up the small key. "His brother-in-law is a detective for the Puerto Rican Police. A guy named Collat. He gave the key to us."

I couldn't see Nels's reaction. He didn't shoot me, at least, so that was something.

"Now, you." He motioned the shotgun toward DJ, who turned to me as if I'd knocked on Nels's window—porthole, I mean—and asked him to come over and stick us up.

"Go on now, brother, turn 'em out," Nels ordered. "I ain't been in the mood to shoot nobody for a real long time, but I'll always do what I hafta."

DJ grumbled, then turned out his pockets. All he had on him were the keys to *Reel Fun*.

"All right, so you ain't got nothing stolen in your pockets. You two boys are headed in the right direction," Nels said, lowering the shotgun, but not to the point that he couldn't swing it up on us in a heartbeat.

I slowly lowered my hands.

"Did you know Luc Baptiste?" I asked.

"He was my next-door neighbor. What do you think?"

"Fair point," I said. "When was the last time you saw him?"

"Few days ago," Nels replied, but it didn't appear he wanted to talk about that. He had something else on this mind. "I got a question for the two of you."

I wasn't in the place to refuse him, and a little dialog was good for earning trust.

"You said Luc's got a brother-in-law who's a detective with *La Uniformada*."

"Sure did," I answered.

"Then why ain't he out here, poking around? Why'd he send

you two?"

It was then that I realized I'd broken one of Collat's rules. His only one. I spoke his name.

But before I answered, Nels seemed to come up with the answer on his own.

"Shit." His shoulders slumped, and the shotgun's choke swayed beside his knee as all the tension drained from his shoulders. For a second, I thought he might tumble backward and splash into the water or whip that thing up and shoot us. "Luc finally got himself into real big trouble, didn't he? He crossed somebody connected and got himself killed."

CHAPTER EIGHT

Our new friend Nels had a lot more to say. And he'd only say it at the nearest bar; a single-story, corrugated steel building with a large patio that was half thatch and half blue tarp. A rusted sign planted in the dirt parking lot read Shell's Bar and Grill.

The place was walking distance from the marina—maybe half a block. The location, across Krum Bay from the desalination plant, ensured it would never be featured on any St. Thomas tourism brochures. Even so, it didn't look nearly as busy as it should have been, given the time of night and the space the building occupied.

When we walked through the front door, my initial assessment was confirmed. The bar was big enough to hold a couple hundred people, but as I scanned the room, I estimated no more than two dozen people inside.

A bouncer sitting on a bar stool across from us nodded at Nels. He was easily as tall as me, and twice as wide.

"You bringin' some new friends tonight, Mister Nels?" He grinned like a schoolyard bully, laying a trap for the squirrely kid.

"I got friends," Nels said, as he turned right and kept walking. DJ and I followed him on a path across the barroom. "I got more friends than you, you grinning, silly, little bitch…" The rest was lost in a stream of Nels's mutters.

My partner made eye contact with the bartender and raised his hand. "Bucket of beers," he said. "Don't care what. Just bring them to our table."

"Bucket!" the bartender cried.

On our left, a pair of sun-burnt tourists laughed over beachy mixed drinks, and a group of local guys who must've just got off work sipped beers and played at a tattered pool table with a beer-warped two-by-four standing in for one of the table's legs.

"You know I got friends," Nels mumbled. "Got one." He pushed open a door along the northern wall, leading us out to the patio. "Had one I cared about a lot. Ain't many people in this world got a friend they cared about a lot."

He led us straight to a table along the patio's leftmost wall, then pulled a chair out, and plopped down. His tanned belly hung out of his open shirt while he glared at the door, his lips twitching like a pair of hooked nightcrawlers while he talked to himself.

I pulled out the chair opposite him and rested my elbow on the two-by-four rail that the sections of thatch and tarp had been stapled to. DJ stood beside us, leaning on a support post.

From where we sat, we had a clear sight line to the marina— Nels's boat, in particular. His eyes shifted that direction.

Two seconds after we took our table, the door popped open behind me. I turned to see a little waitress trucking our way with a glistening metal bucket in her hand. The necks of green beer bottles poked over the top like fresh-cut celery.

"There's my girl!" DJ said with a flirty smile.

The waitress laughed and shook her head as she placed the bucket on the table between Nels and me.

"I'm not nobody's girl," she said in a light island accent. Maybe Jamaican, maybe Haitian or something else—my ear hadn't been tuned to all the different accents down this way. "You just keep that in your head, Mr. Light Blue eyes with your big, hungry smile."

"I never forget good news," DJ answered, not breaking his grin.

She rolled her eyes and laughed. "You got a way about you, don't you? Is there anything else I can get you gentlemen?"

"More." Nels plucked a bottle from the ice and took a long drink. "And keep 'em coming."

"Mister Nels, we're not going to have another incident tonight, are we? Don't want you scaring off your new friends."

"I can handle myself, Beth," he said, halfway into his bottle. "And these two ain't my friends. They're business associates. We're here to talk about business, okay? I can keep count of my bottles when I got business to talk about."

Beth raised her eyebrows at me.

"We're in negotiations," I confirmed, as I dug into my pocket and pulled out a credit card to start a tab. I didn't see which one. I didn't care. I handed it to Beth. "My partner and I are looking for some good marina slips to sell to retirees from the mainland."

Her eyes cut toward the marina in Krum Bay, then back to me, chopping my cover story to pieces.

"You could do better than that, Mr. Big Business Man." She took my card, then nodded in the direction of Nels's boat. "I can't expect that too many folks want a good look at the water plant when they're retiring down to St. Thomas."

I shrugged at her. I couldn't push the lie any further.

"We'll offer market rates," DJ said. "A square price for a square deal. We ain't here to pull the wool over anybody's eyes."

"I'm sure you never sweet-talked a soul in your life." Beth smiled at DJ as if she knew the kind of man he was—and she was probably right. With that, she walked back into the bar, throwing one last look over her shoulder in DJ's direction, catching his eyes following her.

When the door closed, DJ clicked his teeth and looked at me.

"I'm feeling better about our night, Dep." He grinned like a mountain lion coming upon a suburbanite's terrier.

I buried my face in my hands.

How he did it, I'd never know. I was tall and blond and looked good in a wetsuit, according to my wife, but I never had as easy a time with women as DJ apparently had. Then again, I'd never been much of a skirt-chaser—at a bar or anywhere else. Not even before I met Alicia.

A beer glistened at me from the bucket. I took it, the glass cold and wet against the muggy air that seemed to collect on the deck. From the color of the bottles, I was expecting Heineken or Tuborg, but it was called Stag and was from Trinidad and Tobago. I took a drink, and set my eyes on Nels, who looked longingly at his boat. Or Luc's boat, perhaps.

"You and Luc were close," I said.

"He was my friend." Nels continued looking out over the water. "He might've been part of the news, but Luc wasn't like them other ones. Wasn't in it to sell stories. He wanted truth. Said he liked the way it felt to write something a lot of people didn't want him to write." Nels took a drink from his beer, and his mouth curled into a bitter line. "Sometimes I felt like he was the only guy on this whole Earth who knew what was worth doing."

"How's that?" I asked.

He took a long pull and looked me directly in the eyes. "Either of you two in the military?"

"101st Airborne," DJ answered.

"I was Pararescue," I said.

"All right," Nels nodded slightly. "You two see combat?"

"Yeah," I answered. "Afghanistan."

DJ knocked on his titanium leg with his opposite foot.

"I was First Infantry," Nels said. "Vietnam."

"Big Red One." DJ nodded somberly.

Nels pointed his bottle at DJ in affirmation, then took another long pull from it. "Mortarman. Saw my first combat during Operation Cedar Falls in January of '67 and went through it all until we were called back to Fort Riley in '70."

The look on his face suddenly changed, like an old memory had captured and dumped him into a bottled reality like a lightning bug. Then the lid spun off, and he came back to Shell's Bar and Grill.

"Three years on the campaign does something to a man," he said. "Makes you crave death. Not dying, mind you. You just want to lay your eyes on death from time to time, the same way your heart aches for an old girlfriend when you're home alone at night, even though you know she ain't no good."

He looked up at us, holding his next thought. Nels was gauging our reactions. Probably expected us to be shocked, maybe offended that he'd admitted something that would have curdled the sensibilities of polite, decent people.

"You need the gamble," Nels continued. "The excitement.

Theme park rides don't do it. Fast cars and motorcycles work for some fellas. Not me. Gotta be bullets flying, blood, and fire—kill or be killed. Some of my buddies turned to crime after the war. Doing stuff like running drugs and knocking over gas stations. I didn't."

I nodded. I didn't know anyone who'd turned to crime. But I'd drifted from most of the guys I'd served with.

Yet, the desire Nels described was familiar to me. I'd never hurt anyone who didn't deserve it, and I wasn't going to jump into the drug trade, but I understood. Once my body was washed by the wave of pure adrenaline I got when I jumped out of my first airplane, it craved that feeling again.

"Luc understood," Nels continued. "The kid wasn't a vet, but he had that same wild streak in him." He held his beer up in a toast, looked to the sky, then took another drink. "He always kept charging, head-first, at whatever he was onto. That kid loved the rush."

"Do you know what he was working on?" I asked. "Any idea who might've wanted him dead?"

"Yeah," Nels said. "I know exactly who wanted him dead."

My head swung right—to DJ, who looked every bit as surprised as I must have. Did Nels say what I thought he'd said? I turned back toward him.

"You do?" I sat my beer down and leaned closer. "Who?"

Nels looked at the marina again. He studied it for a moment, the murk clearing from his eyes, and his lips pressing into a sharp line. Then, he directed his eyes back to me.

"The elites," he said.

My shoulders slumped.

DJ snickered beside me. I managed to hold a straight face,

not betraying how stupid I suddenly felt.

"Ain't a joke," Nels said. "They're across the whole damned world, killing good folks like Luc—folks who're trying to stand up for what's right and bring attention to the evil things the elites are doing to everybody."

All this time wasted by chasing a dead lead. We couldn't leave until I got my credit card back from Beth and closed my tab. So, I thought I'd entertain Nels's theory for a minute by challenging it.

"And who are these people?" I asked. "And I don't want to hear about the World Bank or the New World Order or shadow governments pulling strings from Cold War bunkers. Give me names. Specifically, who are the elites?"

"I can't name names—they all been scrubbed from the record. They got money and they got ways to hide. They ain't people like us," Nels fired back. "Politicians. Big businessmen. Billionaires. People with the kind of money they won't get ground under the boots of the New World Order."

"Hey, pal," DJ said, "you're talking to two of those right now."

I shot him a look that told him to shut up. I didn't like talking about money.

"And what do these people do?" I asked Nels.

"They put fluoride in the water." Nels grabbed a fresh beer from the bucket. "They drop chemtrails on us from the sky to keep us in line, they put asbestos on dollar bills to keep us buying cancer drugs, and they keep us fat and happy, not thinking too hard about why things are the way they are. They don't want nobody questioning their position at the top, or why the one percent got so much power over everybody else. I mean, hell, look at the drug companies in P.R. After Maria, who was the first ones to get power back?"

"They were," I said.

"The hospitals never lost power," DJ added.

I'd read that most of the big drug manufacturers in Puerto Rico had stores of diesel, backup generators, clean water, and food in the eventuality that a storm like Maria knocked out Puerto Rico's already weak infrastructure. Didn't take a genius to see disaster preparation as a worthy investment here.

"And they ain't curing diseases." Nels brought his beer bottle up, then stopped halfway, struck by a thought. "Hell, you seen them commercials on TV, right? When they go calling out the side-effects of their drugs like auctioneers. I bet you those companies' drugs are the cause of half the diseases people got these days. Drug companies are still companies—they got greed and shareholders whose only interest is the bottom line—and are they gonna stop selling something just 'cuz Grandma Dottie's turning a little green after taking her heart pills? Hell no!"

Froth hung off the corner of Nels's mouth. I felt sorry for getting him so worked up—the man was obviously suffering from something. I turned around and looked through the small window in the door, praying I'd spot Beth. No luck.

Then again, this might be a cry for help from Nels. If Luc Baptiste really were his only friend, I couldn't leave him here alone to wrestle with his grief. He needed someone to talk to. Clearly.

The least I could do was stick it out with him for an evening.

"Did either of you two know that LSD was supposed to be a blood thinner?" Nels asked.

I shook my head.

"Didn't have a damned clue." DJ took his first beer from the bucket.

"Yup. Some Swiss doctor made the first batch looking for a respiratory and circulatory stimulant. After he figured out what it really was, he started sending packets of LSD to doctors and researchers across the world. When word got out that it expanded peoples' minds, what happened?" He slapped his open hand on the table. "Illegal!"

"That's the elites at work again," he said. "They didn't want people to see what kinda grip they got the whole world in. They didn't want John Q. Public to quit worrying about his mortgage and buying a new car every two years. They wanted him to be a white-collar slave.

"But I'm getting off track," he said, then sipped his beer.

"So, you think there was some big conspiracy of mortgage brokers on failed blood-thinners who killed Luc Baptiste?" DJ asked.

I expected Nels to sock him for being a smartass, but he didn't seem bothered by DJ's skepticism. Or mine. I imagine he was used to people not believing him.

"The elites wanted Luc dead because he was always digging in the business of powerful people, and he dug in the wrong spot this time. Or the right spot, I guess," Nels said. "Those folks got a lotta fingers in a lotta pies—they wouldn't think twice about killing off an honest man like Luc. Hell, they'd probably kill someone like him as fast as they could."

My brain searched for any kind of foothold. This was too much to take in right now. So, I leaned my elbow on the two-by-four beside me again and sipped my beer.

"Thanks for cluing us in, partner," DJ said.

I looked at him, wordlessly letting him know he was crossing a line, but he kept his attention on Nels.

"But you got anything more specific to share with us?" DJ asked. "Like, did you see Luc hanging out with anybody you didn't recognize? Maybe catch a glimpse of the guys who went through his boat a couple days back? Did he tell you anybody threatened to whip his ass or hurt him?"

"Well, I did see the fellas that tore his place up," Nels said. "There was three of them, I think. I don't know. Maybe it was two. Or four." He brushed his long hair out of his face. "I called the cops. But they got there after the other fellas left. And they just kinda came and went. Nobody said nothing to me."

Did Collat know that? If the police were called to Luc's boat, there should be a record of it somewhere, and Collat would have access to it. He'd never mentioned it.

Nels's expression changed. He'd remembered something.

"You know what?" He put his elbow on the table, coming closer to me, excitement in his eyes. He tapped the table with his index finger. "I did see Luc in this here bar with somebody I seen at the VA once or twice. It was about a week ago, when I… uh…"

"Had an incident," I said, remembering what Beth had warned Nels about when we sat down. My guess was he'd gotten blind drunk.

"Yeah, an incident," Nels said. "Luc was having a business meeting with this guy from the VA—what's his name? Anyway, there was a voice recorder on the table between them."

"A voice recorder?" I asked. "How big was it?"

"I dunno. Small enough to fit in Luc's pocket. He always had the thing on him."

"Small enough to fit inside a DVD case?"

Nels blinked at me, surprised by the odd comparison. "Yeah, I guess it could, if you needed it to."

I turned to DJ. "Did you see a digital voice recorder on the boat?"

"Man, we tore that thing apart," he replied. "Who's this guy Luc was talking to?" DJ asked. "He work at the VA?"

"No," Nels answered. "No, he's a vet. A Marine who was in Operation Iraqi Freedom. I know his name's Marc, but the Iraq guys don't hang with the Vietnam guys all that much, so I don't know him well. We talked at the Memorial Day cookout this past May for a minute—I know he was a combat engineer who was caught in an IED blast while cleaning up a street or something. Lost his arm. Maybe he knows something about Luc."

Or, at least, he knows what he and Luc had talked about.

"Is the VA open right now?" I asked, looking for Beth over my shoulder.

"They'd be closed by now," Nels answered. "But they open up tomorrow morning at eight sharp."

Looked like DJ and I had somewhere to be in the morning.

CHAPTER NINE

From her office's vantage point in the Hildon Building, Tamara Price could have looked down into the heart of Santurce, San Juan's most populated barrio. If Miss Price were to spin her chair around, she'd have a perfect view of the Bay of San Juan, and all the swollen cruise ships waddling into port near the historic district, spilling out passengers greased up with money, oblivious of small, sick people like Gabriela's daughter, Flor. From Miss Price's lofty office, San Juan was as clinical and orderly as one desired. At this height, there were no street vendors on sidewalks, roasting in the Puerto Rican sun as they fried up mashed plantains for mofongo and prayed to catch tourists' eyes and a few dollars. None of the buildings below moldered or stunk of mildew after Hurricane Maria had blown the island down to its skin.

No one was lame. No one was sick. No one was poor, except through their own failures of effort. People were not jammed into the poorhouse randomly. Misfortune was a compass, always pointed in the right direction.

On the eighth floor of the Hildon Pharmaceutical building,

one could look down and see a perfect world of majestic white sail boats, gleaming black cars, and people with money to burn. To be Gabriela Ramos, sitting in front of Miss Price, was to be inspired by a young woman's capacity for self-determination, wits, and above all else, hard work—the fuel for all fortunes.

If Gabriela had only had the focus and the guts when she was younger—if she hadn't chased boys as a young teenager and sniffed out alcohol in her mother's hutch the way other kids hunted for Christmas presents, maybe she wouldn't have had to come to her boss, begging for charity.

Even before showing up at this meeting—if asking for a handout could be considered a meeting—Gabriela knew her place in relation to Miss Price—six floors down and two promotions up. A supervisor's office held fast to the rung between Miss Price, newly hired vice president of special projects at Hildon, and Gabriela Ramos, Team Lead for Event Planning.

The two of them were of an age. Gabriela was almost thirty. And regardless of what her corporate bio might say, Tamara Price was only thirty on a bad day. Her eyebrows perfectly groomed, her skin radiant under a dusting of foundation, she looked closer to twenty-four, and would probably age at half the rate of Gabriela.

A good face to have for a company, and not only on account of her God-given, wide, clear eyes, and dark, silky hair that always fell just the right way over her shoulders, or her fetching smile that nabbed everyone, or that she was a swatch of "diversity" for a company with a board overwhelmingly stuffed with balding white men.

No, Miss Price was also as sharp as they came. She had an unparalleled knack for pitching ideas to the rest of Hildon's board, perceptively guessing sticking points and objections in the planning phases for each new project, when team leads like Gabriela did dry runs of their presentations on new ideas in Tamara's office.

And Miss Price's eye for talent was unmatched. Gabriela had worked under three different VPs over her six years with Hildon. None of them hired the way Miss Price did. None saw the potential in an applicant's portfolio as clearly, or seemed to understand how personalities fit together on a team, or how best to motivate them to meet the teams' goals.

Meeting goals might've been Miss Price's strongest talent. She always got results.

Put it all together, and you had what seemed an inevitability; one of the youngest vice presidents to ever serve on a major pharmaceutical company's board. So, if anyone, short of the Lord God, could help wiggle Gabriela's daughter into the Anthradone trial, it was Miss Price. After all, the trial was being run by a contractor on Hildon Pharmaceuticals' behalf. An up-and-coming VP would have to have some sway.

"I just don't see how I can do anything to help," Miss Price said. "I'm sorry—I truly am, Gabriela—but I'm simply not in the position to interfere with a trial."

Miss Price's eyes pulled Gabriela's attention from the high windows beyond her. So clear and young, and looking into them brought a pang of knowing Gabriela would miss a young woman's will and energy. All that determination, and earnest seeking.

No crying. No whining. No feeling sorry for yourself. Lord, Jesus, grant me the strength to endure in Your name.

"You understand, don't you?" Miss Price asked. "My hands

are tied. You've been like family to me, and to everyone else at Hildon, Gabriela. I, of course, want the best for your daughter, but using my position to do what you've asked calls into question our entire organization—it's *problematic*."

Gabriela swallowed the lump down her throat and blinked her eyes clear.

"I wouldn't want to cause a problem."

"It would compromise the nature of the scientific study," Miss Price said. "A drug like Anthradone, with all its promises and potential to cure such a rare disease without any other effective treatments—think of how many people have waited for that. Any outside interference could set it back years, and meanwhile, the people who need it won't get it."

Miss Price spoke like a grief counselor. Soft, but firm, giving measured doses of bitter, jagged reality. The world couldn't stop for one little girl.

"There's also a personal risk for you, Gabriela. Even if someone were to know that we discussed this, it would be a serious black mark on your record."

Gabriela's spine stiffened. Her fingernails prodded at the heels of her palms. *Lord save me from myself. Don't let me lose this job. Please, if it is Your design.*

"Hildon would have to let you go, and you'd have a difficult time getting work in the pharmaceutical industry ever again—no one wants to risk undermining science. Think of all the capital we have to invest on an orphan treatment like Anthradone. Research is our biggest exposure to risk, and to open ourselves up to further exposure because an employee pushed too hard from the inside— the margins are already slim, and the consumer base is going to be infinitesimal."

"No—I didn't mean to—"

Miss Price held up a perfectly manicured hand.

"I know you didn't—you're a good mother trying to do everything possible for her daughter. Who among us wouldn't do that? That's why I'll keep our meeting off the record. That, and respect for the work that you've done here. We watch out for our Hildon family members."

Like family. It felt good to be protected by someone who cared. Even if Miss Price didn't have any kids.

"We can't taint the blind nature of a drug trial," she said. "You understand."

"I understand. Of course."

Miss Price smiled sadly from the other side of her big desk. She folded her hands, only to spread them again.

"I'll do anything else I can to help you," she said. "I can dig up referrals for another pediatric oncologist—we can relocate you to any major city in the continental U.S., any city with an outstanding children's hospital—but I can't meddle in a study. It's unethical."

Gabriela took Miss Price's words as well as any mother in her position could have. A new doctor wouldn't do it. Moving across the country with a daughter as sick as Flor might kill her. Her fingernails bit into her palms again, but she didn't make a scene. She wouldn't let herself cry in front of her boss. She had a good job, even if her paycheck didn't cover all of Flor's bills; she was already paid in the eighty-fifth percentile of people who'd held her position for the same number of years she had.

"Gabriela, honey, you seem stressed," Miss Price said. "Do you need to take a personal day?"

"I'm out of vacation days." Gabriela set her eyes on her feet.

The tips of her shoes were dulled with age—something that never would've happened to her four years ago.

"Then you have my permission to take unpaid days," Miss Price offered. "I'll clear it with HR." She picked up the receiver on her desk phone and started to bring it to her ear.

Unpaid vacation? No, that was worse than working—without work to distract her, she wouldn't be able to focus on anything. Not with the knowledge of crippling debt creeping closer and closer by the hour while Gabriela did what? Slept on the couch next to Flor's bed and watched TV?

"That's all right." Gabriela forced herself to look Miss Price in the eyes. She flexed her cheeks, jaw, and every other muscle in her face until her lips formed something resembling a grin.

She pushed herself up from Miss Price's Italian leather couch.

"I'll be just fine, Miss Price." She held the smile. "I appreciate you watching out for me."

Miss Price slowly hung up the phone, cheerfully meeting Gabriela's smile with one of her own.

"Thank you for sparing your time," Gabriela said.

"Sparing my time? Gabbie, we know each other better than that."

Gabriela forced a smile. If she could've seen her own face, she was sure she would've seen the smile as a cold, twitching thing, a fish trying to gulp down its last few breaths.

"Try your best to take it easy, honey," Tamara said. "Everything you are, your clothes, your smile, the way you wait in line at the grocery store—your whole person reflects on the company."

"It does." Then, Gabriela turned to the door, took the lever handle in her stinging hand, and twisted it until the latch let go. She scurried out of Miss Price's office before her whole person reflected the thoughts and feelings, she felt bubbling up inside.

Gabriela strode past the secretary, Luis, without giving him a first look. She felt his eyes on her as she cut toward the small hallway beyond his desk. She felt him watching, taking pity on her, tasting the despair that must've been peeling off her skin until she moved right, into an intersecting hallway, and ran for the nearest bathroom.

Inside the first stall, she gave herself five minutes. Not an extra second would be wasted on tears, on feeling bad for herself or for Flor. There were precious few seconds left.

When the timer beeped on Gabriela's phone, she unspooled a wad of toilet paper. She blotted the running mascara as best she could. A quick prayer to the Lord for strength and guidance, then, she emerged from the bathroom stall, and caught an eyeful of herself in the long mirror over the vanity.

Terrible. Awful. Unpresentable, uneven smudges of mascara under her eyes—it was no wonder she hadn't climbed Hildon. She pulled a paper towel from the dispenser, wet it, and scrubbed.

Before long, all the mascara was erased. She'd left her makeup in her purse at her desk. If she wanted to fix it, she'd have to emerge from this secluded bathroom and face the world again.

Outside, the bathroom, the halls murmured with distant phone calls and the hollow clicks of computer keyboards. No one noticed her. No one cared. They had their own problems.

She wound through the halls, reached the elevator bank, and rode it down six floors.

As soon as the doors opened, the stench of burnt coffee hit her nose, and the chatter of people taking their first fifteen of the day assaulted her ears.

She continued down the main hall of the second floor, toward her team office—the tiny room she shared with her two subordinates, Paul and Martina—a space far too small for two people, let alone three. Thank God the new campus would be opening in a week, sparing them all another summer of swimming through each other's body heat for nine hours a day.

What did body heat matter to Gabriela now? Would Flor still be with her next summer? Would she comment on the sweat stains around the collars of her mother's shirts when the laundry came back?

Or would she be gone?

Gabriela understood why putting Flor in the trial would be frowned upon. But didn't she have Li-Fraumeni Syndrome too? Which was more unethical? Picking out a single person to add into a trial that would probably include hundreds of people? Or letting a little girl die when you had a cure available, because innovation was hard and drug development cost too much money to risk?

Year-end balance sheets meant everything to Hildon. The bottom line must hold. Did their cures pay enough to cover advertising? How about construction of the new campus, and the new hires' salaries? Was the income stream fat enough to satisfy the stockholders' profit margin? And what about compensation packages? Lord help them if they forgot about compensation packages.

Income was soft this year? Buy up another lab. Figure out a new way to use an old drug—and if you could use that old drug to treat an orphaned disease like Li-Fraumeni, you'd go home with a two percent raise. Salami-slice every formula and compound until you had customers using antibiotics to treat gout. Did it matter if Flor were in one trial? Would Hildon's vast corporate web tear from its supports and drop them all into freefall?

No, it wouldn't. But Gabriela needed her job. And, in any case, Miss Price wouldn't help her. Who else could she beg for help?

Nobody.

When she turned into the open door of her team's office, she found Paul hunched over his computer, their team's budgetary spreadsheet open on his screen.

"How'd the meeting go with Price?" His office chair groaned as he looked back at her.

"Fine," Gabriela said. She dug in her purse, looking for her mascara.

"What did she say about getting that banner made for the kickoff celebration?"

Banner? What banner? Who cared about a banner?

"Gabbie?"

Right. *The banner.* Her cover story.

"It didn't come up." She found the black tube of mascara tucked in an out-of-the-way pocket, separate from her hot pink makeup bag. Flor must've been playing in her purse again.

"You said you were going to ask her."

This wasn't going away. She sighed, her hands flat on her desk, and then she turned around to face him. He didn't know about Flor. None of her subordinates did.

"Call the printing company and see if you can get it put on our account. They'll work with us."

Paul crossed his arms. "What's their name again?" he asked.

"I'll find it." Gabriela turned back to her desk, unlocked her computer, then opened the company directory system. Numbers for all of Hildon's vendors, contractors, and researchers crawled up the screen as she scrolled to the entry for M&G Print Services, but a moment after seeing it, she froze.

The next entry sent a flutter up her spine. Markel Research Group—the Anthradone trials.

Gabriela looked over her shoulder, and saw Paul with his back turned, grumbling, his nose six inches from his computer monitor as he pored over whether the napkins at the kickoff celebration should be aqua or turquoise.

She clicked the entry for Markel Research, scrolled down and snatched a piece of paper off a notepad she kept next to her keyboard. After scribbling down the office number, she backed out of the Markel entry, clicked M&G Print Services, took that number down, then gave it to Paul.

A half second later, she was three paces down the hall, fighting every urge to sprint.

Then she slowed as her thoughts coiled around a new problem: where was she going to call Dr. Markel without anyone noticing? She couldn't go back to her car. She'd have to swipe her ID badge at the door, and if someone got suspicious a week or a month or a year from now, she'd have to explain why she took an irregular trip out to her car that morning. No empty offices here—they were behind schedule on the new building, and all the new hires had been stuffed in. Bathrooms were right out. Too many people coming or going.

She opted for a particular broom closet—one crammed in a corner on the opposite end of the building, near an IT services storeroom.

The janitors worked nights, so it was a perfect place.

When Gabriela turned into the hall on the southwest side of the building, she found it empty, the lights off.

Perfect.

Inside, the closet was plenty big for someone as small as Gabriela. It smelled of bleach, latex and dust—something that normally bothered her, but not now.

Her left hand clutched the note with Markel's number. Her right hand held fast to her phone. She'd kept the broom closet light off, only using the light from her phone's screen to illuminate the note.

She tapped in the numbers, her thumbs trembling. Once she had the number in, ready to dial, she paused and prayed. Let the prayers guide her through. Then, she hit the button.

She was barely able to hold onto the phone as she pressed it to her ear.

It rang once.

"Markel Research Group, how may I direct your call?" a woman's voice answered.

Gabriela went numb. She hadn't thought about what she was going to say, much less who she was going to talk to. Should she ask for a supervisor? Maybe the person in charge of planning trials? But what would she do then? Ask them for a spot for Flor Ramos, the girl they'd rejected already? What in the hell had possessed her to zip off on her own and do this? How small she was, how insignificant. No one would listen to her.

"Hello?" the receptionist said.

The veins in Gabriela's ears pounded. She could barely hear herself think. Now or never. *Do it or leave yourself wailing at Flor's funeral about how you had a treatment so close, you were only a few words away from getting it to her. Live with that the rest of your wretched life.*

She had to say something.

"Dr. Markel, please." Right to the top. A big gamble, one she knew could backfire, and likely would. If Markel were the kind of man who micromanaged everything, he'd sniff her out as a liar before she could say much at all. But if he were too detached from his own company, she'd be wasting her time.

There has to be a way, oh Lord. Shepherd me.

"May I ask who is calling?" the receptionist said.

"Yes, my name is Flor Gabriela—" the only two names that came to her "—and I'm calling from the Associated Press wire service. I wondered if Dr. Markel wouldn't mind telling me about a new cancer drug, I've heard he's working on? Anthradone, is it? Am I pronouncing that correctly?"

Gabriela braced for the receptionist's answer. Her hands had gone back to trembling. She noticed everything now—her own breathing, the faint thud of footsteps on the floor above her, and the worrying silence on the other end of her phone call.

"Dr. Markel is currently not in the office," the receptionist finally said. "May I take a message for you, Miss Gabriela?"

Without meaning to, Gabriela breathed a sigh of relief.

"He's not?" She asked. "Is there another way I can reach him?"

"I'd be happy to take a message for you, ma'am."

"Oh, no, that's fine. I'll talk to someone else." Gabriela ended the call.

What the hell was she doing? Impersonating someone to talk to a doctor she didn't even know—one that she had a truly clear conflict of interest with? And what if she *did* get Dr. Markel on the line? What then? Did she sob into the phone and beg him to bend the rules and put Flor into the Anthradone trial?

Another prayer came.

Gabriela stared into the darkened closet. She saw vague shapes in the shadows. She saw a future without light, a barren, gray smear. She saw herself barefoot and shivering, damned to wander through a wilderness of dead plants, dried riverbeds and sulfur, the shimmering heat, the sleepless nights of mourning. A lake of fire.

Her mind pictured Flor, a preschooler, squeezing her thick, black hair together with a rubber band, like a farmer wrestling with a bundle of hay. She tamed her hair, then put a tiara on her head and twirled in the living room of their old house, showing off the ballet steps she'd learned.

Six years ago. Half her daughter's life. She was so full of energy before Li-Fraumeni, when the worst illness Flor ever had was a string of stomach aches that a doctor found out was chronic indigestion caused by a bacterial migration from her gut.

All it took to cure that was a single treatment of Poraxim—another of Hildon's products, which they were happy to sell for a couple hundred dollars.

No one batted an eye about giving her that medicine. No one had yanked it away or told Gabriela it would be unethical to use it to heal her daughter.

Now it was all different.

Gabriela wiped her hand on her skirt, then she opened the closet door and checked the hall. Just as she was about to step out, her phone rang in her hand.

She jumped. Somebody was going to hear it. She shut the closet door and hit the button to silence the phone.

On the screen was a number she didn't know. It wasn't saved in her phone, and it wasn't the number for Markel Research—it was a couple digits off.

She let her phone vibrate in her hand until it stopped, and the screen went dark. Then, she switched her phone over to silent.

As she started to open the closet door, the phone buzzed again.

Same number.

Gabriela couldn't answer. She knew it had to be someone from Markel. Probably an attorney or a fraud officer—she didn't want to face up to what she'd done. How could she explain herself? More lies? She wouldn't be able to keep track of them all.

But when the phone started rattling at her a third time, Gabriela knew this wasn't going away. She had to face whomever it was head on, offer a sincere apology without elaborating too much, and hope that would be enough.

She answered, bringing the phone to her ear.

"Hello?"

"Is this the reporter from the AP?" A man's voice asked. Not the receptionist.

Her heart jumped into her throat.

"Who is this?" Gabriela asked. "How did you get my number?"

"You called my lab and asked for me."

Impossible.

"Dr. Markel?"

"Yes." He was whispering into the phone. Gabriela pictured a man in a dark closet hiding, like her. "You stirred up my receptionist, Angela," he said. "What did you tell her?"

"Just that I wanted to talk to you about Anthradone," she said. "But I don't think that's what upset her, I hung up on her."

The call went silent for a handful of seconds. Long enough for

Gabriela to consider telling him the truth.

"Dr. Markel, I—"

"I can tell you everything you'll want to know about Anthradone, but we can't do it over the phone. How quickly can you come to my house?"

Now wasn't the time for the truth.

If Gabriela could get into the same room as Dr. Markel, she knew she had a better chance of getting him to accept Flor into the Anthradone trial. He couldn't turn away someone in need—not face-to-face.

"Where do you live?"

"West of San Juan," he answered. "I'm on the coast, north of Manati."

Gabriela wanted to leave now, but she couldn't. Not after telling Miss Price she couldn't take a personal day. And she'd have to arrange for Flor's nurse to stay a couple of hours later than usual.

"This evening," she said. "Around 6 p.m."

"Then that'll have to do," he said. "Am I calling you on a cell phone number?"

"Yes."

Silence followed her answer.

Gabriela looked at her phone—of all the times to get disconnected.

She started to re-dial the doctor when an alert to a text message appeared. She tapped it and a message from Dr. Markel's number came on the screen—his home address.

CHAPTER TEN

Tamara Price lifted her head up high, pushed her shoulders back, and marched toward Rachel Little's office door on the top floor of the Hildon building. It would be Tamara's office soon enough, when Rachel Little stepped down, and Tamara, the odds-on-favorite for Hildon's next CEO, took over. She had to act like she owned this place. She had to be confident to inspire the confidence of her future employees. She had to keep the money flowing.

But when she pushed the door open, her icy facade cracked the instant her eyes met those of the man on the other side of Rachel's office door.

He stood in front of the desk. His slicked back, sandy brown hair seemed to absorb the last few threads of light filtering through the floor-to-ceiling windows along the far wall. He shouldn't have been here; it was an unnecessary risk.

The police officer, hat in hand, nodded Tamara's way.

"Tamara!" Rachel did her big greeting, as always, her arms outstretched, ready for a hug, her wavy blond hair bouncing off her shoulders, and the flared hems of her white pants swishing around her naked ankles. She slipped around her desk and came Tamara's way. "So glad to have you here."

Always too familiar for business. Rachel was touchy-feely in ways that seemed premeditated. In any case, Tamara held her arms out for a hug as well, because you *had* to match the other person's energy when in a social situation. Hinting at discomfort meant letting Rachel dominate the room, and that was social suicide. As sure as vomiting on her shoes.

The two women, CEO of Hildon, and VP of Hildon Special Projects, embraced each other like long-lost sorority sisters. It'd been a day since they'd seen each other.

Tamara watched the police officer over Rachel's shoulder. His face betrayed nothing, and his hands were as still as a trained killer's. While he kept his nerves together, so too, would Tamara.

Letting go, but still holding Tamara's shoulder in her hands, Rachel tucked her chin and smiled so warmly, it almost turned Tamara's stomach—that smile had definitely been practiced in a mirror.

"I thought this was going to be a one-on-one meeting," Tamara said, breaking off from Rachel's hug. "I hope I didn't arrive early."

"Oh please, as if you could. You're right on time. I called you down because I wanted you to meet Officer Abalos and his men." Rachel waved a hand from the officer standing in front of her desk to this year's sectional, pushed into the corner, with a pair of uniformed policemen sitting on it. Tamara's blood went hot. What kept her from bolting through the door was the same sheer guts and determination that had put her in Rachel's office in the first place. A meek person didn't rise to the upper echelons of a Fortune Global 500 company the way Tamara Price had.

Both the officers on the sectional smiled affably at Tamara.

"Good afternoon, gentlemen," she forced herself to say. "Welcome to Hildon, and I'm pleased to meet the both of you."

"Officer Abalos," Rachel said as she turned and strolled behind the desk, "I'd like you to meet our VP of Special Projects, and the youngest executive to ever serve Hildon Pharmaceuticals, Tamara Price."

He extended his hand.

Not wanting to make a scene, Tamara took it immediately, and shook.

"Miss Little has said a lot of good things about you." Officer Abalos may have looked white, but his Puerto Rican accent was every bit as thick as any of the other locals Tamara had met.

"She's always flattered me," Tamara said, breaking the handshake. Modesty was always good. Showed confidence.

"Don't let her downplay herself," Rachel said. "Tamara is the brains behind our new campus. She went way beyond her title and has brought it all together in a way that has left even the board wondering where I dug her up."

"You must be a very ambitious woman," Officer Abalos said.

"I love this company and I love the work I do. Sometimes I feel as if I've never worked a day in my life."

"You may feel like that now," Rachel said with a smile. "But when you're running the show, you'll change your tune. Everyone wants a piece of my time, everyone wants more money, everyone wants, wants, wants! It's never ending. There are times where I swear this job will drive me to murder." She gave a playful smile to Officer Abalos. "Just a joke, of course."

He laughed, his eyes meeting with Tamara's.

"In any case," Rachel said, as she sat in the big leather chair behind her desk, "you aren't here to listen to me gripe and I'm sure you have work you need to return to. I only wanted you to have a face to put with Tamara's name, since you'll be working closely with her over the coming days. We'll be in contact to talk about firmer security plans tomorrow."

"And we'll be here." Officer Abalos reached across the desk to shake Rachel's hand. "I'll pass the word to a few watch sergeants who will post off-duty work opportunities for their people. We'll have the manpower you need for a smooth, safe opening party for your new building."

"Wonderful," Rachel said with a smile. "Once you've got an actionable security plan in place, please send it over for our approval."

Orders in place, Officer Abalos headed for the door. The other officers rose from the couch and followed him into the outer office, where Tamara watched Rachel's secretary rise from her desk with a toothy smile, then escort them to the elevator. Tamara closed the door behind them, her pulse throbbing through fingers chilled with sweat.

"So," Rachel said, with an expectant look in her eyes, "are you holding weed on your person, or do you get that jittery around cops just because it makes things more exciting that way?"

Tamara turned and faced her boss, watching as she pulled open the big filing drawer by her knee. Out of it, she brought a bottle of scotch and a pair of glass tumblers.

"I've had some incidents with the police," Tamara said. "Every black girl who grew up in Southwest Atlanta knows what I mean. You don't trust a man in uniform, until you *know* you can trust him."

Rachel poured a splash of scotch into both glasses, then held the other one in Tamara's direction.

"We're a long way from East Point, little darling," Rachel said with a smile. She bobbed the glass, urging Tamara to have a drink with her.

Turning down a drink with your boss was career suicide. Tamara walked over, accepting it from Rachel, who wasn't ready to let it go.

"Besides, every officer you'll see on Hildon's premises from here on out is being paid by us. Handsomely. Nobody on that side of the law with half a brain would do a thing to us. Even after we write the checks, any cop in Puerto Rico who's part of the union will give you and me and everyone else with an impressive title in this building the light touch treatment. You'll see."

Rachel sipped her glass. Tamara did too.

"There isn't something you're hiding from the law, is there?" Rachel asked, with that same rakish smile across her lips. "Right?"

Was she teasing? Or was that smile meant to mask the discomfort of a prying question?

"Dear, it's all right." Rachel stood up from her chair. "I know you're a clean, wholesome type. Besides, everyone here has something they're getting away with or from. Island life, right?" Rachel winked. "Things get wild. The Virgin Islands are a skip eastward from here, and everybody knows the kinds of things that happen over there."

She took another sip from her glass and then walked toward the sectional, beckoning Tamara to follow.

After Rachel took her usual spot—on the shorter side of the sectional, in front of a Banksy original hung on the wall—Tamara took her seat on the longer part.

"In any case, there's no need to worry." Rachel stretched her slender arm across the back of the couch and crossed her long legs at the knees. "The one thing you should remember as you do this job is that a few extra work hours, a couple charitable contributions, a donation to the governor's campaign—all those things are a tremendous value." The meaning wasn't lost on Tamara. Money could buy consideration, time, an attentive ear—all things worth more than a luxury yacht or a private airliner.

"Well, anyway," Rachel gulped the scotch, "there is something else I wanted to get your ear on while you're here. Arlen Burkhart is coming to the kickoff celebration."

Tamara's throat tightened. Without thinking, she almost slouched into the couch, but she forced herself to sit up straight, to ignore the cold hand slipping around her neck.

"He is?" she asked. "Well, that's good. Isn't it?"

"That largely depends on your definition of *good*." Rachel sucked down the last of the scotch in her glass, then got up from the sectional and went back to the bottle on her desk. "He's flying in tomorrow."

"Maybe he wants a little vacation time. He enjoyed himself at the investors' weekend in St. Croix a couple months ago," Tamara said. "We want to keep our investors happy."

"We'll just have to make sure none of the policemen we're hiring get any funny ideas," Rachel answered.

"I thought they wouldn't mess with us," Tamara said.

Rachel raised an eyebrow and poured more into her glass. "Everyone has their limit."

"Why would the police want him? Did he do something on

St. Croix? Or did he get in trouble at home?" Tamara turned her head. "Is that why Mr. Burkhart is coming here?"

"No, nothing like that," Rachel said. "At least nothing I'm *aware* of, though it's not like he comes crying to me when he's in trouble. I'm not into that kind of life. As far as I can tell, he wants a couple days to sit in with the board and to inspect the new campus before it opens. He said he wants to offer his *management counsel*—whatever in God's name that means." She took another swig of scotch.

The cold air in the room suddenly had a deeper bite. Tamara picked up her glass and took a swig as well.

"Does he think we're heading in a bad direction?" she asked Rachel. "Our returns have been through the roof since the new campus announcement, and once we've got it up and running, our new Orphaned Drugs Research Division should bring us phenomenal growth."

"He'd be crazy to mess with the golden goose, but then there are all those rumors that make him seem pretty damn crazy." Rachel shrugged. "He's a whale investor. They're high maintenance. He just wants to throw his big, fat tail around to stir up all the smaller fish. The man owns two percent of Hildon, so we're going to let him."

If he wanted to see the new campus, the responsibility would fall on Tamara—she knew that. She'd be his main point of contact, the walking encyclopedia to answer any and all questions, from what kinds of flowers they'd have growing out by the sign at the entrance to the types of antimicrobial material coating they'd use in the labs.

And she knew it all. "I'm prepared for that," Tamara said. "Send him my way."

"You know I will," Rachel answered with a smile. "But I want to make one thing clear with you, before you spend time entertaining Mr. Burkhart: all those rumors about him are only rumors." Her expression turned serious. "He's never been proven guilty of anything. But if you catch something concrete, bring it to me. Immediately."

"I will, Rachel."

CHAPTER ELEVEN

After our night with Nels, DJ and I headed back to *Reel Fun* with an extra guest. Not Nels, who shambled back to his boat around midnight, but our cute waitress, Beth. Even I couldn't deny DJ's ability to charm.

On the voyage to Long Bay—east on the coast from Krum Bay—I stayed down in the cockpit while he let Beth steer *Reel Fun* from his lap. Within an hour, DJ motored into the marina where I kept my catamaran, *Wayward*. I told him he could stay in the slip adjacent to *Wayward*, since I'd leased it as well.

From there, I took a short walk up the pier, then onto Frenchman Bay Road, where I fell into bed next to my wife, Alicia.

In what felt like an instant, I awoke to sunlight and the sound of laughter from the kitchen. DJ's and Alicia's.

And Beth's.

DJ really brought his one night stand to my house.

Beth seemed like a nice girl, but I didn't want strangers poking around my place.

I grumbled and checked the time on my phone—9:17 a.m.

Dammit! The VA had been open for over an hour.

I rolled out of bed and headed into the master bath to wash the bar stink off me.

Fifteen minutes later, I came out of my room, dressed in a pair of dark blue jeans and a gray golf shirt emblazoned with *Newport Beach PD Memorial Day Cookout* on the pocket. I'd picked it for a reason—if she were up to anything, I wanted her to know she was dealing with a cop.

Past the end of the hall, I saw Beth's profile. She sat on the nearest bar stool, her back hunched over, her hands in her lap, and wearing a hoodie that had to belong to DJ. "Hey, Dep, is that you I hear lurking in the hallway?" DJ called from the kitchen. "You don't hafta be shy, my friend. Come on out and say good morning to the ladies!"

Alicia giggled, which got my blood pumping. I didn't understand why she always laughed at DJ's inane comments—especially the ones about me.

I came marching out of the mouth of the hall. All three of them were at the breakfast bar, which was a chest-high bar top between the kitchen and living room.

Alicia leaned against the counter on the kitchen side, holding a mug of coffee. She looked as sweet as she ever had in her lavender bath robe, hip cocked to one side, blond hair resting on her near shoulder. She'd say she was messy and unpresentable to company. I'd say she was cute beyond belief.

DJ leaned on his elbows on the far end of the bar, grinning at me. He noticed me checking out my wife. I walked around him, opened the cabinet, and took out a coffee cup.

"Morning, everyone," I said, as I carried my cup across the kitchen toward Alicia and the coffeemaker.

I planted a kiss on my wife's forehead.

"DJ said you two closed down the bars last night." She took a sip of her coffee, trying to hide her grin.

"That's a technicality," I said. "More like a person of interest closed down *one* bar, and we were there with him."

DJ threw his head back and laughed. Coffee dripped down the side of his mug.

"Man, they musta beaten the fun out of you at the police academy—the man can't even admit when he had a fun night out." He turned his attention from Alicia to me. "But I know I saw you smiling once or twice when you were talking to old Nels, buddy. He might look rough, but surely the man knows how to have a good time."

"Surely he does," Beth said, her eyes going wide, as if there was more to the story than any of us knew.

"Sounds like somebody else I know." Alicia's eyes settled on DJ.

"Ain't nothing wrong with a man enjoying himself now and again," he protested. "Took me a long time to figure that out. Believe it or not, I used to be as uptight about everything as my man, Dep—" He stopped himself, averting his eyes from me, and took a sip from his coffee.

His jabs were getting on my nerves, but it was too early in the day to verbally spar with DJ. So, I decided to let it slide. I stayed posted next to Alicia, enjoying a hot cup of black coffee.

She elbowed me, but I didn't react.

"It's true," DJ continued, "I used to be a very regimented person. Up at oh-six-hundred, haircut every weekend, the next day's clothes laid across my footlocker each night. Every detail accounted for, every decision by the book, every day predictable and planned from the minute I lifted my head from the pillow to when I pulled my blankets over me and turned out the light. I was as flat and crisp as a pair of ironed socks."

I'm sure I wasn't the only one who had trouble squaring that version of DJ Martin with the man I saw before me. I looked across the bar at Beth furrowing her brow. It was hard to imagine him being one of the guys at the very pointy tip of the spear of American military muscle.

"That must've been quite an eyeful," Beth said. She pinched a lock of his hair, pulling it away from his face. "I could almost picture a respectable young man under all this mess. And under that man, a wild party boy who loved to play with girls' hearts."

"Truth be told, I kept myself in lockstep. If I didn't, I'd have had some butter-bar second lieutenant chomping my ear off about why I was three minutes late to morning PT for all *that* mattered." He shrugged. "The Taliban might've blown my leg off, but they knocked the stick out of my ass too."

I didn't quite know what to make of that, and from the perplexed looks of the two women, they didn't either. Was it a joke? Did he want our sympathy? It was difficult to comprehend how a man losing his leg could think of that as a good thing.

My eyes wandered up to the clock above the bar. It was 9:38.

I gulped down a mouthful of hot coffee. "The VA opened at eight this morning." The coffee burned my throat, but I didn't care. "We need to double-time it over to Charlotte Amalie."

"You need a ride home?" DJ asked Beth, making eyes with her. "Ain't got a car to take you anywhere, but *Reel Fun* can get you to any side of the island without a problem."

She smiled at him. "You're sweet, DJ, but I can get a ride all on my own. I don't need you to trouble yourself if you've got a job to do. I'll call my sister to come get me."

He smiled back at her. "You're just a peach, ain't ya? But you don't need to bother her. I'll get you home."

"DJ," I said, "we *really* need to get out to the VA."

If that Marc guy was hanging around like Nels said, we needed to talk to him as soon as possible. Leads didn't stay warm for long, and he could have already been there and left. We knew nothing about what treatment he got there or how often.

"I appreciate you," Beth said to DJ. "But you have work to do, and you better get to it. Don't keep things held up for me. I'll call my sister, then walk down to the marina and wait for her."

One problem taken care of, I thought. At least I wouldn't have to leave Alicia here alone with Beth.

"You don't have to do that," Alicia said. "We've got plenty of coffee to drink—I'd never finish this whole pot on my own." She waved a hand at the coffee maker, which was only a quarter full. I'd seen her drink more than that in a single morning. "We can sit out on the porch while your sister is on her way over."

"I wouldn't want to keep you from your morning."

"You're not," Alicia answered. "I'm always up for good company." She grinned at DJ. "You couldn't possibly be as boring as this one-legged pirate."

"Yaarrgghh!" DJ said. "I resemble that remark."

If anything, I wished Alicia were right and DJ would take it a little slower.

"We both know you'll start crying about how much you miss me as soon as I step out that door," DJ said, pointing toward the sliding glass door overlooking the Caribbean. "I know living with Jerry would have me pulling my hair out every minute of the day."

I put my coffee mug in the sink and left the kitchen.

"Jerry—" Alicia started to say, but I didn't stop. I walked toward the deck door, got my shoes on, then laced them up while I sat on the couch with my back to the others.

"Don't worry about him," DJ said. "He's sweating out all the beer from last night. A little sunshine, a little ocean, and a whole lot of chasing down a murderer is gonna get his spirits right back where they should be."

I rose from the couch and turned toward DJ. He gave me a look that told me he knew he'd crossed the line, but he didn't care.

"Let's get going," I said, heading over to give Alicia a quick kiss.

Then I turned and walked out the back door. By the time I was down the wooden steps leading from the porch, DJ was thumping down from the top.

"Don't worry about us; we've got this job locked down real tight. Everybody's cool, everything's gonna be smooth sailing," he called back to Alicia and Beth. "We'll be back in time for dinner."

CHAPTER TWELVE

D J was right about one thing; getting to work on Luc
Baptiste's murder did have me feeling better. Living on St.
Thomas, the sunshine and the briny air were nice perks, but
nothing cleared my head like work.

The VA office on St. Thomas sat about a quarter mile inland
from Crown Bay, in West Charlotte Amalie, not far from the
Yacht Haven Grande Marina in Long Bay.

Reel Fun cruised westward through Long Bay, keeping close to
the shoreline, steadily dodging the other craft that seemed to cut
every which way around us. DJ guided her through Haulover
Cut—a narrow, man-made channel between St. Thomas's
southern shore and the north coast of Hassel Island. I held my
breath while reefs closed to within ten yards of us on either side.
Hassel was a pretty place—a roughly 140-acre island mostly
owned by the Virgin Islands National Park and a handful of
private estates, with a rocky shoreline and small stretches of sand
beach.

To the west of Hassel, nearer the mouth of Crown Bay, lay
Water Island—another high-dollar piece of real estate shared by

a hundred or so people. The island's name told you all you needed to know about its importance in the early days of exploration. Ships from all countries, tradesmen, pirates, privateers, and warships all stopped on Water Island to replenish their stores from the many freshwater ponds located there.

After navigating through Haulover Cut, we continued our westward course, following the contours of the beachhead, the sticky air hissing past our ears and the Bimini hardtop holding off sunlight so bright that looking at *Reel Fun's* bow without my sunglasses felt as if I had almost seared my eyes.

Within a few minutes, we were close enough to Crown Bay Marina to see they had a few open spots for day docking. DJ pulled the throttle back to idle, then pushed his hand flat on a piece of the high-gloss, white dash to the right of the boat's wheel. Like magic, a door rose up, revealing a compartment holding a GPS, start/stop controls for both engines, fuel pump, anchor controls and one of *Reel Fun's* two marine radios.

DJ twisted a knob on the smaller VHF radio, then brought the mic to his mouth.

"Crown Bay Marina, this is *Reel Fun.* Tell me where I can tie up." His finger let go of the button on the side of the mic. The radio cracked, and a few seconds later, a woman's voice answered.

"*Reel Fun,* proceed to VHF 12 for more instructions."

DJ quickly changed frequencies on the radio. "This is *Reel Fun,* waiting for somebody to boss me around."

"This is Darla at Crown Bay Marina, ready to boss you around, skipper. What're you looking for, *Reel Fun?*"

"How long you think we'll be here?" DJ asked me.

I shrugged. "Back by dinner time, right?"

He nodded agreement.

"Just looking for a day slip and about six hundred gallons of diesel," he said into the radio. "Got something like that?"

"Always do, *Reel Fun*," Darla answered. "Go to the first face dock and Glen'll get you squared away with fuel."

Reel Fun slowly pressed forward into the marina. Ahead, I saw the low, colorful buildings of Charlotte Amalie West. Off our portside, a familiar-looking sailboat motored out into Crown Bay. I caught the name—*Lady Lesley*—and remembered emailing back and forth with the owner, Ron, a few times before I found *Wayward* back in Yacht Haven.

Lady Lesley was a beautiful Tayana 37 that had sailed up and down the eastern seaboard since being commissioned in 1987. According to Ron, she'd spent the last decade shuttling between a rental off Elbow Cay in the Bahamas, and a place down here in St. Thomas.

I saw Ron on deck, working hand-over-hand to unfurl a stay-sail. I waved and he shielded his eyes from the sun at my back, then smiled and returned my greeting.

"Hey, Dep, quit waving at the neighbors. I need you to hop your ass down to the cockpit and get the lines ready." DJ spun the wheel, turning the bow to starboard, aiming for a place on the fuel dock behind a converted tugboat.

Why couldn't I have been partnered with somebody like Ron? A friendly, competent guy. I didn't have time to dwell on it, though. I dutifully climbed down the flybridge ladder and brought the lines out of storage. As soon as I had them out, I looked up at the dock and saw a bow-legged, sun-scorched man who couldn't have been a day under seventy holding his arms out.

"Toss me a line, son," the old man called, his arms spread wide like an anhinga drying its wings in the sun. "I'll get you tied off and filled up."

"Glen?"

He nodded.

I tossed the line high, trying not to hit him in the face. He ducked a little to the side and caught it over his shoulder with practiced ease.

Glen was as good as his word. He got us tied up, and once DJ opened the fuel door and removed the caps for him, we headed up to the dock office, paid for our day slip and six hundred gallons of diesel, then headed inland. Darla said Glen could pull DJ's boat forward using the dock lines, so it would be out of the way of the fuel dock.

I couldn't see how one old man could handle that on his own. Surely, the marina had another dockhand somewhere to help the old guy out.

We walked up a set of concrete steps from the marina office. I heard DJ grunting behind me as he pulled on the rail with each step. The hangover must've been roasting him from the inside out, and I doubted he'd gotten much sleep the night before.

Part of me wanted to let him twist in the consequences of his own poor choices, but I couldn't leave a guy who only had one leg hanging. So, I turned and reached out a hand.

"I'm fine," he said.

He wasn't. Sweat glistened across his forehead and his skin would've been green if he wasn't so red. Anyway, I didn't push it. I left him alone.

I walked up the rest of the steps, then stopped at the top. Ahead of me, I saw roads and traffic and strip malls dressed in colorful, chipped paint. With the drugstore on one corner, the grocery store on another, and a check-cashing place sharing the same building, Charlotte Amalie West looked like any other small town in America, except for the paint.

That, and the hills of St. Thomas, smothered under dark-green rainforests.

Halfway up the hills, I saw a scattering of homes spaced far enough apart to be considered "private," but not so far, they were remote. Big decks and windows and white roofs seemed to push through the thick canopy, as if the houses were gasping their last breaths before being smothered by foliage. Here and there, blue FEMA tarps replaced the white rooves on several homes.

I took out my phone and looked up the VA's address, then copied and pasted it into my GPS app.

Crown Bay Marina was close to the VA office. Less than a mile. I could make it without breaking a sweat, even as the sun rose overhead.

"My phone says we've got a little over half a mile from here to the VA." My eyes darted from DJ's titanium leg to his face. "Want me to call a cab?"

"What do you need something like that for? Bone spurs?"

"I'm trying to have a little compassion for my fellow man, DJ. That's all. I just thought you might prefer riding in a car to walking in the heat with your leg thumping around."

"Save your compassion for somebody who needs it. Just point at the VA."

I jabbed my arm northwest like a spear.

"Then let's get going," he said, walking past me. "We don't want our lead getting cold, right?"

We crossed the side street leading to the marina, made our

way through a parking lot and hit Moravian Highway just beyond it.

Ahead of DJ, and having already crossed the highway, I stepped into a narrow parking lot attached to a blocky structure. The lot was big enough for one row of parked cars and space to drive around them but not much else.

The building looked like some of the cheaper apartment complexes I'd go past whenever I had to drive up to LAX to fly somewhere. No detail to it, no frills, nothing but four white walls, a roof, and however many windows it took to keep the place from looking like a prison.

A half dozen sets of doors punctuated the walls every twenty feet or so. I spotted one set that displayed a pair of window stickers of bald eagles holding American flags in their talons, soaring over the Rockies, and knew it was the VA without even seeing the small print on the door.

Going straight for the entrance, I walked between a Jeep and a Kia, then stopped to see where DJ was. He'd crossed the highway and was hobbling up the narrow strip of grass between the road and the parking lot.

An intense guilt swelled in me. I shouldn't have been pissed at him. Not for anything he'd done. Life was hard enough for him without me holding a stupid grudge or being thin-skinned about every prickly word he had for me. For God's sake, I used to jump out of airplanes in full scuba gear, then swim to shore and ruck a half dozen miles through the Florida swamp. I should have been able to handle a ribbing.

When he moved between the Jeep and Kia, I pulled open the VA's front door. A blast of chilly air rolled out, feeling like heaven on my bare skin. I soaked in the AC while DJ shuffled to the front door. When I followed him in, I found myself in a small waiting room. Ahead, beyond DJ, was an empty receptionist's desk. A hallway branched off to the left of the desk, then led to the back of the building. "We should wait for somebody to come up front," I said.

"Why?" DJ set himself in the direction of the hallway. "We're both vets."

Before I could argue the point, my phone rang. I pulled it out of my pocket, my eyes on the back of DJ's head, swiped my thumb across the screen without looking and brought the phone to my ear.

"This is Jerry."

"Jerry," a man's low, silky voice said, "it's good to hear your voice again."

A chill sank through my gut.

"Arlen."

CHAPTER THIRTEEN

I smashed the heel of my palm against the door frame as I stomped outside, where the Caribbean sunshine gnawed at my forehead with a deeper bite than it had just seconds ago. Arlen Burkhart was the last person I wanted in my ear. Especially now.

"You've got some real balls, calling me," I said. "How'd you get this number?"

"I only called to talk to you briefly," Arlen said calmly. "I don't mean to freak you out, Jerry, but that's unavoidable sometimes. That being said, I think it's important that the two of us say some words to each other. All I'm asking for is thirty seconds of your time."

"I'm not giving you anything," I said. "The last time we spoke, I made it crystal clear that you don't get a single second of my time ever again. Then I moved across the country, which I assumed would get my point across. Apparently, I assumed wrong, because here you are, calling me."

"That's exactly *why* I'm calling," he said. "I thought I owed you a warning that the distance between us is going to shrink.

Considerably."

"No, you stay away from us. You have your part of the country, I have mine."

"I understand why you'd feel that way," Arlen said. "And in a perfect world, I'd be able to honor your wish to stay away. But, Jerry, this is reality. And the reality is I'm a businessman. I have business interests across the world that need my presence from time to time. In this particular instance, there's a pharmaceutical company in Puerto Rico that has asked for my guiding hand. Maybe you've heard of Hildon Pharmaceuticals? I own a two percent share, so our personal enmity has to take a backseat—as uncomfortable as it may be."

Puerto Rico? How did he know we were in the northern Caribbean?

"I don't want to, but I have to invade the neutral zone to see to my financial interests." he said. "I'm genuinely sorry for the problems that might cause you."

I barely heard him over the boiling rage between my ears. That whole spiel about being a businessman who had to see to his financial interests was all a lie.

Arlen could have zipped to Puerto Rico and back without me noticing. Wasn't like he needed a place to stay. He'd only called because he wanted to get close to me.

He wanted to try drawing me in again.

"Since when?" I barked at him.

"Since when, what?"

"Since when did you become a two percent owner in a Puerto Rican company? Was it after Alicia and I decided to move here? Or did you do it years ago, and this is another of those weird accidents that always seem to happen in the way you want them to?"

"You are free to look at events through whatever lens you prefer—it's not my place to convince you about what's chance and what's intent, Jerry. And really, why would I try? You'd never give me the benefit of the doubt," he said. "Things happen as they happen. That's all."

How typical of Arlen to try and twist this around on me by implying I was being paranoid about him. Shirking off all responsibility and projecting his misdeeds onto other people was his go-to defense. What a funny coincidence that all these unconnected things were coming together right here, right now, putting him closer to me.

I ground my teeth and spat on the sidewalk.

"It drove you crazy that I walked away," I said. "From the minute I looked you in the eye in your office and said I was exiting Snyder & Burkhart, you've been scheming up ways to pull me back in and put my whole family under your thumb to make sure I stay for good. You couldn't handle that I *chose* to walk away from you. You still can't. Now that I've moved out of Orange County, you're trying harder to bring me back."

"I remember what I said in the heat of the moment," Arlen allowed. "You don't have to remind me. It wasn't my finest hour, and I've lived with that guilt for the year you've been gone. Truth be told, yes, I would like you back home, Jerry—I want you back where you belong. You know you'd be happiest here.

"But you're a man who's made the choice to walk his own path. I respect that now. I respect that more than you'll understand. But my coming to Puerto Rico has nothing to do with my personal life.

"Hildon is expanding aggressively, and they've requested help from experienced, steady hands—from people who know how to make deals."

"You've sure made a couple doozies," I said, and heard the breath being snatched out of his throat. Maybe it wasn't fair of me to say something like that to him, maybe it was. I didn't care.

"Just stay the hell away from me," I said. I punched the *End* button on my phone's screen.

From the sidewalk in front of the VA office, I looked south, out to Crown Bay. White ships milled through the shallow waves, glinting under the Caribbean sun. My mind's eye saw Arlen, standing near the bow of a mega yacht, binoculars pressed up to his eyes, his dark gray hair tucked behind his ears as the wind tousled the ends, his mouth puckered at the center of his goatee. He wore a pair of loose-fitting, white linen pants that flapped against his legs as he stared at me.

But, no, that was delusional. Arlen would never watch me. Not himself. He'd hire someone else to do it.

"Whoever Arlen is, I think I might like him," DJ said, startling me. "Think you could give him my number? I think he and I might have a lot to chat about."

He leaned halfway out of the VA's front door, a toothy grin on his face.

"Leave it alone," I said.

DJ cocked the edge of his smile as he held the door open and let me back inside.

"Did you check out the hallway?" I asked.

"I did."

"And?" I asked.

"It's a pharmacy. Some folks back there," he said. "Lady behind a sliding glass window. Probably a nurse or something—

but she was on the phone, so I didn't talk to her. I decided to come check on you instead."

"Let's go talk to her." I looked over my shoulder, scouting the bay one more time. I didn't see anything new.

Past the small foyer at the front doors, a hallway led further into the suite, where it ended at a T-intersection with a waiting room on one side, and a big, open, darkened assembly area on the other. It looked like some kind of ballroom or empty mess hall.

From the smaller room, I heard a man's voice spinning up intensely. DJ and I stepped in, then I turned right and saw a tired-looking woman in scrubs on the other side of a sliding window with filing cabinets arranged behind her. A guy in a wheelchair stopped in front of the window, the back of his neck as red as burning coals. A meandering scar in the shape of a question mark twisted around his ear.

"Sir, I've told you, that's an off-label use for that prescription," the woman behind the counter said. "The VA doesn't cover it. What do you want me to do? Call up Congress and get it fixed?"

Her words were like a trigger for the guy in the wheelchair. As soon as she'd said it, he swung one meaty hand upward like a hook, latching it onto the bottom guide of the sliding window.

"I served my country!" he howled, as he hoisted himself out of his chair, pulling closer to the woman behind the counter. She appeared more annoyed than scared. "This is how you repay me? This is what my government does? I want what was promised to me when I served!"

I jumped in before the guy did something he'd regret. My arms went around his waist. He didn't let go of the bottom of the window. Not at first. I shook him once or twice, then DJ came up beside me, grabbing the guy's hands and unhooking him. We guided him back to his wheelchair.

All the while, he barked and carried on about honor and service and hanging his ass out of a tank hatch. Even as I sat him down in the chair and clamped my hands on his shoulders to keep him in place, he continued to jaw at the woman behind the counter.

Then, I heard the glass glide shut behind me.

His head snapped around to me.

"What'd you go and do that for, you stupid son of a bitch? You think Bernice needs your help? She's the one screwing me out of my damned meds!" He cupped his hands around his mouth and shouted at the closed window. "Medicine prescribed to me by a Veterans' Administration doctor!"

"You can yell as loud as you please, pal," DJ said with a chuckle. "She ain't opening that window again anytime soon."

The guy shot a mean look at DJ.

"She's just working the counter," I said. "I don't think she's here to screw you out of anything."

"Then why is she telling me I gotta pay eight grand for my new meds?" he asked me.

"Eight thousand a year?" DJ asked.

"A month!" the man roared.

I understood why he was pissed.

"That can't be right," I said. "They probably bungled some paperwork somewhere."

"Yeah, this is all just a big, bungled mess of paperwork—not a system designed to screw guys like me out of stuff I was promised." The man inclined his head at me and grinned. "You sound just as naïve as I was when it was my turn to pull some other ranting bastard out of that window a year or so back. Make no mistake: this *ain't* no bungled paperwork. They're doing this on purpose."

He rubbed the top of his head. His hair was buzzed close to the scalp and the tips of his fingers sounded like kitchen matches being struck.

"Guess I shouldn't be so mad at Bernice," he admitted. "Sorry, Bernice!" he shouted at the frosted glass window. Nobody answered. He shrugged and turned his wheelchair toward the doorway DJ and I had come through. "Not like she's behind the counter pulling my benefits away from me. Hell, she probably has to deal with the same crap as me, just with some other poor grunt having to put their face on it.

"It's a helluva thing." He started to wheel out of the room and down the hall. "Get a piece of shrapnel stuck in my head, and that somehow *still* ain't good enough."

DJ and I followed behind him. Something told me this guy probably knew the man Nels told us to find.

"Ain't nothing good enough when there's taxpayer money going into it—that's what I learned from serving," DJ agreed. "They tell you up front that if you put your body on the line for them—if you fight hard for two years, or four years, or whatever—they'll take care of everything else. Turns out 'taking care of everything' means doing the bare minimum, according to whatever some bunch of politicians think."

"Hooah." Wheelchair Man nodded.

"Hooah," DJ answered. Then, without prompting, "Hundred-and-First Airborne."

Wheelchair Man continued to glide forward, pulling up a

sleeve to reveal the black and yellow shield and horsehead tattoo on his arm. "Cavalry."

DJ hobbled a step quicker as we hit the dog leg left, leading into the foyer by the front doors. He reached in front of Wheelchair Man, then shook his hand.

"How about this one here?" Wheelchair Man's thumb gestured over his shoulder at me. "Looks like he's still got all his parts and pieces. Does that mean he was dumb and lucky, or does that mean he was smart enough not to sign up like the rest of us?"

DJ opened the door.

"Air Force," I said.

"Chair Force," Wheelchair Man repeated.

"Pararescue," I fired back.

His hands clamped the wheels of his chair. He came to a stop, then rotated to look me in the eye.

"A PJ? And you're not missing a single piece of you? Wait. Pull your jeans up," he said.

I did, showing my bare ankles above the tops of my sneakers. I knew what he was looking for: a prosthesis. He wanted to see if I'd been wounded in combat.

"Dumb and lucky," I answered.

"Some of the stories I heard about you PJs makes me think you might be the dumbest, luckiest guy I ever met." He laughed, then resumed rolling through the foyer and out the front door. He cut left, then stopped on the sidewalk next to an ashtray pushed up close to the wall.

The sun was higher and brighter than seemed possible. I shielded my eyes and gave the bay another glance.

"How come I've never seen the two of y'all around here before?" He reached over the side of his wheelchair and pulled the ashtray next to his left wheel.

"Never cared to show up," DJ said. "My social obligations got me too busy."

I kept my answer to myself. This place wasn't for me. I hadn't been wounded—profoundly or otherwise. The worst injury I'd had during my enlistment was a high-ankle sprain from a rough landing during a night jump; my foot clipped a stump just outside the designated LZ when I was doing drills at Hurlburt Field.

"Well, I'm glad you came by today." A cigarette bounced between the man's lips as he spoke. He lit it, then held his hand out to DJ. They shook again.

"My name's Andy," he said.

"DJ Martin," DJ answered.

Andy held his hand out to me. I hadn't noticed the black, fingerless gloves he wore. The palms were padded and had been smoothed against the wheels of his chair. His fingers were covered in thick calluses.

I took his hand firmly and shook. "Jerry Snyder."

"We've got a meeting coming up pretty shortly here," Andy said. "If you two wanna stick around, I'm sure the boys wouldn't mind since you both had respectable jobs. We've had a few POGs try to boohoo their way through stories about papercuts and carpal tunnel. They get froze out pretty quick." He shrugged. "Sucks, but that's how it goes."

I grinned at his use of the acronym POG. I hadn't heard it in a long time. It was a derogatory term for military personnel who worked in clerical jobs. Although, by definition, I was one of those "People Other than Grunts" myself. Pararescue was tough, but we weren't ground pounders. We almost always flew to where we were going.

"Actually," I said, "DJ and I are looking for someone. We heard we might find him here."

Andy raised his eyebrows. "Oh yeah? One of you got a battle buddy you're trying to find?"

"Not exactly. His name is Marc. He was a combat engineer. An Iraq veteran."

Andy took a drag of his cigarette. I could almost see the thoughts rumbling around behind his eyes.

"You two cops or something?" he asked, eyeing the Newport Beach PD shield on my shirt.

"No," I said. "We're not cops. I used to be a cop, but not anymore."

"He's a dry drunk now, know what I mean?" DJ said with a smile.

"We want to ask Marc about a guy named Luc Baptiste. He's some journalist, and somebody told us Marc talked with him a couple days ago. We just wondered if he knew where Luc had gone."

"Your friend is missing?" Andy took a drag off his cigarette and rubbed at the scar behind his right ear. "That's a familiar-sounding story. If you two feel like sticking around an hour or two, Marc should be at today's meeting. Bet you could talk to him afterward."

"The rest of our morning's clear," I said.

"I just had something come up," DJ said.

I looked to my right, straight into DJ's eyes. Now wasn't a time for jokes—we were on the verge of picking up a new lead in Luc Baptiste's murder, but to do that, Andy wanted to know we were trustworthy.

We couldn't screw this up by not throwing our guy Andy a

bone.

I had to say something to him. But I knew he'd take it the wrong way, and I didn't want to make a scene. Regardless, DJ could probably benefit from a meeting or two to chill him out.

"You can't cancel?" Andy asked DJ. "It's good for the soul, amigo."

DJ offered no further explanation.

Andy cracked a smile and nodded. He'd dealt with guys like DJ before.

"You know, DJ, I used to be like you." Andy leaned away from us and dabbed his cigarette out in the ashtray. "I'd wake up every morning, running on two hours of sleep—if my anxiety lets me sleep at all. I'd put on my meanest face, and I'd roll out into the world, anyway. Come hell or high water, I was *not* going to let some touchy-feely sniffles get the better of me. Stuff it down and go forward, right? That's how I got through basic, and NCO school, and God only knows how many bomb defusings and firefights."

Andy inhaled deeply. His forefinger traced the scar around his ear once more as he looked over Long Bay. Then he exhaled.

"After all the surgeries were over, I came down here as soon as I figured out how to be independent again," he continued. "I figured I could just go to a paradise like this—the furthest thing from where I grew up in Bismarck—and then I could use this new environment to reset myself. Leave my old habits and my old problems behind. I could figure myself out. Deal with it all on my own." He shook his head and chuckled softly. "Man, I was wronger than wrong.

"How many years did we spend getting the idea of relying on other people hammered into our heads?" He nodded at DJ, who remained still. "The Army taught us we were stronger together, and when I needed to take that lesson to heart the most, I didn't." He pointed through DJ, toward the VA's front door. "The people coming to that meeting are my brothers and sisters. I can rely on them. I can trust them. They've helped me more than my *actual* brothers have. And if you'd have them—if you can be open and honest with them and give *them* a shoulder to lean on some-times—I know they'd do the same for you."

DJ stared forward. He hadn't moved a muscle, hadn't even looked in Andy's direction. Did any of that make it through?

"I'm gonna head to my thing," DJ said to no one in particu-lar. "Call me when you're done in there, Dep."

He stepped off the curb without a glance at me or Andy. I waited until DJ had slipped over the thigh-high wall between the parking lot and the strip of grass that led to the highway before I said anything to Andy.

"Sorry about him," I said.

Andy smiled politely at me, taking a breath through his nose. "Nothing to be sorry about, man. He ain't the first vet who's snubbed that offer. It happens. I want every vet like DJ to see that it's all right to ask for help. But I can't baby him, either. If I start chasing after him, pleading with him to reconsider, telling him it's for his own good, you think that's gonna make him change his mind?"

"Probably not."

"Definitely not," Andy countered. "I learned the hard way that if you want somebody to listen to you, you can't bully them into it. You gotta establish mutual respect. You gotta let them come to you. But that doesn't happen unless both sides are ready."

"And DJ's not ready," I said.

CHAPTER FOURTEEN

I followed Andy into the VA office and then into the big, empty room at the end of the hall opposite the pharmacy, where DJ and I'd kept Andy from climbing through the window.

Arriving in the room before anybody else, I helped by setting up metal folding chairs, while Andy instructed me where and how many to put out. Shortly after I put down the first chair, other men and women began to filter in and help arrange the room for the coming meeting. To my eyes, they ran the spectrum of everyday people: some dressed in collared shirts with slacks and neat haircuts, others in T-shirts, tank tops, shorts, jeans, flip-flops, sneakers, and prescription shoes.

These vets just weren't the thick-necked, high-and-tight, twenty-somethings they may have been when they'd served. Just as they'd been remade in basic, they were now in the process of being remade again by civilian life. Some were clearly struggling to adjust to their new identities.

After the chairs were set up, I took a seat and waited on my own. Andy brought a handful of the other vets over, introducing them. Each of them gave me a first name—Mike, Jose, Daryl,

Melissa—a service branch, and the particular unit they were with or job they performed.

Andy introduced me as PJ Jerry.

I was amazed at how unbothered they were in telling their stories. They were often tales rooted in abject boredom, suddenly punctuated with unbelievable violence caused by roadside bombs and surplus Soviet munitions leading to a new scar or permanent disability.

Listening reminded me of the sound a Humvee made when it rolled, and its roof collapsed like a milk carton, or how, five yards away, an IED was hot enough to singe the hair from the back of your neck, or how you had to cradle a man suffering from burns like you'd cradle a newborn, because grabbing him by the wrists and dragging him to safety would make the skin peel off his arms.

Going to the meeting, visiting with fellow veterans months or years after their life-changing injuries, was an experience I didn't expect to have when I hurried out of bed this morning.

And here I was, sound of body, the worst kind of voyeur. Lower than a Peeping Tom. I felt like I'd snuck into a widow's closet to watch her cradle a yellowed photo of her long-dead husband while she cried herself to sleep.

Regardless, I kept my seat when the meeting started. If I got up and left, they'd be insulted, and I needed this lead in the Baptiste case.

Andy rolled past my right, toward the front of the semicircle of chairs, the windows overlooking Long Bay at his back. The easy chatter in the room died down.

"Morning, everybody," Andy said. "We have an FNG with us today."

Several of the guys laughed at the acronym for a fucking new guy, a moniker given to any new person in a military unit. I grinned, taking it in stride.

Then, Andy gave the floor to me, motioning me to the front. I hesitated. I didn't deserve to talk. These people had given much in their service—their bodies and minds, and I had come out whole. I wasn't supposed to be here.

"Aww! The new guy's shy!" They all laughed, and Andy motioned me to stand up. So, I did.

"My name's Jerry," I said. "I'm from Newport Beach, California and I used to be a cop."

A couple of the guys jokingly booed me. I laughed it off.

"I'm an Air Force vet," I continued. "I enlisted in 2006, after a couple years of being bored to tears in a college classroom. While I was in college, at a career fair, I met a lieutenant at a recruitment table. He seemed like an all-right guy, so when he asked me to listen to him give a presentation after lunch, I did. Me and a dozen other people sat in a big lecture hall and listened to him tell us about the different jobs we could do in the Air Force. Either after graduation, or in case there was—you know—anyone thinking about dropping out. I guess I didn't have any concept of different jobs in the service. I figured, Air Force—you're gonna fly a jet or bomb somebody."

They all laughed. I figured a lot of them related to how green I'd been then.

"But when that lieutenant talked to us about Pararescue School, about how it constantly challenged enlistees to do some of the most dangerous work the military had to offer—and to do it anywhere on the planet—I was in."

The hair on my arms stood up as I remembered that guy—a man named Simpson—and the way his service blues commanded the full attention of a room of college kids.

"I wanted to be the guy who was dropped in behind enemy lines," I continued, "to find somebody who was hurt, and bring them out alive. I wanted the hardest challenge I could find, and I wanted to do some good. After I got out of the pararescue pipeline, I served three tours in Afghanistan doing just that."

"One after another?" Andy asked me in disbelief.

"I'm lucky, and dumb," I said, grinning. "But not crazy." That got another laugh from the group. "The first time I deployed was early in '09. Then toward the end of 2010, and again in 2012."

Andy whistled. "And you came out without a damned scratch."

A lump swelled in my throat. I swallowed it back. Then, my eyes met with those of a man I hadn't been introduced to. He sat in the chair nearest the door to the hallway. There was something familiar and terrifying about the way he looked.

He was average height, with a stocky build and dark hair going gray around his temples. He had only one arm, and an intensity to his eyes that pierced into the core of me.

I looked away.

"That's my story." I plopped back into my chair.

"Well, all right," Andy said. "The man knows when his story ends. Always happy to meet somebody from Pararescue."

A couple guys near me made grumbles of agreement.

The guy to my left clapped me on the knee. "A PJ saved my brother's life."

I nodded, but I barely heard him. My attention had drifted over to the one-armed man with the piercing eyes, then back to Andy.

The rest of the meeting went about the way I assumed a support group for veterans would. Guys shared their stories about struggling with everyday things most people took for granted— tying shoes with one hand, bottling up anger around loved ones, navigating a grocery store while fighting the temptation to sock some obnoxious kid in the nose. Then Andy made announcements about new VA services and a fishing trip the following weekend, sponsored by Hildon Pharmaceuticals.

The meeting ended with a prayer led by Mike, one of the guys Andy'd introduced me to. We said amen, and everyone dispersed.

I got up from my chair and approached Andy, who was finishing up some business with the guy who had to stop himself from punching the second grader in a grocery store. Behind me, I could almost feel the one-armed vet lurking around; he had on a pair of hard-soled boots that made a very distinct sound against the floor. I made sure I didn't look in his direction.

Done talking, Andy met me with a smile. "How'd it feel, man?"

"Getting up in front of people and talking was never for me, but I'm happy to come back—if you'd like me to be part of the group."

He cocked his eyebrow at me. "The hell are you talking about, Jerry? Of course, we want you back. Why wouldn't we?"

I stepped closer and lowered my voice. "My story is next to nothing compared to some of these other guys. I'm still walking around like going to Afghanistan was a long camping trip with colorful locals."

"Aw, hell." Andy waved me off. "More than half of them said the same damned thing after their first day. There's always some poor bastard that got it worse, right?" He grinned and slapped the armrest of his wheelchair.

"You keep coming, you'll settle in. You'll see how all these people respect somebody who's been there, whether you've got lead stuck in your guts or not. Since you were never hit, they might give you some guff about being lucky, but they only kid the guys they want to stick around."

It was nice of him to say that, but when I turned around and scouted the room again, I saw a place I didn't belong. By now, the men and women who'd come to the meeting had broken off into smaller groups, talking and joking in low voices and drinking coffee, some already halfway to the door, others grabbing a cup for the road.

"So, which one is Marc?"

"I knew I forgot something!" Andy smacked his forehead. "Hey Marc!" He called toward the coffee station.

The one-armed man with the piercing eyes turned around. When his eyes met mine, that same feeling of wariness jostled in my belly. "Need something?" Marc sounded punchy. Nothing too obvious, but his words were half a step slower than most people's.

"This is Jerry," Andy said. "Jerry, this is Marc Herrera."

I held out a hand to Marc. He took it with a thin, clammy grip, and barely shook.

"My dad was a PJ in Vietnam," Marc said. "I had a lot of respect for the Air Force, growing up."

"But not enough to be an airman," Andy chimed in with a laugh.

"Flying terrifies me." Marc cracked a tired smile. "So, I en-listed in the Marines—but that didn't do me any good when I realized I'd be flying as part of my deployment."

We all laughed. Now that I'd talked to him, I wondered why Marc gave me the heebie-jeebies. He seemed like a good guy, only worn down.

"Jerry's been asking about you," Andy said.

"Oh, yeah?" Marc's disposition changed instantly, like he'd found out I wasn't just chatting with him, I was knocking on his door to sell him on a new religion.

My cop sense told me I was going to lose this guy quickly, so I had to get to the point.

"Did you know a man named Luc Baptiste?"

Marc crossed his remaining arm over his chest and furrowed his brow.

"Did *you* know him?" Marc asked. He nodded toward the Newport Beach PD badge on my shirt. "Are you a cop down here?"

"I'm not a badge anymore," I reminded him. "I'm strictly doing private work now. I've been asked to look into his death, and I heard the two of you met at a bar near Krum Bay shortly before Luc disappeared." I didn't know when Luc disappeared for sure. I didn't even know the date he'd met with Marc, but sometimes you had to fish a little deep to see what came up for the bait.

"You think I killed him?" Anger flashed through Marc's eyes.

It was then that I realized what unnerved me about him. Marc reminded me of my father shortly before he died.

From a brain tumor.

"How long have you had your cancer?" I asked. And I shouldn't have.

Andy almost held back his gasp. "Let's come back to this

later."

"Too long," Marc snapped the answer at me. "And too many times. For all that it matters, I've got enough trouble. I don't need to go around killing people."

"No, of course not," I said. "Look, I'm coming at you wrong. Luc's family wants to know what happened to him, and I'm trying to give them the best answer I can find. They don't have the faintest clue about what he was working on, but I thought you might know. Luc wrote an article in *The New York Times* that upset some yahoo over in Culebra. He's my guy right now, but I'm doing my best to follow up every lead. I just want to be able to tell Luc's family something as soon as I can."

The fire behind Marc's expression cooled. "What's his family like?"

"He's got a sister—she's married. The brother-in-law put my partner and me on this. He and his wife are more worried about Luc than they're willing to admit. I can tell."

"A sister?" Marc's eyes drifted upward, carrying the far-away look of a man struggling with himself. After a few seconds, he came back to the room in the VA. "Luc asked me about my cancer."

At least I wasn't the only one.

"He asked me how long I've been dealing with my glioblastoma. How many times I've been diagnosed with cancer and all the medications I've taken in the last five-ish years, including the stuff I'm taking now."

I tried to think of who would want Luc Baptiste dead for putting together a human-interest story on a Marine with cancer. My mind flipped through the different angles: the best I could think was that Luc had tried to expose the VA by showing how ineffective they'd been against Marc's brain tumor.

Hardly anything was effective against glioblastoma. That wasn't the VA's fault. Most people didn't last longer than a year and change with treatment. The curtain fell much, much quicker if it went untreated.

Garner's losing money because of Luc's article in *The Times* seemed a much more compelling motive.

"Did he ask anything else?"

"He wanted to know how much I'm spending on meds and treatments. Enough to make me seriously consider stopping treatments." He blinked and held his eyes shut for a moment.

"Before you ask, I don't know why he wanted to know all those things." Marc opened his eyes and looked blankly at me. "Said he was working on something but wouldn't tell me anything about it."

"Then why'd you take the interview?"

"I needed money, man. He paid me."

Marc rubbed his eyes. My father's face flashed through my mind. Haggard, with one eye drooping, a trembling hand brushing over a forehead that seemed to have aged twenty years in two months.

"Did you talk to him about anyone?"

"What?" Marc blinked at me. He seemed out of it, a step deeper into the fog than he'd been a moment ago. "What did you say?"

"Marc, why don't you sit down a minute?" Andy asked.

He looked vacantly around himself, once, twice, and on the third time saw the chair directly behind him. He put his hand on it, wobbled for a moment, and then lowered himself down.

"I'm okay," he said.

"Did you drop any names during your conversation with Luc?" I asked. "Maybe give him someone else to talk to?"

"Did I?" He blinked, thinking. "Yeah, I did. This doctor. This doctor who I saw on account of my oncologist."

I exchanged a glance with Andy, who twitched his nose at me. Marc wasn't the only one getting lost.

"You mean your oncologist referred you to another doctor?"

"Look," Marc sat up in the chair and wiped some sweat from his neck, "my guy said I could go talk to this other doc, and he'd give me some special treatment that would cure me."

"Cure your cancer?" No way would any doctor worth his degrees make that promise. Either Marc was being led on by someone looking to wring him dry, or he was more delirious than he seemed in that moment.

Assuming Marc had been seeing an actual oncologist for treatments, pushing scams on the side was a huge risk to a legitimate doctor's reputation. Unless he was running a side-hustle with whomever he sent Marc to. But then, where did the money come in? Identity theft? Theft of VA benefits?

"Something like that," he said. "I don't know. It sounded weird from the start, but with this tumor eating my brain, I'm willing to do weird stuff, you know?"

I nodded.

"He gave me this doc's address," Marc said. "So, I figure, why the hell not? What am I gonna lose by going? I went. I'm barely five steps inside this other doc's house, and he says hello to me, then without taking a breath, he says he wants to give me an injection right there in his living room. I hesitated. He pulled out the needle and tells me to roll up my sleeve. But I'm scared of needles, so I tell him, 'hell no!' I've seen how this movie ends.

And it's not with me getting up and feeling better."

Scared of needles and airplanes.

"So, you sent Luc after this guy before he disappeared?"

Marc nodded.

"What's his name?"

"Markel."

I scratched the back of my neck while I thought about all the things Marc Herrera had given me to chew on. His story about this mystery doctor didn't add up. Too many fuzzy details, and since he was, reportedly, the last person to see Luc Baptiste alive, he wasn't clear of my suspicions.

Maybe, close to death as he was, he didn't care about stirring up more trouble for himself. It'd all be over soon, right?

Given that Marc was terminally ill, I didn't think he'd run. His body wouldn't take it. Then again, he might be happy to kick off if he'd killed Luc. In any case, if he tried to slip away, someone at Armstrong could dig up his home address or a boat registered in his name, and I'd find him.

The next move I needed to make was to check his story. Luc's bundle of threats and court documents was back on *Reel Fun,* and it might have something from Marc Herrera or Markel. Or both.

"You remember Dr. Markel's address?" I asked.

CHAPTER FIFTEEN

After lunch, Miss Price piled on the work. She was uncharacteristically anxious, calling down to Gabriela's desk to share every thought she had about the new building. Was she feeling guilty about blocking Flor's spot in the Anthradone trial? Or did Dr. Markel call to tell her about his conversation with Gabriela?

No, it couldn't be that. Why would he call Miss Price? She had nothing to do with handling the research labs. He'd call the compliance office, and they'd bring Gabriela in right away.

Miss Price must've been worried about the new headquarters. Gabriela couldn't fault her. Miss Price had a lot on her plate. Gabriela would've been zipping around her office too if her nerves weren't already shot in anticipation of her meeting with Dr. Markel.

But she had to play it cool. She had to check up on contractors, and adjust orders to caterers, and make sure the down payment got into the band's bank account, and she had to source a sixty-foot projector screen. Miss Price's eyes had bugged out at the last three quotes Gabriela had given her for the projector screen, but she wasn't willing to compromise on size, so Gabriela had to continue the search. Amid all of that, Gabriela arranged for Flor's day nurse to stay into the evening. Hopefully, she'd be back from Markel's by nine that evening.

One task rolled into another, until she found herself alone in her windowless room when a break in the action finally came. Gabriela checked the time on her phone.

Already 5:45.

She should've been gone an hour ago! God have mercy on her if she lost her only chance at meeting Dr. Markel. How would she ever look her little girl in the eye again?

Gabriela grabbed her purse and bounded out of her chair. She slapped the light switch off as she went out, then zipped down the hall, her heart thrumming in her throat while the stale office air rushed past her ears. Running through the door to the staircase, she took the steps down two at a time, getting to the main floor faster than she'd believed possible.

There, she pushed through the staircase door, then briskly strode through a lobby decked in marble, steel, and glass.

Once outside, she pulled out her phone and copied Dr. Markel's address into her GPS app. The tropical air outside rested heavily on her shoulders, sticking to the back of her neck, and putting a chill in the light breeze blowing across her skin.

Her car was one of a dozen still in the employee lot, about two hundred feet away.

She ran past Miss Price's Lexus, and past four more empty rows of parking spaces before she reached it.

Gabriela's used Kia stuttered to life as soon as she turned the key. She slapped the car into gear, started the directions in her GPS app, then rocketed from the parking lot.

First, she headed east, then south toward the highway, which cut through the more densely populated part of the city. There, the side streets just off the highway's shoulders were quilted with mismatched asphalt patches, and the historic hotels, shops, and colorful murals in Santurce yielded to apartments, convenience stores, and cubic houses still bearing the scars of Maria's fury three years on.

South of there, she crossed the Martín Peña Channel. Then the road followed alongside the Rio Piedras for a few miles before the highway crossed over the river and bent westward.

Her phone said Manati was half an hour away. Most of the drive would be through San Juan's suburban sprawl—more squat, blocky houses and strip malls filled with mom and pop operations tucked against jungle and rocky hills. More murals and tarps on roofs and patchwork asphalt.

Seeing the areas west of San Juan came as a welcome change of pace—she and Flor hadn't left the city in almost a year. But the real treat was being out from all the tall apartment buildings. Out on Highway 22, where the road overran the trees, she had a perfect view of the westward Puerto Rican sky. Ahead, the setting sun had all but disappeared over the horizon. In its wake came bursts of pink, orange, and deep purple as vibrant as her little girl's smile once was. The hand of the Lord painted this air, leaving His radiance upon it, His glory for her eyes to see and for her heart to follow into the arms of mercy and healing, to remind her that life had once been kind to her, and it would be again. Not only for herself, but for the fruit that she'd borne in the back room of her family home when she was still a child, too.

Even after years of heartache and despair—after hurricanes and watching her little girl wilt before her eyes, Gabriela Ramos couldn't stop herself from being awed by the majesty of God and

His message that no matter how hard things became, how murky they seemed, nothing could ever close that wide-open sky.

She continued westward, alternating her attention between the road and the sunset. Eventually, she turned off the highway, taking the only exit—heading south toward Manati. A half mile down, Gabriela's phone told her to head west onto Highway 2, which took her along the northern edge of Manati, proper.

This town was unknown to her. She didn't know anyone who'd come from Manati, or even anyone who'd spent time there. The houses and buildings were compressed to one story for the most part, and the structures weren't as densely packed as in San Juan. Before she could get a good feel for the place, her phone told her to turn northward, up a two-lane highway. Outside her car, buildings and pavement gave way to forest so dense and dark, she couldn't see anything but walls of green leaves and dying branches lit by her car's headlights and dripping with shadows.

She passed through a *barriada*, where only a few streetlamps still worked, leaving nearly every intersecting road she looked down cocooned with darkness. These few working-class neighborhoods to the north of Manati likely had irregular power—which, on a given day, was probably off more than it was on.

Moving north, the houses spread farther apart and became bigger. Compared to the houses she'd passed a few blocks before, most were lit up like Christmas trees. She saw no blue tarps glistening with moisture under fading twilight, or loosely piled lumber in vacant lots, or balls and bikes thrown down by children wherever they stood when their mothers called them in. Three miles down the road, she was guided into another thick stand of jungle, where her phone instructed her that she would turn eastward in a quarter mile. Gabriela strained her eyes into the darkness ahead, looking for a lamp post, street sign or mailbox, or some hint of a way forward.

She saw nothing until the moment her phone told her to turn, when a small notch cut through the trees caught her eyes, holding the way open for a one-lane dirt road. She hit the brakes and swung the wheel, making the turn.

The road ahead was frighteningly dark; leafy branches hung out over the narrow road, blotting out the stars. On either side, thick vines and heavy foliage crept closer. If she had to stop and get out for some reason, she doubted she would have enough room. Fortunately, it didn't come to that. Half a mile down, the dirt road turned to blacktop so smooth, she could feel it caressing the dirt off the tires of her Kia. The forest peeled back as well, held off by a large stone arch over the road with massive flower-pots at its base.

When she passed under the arch, it was as if the whole world opened up to Gabriela once more. Stars twinkled overhead, the driveway looped around a large flower garden bursting with color, and in the middle of that, she saw a two-tiered fountain spitting into the air. The lowest tier was a circular bath, its edge hovering a few inches above clumps of red tropical flowers. The top tier supported a caduceus staff—an emblem Gabriela saw at every hospital, on the sides of ambulances, stitched into lab coats, printed on the labels for Flor's medication; two snakes twisted around the staff, with wings spreading from the staff's head. It looked angelic, until a heavy feeling settled over Gabriela, burning hot as pitch, and the faint smell of bleach over a dusty hospital floor came to her.

How much did that thing cost? Had to be the same as one or

two chemo treatments for Flor. Or ten, for all Gabriela knew.

Judge not. She took a deep breath.

Still, she couldn't help but feel slighted. Was this the kind of crap this doctor spent his money on, while Gabriela scrimped and saved and struggled?

She was close to stomping on the pedal and ramming that stupid fountain into the porch and through the front door. Then she'd jump out of the car, scramble through the hole in his house and grab whatever medication he was, undoubtedly, going to rake her over the coals for.

Imagine that, she thought. This beautiful house with its front teeth knocked in—this house that Dr. Markel probably treasured as much as anything in his life. The mound of broken glass and concrete Gabriela would leave behind her, the shards and dust of another man's dreams.

She snapped herself out of her terrible imagery. *God help me,* she thought, *when did she turn into this person?*

She followed the drive around the fountain and into a turn-around, parking between a gleaming black Mercedes Benz and a huge SUV.

Of course, her brain started to crawl into thoughts about how expensive both those cars must be to drive, and insure, and what it meant for one person to have all this wealth while so many other people had barely enough to live. People dying to keep their families from the kinds of debt that denied opportunities across generations—the kind of debt that kept a child's mind as empty as her belly.

If the cash put into either of those cars were put toward...

Gabriela closed her eyes tightly, ran her tongue along the bottoms of her teeth, and willed herself to stop imagining scenarios and do what had to be done to save her daughter.

Before she got out of her car, Gabriela prayed, then pulled the visor down and checked her makeup in the mirror. Her lipstick had gone dull, so she reapplied, then noticed that her mascara could use some touching up. She started to reach for her makeup bag in the pouch behind the passenger's seat, then stopped herself.

Through the back window, she saw the house's big front porch, elevated about four feet off the ground, the steps leading to a front door with opaque cast-glass that looked like ripples on churning seas.

It was open.

Gabriela shook her head. If she left her front door open, she would've been tied up and tossed in the bathtub while somebody cleaned her place out in thirty seconds flat. And the police wouldn't be able to find a suspect if he'd left behind a note signed, dated, and stamped by a notary.

Out of her car, she started toward the front door. The fountain bubbled to the right of her and bugs dove at the lights hidden behind the flowers, looking for the darkness behind them, while coqui chirped and laughed from the security of the undergrowth off the driveway.

At the first step, Gabriela became acutely aware of the rising and falling of her chest, the sticky air in her throat, and the movement of her ribs and her diaphragm. Her tiny, mortal body both pushed against and gulped something primordial, something that would be around long after she was dead and buried.

The wind's supremacy could kill her with the brush of a breeze—and almost had more than once—but she needed it. Every second she was alive, she was a minute from death, until she took her next breath and restarted the timer. She existed at the mercy of something far more powerful, and always would.

Her eyes met the open door ahead. Her brain switched to Flor, then to Dr. Markel.

She climbed the rest of the steps, then stopped on the porch, which extended all the way to the corner of the house. To her left, a splash of light coming from a Tiffany lamp at the center of the house's big front window spilled onto the porch. It sifted through strands of wicker in a pair of chairs sitting on the porch. Beside the chairs, shadows from a large wood table cloaked the rest of the porch in darkness.

Through the front window, she saw a sitting room with a TV as big as a mainsail, and wall-sized bookshelves speckled with beachie knick-knacks like driftwood and conch shells and a dried seahorse pinned under glass. She pictured herself in that room; Dr. Markel sitting on the antique rocker in the corner, his legs crossed at the knees as he studied her over a pair of glasses perched on the end of his nose. She could see him shaking his head and dismissing her when Gabriela explained that she wasn't a journalist, but a desperate mother with her hands out.

She would be shooed away without a second thought.

Gabriela paused and prayed. God would get her through. He always did.

Standing less than a pace from the door, she peered into the open crack. The entryway waited on the other side. Past it, she saw a shard of a room, well-lit with pebble-glass cabinets high on the walls, and the faint shape of a stack of white plates behind the glass.

A kitchen.

That thought tapped the threads of Gabriela's soul, reverberating deep inside her.

Dr. Markel was a person. He ate. He kept a tidy home. He sat in his chair and read books by the light of his Tiffany lamp in the front room, where he could see his gaudy fountain.

A nugget of humanity existed within him. She could work with that. Gabriela's hand moved to the vertical wooden handle of the front door, made to look like a weathered ship's mast. It was warm.

Bang.

Her hand recoiled from the door handle. A sharp sound reverberated inside her skull. What was that? A firecracker? A power transformer blowing? But the lights were still—

A woman's scream came next. Gabriela's blood went cold.

Bang. Bang.

The scream stopped.

A gunshot. In a haze of panic, she stepped back, blood scurrying from her brain, every instinct in her body begging her to press herself low and get as far away from the gunshots as possible— and God in Heaven! That bone-chilling scream.

Footsteps pounded inside the house.

A shadow fell across the cabinet doors, coming closer. Her conscious mind was no longer in control—it was being devoured by fear, her instincts alone driving her to act. Gabriela darted to her left. The thick shadows near the table drew her eye. She balled herself up, pulling the darkness over, then turned around, her back against the house.

Stay here. Stay quiet. Don't move, don't think, don't breathe.

The porch rattled under her. Footsteps came nearer, like a stormfront crashing over the water. Suddenly, the back of a man's figure came into view; then he turned right at the bottom of the steps and trotted past her.

She saw him in profile. The man wasn't tall, but he was upright, with good posture; a muscled, broad-shouldered man. His long, dark hair was swept back from his face, and the light from the lamp in the window behind Gabriela revealed a lean, hollow cheek, a deep-set eye and angular nostrils that bestowed him with a murderous intensity.

She flattened herself against the wall. Why did she look? Why would she risk bringing herself out of hiding?

Had he seen her? Did he hear her? Was he coming back?

She was as good as dead. He was going to shoot her. Wait. If he was going to shoot her, why hadn't he done it earlier? He needed more ammunition—maybe he'd only had enough for the doctor and his wife. Three bullets? Why would he only bring three bullets? Would he know the exact amount he'd need to plug up a shrieking woman after she saw her husband killed in front of her?

Stop. Just stop.

A hellish orange glow appeared across the fountain. The snake-and-staff at the top turned fearful, and the walls around Gabriela reflected the same quivering, orange light. Her deep, dark shadows began shrinking. She couldn't see where the light came from—only that it appeared, eating the only thing keeping her safe.

She pulled her knees tighter. Her ribs were a girdle around her lungs, her minute of life being squeezed away. The flickering orange light crept toward the toes of her flats, then touched them. The gate holding back the invaders from her body fell, and a burning terror rushed from her feet to her heart, seizing control of her soul and lashing it with hellfire. The light retreated. It slid against the railing far to her right.

The orange light pressed toward her. It advanced across the porch's ceiling. She thought she'd been spotted—that a porch light had come on, and the man with the gun had come to shoot her.

Until she saw the fireball.

The fire soared over her, then crashed through the front window above and behind her. Glass rained down on Gabriela's head. She squeezed her eyes shut. Cold stung her unprotected arms and the back of her neck and scalp.

She opened her eyes to see a long shard of glass embedded in her right forearm. It bled freely. And before she knew it, a swell of heat pressed down on her.

She jumped up from her hiding spot, her eyes drawn to the inside of the house. Through the broken window, she saw books burning. The big TV screen warped and bubbled. The seahorse's glass shroud popped and cracked from the explosive heat.

Flames overran the front room.

CHAPTER SIXTEEN

I tried calling DJ after I'd left the VA office, but he didn't answer, and I wasn't in the mood for calling more than once.

A lot of things had come at me this morning, and I needed some DJ-free time to decompress. So, I walked down toward Crown Bay until I found a little mom and pop seafood stand near the shore.

The stand was all kitchen, save the counter, which was a half-height wall open to a wooden deck where three round, steel-wire tables sat. A frond-thatched roof topped the deck, giving some shade from the early afternoon sun.

The owners were a nice, retired couple from Michigan named Sheryl and George. They said they'd sold their property where they'd once raised emus, rheas, and three boys, then moved down this way for the year-round motorcycling weather. Sheryl and George were a fix for all the thorns pricking me. She was empathetic, conversational, and outgoing, and I could tell that George, despite keeping his back to me while he cooked up a basket of conch fritters and not saying much, was a man with a good heart who put his soul into everything he did—including running their little restaurant.

After a few minutes, he popped the fritters out of the fryer, and sat them in a small plastic basket for me. I took my order, added a cold Miller High Life to it, then ate at one of the tables while I watched a cruise ship pull into port.

Thousands of people disembarked onto St. Thomas on any given day. My mind wandered past them, past Luc Baptiste and all the people glad to see him dead, then idled near Arlen.

Over my life, I'd wasted plenty of mental energy on that man. Coming to the USVI should have been the end of it, but the past had a way of staying close behind.

Arlen never did what other people told him. I should've remembered that when I'd stormed out of his office in Irvine.

All that thinking and drinking, and before I knew it, an hour had gone by.

I set my third High Life bottle on the table.

"How do you feel about another beer?" Sheryl asked me while she scrubbed the counter.

"I'm feeling like I have to get back to work." I sighed and rubbed my hand through my hair.

She flapped her hands at me. "Oh, come on. Who's dying?"

I couldn't answer her question. I pulled out my phone and called DJ again.

He answered. "How's the Pity Platoon getting along, Dep? Anybody cry about their daddy not giving them a pony?"

"If you were there, you'd know."

"I'll let that mystery be a mystery," DJ said. "You got an upper limit to how much human suffering you're willing to take on?"

"We need to ship out," I answered. "I've got another lead to follow."

"That mean we're giving up on Nick Garner? I always thought he could do with a federal sentence to get him to knock off all that phony garbage he's pushing."

"He might stand in front of a judge yet," I said. Though from the things Garner had implied about DJ, I wondered if the two of them wouldn't be right alongside each other. "For now, I've got a line on a doctor over in PR. Luc was asking around about him."

"Need a charter fishing boat to take you over? I'll rake you over the coals on rates, but I'm your only option, so too bad."

"We'll negotiate terms later," I said. "I'll meet you on *Reel Fun*."

Done talking, I settled up the bill and left George and Sheryl a nice tip. The food was good, and I had a feeling I'd be back their way.

I walked west and arrived at the marina within a few minutes. *Reel Fun* bobbed among the other boats, her tuna tower sticking up like a radio antenna at the top of a dry hill in Chino.

I boarded her, checked in the salon for DJ, and didn't find him. But I didn't have to wait long. He was back on the boat about the time I sat down on the flybridge settee.

"How was the walk?" I called down as he stepped onto *Reel Fun's* swim platform.

"Invigorating," he belched.

When he started up the ladder, I reached a hand down to help him get up the last rung, but DJ ignored it and pulled himself up. He made for the skipper's chair, while I took out my phone, unlocked it and pulled up the note I'd jotted down with that doctor's name and address.

"Now that you're good and greased up, what do you say

about following our next lead?"

"Fine idea, Dep. Fine, indeed."

"Doctor James Markel," I said. "He lives north of Manati, which is west of San Juan, if memory serves."

"Got his address?" DJ started the boat.

I handed him my phone. He pushed down on the nav-console, opening the compartment to his GPS chart plotter, then tapped my phone's screen to get the latitude and longitude and entered the coordinates into the chart plotter. He seemed to study the screen for a moment, comparing it to my phone's GPS—I couldn't see what he was looking at.

"The chart plotter says it's about a hundred nautical miles from here. Looks like his place is right on the coast." He turned, handing my phone back to me. "Lucky for you, you hired yourself a very comfortable charter."

I hopped out of the settee, then tapped the fuel gauge. "A charter with full tanks."

Down the flybridge ladder, I hit the aft deck, then untied our lines from the dock while I prepared myself for the task ahead. Two hundred miles round trip would suck most of the fuel from DJ's tanks. It was going to be another late night.

Once I was back aboard, DJ motored us out, taking us south-west from Crown Bay as I dutifully coiled the dock lines and stowed them with the fenders.

Once out of the bay, we moved generally westward, passing the Flat Cays, then Savana Island and finally turning slightly north of west to cross the ten or so miles of open water between there and Culebra. The sun was fat and red as we cleared the water from Culebra to Puerto Rico, then traced along Puerto Rico's north coast, the lights of San Juan coming into view. In the three hours since we'd left, DJ hadn't said much of anything. My own thoughts kept circling back to Arlen.

As we passed San Juan Harbor, with the sun starting to dance with the horizon, I noticed DJ's eyelids getting heavy. I'd almost forgotten he hadn't slept, and the monotonous drone of the engines and bow waves were enough to make anyone sleepy.

"You want me to take the wheel, Captain?" I said over the wind.

He looked at me, blinking, his eyes red. "Not a chance, my man. I got it."

So, he kept it.

Another hour passed before he looked down at his chart plotter, the glow from its screen lighting his features in the darkness. He gently pulled back on *Reel Fun's* twin throttles until the boat's wake caught up to us, lifting the stern.

The wind disappeared and the air felt heavy. When the sound of the engines dropped to a low rumble, I became more aware of the night—the waves splashing against *Reel Fun's* hull and against the rocky shore to my left, and the billions of stars over our heads. Alicia and I had become entranced with the night sky after moving to the islands. Sitting on the back deck and looking up, we were much more comfortable than we were around others or watching TV.

I couldn't explain why. Some people were troubled by knowing the world was insignificant compared to the empty vastness of space—Earth comprised less than half a gnat on the celestial windshield. That idea gave me comfort. It reminded me that all this trouble came and went, and the universe continued to move forward. Time kept ticking.

"Get out the NVs." DJ motioned toward the compartment

under my seat. "Tell me what you see."

I rose, lifted the settee cushion, and recognized the hard case with his night vision binoculars inside. I put the case on the flybridge's deck, then pulled out the binos.

DJ cut *Reel Fun's* lights. I put the binos up to my eyes and scanned the coast.

"Nothing's glowing at me, Captain," I said.

"Make sure you're in the right places."

"We're looking for some doctor's house. With these binos, it should be like looking into headlights. And since it's on the coast, he's probably got a dock. The dock should be lit up."

"Like that one?" DJ pointed westward.

I pointed the binos over the bow, then had to pull them away from my eyes when the screen flashed white from bright light just up the coast. Through the darkness ahead, I saw exactly what I expected to see: a well-lit jetty.

"Exactly what I told you would be there," I said.

His only answer was to push on the throttle. *Reel Fun* lurched forward, and I was thrown backward, catching myself on the top of the still-open settee compartment.

I pulled myself steady and sat on a different part of the settee, then brought the binos back to my eyes.

I spotted something.

The light would've been hard to see with the naked eye, even as dark as it was, but the IR sensors picked up a faint glow. It was up on the coast. A shimmer in the trees.

Fire.

CHAPTER SEVENTEEN

A Molotov. That's what Gabriela had seen flying through the air. Standing at the broken window, looking at the destruction it caused, left her mesmerized. Never in her life had she seen a house fire. Ribbons of flame crawled up the spines of leather-bound books, a wild streak of fire gorged on the hardwoods and the carpet, spreading at the base of the bookshelf as it simultaneously crawled upward.

The heat gnawed at her skin. God help her, shouldn't she be afraid? Shouldn't she feel some kind of empathy? A man's home, his footprints, his memories, his passions, his comforts, were being devoured right before her eyes. Dr. Markel might've profited off Flor's misery, and a thousand other girls like her, but even *he* didn't deserve to have his home turned to ash.

Gabriela watched in fascination and horror. The flames seemed to leap from the bookshelf in fits and starts, crawling up the far wall, while at the same time, writhing across the floor like the serpent slithering over the roots of the Tree of Knowledge. Part of her wanted to be taken by the flames. The pain would be all-consuming. It would drive her insane, engulfing her body, her mind, erasing her sense of self as it overwhelmed her senses and burnt into her brain.

But it would be over. She would be cleansed. Her mortal husk would be shucked, and her spirit would be free to revel in Glory on Highest, to bath in the light of eternity, to know the face of grace. She reached out. A leaf of flame brushed against her finger.

Gabriela reeled her arm in. What in God's name was she doing? Standing in front of the fire like an idiot, losing her mind? But for the grace of God, she hadn't already been shot down.

Turning from the fire, she stepped to the edge of the porch. She looked left, then right, and saw nothing but the fountain and the cars.

He was gone. Or hiding, waiting to kill her. Her hands trembled at her sides, so she grabbed the rail around the porch. If she could stay out of sight and get to her car, she could get away.

But… what then?

Back home to Flor?

At that moment, Gabriela held her last bead of hope. She could turn tail and run, or she could bite back her fear, risk herself against the fire, and fight for Flor's life. The moment she'd called Dr. Markel's office, she knew she had to press forward at all costs. This was her one shot at righting the wrongs of her life, of undoing her teenaged mistakes. Her justification for leaving her family back in the Dominican Republic was to give her newborn baby Flor a better life. Well, this was it, and this one chance was more than most people ever got.

Whether there was a murderer in the house, or a fire, or if Dr. Markel, himself, turned her away at the door screaming, pointing a gun in her face, Gabriela Ramos wouldn't run.

She moved to the open front door. Inside, fire painted the rightmost entryway wall and inverted waves of flame rolled across the ceiling. Dr. Markel and his wife had to be in the back of the house near the kitchen.

She took a step forward, wondering if she could get past the fire, but a few feet in, the heat puckered her skin.

There had to be another way in. A place like this had to have a big porch and big windows for looking at the water on the backside of the house.

Gabriela hurried down the front steps, turned right, and ran through a flower bed. She hooked around a corner, followed the driveway past the garage, and came to a stone-paved path through a garden running parallel to the back of the house. To her far left, through the trees bordering the rear of the property, she saw lights tinkling far away. Below, she could hear the wash of waves assaulting the beach.

The garden gave way to a raised wooden deck. Gabriela sprinted up the pair of steps leading onto the deck and ran as hard as she could toward a pair of glass doors leading into the back of the house.

Through the back doors, she saw the fire had spread quickly. Smoke licked the walls and chewed the ceiling. She would have been able to see the front entryway, except for a partition wall on the right being blackened.

Suddenly, movement down low and to her left caught her eye. A man's foot dragged on the floor like a wounded animal. She couldn't see beyond the midpoint of his shin, but it had to be Dr. Markel.

Gabriela grabbed the doorknob. Her hand was slick with rivulets of her own blood, the knob was hot to the touch, and it wouldn't turn.

The door was locked.

"Dr. Markel!" She banged on the glass, hoping he'd see her and could unlock the door.

He didn't.

Gabriela turned and scanned the back deck. Maybe there was another entrance, or an open window, or a key left on the edge of the hot tub.

She checked, but nope. None of that.

However, there were deck chairs.

Gabriela grabbed the first one she saw. It was wicker wrapped around a steel frame, and it had some heft to it.

Wasting no time, she gritted her teeth, picked up the chair by its backrest, wheeled on her heel, and smashed the chair into the back door.

The glass cracked, but it didn't break. So, she laid the chair on its back. She grabbed it by the legs. Holding it at her waist, she took a couple of steps back, and fixed her gaze on the door with a determination she hadn't had in a long time.

Way back in her high school days, Gabriela had been the captain of the school's varsity softball team. She was a hitter and a threat to sock a ball past the fence any time she was at the plate. Here, on Dr. Markel's back porch, feeling the heat upon her face, she squinted at the door like it was the deadliest close-out pitcher she'd ever gone against.

Everything rode on this at-bat.

She saw it coming, low and just a little outside.

Gabriela set her shoulders, cocked her hips, then stomped her leading foot as she brought the chair around like she was going to knock the cover off the ball.

The hard, arched back of the chair smashed through the glass, and kept going until it crunched a second pane of glass, then tore into the blinds, and finally stopped when Gabriela jerked back on her swing, killing the chair's momentum.

Her shoulders hurt more than they had in an exceedingly long time. She was no longer the conditioned athlete of her youth, but she didn't have a second to stop and think about it. She ripped the chair free of the blinds. Tiny knives of glass came with it, most of them missing Gabriela, save a few splinters that caught in the legs of her pants. She was so pumped full of fear and adrenaline, she hardly felt them. Using the chair, she knocked out a few errant spikes of glass from the door before crouching below the smoke and stepping inside.

On the floor, Dr. Markel cradled his wife. She was as pale as moth wings against the spread of crimson beneath them. Markel kissed the top of her head and muttered something Gabriela couldn't hear over the growling flames.

Mrs. Markel was still. And all that blood. Gabriela knew that she hadn't heard her husband. She was already gone.

"Dr. Markel!" Gabriela shouted, then coughed as smoke fed into her lungs. She lowered her head, catching him glancing at her. He turned back to his wife, holding her tightly and muttering.

She wouldn't be ignored. Not after all this. Gabriela dropped to her hands and knees and crawled toward him. She grabbed his foot, then used his legs as a guide through the thickening smoke of this man-made hell.

At his shoulder, Gabriela's fingers slipped over wet, warm blood. His T-shirt was spongy and sticky. God, she hoped it wasn't Dr. Markel's blood.

"Please! I need to talk to you. Do you have any Anthradone here?"

"Anthradone?" His voice was a throaty rasp. "Who the hell are you?"

"I talked to you on the phone," she said. "I'm the reporter—actually, I'm not a reporter, I'm—"

Why was she wasting his time? She had to get him out.

"It's not important," Gabriela said. "She's gone, Doctor! Let her go. We have to get out of here—you're dead if you stay here."

He turned his head and looked directly at her, his pale blue eyes holding Gabriela's own. It was funny, the way a person's eyes said so much more than words ever could. About who someone was, where they were going, and what they wanted now.

Dr. Markel's eyes told Gabriela he wasn't leaving his wife's body here.

"My daughter has Li-Fraumeni," she said. "Please, you have to get out of here so you can help her!"

A blast of wind rushed up from behind. A deafening thump came behind it. Instinctively, Gabriela screeched and covered her head. Bits of ash and ember shot past, and hands of smoke took hold of her throat.

She coughed and hacked, looking behind her. The partition from the entryway had come down, revealing nothing but smoke as black as a new moon, cut by the deadly orange shimmer of a column of flame, roasting the back of her.

"Dr. Markel, my little girl still needs you!" Gabriela shouted over the fire. "There are people everywhere who still need you—you can't stay here!"

Gray ash settled over him.

She grabbed Markel's arm and yanked him away from his wife. He didn't fight her.

Because he couldn't have fought her. A splotch of dark red showed through the ash that covered him—and it was growing.

Dr. Markel had an open wound across his belly. He'd be gone within minutes.

"I can't go with you," Dr. Markel strained to speak. "I'm sorry."

Then she'd already lost, hadn't she? Before she'd come in this house, and risked her life against the fire, she'd lost. Her chance to cure Flor was gone. Gabriela lowered her head until it rested on Dr. Markel's elbow.

God in Heaven, after all you've shown me, why would you take it away like this? Why would you take my little girl?

A hand weakly brushed against her forehead.

She lifted her eyes to see Dr. Markel struggling to say something. His mouth moved, but nothing audible came out. He motioned with his eyes. He wanted her to come closer.

Gabriela brought her ear to his mouth.

"In my office," he said. "Laptop."

She pulled away from him. "Laptop?"

He nodded, slowly.

"Where's your office?" She checked the room around her, but the smoke curtained anything beyond a couple feet.

He turned his head to her right, his eyes focusing on something only he could see.

"Where?" She shook him. "Where is it?"

He moved like a rag doll. He was too weak to answer.

Gabriela peered to her right again and saw only smoke and

darkness. Terror stung her like a red-hot pitchfork when she thought about going deeper into the smoke.

His office. It had to be in his office, and whatever was on that laptop, it was worth Dr. Markel using his last bit of strength to tell Gabriela about it.

So, she began to crawl into the smoke.

Moving through the heavier smoke was as bad as every living thing implicitly understood it to be. You didn't have to train a dog to avoid fire, you didn't see birds perching on burning trees, or hear about horses running into burning barns. Every human, every animal, knew. Gabriela suddenly had a little understanding of what motivated a firefighter to enter a burning building. Not doing so could mean the loss of innocent life.

When she looked back and realized she couldn't see Dr. Markel, or the back door, or even her own feet, a deep, primal fear took hold of Gabriela's heart—something more elemental than what she'd felt outside, where that gunman lurked, something that bit deeper than the first time Flor was diagnosed with cancer.

The fear threatened to chain her to the doctor's living room floor. The devil called her name. He tempted her to stop and rest, to forget about her troubles, to stop struggling so damned hard.

Gabriela scrambled forward, holding her blouse over her face with one hand. She shut her eyes and held her breath until her head bumped against the wall. Then she backed away, reached out with her left hand, and felt a door frame, then felt an opening to another room.

She went in.

Here, the lights were off, and mercifully, the smoke wasn't as thick, though not by much—it was thick enough to make her cough and wheeze. Gabriela moved forward, keeping her right hand on the wall, terrified to break contact with it and lose her way in the smoke. Suddenly, the top of her head bumped into something. It felt like another wood thing. Maybe a bookcase, or some kind of table or, she silently hoped, a desk?

She reached up, and her fingers immediately wrapped around a familiar shape—a pen—a whole mess of them. They spilled out and came crashing down on her head, and her heart felt lighter—she'd found the doctor's desk!

A spill of light appeared against the ceiling, like someone clicking on a weak lamp. She rose up on her knees, until her eyes were level with the top of the desk. She saw a blurry reflection against a picture frame on the wall.

Then her brain put it together—the light came from a computer screen!

Both her hands swiped across the desk. They latched onto something hard and thin, and then they pressed it down until it shut with a click.

She snatched Dr. Markel's laptop off the desk, sending a dozen things flying in every direction, and yanking the power cord loose. She didn't care. She had his laptop. She had the key to saving Flor's life, right here in her hands.

Wait. What did he actually have here? A formula? What was she going to do with a formula? She couldn't synthesize the drug herself. She didn't know the first thing about it.

No, no, there had to be a way. The Lord would open a way.

Maybe she could take it to one of Hildon's competitors. She could sell it to them for money to pay off all the medical bills and work out a way to get enough Anthradone to cure her daughter, or she could ransom the formula back to Hildon. She'd get fired, but what did she care? So long as they gave her the Anthradone to cure Flor.

Flor mattered. Not a paycheck. At least, not one from a

pharma company.

She hacked up a deep cough that sent her doubling over and catching herself against the hardwood floor with her elbows. She kept the laptop clutched to her chest.

All of this would be worthless if she didn't make it out of the house.

Gabriela looked left. Hellish light danced against the wall opposite the door she'd come through, and smoke belched into Dr. Markel's office. She went toward it awkwardly on one hand and both knees, still holding tight to the laptop, then looked out and saw nothing but a black-gray curtain backed by flame.

Dr. Markel's body was in there, somewhere. God rest his soul.

She turned around and, as she worked her way toward the desk, she noticed a beacon of hope shining in through the smoke.

Gabriela crawled toward the light. She came to another wall, and felt her way around it, until she realized she was at a window—and it was open. Her free hand pressed against the window screen until it ripped out of the way.

Hoisting herself out, she tumbled through the window and escaped the house, landing on her back in a flower bed.

She lay there for a moment, her lungs sucking in clean air and pushing out the smoke as best they could. Her arms were numbed from the cuts, her eyes stinging, her heart bouncing in her chest.

Her journey out of the fire and flame was a miracle. God's will was good, and she owed Him more than she could ever repay. She would sing His glory from now until the end of days.

She watched the chimney of smoke crawl up into the night sky, listened to the flames hollow out the house, felt the thud of what must have been a large beam falling to the ground some-where inside.

The weight of something pressed on her hip. She lifted her head to see what it was and saw the laptop. Did she wreck it in the fall?

The machine was dirty. When she opened the lid, the screen was smudged with blood and soot—likely from when she'd grabbed it off the desk—but she had a login screen.

The laptop still worked.

She snapped it shut, then got to her feet. In front of her, the fountain shone white above the hidden spotlights, the caduceus wings spread. The angel who led her out of the fire.

Thank God Markel had spent so much money on that awful fountain.

She shook her head, then stumbled across the driveway to her car. Once there, she opened the back door, wrapped the laptop in one of Flor's blankets, and carefully laid it on the floor behind her seat. It had to fit snugly; she couldn't have it rattling around on the drive home.

Then, she got behind the wheel, started the engine, and slowly backed out.

When she cleared Dr. Markel's big SUV to her right, she saw what remained of the house in her rearview mirror. The porch and everything on it were lost in the flames. Fire beckoned to her from the open window of Dr. Markel's office.

The whole house would be gone within moments. She couldn't have been in there longer than five or ten minutes, and the fire had spread pretty much everywhere.

She coughed again and put the car in drive. She looked up, checking the fires in her mirror one last time.

Then her throat went tight. A man's figure stood in the driveway directly behind her. Before he had a chance to shoot her, she stomped the gas pedal.

CHAPTER EIGHTEEN

"Trouble," I shouted over the wind and clapped DJ's shoulder. Then, I pointed in the direction of the fire. It was plain to see now, even without night vision.

As we cleared the last outcrop of rock, we both realized that the fire burned directly above the jetty.

DJ shoved the throttle. *Reel Fun's* engines screamed like a wild cat. I ran to the flybridge ladder, then quickly down to the cockpit, and burst into the salon. DJ wasn't a diver, but I was. He let me keep some equipment on board.

I yanked up the cushion on the starboard settee, found my stuff, and dug out my mask, fins and booties, swimsuit, and a small, single-strap plastic shoulder pack lying on the floor. Quickly, I changed out of my clothes and into my swimsuit and booties, then put the pack on so that the strap lay across my back and the bag fit on my chest. Finally, I opened the pack, took out a neon green glow stick on the end of a lanyard, snapped it, and put the lanyard around my neck.

A set of handheld, waterproof VHF radios waited on a charging cradle in the master stateroom. I snatched one up, turned it on to make sure the battery was charged, then turned it off and stuffed it in my pack.

On my way to the aft deck, I scooped up my mask and fins.

Reel Fun slowed to a halt just as I finished putting my fins around the heels of my booties.

"Channel 3, DJ!" I called up to the flybridge as I got to the swim platform. "I'll make contact when I'm on the jetty."

"Roger that," DJ answered.

I adjusted my mask over my eyes, then held it tight with my fingertips as I took a big stride off *Reel Fun's* swim platform. I scissored my fins instantly, my face barely going below the water.

When I surfaced, I pointed myself in the direction of the jetty. The lights made it easy to spot, and if I somehow didn't see them, the fire burning up the hill from shore was plenty to guide me. I estimated two hundred yards to the end of the jetty from my position. If the current cooperated with me, I'd be there in under three minutes.

As I swam, I noticed at least four different boats moored to a dock farther along the jetty, nearer the shore. A yacht about the size of *Reel Fun*, a much smaller boat about fifteen feet long on the opposite side of the dock, a fifteen-foot trawler and a Cigarette boat painted some kind of dark, high-gloss finish that reflected the firelight. After I pulled myself up the ladder hanging off the end of the jetty, I took off my mask and unsnapped the heel straps from my fins, my eyes on the fire all the while. It must've doubled in size in the time it took me to swim from *Reel Fun*. I hoped to God Marc Herrera hadn't got some idea about luring me out here to get rid of the pesky guy asking too many questions.

Out of habit, I checked my surroundings. Other than the fire, the boats ahead of me, and *Reel Fun* behind me with her running lights on, I couldn't see much with the jetty lights shining in my eyes.

I unzipped the pack on my chest, then took out the handheld. "I'm on the jetty."

"I see ya," DJ answered.

"Moving up to the fire now. I'll keep you posted."

"Roger that."

Leaving my mask and fins behind on the end of the dock, I moved forward. With each step I took on the wooden jetty toward the shore, my pulse pounded harder in my ears.

I batted back the creeping fear that I was walking into someone else's kill zone. My eyes kept close tabs on each boat's deck. My mind was eager to grasp onto the shadows playing across bows and decks and turn them into human-shaped figures.

As I passed between the boats—the Cigarette boat and the yacht on my left, and the smaller boats on my right, I saw no lights and doubted anyone was inside them. I stepped off the dock and onto the rocky shore, the sense of foreboding growing stronger.

A path meandered up the shallow cliffs ahead of me. It was made of sand poured behind railroad ties to create steps, with lights on posts marking either side of the trail. It went about ten yards ahead of me, rising up ten feet to the top of the rocks before it cut suddenly right, still climbing upward.

"I'm heading up to the house," I said into the radio.

"Copy that," DJ answered. "Just don't get roasted alive. I'd hate to have to tell your wife you cooked up worse than a toddler's campfire marshmallow."

"Well, we wouldn't want you to have to go through that, would we?"

I started up the trail, reaching the dogleg, where the fire's heat strongly suggested I go back to the water. But I continued on.

Five yards farther, I followed a switchback in the trail. A few more paces, and I came to the top.

Half the house was engulfed in flame and the darkest smoke I'd ever seen. A hint of a wooden deck became visible, which made me think I'd come around the backside of the place, but I couldn't be sure. What I thought was the deck could've been the interior floor exposed after a wall caved in.

The heat was relentless. It made my eyes pucker, and the bare skin on my stomach, arms, and legs tingled with goosebumps. As I stood there in awe, part of the roof caved in. It hit the ground with a heavy sound that reverberated up the soles of my feet and into my gut. Embers twisted into the sky, and an intense wash of heat passed over me.

Another urge to run the way I'd come from hit me. It was the natural human thing to do when confronted with danger, but I was trained as a pararescue operator. Years of instruction and drilling had molded me into the kind of guy who had to go check for survivors. Only fools and heroes ran into a burning building. I was neither; it was my job.

So, I went left—around the quarter of the house that hadn't been swallowed by the fire. Here, a strip of grass a few feet wide had been cleared between the house and the brush to my left.

I passed by a closed window and tried to peer inside. I couldn't see a thing. The inside of the house was probably so choked with smoke, I wouldn't have seen my own hand in front of my face.

"Dr. Markel!" I shouted at the window, hoping he was somehow on the other side and able to answer me. There was no response. I continued around the front of the house.

A big, white fountain was the first thing that caught my eye. The two-tiered water feature housed a sculpture carved to resemble a caduceus staff.

A pair of taillights suddenly came on, grabbing my attention. A navy blue SUV—a Kia—and I couldn't hear the engine running over the roaring fire, but it slowly backed out of a spot on the driveway.

It curved around the back of the other car, and thanks to the lights on Dr. Markel's fountain, I got a look at the driver—it wasn't Marc Herrera.

A woman sat behind the wheel. She had dark, frizzy hair and a round face. She looked petite, harmless, and scared to hell and back.

"Hey!" I waved my arms.

She didn't see me. But she knew something, and I didn't want her running off. I ran toward her.

Just as I passed the fountain, she looked at me in the mirror. I guess I spooked her, because the Kia's engine revved, the tires yelped, and she took off.

Then, the Kia came to a sudden, violent stop.

A stone archway stood on the far edge of the driveway. The arch was grounded a foot on either side of the exit and the car had crashed into it.

"DJ, get to the dock, ASAP! I've got someone in need of medical attention."

My instincts took over. I ran to the car and peered inside. The woman was slumped against the airbag from the wheel.

"Ma'am," I said, yanking the door open, "can you talk to

me?"

She muttered. I couldn't hear her over the fire, and she was covered in soot and ash, but if she were talking, she was alive and conscious. Her hands and arms were bloody, but I didn't see any other obvious injuries.

"You were in an accident," I said, "I'm a trained medic—I'm going to take you out of the car."

I reached across her, intending to get my hands under her armpits to pull her out, but instead, my finger brushed across her neck, and she flipped out.

She screamed like a banshee and slapped at my arms, then tried to push me away. But she had as much strength as a newborn puppy.

"Come on, lady," I said, as I took a firm hold of her and pulled her out of her seat. "Just relax!"

"No!" she screamed hoarsely, then coughed while I lowered her to the ground, and leaned her up against the rear wheel of her car. When the coughing quit, her first words were, "Where's the laptop?"

"Ma'am, if you had a computer in that house, it's a puddle now. I'm sorry."

"No…" she moaned. She was out of her mind. But when she came back around, I wanted to make sure she was with DJ and me.

I took my green glow stick in hand and used its light on her face. Her hair was singed in places, a trickle of blood ran from her nose, a bump on her forehead would be the size of a baseball in ten minutes, and she had black marks around her mouth like runny mascara.

"Were you in that house?" I asked. "Do you know Dr. Markel?"

"The laptop." Her eyes fluttered. I was afraid she was going to pass out, but she rubbed her face, blinked, and when I raised the glow stick between her eyes, her pupils constricted evenly. Good sign.

"Do you know how the fire started?" I asked, as I ran the glow stick farther down her body, checking for any other serious wounds or burns. Her blouse was dotted with blood, and the knees of her gray slacks were soaked with it. "Is there anyone else inside the house?"

"Dr. and Mrs. Markel," she said, half awake. "They've both been shot."

Shot? The word made my arm hair stand on end.

"Did you see who did it?" No one else was around that I noticed.

"Yes," she answered. "I don't know who—" she trailed off. "He gave me a laptop."

"The shooter?"

She coughed again. "No, Dr. Markel gave it to me."

The glow stick passed over her right arm. A shard of glass captured the light. She must've busted through a window to get out of the house.

"You have glass embedded in your arm," I said, as I passed the light from her right arm over her left. "Both of them."

I reached into my pack, took out my first aid kit and popped it open. I wouldn't have enough bandages and gauze to cover every cut on her arms, but I'd do my best to cover the deepest ones. None of them seemed to be bleeding any more, at least, but I was sure that'd change once I pulled the larger shards of glass out.

"Take my hand," I said, extending my left to her right. When she gave it to me, I took hold firmly. "This is going to hurt, but that big piece has to come out before you can move. I want you to squeeze my hand with both of yours, okay?"

When she nodded her understanding and gripped my hand, I pulled the glass dagger from her forearm. She bit her lip and pushed her head back against the fender.

"What's your name?" I ripped open the packaging on the only bandage in my kit, then started wrapping the large cut on her right arm.

"Gabriela Ramos." She sounded half asleep. She started to sag against the tire, then jolted upright. "The laptop! Get the laptop!"

She grabbed the strap of my bag and pulled me closer. I don't know where this sudden burst of strength had come from, but it crackled in the whites of her eyes as she stared me down.

"Get the laptop. Do *not* leave it behind."

"Okay, ma'am. I just want to make sure you're stabilized first." Suddenly, the strap of my bag went slack again. Her hand dropped to her lap, and a wet shimmer appeared in her eyes.

"Please, sir, you have to get the laptop." A tear cut a clean swath down the soot on her cheek. "It's for my little girl. She'll die without it. We can't leave it here!"

"She'll die without your laptop?"

"I told you it's not mine," she said. "Dr. Markel gave it to me. He said the cure was on it."

I almost asked her what she was talking about, but odds weren't great I'd get a coherent answer. Now wasn't the time to press her.

"Okay, Gabriela, where's the laptop?"

The tension in her shoulders relaxed.

"Behind my seat," she said. "Wrapped in a blanket."

I reached up and grabbed the handle for the rear door, then pulled it open. Sure enough, when I unwrapped a pink and purple comforter with a cartoon character on it, I found a jet-black laptop.

"You got this from the man who lived here?" I asked, while I turned the laptop over and checked it for damage.

"Yes," she said. "Is it still working?"

"It's in one piece." I opened the lid, but the screen didn't come on. "It's not turning on."

"It's not?" She planted a hand on the driveway, trying to push herself to her feet, but she didn't have the strength to stand.

I knelt next to her. This laptop seemed to mean everything to her—and if it belonged to Markel, I needed to get it back to *Reel Fun* regardless. I gently sat it on her lap.

"You hold onto it for now. We'll get somebody to fix this thing up," I said. "Don't worry."

She smiled at me. "Thank you."

"Hold your thanks. You'll hate my guts after I pick you up and move you out of here."

She didn't appear concerned. "Are you a doctor, too? And how did you find me?"

"I was in the Air Force—Pararescue," I answered. "Dr. Markel is wrapped up in some kind of trouble. I hoped to talk to him before—" I looked at the fire. "I guess I was too late."

"He's dead now," she said without any hint of emotion. She was drained. If she were close to Markel, all the grief and mourning would come pouring out once she had some rest and some time to reflect.

I closed up my kit and returned it to the pack on my chest. Then I sized Gabriela up.

"How's your neck feeling? Stiff? Sore? Can you move it okay?"

She rubbed it, stretched to her left, and grimaced.

"Just try to relax." I scooped her into my arms.

"What are you doing?" She clutched the laptop to her chest. "You're hurting me."

"I said you wouldn't like me."

For a moment, I considered going right, across the driveway, and around the same side of the house from where I'd originally come. The tips of flames teased the brush near the house, so going in that direction was the surest way to come out of this without eyebrows.

I went straight—around the part of the house that was little more than hot coals and blackened wood.

Three or four yards from the house, a powerful heat began to push back at me. I went as wide left as I could. I had no desire to bake the insides of my lungs.

Once we came around the back of the house, my next challenge was getting down the path that led to the dock. With Gabriela in my arms, our combined center of gravity would make for an awkward trip down, but I had no choice. I slowly negotiated down the railroad tie steps and made it all the way to the bottom without breaking anyone's neck.

To find that DJ wasn't there.

"DJ?" I said into the radio. I waited for a response.

Nothing.

"I've got wounded," I said. "I need a pickup at the dock."

More silence.

"DJ, where the hell are you?"

"I met a new pal." I heard the howl of wind whipping past him as he yelled into his radio. "We're having a little disagreement between friends—don't get your panties in a twist."

I carefully laid Gabriela on the dock, then squinted northward, looking across the water.

Then, as a wave dipped or crested, I saw a low, steady cone of light moving left to right in the distance. *Reel Fun.* DJ was out there with a fishing spotlight.

"Another boat took off from the dock when you were warming your hands by the fire," he said. "I offered a neighborly hello, but he ain't too friendly."

The yacht and the two smaller boats were still tied up in front of me.

"The Cigarette boat?"

"Nobody gets one past you. You're as sharp an investigator as they come," DJ answered.

"Let him go," I said. "There's no way you can catch up to him, and I need you here."

I squeezed Gabriela's hand. "Still comfortable?"

She said nothing. My head went to the worst place—that she'd died here while I waited for DJ, but I felt a pulse. She'd passed out.

"DJ?" I said into the radio.

"All right," he said. The spotlight cut out. "I'm bringing *Reel Fun* around."

CHAPTER NINETEEN

O nce I got Gabriela comfortable on the boat, I had a decision to make. She needed medical attention but taking her to the hospital would involve a lot of questions that I didn't have answers to. She was bleeding from several cuts, but I didn't think it was life threatening and aside from the pain, DJ and I were both trained in battlefield first aid and could treat the cuts and stop the bleeding.

The other option was to take her back to St. Thomas.

I called Alicia. She had to get out our big medical kit from the hall closet. We had a patient coming over. The next three hours on *Reel Fun* were spent keeping Gabriela comfortable and awake. DJ had me put her down on the aft settee in the salon, explaining that it would be more comfortable. There, I kept watch on her, giving her fluids, talking to her, making sure she wasn't in too much pain, and letting her clean her face with a washcloth.

Most people wouldn't be able to handle a three-hour ride at full throttle like that. DJ had been right; though the ride was rough, looking forward to the master stateroom and how much it was rising and falling in the chop, it was a lot smoother in the back of the boat. Gabriela held up remarkably well, hardly ever complaining when a cut on her arm reopened, or when she went into a coughing fit and hacked up something oozing and black as coal. She was a tough lady, and she had my respect. I'd recovered airmen who had been through less than she and griped about it ten times as much.

When we finally motored into my extra slip at Long Bay, DJ helped me get her off the boat. Alicia was there, parked at the marina office with our car, just like she said she'd be.

She held her non-medical questions until all four of us were back at the house, and Gabriela had been laid on towels spread over the tiled floor in our living room while we cleaned needles and prepped sutures in the kitchen together.

"Where'd you find her?"

"A doctor's house." I threaded a needle and laid it on a baking sheet covered with a dish towel on the counter to my left. "I didn't expect to find her there, but I couldn't leave her."

"I know you couldn't." Alicia turned to me and whispered, "What's with the laptop? She's been holding onto it since I picked you guys up."

"She says there's a cure she needs on it," I answered.

Alicia's eyes darted back to Gabriela. "Is she sick?"

"Her daughter."

"That matches up," Alicia said, looking her over.

She finished prepping the last needle, then put it on the tray. I followed my wife out to the living room, then set the tray down on an end table near the couch.

"All right, Gabriela," Alicia started, "I'm going to undo some of the dressings on your arms and figure out where exactly we need to put in stitches. Is that okay with you?"

Gabriela looked up at DJ, who was holding her hand.

He clapped her knuckles reassuringly. "Don't you worry now," he said. "Alicia's a good woman, and a hell of a nurse. Next time I lose a leg, I'm gonna make damned sure she's the one sawing it off."

He and Alicia laughed, but Gabriela furrowed her brow and shot a pleading look at me.

"We're not taking any limbs off," I said. "Don't worry."

She nodded; her eyes calmer than I'd seen them all night.

Alicia went to work. I helped with handing her fresh needles, keeping the sutures ready, and passing over syringes full of lidocaine. Of the two of us, I was the more widely trained, but methods on the battlefield put expedience before comfort and a PJ was more a jack-of-all-trades. As an RN, Alicia had better bedside manner and a deeper knowledge of this kind of procedure.

Two hours, and more stitches than I cared to count later, Alicia sat back on her heels, took off her latex gloves, combed a strand of hair behind her ear, and finally wiped her brow.

"You did great, Gabriela," she said, while I re-dressed Gabriela's arms with fresh bandages. DJ and I helped her get to her feet, then eased her down onto the sectional nearby. Her cheeks flushed and a lock of her dark hair clung wetly to her forehead. She looked ready to pass out.

"Do you have access to any kind of antibiotic?" Alicia asked her.

She shook her head.

"I think I can get you some topical cephalexin. I'll make a phone call in the morning." She turned back to our guest. "For now, how about something to eat?"

"Yes, please, thank God," Gabriela said.

"I'll whip something up." Alicia started toward the kitchen. "I can't promise gourmet, but it'll be edible."

While my wife worked in the kitchen, I reached down and grabbed the laptop off the floor next to the bloodied towels, then sat it on Gabriela's lap.

Her hands locked around its back edge and pulled it close.

"I heard a rumor Dr. Markel was pushing a cure for cancer," I said.

She cocked her head at me. "Who told you that?"

"That's not important. What's your relationship with Markel?"

"My *relationship?* He's a doctor with a treatment that'll save my daughter's life. That's where our relationship begins and ends. Do you think I was participating in something improper with him?" She was getting her hackles up.

I was never good at hiding my skepticism, and she was picking up on it.

"Forgive the deputy," DJ said, physically cutting between Gabriela and me. "The man doesn't have a badge no more, but he's a cop at heart. That makes him an unrepentant asshole. We was both wondering if you could tell us a little about that drug you wanted, and maybe a couple things about the good doctor."

She licked her lips and nodded. Then she crossed her arms, but immediately uncrossed them, aware of her bandages.

"You have to promise not to tell anyone at work," she said. "If my bosses knew I was there, they'd fire me."

"So, you don't work for Dr. Markel?" I asked, nudging DJ out of the way with a hand on his shoulder.

"Dr. Markel ran a lab contracted by Hildon Pharmaceuticals,

which is the company I work for. Over the last year, his lab has been conducting public trials on the drug my daughter needs. I applied, but we didn't get accepted."

"What's this drug called??"

"Anthradone," she said. "Flor has a rare genetic disease called Li-Fraumeni Syndrome."

"What's that?" I asked.

Her hands went to the laptop, tightening around its hinges.

"A person's body is making cells all the time." She swallowed hard, then continued. "Sometimes, even in totally healthy people, these cells go bad and turn cancerous. It happens a lot, in fact. A lot more than you may think. The only reason you and your wife and your friend here," She motioned toward DJ. "The only reason you don't have cancer is that a normal body makes a certain protein that's really good at killing cancer cells. Doesn't always work, but it usually does."

"People with Li-Fraumeni have a problem with that protein. If it's there at all, it doesn't work. And they get..." Gabriela noticeably shuddered. "...tumors."

Suddenly, tears welled in her eyes. A droplet hit the laptop, then rolled toward her.

"My daughter is twelve years old. She's had cancer three times in the last three years. I've had to watch my precious baby get poison pumped into her, and seen radiation bombarding her little body. I've had to put food in her mouth when she was too weak to do it herself, I've had to buy her clothes for girls half her age because everything else falls right off her. I've picked up clumps of hair from her pillow while she's moaning in the middle of the night with a chill."

She stopped and rubbed a knuckle across her eyes. DJ came

to her side, picked a tissue from the box on the end table, and gave it to her.

"Thank you." She smiled through her tears, then blotted at the corners of her eyes.

"After years of going through all that, I hear there's a cure for Li-Fraumeni, but she can't have it because I work for the company making it."

I frowned. I didn't have any kids, but I wanted them some day, and I could only imagine the depth of her pain.

"What is that?" she asked. "I put my time and effort into helping them make the thing, and when my daughter *needs* it, suddenly she can't have it because… why? Aren't we making treatments to make people better? Isn't she a person who needs to be better? And if Hildon isn't doing that, then what *is* it doing?"

"I knew I wasn't supposed to contact Dr. Markel," she said, "but what else was I going to do? Stand around and watch my only child waste away? When I *know* there's something out there that can save her?"

Gabriela's jaw flexed. Her hand balled into a fist, and then she relaxed it and took a breath that seemed to shake her from her core outward. Then, another coughing fit came.

I waited until she was finished.

"Dr. Markel invited you to his house."

She blinked at me. "How did you know that?"

"You're not the only one," I said. "I met another man with terminal brain cancer today. His doctor referred him to Markel, and Markel invited him to his house."

"Did he go?"

"Sort of," I answered. "What happened back there, anyway? Did you set fire to his house?"

She began to sob again. One hand gripped the arm of the sectional, barely able to grasp it, the other clung firmly to that laptop.

"Maybe we should give the woman a break." DJ put a hand on her back. "She could sack out here on the couch for the night, and we can ask her questions in the morning. We all need some sleep."

I didn't want to wait. The human mind was too quick to forget things, to confuse one memory with another and change stories. A short man became average height, a white shirt turned yellow. Especially after sleep. She needed to tell me everything she knew as soon as possible.

Gabriela shook her head, and leaned forward, breaking contact with DJ. "I want to talk now, while it's fresh in my mind."

Her elbows rested on the top lid of the laptop, her palms upturned, and she gazed at the wrappings on her arms. The whole room stayed silent, except for the sounds of Alicia plating something in the kitchen behind us, and the steady churn of waves outside the house. I smelled coffee percolating.

"I heard them get shot," she finally said. She knitted her hands and squeezed her fingers together as tightly as they'd go. "Dr. Markel and his wife."

"Did you see it?"

She shook her head. "I was outside—at Dr. Markel's front door. It was open. And I was about to go in when I heard his wife scream." Her eyelids closed tightly, reliving it. "I'll never forget that scream."

How did you ask a woman who had been through as much as Gabriela to sit on your couch and spill her guts while you nodded your head like you understood? I didn't know. I never knew. As a former detective in Newport Beach, I was supposedly an expert at this sort of thing.

No one had trained me in Emotionally Wounded Mother Counseling. Not at the academy, not in school, and not on the job. And, as far as I knew, Armstrong didn't have an expert on staff.

I put my hand on both of hers. Our fingers were a tangled ball of knuckles and nails. We were together.

"You'll get past that," I said. "You're a strong woman, Gabriela—I can see that plain as day. Over the long run, a scream isn't going to do you in."

She turned her face to me. Tears streamed around the contours of her cheekbones and a weak smile flashed across her face, then vanished.

"Thank you." She placed her thumbs on my knuckles. "I hope that's true."

Alicia came around the back of the couch. I perked up as soon as a tray clinked on the coffee table and I saw the carafe, the mugs, the sliced fruit, and coffee cakes.

"I didn't know what to make but on a night like this you can't go wrong with coffee and sugar, right?"

"Definitely not." Gabriela wiped the tears from her eyes. I let her take a cup and a square of coffee cake first. "Thank you. And can I have a glass of water too?"

"Of course." Alicia walked back to the kitchen.

I grabbed a cup off the tray and helped myself after Gabriela. Alicia came back with the glass of water. Gabriela chugged it down, then put it on the table next to her barely touched coffee, and nearly gone slice of coffee cake.

"Can I ask you a few more questions?" I said.

She nodded.

"Did you see the person who shot Dr. Markel and his wife?"

"He was a white guy," she said. "He looked like—who was the guy who played that crazy banker in the 80s movie? He was Batman too."

"*American Psycho?*" DJ said.

"That's the movie," she answered. "What was the actor's name?"

DJ snapped his fingers a few times while he thought.

"Christian Bale!" my wife shouted out from behind me.

I turned around and looked at her.

Gabriela bounced upright and pointed at Alicia. "That's him!"

"When have you seen those movies?" I asked her.

"You haven't seen either of those flicks?" DJ asked me. "How in the hell does a guy your age not see either of those movies?"

"Most guys my age don't have the responsibilities I do."

"And that's a damned, crying shame. More to the point, the guy you saw, Gabriela, had kinda slicked-back brown hair, right?" DJ asked.

"He did," she said. "And he had a masculine jaw, and a well-proportioned nose."

"Like he was a model or something?"

She nodded and shivered as a chill skittered down her shoulders.

"He threw a Molotov cocktail through the front window of the house. Right over my head, where I was hiding. After I got myself back together, I knew I had to get inside and see if Dr. Markel was still alive."

"Was he?" I asked.

"He'd been shot through the belly. His wife was gone when I got there—I had to break through a glass door with a patio chair—but when I told him who I was, he told me to take this laptop. There is something on here he wanted me to see—something important."

"But you can't get into it," I said. "And even if you could, it's what—a drug formula? Are you a chemist?"

"There are people out there who might be able to make it for me."

A stolen formula taken from a dead man's home may as well have been nuclear for any legitimate chemist. Hildon wasn't likely to let their intellectual property loose in the wild.

"Might be some folks Armstrong knows who can take care of that for her," DJ said.

Armstrong wouldn't want whatever was on the laptop; of that I was certain. It'd threaten the organization's mission.

"Did you see the guy leave?" I asked. "The shooter."

"I was only thinking about getting to Dr. Markel—I was thinking about my daughter."

I nodded. "But you did see him. And after seeing him, how long was it until you saw me?"

"I don't know..." Gabriela picked at one of her bandages. "Ten minutes? Maybe a little less?"

DJ grumbled. He crossed his arms a little tighter and knitted his brow. "He was on the Cigarette boat we let get away."

I didn't say anything. He was sore about having to leave his chase to come pick us up from the dock, but I wouldn't apologize for trying to save Gabriela's life.

"I'm sorry for the trouble I caused you all." A plump tear let go of Gabriela's chin.

"It'll be all right." Alicia rubbed her back and whispered to her. "It'll be okay."

"Do you think I can get back to my daughter tonight?" Gabriela cupped her face in her hands, then lifted her eyes and looked at me. "She's back home in San Juan—her day nurse agreed to stay late with her, but I didn't tell her to plan on sticking around *this* late."

"Of course," Alicia said.

"Sure," I agreed. "We'll bring her back here. We've got an extra bedroom the two of you can stay in while everything gets sorted out."

"Stay here?" Gabriela asked.

The idea seemed to unnerve her. I was a stranger, after all. A man who had come from nowhere and saved her life, but a stranger.

"I think it's smart to play it safe. At least for a few days, while you recover."

Her mouth tensed as she thought about it, then she nodded.

"Jerry." DJ jerked his head toward the deck door. "We need to chat a minute."

I stood up as he opened the sliding door, then went out.

The night was clear, with a million stars raining light onto St. Thomas, and the air caressing the back of my neck was welcome. I didn't realize how humid the inside of the house had been. I paused, taking a second to tug up the back of my shirt and wipe my neck clean.

DJ leaned on the railing overlooking the trees and the hill that ran down to the beach below. I slid the door shut, then pulled up a deck chair, rested my ankle on my knee, and waited for him to start.

"We just stomped our collective foot down on a real big pile of shit," he said, in the gravest tone I'd ever heard him use. "Our first priority has got to be moving on without flinging it all over ourselves. Right?"

"Not the metaphor I would've used, but, in principle, I agree."

"We gotta smoke out that Christian Bale-looking fella."

"After we go back to PR, sure. But before we do anything, we have to make sure Gabriela and her daughter are safe."

"All right, so take your boat and pick her up."

"You have to take us in *Reel Fun*."

He stiffened up. His lips went thin under the whiskers of his mustache. "*I* have to take you?"

"Don't make me repeat myself. Besides, what else are you going to do now? We both agreed that the other guy took off in that Cigarette boat. So how are you gonna find him, genius?"

"I got his boat's name. That's all Armstrong needs to find out where it's docked. Hell, they might even be able to tell me everywhere it's been since it touched water. That man already killed two people that we know of—and it don't take a genius to see there's some kinda link to Luc Baptiste. If we catch the murderer, we can beat some new answers out of him."

Blood was in the water, and DJ caught a taste of it. We were headed toward another unprofessional disaster.

DJ probably wouldn't see it my way, but I knew the only way we'd catch this guy and get information out of him would require deliberate actions, the smart approach; something DJ wasn't familiar with. "No, we're not doing that," I said. "We're doing this the right way—*after* we make sure Gabriela and her daughter are safe."

DJ grunted. He didn't agree. I didn't care.

"Do I have to remind you that we're only on this whole thing on account of Detective Collat? You think he'd appreciate you knocking this guy's brains across the deck?"

"Oh, right," DJ said, throwing his hands up. "That's why Collat put us on this. So we can have our murdering friend booked, tried, and convicted by a jury of his peers. Well, I got an APB for ya, Deputy Snyder. Whoever did this ain't *got* no peers. If this fella had something to do with Luc Baptiste's murder, he's outside the place where Justice's fingers can take hold of him, because the cops don't wanna look into it."

I knew he wouldn't see it my way.

"No one is above the—"

"Open your damned eyes, Jerry!" DJ shouted over me. "Collat didn't hand this to us because he thought we needed to stay sharp. He did it because the cops are *crooked*. You think this is about some retiring detective who couldn't be bothered about another murder? Even you ain't *that* stupid!"

Insulting me on the back porch of my house while my wife and a guest were only separated from us by a pane of glass was something I could barely tolerate.

He deserved to get socked, but I didn't want to punch a cripple.

"Only way this gets done correctly is if we do it by our own hands," DJ said. "We don't leave this up to the law, or Collat, or Armstrong, or anybody else. Get me?"

I glared at him.

He came off the railing, hobbled a couple steps toward me, and leaned his head forward.

"You get what I'm saying, right, Jerry? To do this the right way, you and me got to be together. And we got to be together all the way."

"All the way?" I rolled my eyes, then got up from my chair, turning my back to him. "You're talking about trying to kill this man."

"It's what he deserves."

DJ was right to assume our guy had protection from the police, or someone above them. The cops were likely at Dr. Markel's house now, doing an investigation. Soon, they'd run the plates on Gabriela's wrecked car. They'd identify her. And it wouldn't surprise me at all if our murderer magically appeared at her front door moments before the police.

My hand clenched the wooden rail of our deck. The wood posts groaned and squeaked near their bases. I wiggled the railing and listened. Given enough opportunity, I could shake this whole thing loose with my bare hands. No matter how strong the wood, or how many nails and bolts were used—no matter how well put together anything was, eventually something would come and break it apart.

I turned around to face DJ. "A man like you needs to take it easy. There'll be a fight you can't win. Maybe not this one. Maybe not the next one. But there will be one, sooner or later."

He laughed. "All right, Jerry. Thanks for being my babysitter."

DJ turned around, then knocked on the glass back doors. Alicia's eyes swung off Gabriela and to him. He smiled and waved, then walked down the steps.

When I went back into my house. Alicia looked up at me from the couch, puzzled.

"Is DJ coming back?"

My eyes met Gabriela's. "How close can we get to your house by boat?"

"There's a public marina not far from my apartment."

"Good."

"Who's taking us?" Alicia asked. "DJ just left—is there someone else at Armstrong coming to pick us up?"

"There probably is," I said. "But there's no telling who, or how far away they might be. We don't have time to wait. We're taking ourselves."

"But you still haven't had your lessons with that captain you talked to—you don't know how to steer that boat at night."

"I'll have to figure it out," I said.

CHAPTER TWENTY

S quatting in a patch of hand leaf bushes near the shore, Patrick Edwards watched through the viewfinder of his DSLR camera as Jerry Snyder and DJ Martin had their lovers' quarrel. Edwards pointed the directional mic mounted on his camera at the back porch of Snyder's house, but he couldn't hear a damned thing over chirping insects and a clutch of coquis whistling from the trees. Patrick shifted his weight, trying to find a dead zone for his mic, when something grabbed hold of his shirt. A stupid catch and keep plant hooked into the fabric of his sleeve. He bit back the curse bubbling in his throat, then peeled the vine's thorns away a few at a time.

Beneath the sleeve, Patrick's skin was hot and dry as old tar paper. He'd have to go to a clinic and get antibiotics after he finished his job tonight. Just as well. Medical expenses were covered under his contract, and he could get that rash on the back of his knee checked out at the same time.

Jerry Snyder was a cheap bastard. He had the money to get the weeds pulled from his property—hell, if Patrick had half of what Snyder was worth, he would've turned the whole property into a private grotto with topless chicks and enough rum to keep half of St. Thomas wasted around the clock.

On the deck, a brusque gesture grabbed Patrick's attention. DJ Martin puffed up and grabbed the ends of his long goatee, furiously combing his fingers through it. Snyder didn't notice. Most people wouldn't have. Took a trained eye to see Snyder and Martin were miles apart.

And Patrick Edwards had a trained eye—his whole livelihood depended on it.

Patrick grabbed his camera and snapped a couple dozen pictures of Martin turning his back on Snyder, rapping on the glass door, and waving bye-bye to Snyder's wife and the woman on the couch.

He captured more of Snyder's wife flashing a smile that'd kill a man with a weak heart, then returning Martin's wave before the camera's viewfinder fogged up.

Reluctantly, Patrick lowered the camera and wiped it with his shirt. Christ almighty, Snyder's wife was really something. Patrick always loved the jobs with fringe benefits. He brought it back up just as Martin zipped down the steps.

Patrick put down the camera, carefully avoiding a catch and keep branch. Then he reached into his pocket and took out his phone.

He dialed his old buddy from the Coast Guard, Mike Scheetz, who'd been a reliable contact when Patrick needed to identify a random. Mike had a cushy job at Customs and Border Patrol in San Juan harbor, and a gambling problem that needed more to eat than his government paycheck supplied.

The phone rang once.

"What are you doing calling me in the middle of the night?"

Mike grumbled.

"Offering to pay you five hundred bucks for five minutes of work," Patrick answered quietly.

He heard Mike's chair creak. Already in his office, perfect for a quick turnaround.

"You're gonna get me thrown in the can, you know that, right? Hell, they might drag my ass to Guantanamo."

"If you don't want the job, don't take it," Patrick said.

"I want the money, is what I want."

"Jesus. Always about the money. Is there any point where you don't bend me over a barrel every time I ask you to do honest work? Don't they pay you enough to scratch your balls all day?"

He laughed. "It's a seller's market, brother."

The point wasn't lost on Patrick. His client had plenty of money, anyway, so it wasn't the overhead creating problems, it was the haggling.

"One thousand, final offer."

Mike whistled. "That's the most you ever said right off the bat. You're hot for an answer, ain't ya?"

"Fifteen hundred, prick. Triple the going rate for something you can do in thirty seconds if you knew how to use a keyboard the right way."

"Sold. And I'll look the other way on that disrespect of my personal style."

Through Mike's end of the call, keyboard keys clicked one by one as he hunted and pecked, probably logging into the DHS database used for facial recognition software. He might be stupid and slow and an asshole, but Mike Scheetz was Patrick's ace in the hole, as much as he didn't want Mike to know it.

None of the other PIs working the Virgin Islands and Puerto

Rico had access to DHS's database. Patrick needed an edge to set him apart in a competitive industry.

"I'm logged in. Send me a picture."

"Have it to you in ten seconds. Do your work quickly. I've got a big fish on the line."

"Aye, Captain." Mike hung up.

Patrick turned on the screen on the back of his camera, scrolled to the clearest photo of the Snyders' mystery guest, then pointed his phone at it and snapped a picture. He texted it to Mike.

While he waited for Mike to ID the woman, he pulled out a second phone. A burner. Patrick kept a drawer full of them back in his office, and on each job, he took one for himself, and gave one to his client. Best way to ensure operational security.

There was a single number in his burner's contacts. It belonged to the other phone he'd given to his client—a person he codenamed Condor. Patrick wrote him a text message.

Jane Doe at Snyder's. Working on ID. Martin likely returned to vessel Reel Fun. *Can have employee keep tabs on* Reel Fun. *Yes/no?*

While he waited for Condor's answer, Patrick lifted his camera back to his eyes. He wasn't going to let Snyder wander off. A year's worth of mortgage payments rode on this job.

Snyder paced the back deck, rubbing his forehead while he alternated his gaze between his feet and the sky. Then, after a few laps back and forth, he slid open the back door and went inside.

Patrick's burner buzzed in his hand.

He brought it low to the ground again and checked the text from Condor.

Leave Martin, it read, *only concern is Snyder. Who is Jane Doe?*

Understood, Patrick texted back.

Through the binoculars, he watched Snyder open the sliding door and say something to his wife and the guest on the couch. She had the dark, tightly coiled hair of a Dominican. Whatever Snyder said, all three of them leapt into action. They moved like the place was burning down—even the Dominican woman with her arms all bandaged up.

All three of them slipped out of sight, somewhere deeper in the house. When Patrick's phone buzzed—likely Mike's ID on the Dominican—he ignored it, keeping watch for Snyder, waiting for him to re-emerge through the back door. When he finally did, he came out with his wife and the Dominican woman following.

Patrick pulled out the burner. *Going to dig around soon,* he texted Condor. *Will contact you with all findings.*

CHAPTER TWENTY-ONE

"**Y**ou don't know how to sail," Alicia reminded me, as we carried the last of our things down to the boat.

I reached *Wayward* and stepped aboard, dropping my bag on the cockpit settee. Then I turned to help Alicia and Gabriela aboard.

"Gotta start sometime. Anyways, the boat's got engines," I said. "I've driven one before."

"Your dad's bass boat on Castaic Lake doesn't count," Alicia commented as she stepped down. "This boat's wider than his was long."

I fished the key from my pocket and unlocked the door to the salon, sliding it open. "A boat's a boat. Goes on water, dips in the waves, feels good to sleep on. We're also short on options."

Gabriela looked around the cockpit with its large, covered seating area on one side, curved stairwell up to the bridge on the opposite side, and the big, stainless steel grill at the stern.

Then her eyes drifted upward to *Wayward's* eight-story mast. "You own a sailboat but don't know how to sail?" she asked, a look of amazement on her face.

"It's a catamaran," I said, side-stepping the question. "Pick out a stateroom, then come up to the bridge."

Before going up, I stepped back over to the dock and disconnected the shore power and water, then went inside and turned on all the batteries and necessary breakers, including the house lights. The women were just coming up from the two opposite hulls where the cabins were located.

"Get the dock lines," I said to Alicia. "Gabriela, all I want you to do is help me watch and not run into anything leaving the harbor. Can you do that?"

"The broker said the boat can sail faster than it can go on just the engines," Alicia said, moving toward the dock.

"I can sail," Gabriela offered.

I looked at her in a different light. "Maybe," I said. "But I don't want you opening up any of those stitches, so let's stick to the easiest passage. *Wayward* has twin 110 horsepower diesels that can get us to San Juan by dawn."

Gabriela and I climbed up to the helm and I started the engines. She'd finally called her sitter to explain that she'd be back by morning. The woman had already figured out that she was staying the night and Gabriela had awakened her.

Alicia cast the dock lines up onto the side deck, and once she was aboard, I put the two throttles into forward idle. The wind had us against the dock and the fenders started rubbing, making the squeaking sound of rubber on fiberglass. I quickly shifted back to neutral, the sudden realization coming over me that I should have already learned all this.

"Shift the left engine into reverse for a second," Gabriela said. "That will move the bow away from the dock."

She sat on the bench on the left side of the expansive flybridge, watching me. I gave her a side-eye, then nodded and reversed the port engine for a tick. With the left engine pulling backward, the front of the boat moved away from the pier. I shifted the engines to forward and watched over the twin bows as *Wayward* moved away from the marina.

"You wouldn't happen to know how to use a GPS, would ya?" I asked Gabriela, as Alicia joined us.

"I'm not good with electronics," she admitted.

"I have the manuals," Alicia said, sitting at the dinette behind the helm seat, and turning on a small lamp built into the table.

Gabriela joined her and the two began poring over the books. Fortunately, I had a straight shot southwest out of the marina for several miles before I'd have to turn west. There were boats anchored there, but they were to one side or the other, away from the deeper channel.

"Here!" Alicia said, carrying one of the manuals to where I stood at the helm. "It's a chart plotter, not a GPS. Well, it has GPS, but not like a car's. It won't tell you which road to take, only the direction to get there. We have to add waypoints around obstacles."

She turned on the larger of the many electronic screens. I knew from watching DJ that it showed a nautical chart with water depths.

Alicia scanned the manual, then set it aside. "Oh, thank God. It's a touch screen."

With Gabriela's help in locating the marina near her apartment building, and after several minutes and a few do-overs, Alicia had a course laid in that would keep us from wrecking *Wayward*. All I had to do was follow the red line. I looked down at the screen for a moment, familiarizing myself with the location of the depth reading, speed indicator, and time to each waypoint.

"It's eighty miles, give or take," I announced, pushing the twin throttles down. "About six hours at cruising speed. You two go get some rest."

"How do you know the cruising speed?" Alicia asked, flipping through the manual.

"A man's gotta know, baby," I said as I settled back into the helmsman's chair.

My wife rolled her eyes at me.

In truth, the saleslady and I had had long conversations about top speeds and cruising speeds. Other than the color of the hull, speed was the one thing I hung my negotiator's hat on. I knew how much I wanted, and I soon knew what each boat had to offer.

Wayward could run all day at fifteen knots. The top speed was eighteen.

Gabriela started toward the steps and Alicia leaned in close, putting a hand on mine on the wheel. "I hope you're not planning on driving all night, hotshot."

"I could use a break in a couple hours."

She put her other hand on my cheek in the darkness. "Yeah. I can do that."

Then she kissed me, and I was alone on the bridge in the darkest hours of night. We'd reached the opening to the channel and there was nothing ahead but water I couldn't see, nothing around *Wayward* but the murmur of her wake and the whispers of winds slipping around her. I set the autopilot, then moved around the bridge, extinguishing all the lights. The chart plotter would have to be on, but it had a dimmer, which I turned way down.

I stood at the helm, my hands on the wheel, absorbing the

nearly imperceptible rhythms of *Wayward* as she worked to cradle us over the Caribbean Sea.

The chart plotter shined upward like a spotlight. I blinked my eyes, looked at it and noticed we were fast approaching the first waypoint. I blinked again, then made a mental note to find some of those night vision goggles like McDermitt had worn the night he and DJ had rescued us from the cult on Norman Island. Or at least a pair of night vision binoculars like DJ had. Might be easier on my eyes.

The first waypoint was only two miles out of the harbor, just past a flashing green buoy, which I tried to keep my eyes away from. Once past the outer channel marker, I turned off the autopilot and spun the wheel to follow the red line.

The next waypoint would be off the northeast tip of Puerto Rico, which lay sixty some miles ahead. I zoomed the plotter out and saw that the red line passed well to the north of Culebra and all the little rocks and islands surrounding it. I checked *Wayward's* speed, adjusted her heading, then set the autopilot again. It had a fine-tuning control, and I adjusted it to a heading of 285° magnetic. Watching the chart for a few minutes, I made sure that we stayed right on that red line. Then I sat down at the helm and started the long wait, watching the horizon for the lights of any other boats or ships.

I found the switch and activated the navigation and steaming lights. The latter were mounted way up on the mast and provided a little light on the water, without ruining my night vision. The red and green navigation lights were invisible from the bridge, but I could detect a slight glow on the water to either side of the bows—green on the right and red on the left.

Time passed quickly, sitting alone with my thoughts. I was

almost certain that Luc's murder was tied to the murder of Markel and his wife. Was Markel selling his so-called cancer cure to anyone he could dupe into buying it? Maybe he'd ripped off the wrong guy.

Luc Baptiste was an investigative reporter. Maybe he was going to expose Markel's scheme, so Markel had him killed. That would explain why he'd talked to Marc Herrera. Luc could've already known that Markel had tried to rope in Herrera.

Maybe Anthradone was Markel's dummy cancer cure. Hildon Pharmaceuticals thought it was real, but they wouldn't be the first big corporation to get roped in by a con man. Theranos and Elizabeth Holmes had proved that tricking investors into buying thin air wasn't impossible.

Could be an investor figured out Markel's game and took him out to save the public embarrassment of a court case. I knew of plenty of guys in the finance world with egos big enough to try something like that.

As I continued to mull the possibilities, I noticed an occasional splashing sound off the right side of *Wayward*, inconsistent with the steady swish of the bow wave.

The fenders, I thought, then rose and took another look forward into the darkness before going down the stairs to the cockpit, then up to the side deck. I quickly pulled the fenders up and stowed them, then returned to the bridge.

Soon, I heard the door to the salon slide open, then close again. I checked my watch; two hours had passed since we'd left St. Thomas. I checked the chart plotter, zooming out so I could see Puerto Rico. We were a third of the way there.

Alicia approached me from behind and slipped her hands around my waist, then kissed my neck. "Your watch is up,

Captain. What do I need to do?"

"I have the autopilot on," I replied, putting my hands over hers. "It hasn't strayed from the red line for two hours and it's at least two more hours to the next waypoint. Just watch out for any boats. If you need to adjust course, you have to switch the autopilot to standby. I saw a cruise ship way out on the horizon a while ago—that's it."

"With the engines running, I was able to turn on the air conditioner," Alicia said, looking at the gauges and plotter. "I gave Gabriela two Ibuprofen and she's resting comfortably in the bigger cabin in front on the right side. Go down to our cabin and get some rest."

"I can sleep up here. The night's cool, and I just need to rest my eyes a bit."

I piled a couple of throw pillows into the corner of the dinette and stretched out, closing my eyes.

"Are we doing the right thing?" Alicia asked quietly. "I mean, we know nothing about Gabriela. She might have killed the doctor herself."

"I believe her story."

"Hmm," Alicia replied.

And that was all. Before long, my mind drifted and it seemed like only a few minutes had passed when Alicia shook my foot and called my name.

I sat bolt upright. "What's wrong?"

"Nothing," she replied, putting a finger to her lips. "We're just a few miles from the next waypoint."

An hour later, with the first faint light of dawn blushing in the sky behind us, I turned off the autopilot and turned into San Juan Harbor. Remembering the sunken boat that DJ and I had seen, I was glad to realize it was getting light. We'd made it.

Shortly after sunrise, Alicia and I got *Wayward* tied to a dock at a marina near where Gabriela lived, then we woke Gabriela up and the three of us double-timed it to the marina office.

After paying the dockmaster for a full day, we crossed from wooden planks onto concrete, then up a set of concrete stairs that took us past the sea wall and onto a wide sidewalk next to a six-lane street. At this time in the morning, the city was just waking up, and only a single car passed by us. An unbroken line of vehicles was parked on the shoulders of the road in either direction.

Gabriela stepped off the curb to cross the street. Alicia and I followed, not bothering to check for traffic or waiting for the crosswalk signal to change.

A woman's clothing store was located on the opposite corner. When she stepped up onto the curb in front of it, Gabriela went left, then turned into the first alleyway she came across.

I was a few steps behind, peering into the smudged front window of the store. A single emergency light flickered in the back corner and a mannequin lay on its side below, dusted with cobwebs. Nobody had been in the place for months, at least. The same as Gabriela and my wife, I turned left into the next alleyway. They were both moving along the opposite side. I jogged to catch up, then came out on a side street, where clean laundry hung overhead, suspended from lines, and draped over balcony railings—a hallmark of poor neighborhoods the world over. A pack of kid-size bicycles was chained to a long, steel stand, and soccer balls and baseball bats mingled at the foots of stoops and in gutters lined with cigarette butts and sludgy sand.

I caught up to the women as Gabriela punched a code into

the keypad next to the big glass doors at the base of one of the buildings. A buzzer sounded, the lock clicked, and she pulled open the door. We moved through a lobby haunted by the funk of mildew, dust, and cigarette smoke that usually characterized cheap second-hand stores. Past the only bank of elevators, Gabriela opened a steel door.

When we climbed the stairs and reached the third floor, she pushed the bar latch on the door, and we came out into a hallway. Then she led us all the way down to the last door on the left. She had trouble getting her keys out of her pocket.

"May I?" Alicia asked.

The lines in Gabriela's face deepened as her mouth stretched into a line.

"Is it this one?" Alicia pointed at the pocket on Gabriela's left hip.

"Yes. And thank you."

"Trust me, when I was a nurse back in Newport Beach, I had to do a lot worse than this." She reached in and fished out the keys. "Stuff they don't talk about in nursing school until you're a couple of semesters in. They must figure you're committed by then, and you won't walk away."

Gabriela pinched one of the keys between her thumb and forefinger. She fiddled it into the lock, then turned it until it clicked.

The door came open, and I heard a TV droning. A matronly Hispanic woman sat up in a chair and started to say something, but Gabriela put a finger to her lips.

"Shhh," she hushed. "*Gracias por quedarte, Clara ¿Qué te debo?*"

Clara eyed me suspiciously as she stood and waved a hand over Gabriela's hand inside her purse. "*No, no,*" she whispered.

"*El viernes estará bien.*"

Then the sitter hurried out of the apartment. A lamp clicked on, revealing the rest of the small apartment; a kitchen on the left with a dinette table, and on the right, a couch against the wall—the living room wall, probably.

When Alicia and I went inside, something else in the living room caught my eye. A bed. Right in the middle of the room, covered in blankets with a steel pole beside it. I thought it was a lamp at first, but then I realized that, no, it was an IV stand. A plastic tube stretched down to the pile of blankets.

Gabriela walked up to the bed and turned the sheets down, folding them over a few inches at a time.

A girl's face peeked out. She was asleep, and she had the same dark, wavy hair as her mother, but it lay flatter on the pillow, like a body stripped down to the bones. The girl also had her mother's round face and button nose.

"*Florita,*" Gabriela said softly, just above her daughter. She kissed her forehead. "Wake up, little girlie." She stroked her daughter's cheek, then Flor began to stir.

Her eyes fluttered open.

"Mama?" An arm as thin as a chicken bone reached up. Long, spindly fingers wove into a lock of Gabriela's hair.

"Hey, baby," Gabriela said.

"What time is it?"

"It's very early in the morning." She kissed Flor again, who hadn't noticed Alicia and me standing beyond the head of her bed.

"Where were you yesterday?" Flor asked. Then she gasped. She sat up in bed shakily, but managed to hold herself there without toppling over. Her hand brushed across the bandages on

Gabriela's arms. "Mama, what happened to you? Are you okay? Were you in the hospital? Why didn't you call me? Did someone hurt—"

Gabriela pressed a finger to her daughter's lips, quieting her.

"Mama's all right. I got a little hurt, but some people helped fix me up." She nodded toward me and Alicia.

Flor's head whipped around. She had the same muted expression I'd seen on Gabriela's face when I pulled her out of her wrecked car and sat her beside it; both like mountain cats perched on a boulder, watching land developers pat out a new lane, bisecting the range they and their ancestors had hunted for millennia.

That expression quickly changed. Flor curled her lip and scrunched up her nose.

"Who're you two people? What'd you do to my mama?"

"Flor!" Gabriela said.

I kept my mouth shut.

"It's okay." Alicia held her hand out, slowly walking up to Flor, who looked at my wife like she'd offered a diseased rat.

"My name is Alicia Snyder."

Flor reluctantly took her hand and shook.

Alicia motioned to me. "This is my husband, Jerry."

"And why are you here?"

"Well, Jerry found your mother. She was hurt. She was near—" Alicia stopped when she noticed Gabriela shaking her head, warning her not to finish that thought. "—near our house. Her car broke down."

"I hit a tree," Gabriela said. "I worked late last night, and I guess I was more tired than I realized. That's like me."

Flor looked in her mother's direction. I only saw the back of her head, but my imagination filled in the blank. She wasn't happy. Then, she rotated her face toward Alicia, her brow knitted.

"Near your house? So which neighborhood was that?"

Alicia looked to Gabriela for help.

"You're being very unkind to our guests," Gabriela said.

"Which was it?" she asked. "Breakdown or car accident?"

"I guess I didn't see the car." Alicia shrugged, trying her best to cover for Gabriela. "I just assumed."

"So, you put those bandages on my mom?"

"Yeah. With Jerry's help."

Her scrutiny bounced from Alicia to me.

"Are you two doctors or something?"

"I'm a nurse," Alicia answered. "Jerry was in the military."

"What, like a medic?"

"Something like that," I said.

"And even though you had to bandage her up, you thought her car broke down?"

Alicia looked to me for help. She wasn't a good liar.

"So, where's the car now?" She turned to her mother. "You never said where this happened."

"The car's wrecked," I answered.

"I didn't ask you."

"I know."

She glared at me. For a kid hooked up to an IV bag in her living room, she had a hell of a spark plug in her.

"We don't have time to sit and discuss anyway, honey." Gabriela coiled the spare line hanging from the IV bag. "I need to get us packed."

"Packed for what?" Flor accepted the coiled line from her

mother.

"We're going to stay with Jerry and Alicia for a little while. On St. Thomas."

"So, you *aren't* from around here."

"We're going to help you and your mom get around," I said.

She glared. I didn't care.

The important thing was getting on the move. The police were bound to have gone to Markel's house by now, and they'd probably run Gabriela's plates. They could come knocking at any time.

Gabriela started toward a hallway across from the front door. She turned left, and I heard a closet door slide open.

"Who are you two, *really*? Does my mom owe you money? Because we don't have any."

"I'm *really* Jerry. And this is *really* my wife, Alicia."

"Whatever." She swung her legs over the side of her bed. Her pink sweatpants hung loosely around her legs, and her matching hoodie billowed from her shoulders like a jellyfish riding a riptide.

One hand firmly held onto the rail of her bed as Flor got to her feet. Attitude or not, it was hard for me to see a kid in such a bad way. It never got easier.

My wife took my hand. Her mind must've been circling the same dread as mine. There were a million scumbags and jerks ahead of Flor on the Big List of People Who Should Have Cancer.

Hell, there were a lot of *good* people who should've been ahead of Flor. I counted myself among them. At least I'd experienced some of my life. I'd been around the world. I'd had time to make my own choices, and wrestle with them in my moments of deepest sleep. I'd discovered who I was. I'd known love. Flor was only a handful of years into dressing herself.

"Alicia?" Gabriela called from the hallway. "Can you come help me a minute?"

My wife turned to me. I nodded.

She walked past Flor and her bed, heading toward the back bedroom. I heard her say something to Gabriela. I'm not sure what.

"Your wife is pretty."

I decided to play it as a genuine compliment. "Thanks."

A second later, Gabriela and Alicia came buzzing down the hallway, each pulling a rolling suitcase. Additionally, Gabriela wore a backpack.

"We're ready," Gabriela said.

"Four days of clothes?" I asked.

She nodded.

"And all necessary medical supplies?"

She nodded again.

"Including toiletries?"

"Yes," she said, as she went past me and grabbed the knob on the front door.

"Great. I'll carry up the kid."

"Carry who?" Flor tried to walk after her mother, but her legs shook like a newborn fawn's. Her knees gave out just as I scooped her up in my arms.

She was as light as driftwood. I clenched my jaw, forcing myself not to think too much about it. I had to get past it—I'd seen worse. Afghanistan and Somalia had some tough rescues. None of those places were the US.

I adjusted my left arm to try and support Flor's head more. As weak as she was, I didn't want her breaking her neck.

"Can you grab your IV bag off the stand?" I asked her, as I walked around the foot of the bed so she could reach it.

She lifted it off the hook and rested it on her belly.

After we left Gabriela's apartment, we retraced our steps back to the marina. *Wayward* was there, waiting for us.

Once aboard, I laid Flor down on the couch in the salon, then took her IV bag and hung it on a towel hook in the wall above her head. While Gabriela stayed at her side, Alicia pulled out some fresh bedding, then the two of them put it down, making sure Flor was comfortable. I went up to the bridge and started the engines, then climbed down, untied all our lines, and pulled in all our fenders.

A moment later, I was back on the bridge and motoring away from the marina.

CHAPTER TWENTY-TWO

Following our breadcrumbs on the chart plotter from our trip over, I steered *Wayward* through relatively calm seas on Puerto Rico's windward side, going into headwinds. The morning sun was just a few degrees south of our almost due easterly course. Along our route, we passed the governor's summer home, which DJ had once pointed out to me—a white, domed building in a stand of trees at the top of the ridge leading down into the sea. *Wayward* continued around the Cabezas de San Juan Nature Preserve, a run of land jutting off the northeastern corner of Puerto Rico.

Catching an eyeful of Puerto Rico's rocky northern coast as I pulled a shade down to block the sun, I remembered the morning sunlight skipping over valleys hidden by the tanned, dusty peaks of Afghani mountains.

My mind liked to gravitate toward that cluster of images—of smoky villages hewn in mountain sides, a man butchering a goat carcass in front of his shop, smiling hello, a mother and her two young girls hauling rolls of a brightly colored fabric as our convoy rumbled past, a boy, no older and barely stronger than Flor, a dinted Russian AK slung over his back.

I also remembered the countryside. The Hindu Kush Mountains had ancient majesty.

More than once, when I'd finished last watch, or woke before dawn, I caught myself wondering how many times I'd looked directly at a forgotten Kushan or Buddhist tomb buried under centuries of stone and dust, where some ancient governor or general or priest had their body secreted away.

The way light played here, off the coast of Puerto Rico, when the sea was like a glittering balm for all the pains in my head, and the air crisp enough to make me believe I'd never need to sleep, and never have to experience those memories again, made me understand why I was drawn here—why this place became my refuge from a life wrenched apart by things I was afraid to think about, out of fear they'd taint the water and the air and I'd never find the peace I needed.

I turned the wheel until *Wayward's* bow pointed east-southeast, heading against the winds coming out of the Caribbean. Then I set the auto-pilot, went down to the cockpit, and stopped. I cupped my hands over my eyes and took one last good look at the water ahead.

I hoped I'd learned from my mistakes in Newport Beach. That I could be strong enough to safeguard everything my eyes saw now, and more. I stepped down off the side deck and through the door to the salon. The girls—my wife, Gabriela, and Flor—had fallen asleep on the settees.

Quietly, I crept into the galley and dug in the cupboards until I found the coffee maker Alicia had stowed away. I didn't know how long the calm seas would last. There was a way to tell from all the navigational and weather equipment up on the flybridge,

I'm sure, but figuring that out would be asking too much of myself. Lucky for me, I hadn't scraped the hull across any sandbars yet.

Once I got the coffee going, I retraced my steps toward the flybridge. Then I stopped. Gabriela was awake.

"You making coffee?" she asked in a drowsy whisper.

"We wouldn't get much further if I weren't," I answered.

She cracked a smile, then combed her hair out of her face. She stretched, and I motioned for her to follow me out to the cockpit.

Out back, I took a seat on the settee.

She stopped at the doorway, then rubbed the bandages on her arms.

"Want something to cover up?" I got up, then pulled open a storage compartment beneath me. Knowing Alicia, she'd stashed a coat somewhere. She'd catch a chill in a sauna.

The first compartment I opened contained some extra dock lines, a cooler, and a brand-new tackle box—which I'm guessing was supposed to be a surprise for me. I closed the lid and pretended I hadn't seen it.

I opened the next compartment to my right and found it empty. The one to the right of that had a pair of sandals, sunscreen, life jackets, and some pool floats.

"Hmm. No luck." I scratched my head and turned to Gabriela. She was gone.

Inside the salon, she was nowhere to be found. At least not that I could see from the cockpit. Maybe she'd gone back to bed.

Oh, well. So long as I didn't hear a splash over the side, I knew she was safely on *Wayward*. I went back up the spiral staircase to the flybridge and sat down in the captain's chair.

A moment later, I heard bare feet coming up the stairs and turned in my chair to see Gabriela, wearing my extra fleece jacket, and carrying two coffee mugs.

"I helped myself," she said, as she handed the half-empty mug over to me. "The coffee wasn't done yet. I hope you don't mind."

As soon as I took the mug, I became keenly aware of the cold in my fingers. And, as I relaxed into the helm seat, I realized how damned tired I was. I didn't need a lot of sleep, but even I had my limits. I must've been running on adrenaline for the last four hours.

"So long as you keep bringing me coffee, you can borrow any coat of mine you like."

She sat down on the port settee. I raised my mug to her, she returned the gesture, and we both took a sip of jet-black coffee.

I usually took my coffee with cream, but we didn't have any on the boat. I made a mental note to pick up some of that powdered stuff to keep in the cupboard.

"Nice view all the way up here." Gabriela turned her face to the wind, which swept back her hair. "Nice just about any place you go on this boat."

"I'd like to say that's the reason I bought it," I said. "But I never thought of it at the time."

"Why did you buy it?"

I took a sip of my coffee. Armstrong had recommended I buy one in case I needed to get lost in a hurry. And Travis Stockwell had helped me pick it out. Something with a lot of hidden storage.

"Scuba," I said. "And pleasure cruises."

Gabriela lifted her eyebrows. "Looks real pleasurable. You've got a lot of boat here."

"Fifty-three feet," I said. "Do you own something?"

She nodded. "Well, I did, anyway. Until I couldn't afford to keep it in usable condition. I sold it about three months before Maria, thank God. I heard it sank."

I nodded. Then I noticed something different about Gabriela. It took me a second before it dawned on me that she wasn't holding Dr. Markel's laptop.

"Where's the computer?" I asked.

"Down on your desk." She unspooled a deep sigh. "The battery was loose, which is why it didn't start when we tried it. I fixed that problem, but now I've got a new one: I don't have the password for it."

She ran her fingers through her hair, letting the wind pull the strands apart. Then she blew into her coffee cup before taking a tentative sip.

"All I've got now are problems," she said. "And one has become more immediate than the rest."

Flor's treatments? Finding someone to create Dr. Markel's drug? Something told me she wasn't talking about either of those. I racked my brain for a moment; then, to my discomfort, the answer shook loose.

"Your car," I said. "We had to leave it at Dr. Markel's house last night."

By the worried look on her face, I knew I was right.

"I have to turn myself in, Jerry," she said.

As much as I wanted another answer, none existed. She was right.

Wayward's fuel tanks were three-quarters full, I knew how to operate the water maker, and with our four solar panels and batteries, we'd be good on power for the foreseeable future. But making a run for it wouldn't help anyone. It wasn't what I wanted to do, and, more importantly, it wasn't what Gabriela wanted.

Though it would keep the police from embarking on a manhunt, turning herself in created different problems. Namely, what we'd do with Flor. Luckily, I had control over that one.

"We can take care of Flor," I said with my eyes on the horizon ahead. "While this whole thing gets sorted."

Presumptuous of me, and I knew it. What made me think Gabriela trusted me with her daughter? And if she did, why would Alicia go along?

Because our choices were made for us.

No one would ever accuse me of taking the path of least resistance, but wasn't it kismet that my wife had once been a pediatric nurse at the Children's Hospital of Orange County? And now, a little girl needed her help.

I couldn't deny that the second I pulled Gabriela out of that smashed car, I knew what I was getting myself into. Maybe it wasn't at the forefront of my mind, but as a Pararescueman, I understood the responsibility I was taking on by saving her. *That Others May Live* was more than a motto on a patch to me. After retiring from the Air Force, I'd made it my life's goal.

I had to care for Gabriela to the end. Not a little bit, not halfway, and not most of the way. To the end. And in this case, that meant taking care of Flor, too.

When I slid my eyes away from the smooth waters ahead, back to Gabriela, I genuinely wondered if she'd take my offer or not.

Her face was without expression. She hadn't guarded her emotions back at the house when she'd talked to DJ and me.

Maybe she'd been rattled by exhaustion and shock. Or perhaps she was now.

"Gabriela?"

Her eyes focused on me. Her chin quivered, and the coffee cup tumbled from her hands, splashed across the deck, and rolled aft. She gasped while I got up, pulled the sprayer out of the sink behind me, and hosed the coffee off the floor and off the cockpit Bimini.

"I'm sorry," Gabriela said, wiping her eyes. She motioned at the coffee cup. "I didn't mean to mess up your boat."

"Don't worry about it." I picked up the cup and put it on the dinette. "This would be one sad boat if it couldn't handle a little spilled coffee."

She pinched her lips together, then fiddled with her hands. "You're doing so much for me," she said. "Why?"

Because I needed peace.

"Because it's the right thing to do."

Gabriela halfway leapt from her seat. She stopped when she met me, wrapping her arms around my ribcage, and pulling me close. Her arms and shoulders bounced as she sobbed. Were it not for my jacket, I would've felt her breath too, and the warmth of her tears.

She'd been holding onto this sadness at least since we'd met, but likely longer than that. Life couldn't have been easy, being a single mother with a child as sick as Flor.

I put my arms around her and let her get it all out. We stood on *Wayward's* bridge, me patting the back of her head and gently rocking her while she cried, for a couple minutes at least.

Then, when Gabriela seemed to be on the backside of it, I stood her up straight, held her at arms' length by her shoulders and looked directly into her eyes, the whites shining like polished silver.

"I swear to you that I will get you through this," I told her. "All you have to do is hold on and keep being strong."

She nodded at me.

All I had to do now was explain to Detective Collat that I was bringing him an innocent woman and hope that he'd understand.

CHAPTER TWENTY-THREE

DJ Martin stood on *Reel Fun's* flybridge, his hands twisting on the ship's stainless-steel helm while he navigated through the dark. The boat was two-and-a-half miles due south of French Bay—the spot where he'd untied and rocketed away from Jerry's slip in the marina.

His hands still tight on the wheel, DJ pulled into Mouillage Cove on the leeward side of Buck Island. It was a U.S. wildlife refuge, popular with snorkelers, bird watchers, and party cruises for its calm waters and exotic fauna.

Jerry was being a moron. What did he think was going to happen if they took this to the cops? That they'd swoop in, play by the rules, and everybody would go home happy?

Somebody in *La Uniformada*—of which their trustworthy and upright buddy, Detective Collat, was a member—would lose a bullet casing or smudge a good fingerprint, or just plum forget to file a piece of critical evidence. Or they'd just be too near to retirement to do the job right.

When the inevitably "speedy" trial rolled around, some months or years later, it would be "discovered" that the murderer had mistakenly been released from custody shortly after being arrested, and nobody had the faintest clue where he'd gone.

No thanks. If Jerry Snyder wanted to wrestle that snake, that was on him. DJ wasn't there to have a turn after Jerry. He was there to get a job done.

To that end, he'd cut the throttle on *Reel Fun*, then shut off the engines. He dropped anchor in Mouillage Cove, got up from the captain's chair, and eased himself down the ladder from the fly deck.

In the salon, he took his sat phone from the charging cradle stuck to the galley wall, carried it out to the cockpit, where it would get a signal, and pulled up the number for Armstrong's S&R division.

Support and Research existed on the back end of Armstrong Research's operation. Staff members weren't public facing, and, as such, DJ couldn't place names to faces. But he knew they were there, and he knew they were damned good. If a boat could be tracked, the folks at Armstrong S&R would find it.

The sat phone rang twice before someone picked up.

"Armstrong Research," a young man's high-pitched voice said. DJ pictured some twenty-two-year-old kid with a bad haircut and a thick pair of glasses reflecting a computer screen.

"Hey," DJ said. "This is DJ Martin. I need y'all to track a boat for me."

"I'm sorry, Mr. Martin, but I think you've dialed the wrong number. We're an oceanographic research company. If you need help locating a specific vessel, please consider contacting the Coast Guard or the local police."

"I'm not here to report illegal dumping," DJ said. "I want to find a boat, and y'all in the S&R division are supposed to support me."

"I'm sorry, sir, but there is no division of that name here."

"Don't play that with me—this is DJ *Martin*. You got that? Martin! Can you square up with me a second and just do what I ask?"

"Sir, I—"

"No, don't give me an excuse. I need a boat tracked. Put your fingers on that keyboard in front of you, and type in this boat's name."

"But, sir," the S&R nerd said, clearing his throat, "sir, we don't offer a service like that to the *general* public."

General public? The hell did that mean? DJ had been through all the Armstrong training. He'd been on ops, he'd met other members of the team, what else—

"Aw, hell." *The pass phrase.* He wanted a pass phrase. "I forgot my pass phrase. Gimme a sec—I got it here."

DJ shuffled over to the tackle locker on the boat's starboard side. He remembered scribbling the new pass phrase on the back of a bar napkin the last time he'd met up with Stockwell. When was that? Last June? Was it really seven months ago?

And what bar was it?

He opened the locker and sifted through all the crap he'd stuffed in there. Brass casings, empty nicotine gum packages, girls' numbers... Then, he found it. Scribbled in fat, black handwriting, inside a beer ring on a napkin from a place called *The Thirsty Gull.*

DJ held it up to the light and blinked until his eyes focused.

"You ready?" he said into the phone.

"Yessir."

"Uhh..." It was upside-down. He dropped it on the counter,

then twisted it right-side up. "Blue tang on the deck."

"Blue tang confirmed," the researcher answered.

The tightness in DJ's chest let loose. Until then, he hadn't realized he'd been holding his breath.

"So, Mr. Martin, what's the name of the boat?"

"Boy, you're gonna turn my hair gray," he said. "Don't call me Mr. Martin. Just DJ."

"DJ," the operator repeated.

"Good going. What's your name, son?"

"It's Chip."

"All right, Chip, I don't—" DJ stopped cold as a new thought burst into his head. Something he couldn't ignore. "Belay that boat stuff. You wanna look into something for me real quick?"

"That's why I'm here, sir."

"Call me DJ. Hey, you know I've been working with Jerry Snyder, right?"

"No, DJ, I'm not cleared for that information. Mr. Armstrong likes to keep all data about his teams restricted to the upper ranks of the organization."

"Well, now you know, man. That's a little secret we'll keep between us. Anyway, Jerry was getting hassled by this guy, Arlen. You think you can dig up some information on him?"

"Do you have any other identifiable information on this person?"

"His first name. Guess he knows Jerry pretty well, too."

"It'll take me some time to find out more."

"But you think you can?" DJ didn't expect much of anything. Matter of fact, he couldn't say why the idea had occurred to him—he shouldn't care about the problems of some tight-ass prick like Jerry Snyder. He'd probably wash out of Armstrong by the end of the year.

"Yessir, I can, given enough time."

"Then take the time you need. Treat it like a long-term thing, man."

"I will do that—did you still want me to check on that boat?"

"That's why I called. Now, I don't have the full name of the boat, but I know it's harbored in Culebra. I hit the back end of the boat with a spotlight and caught the word *Daze*. That's delta, alpha, zulu, echo—you catching all this, son?"

"Daze, yes sir."

"DJ."

"Yes, DJ."

His name tripped out of Chip's mouth, but that was okay. The kid probably was nervous as all hell just talking to somebody.

"I think that *Daze* is part of a multi-word name. I'm not sure how many words are in the name, but *Daze* was kinda off to the starboard side of the boat. Now, can you match something with just—"

"*Purple Daze*," Chip said. "Registered in Culebra to Southern Cross Marina and Boat Rental, LLC. I've got pictures of it here."

DJ choked on his own spit. What a damned fine way to figure all that out. Unbelievably fine. Too easy to be any good.

"DJ?" Chip's voice thinned. "DJ, are you okay?"

"I'm fine. Just thanking my luck."

"Would you like photos of the boat? I can have them sent to your secured Armstrong email address."

"Cigarette boat, right? Purple as a grapefruit?"

"Grapefruits aren't—"

"You did good, Chip." DJ's mind had already moved on. "You're a commendable addition to Mr. Armstrong's outfit, or business, or what have you. I gotta go."

DJ ended the call.

Purple Daze out of Culebra. Southern Cross Marina. Had to be that, didn't it? Maybe DJ's luck wasn't that rotten. Had to be a little something usable still in there, but did he want to use it now?

Of the five hundred people who lived on the island, he knew of only one dropout of the Timothy Leary school of hard knocks living there. His friend Bobby Blount was obsessed with having as many boats as he could get his grungy fingers on and naming them after his favorite hippie songs.

DJ put the sat phone in his pocket and walked back into the salon. On the way forward, the mirror in the head grabbed him by the beard and yanked him over.

His whiskers looked salty; his skin dressed in a rind that could've peeled off him.

A shower. Just a quick army shower. Water on. Water off. Soap. Rinse. A minute to catch his breath and put his thoughts in order, then figure out his next move. Turn back, tail-tucked, and tug on Jerry's sleeve? Or go to Culebra, then figure out why some cold-blooded murderer was driving around a boat that belonged to one of DJ's oldest buddies, Bobby the Blunt.

CHAPTER TWENTY-FOUR

Reel Fun cleared the twenty-five miles between Buck Island and Culebra in under an hour. As his boat approached the mouth of Ensenada Honda, or Deep Cove, or Big Cove, or whatever you wanted to call it, DJ pulled back on the throttles, and carefully navigated through the channel between the reefs and into the island's biggest inlet.

From there, he held a northwestern course, until he passed Cayo Pirata on the leeward side. Then he hooked around the little island, guiding *Reel Fun* due north, toward the golden light of Southern Cross Marina.

His buddy Blunt's place.

Though he'd never gone to Blunt's marina, or home, or seen him outside a bar or Garner's place, DJ had an open invitation to stop by Blunt's marina whenever he liked. Or at least, DJ assumed he did. Blunt had never said it, but if his buddy complained about *Reel Fun* being docked in one of his open slips, he could shove it right up his ass.

What kind of ignorant fool named a marina in Culebra "Southern Cross" anyhow? That was like sailing to Cape Town and hitting up a place called The Big Dipper Bar and Grill. Most people in the Southern Hemisphere didn't know the Big Dipper. A man in Cape Town couldn't stand on his back porch with his kid and point it out in the night sky. DJ maneuvered *Reel Fun* into the first slip he saw. He backed it in, fitting snugly between the docks. The waters in Ensenada Honda were particularly easy going, so he didn't have much trouble dropping fenders and getting tied without Jerry there to be his deck hand. With the boat secured, DJ went into the salon to go pick out a new friend.

The first thing he'd done when he'd bought his Viking 48C was figure out where all the hollow spaces were. He didn't need many, and he didn't need them to be cavernous—only a few spots a couple feet wide and a couple feet deep that didn't draw the eyes of a casual observer.

Those cavities weren't hard to find. With the right kind of stud-finder and a free weekend, a diligent captain could pick out a couple on about any boat.

On *Reel Fun*, one such spot was in the galley.

DJ got to a knee. Then he pressed his fingertips against the crease where the bar cabinets met the galley's laminate flooring, smoothing the crease with his hands until his fingers found the irregularity he was looking for—a small rope. There was less than an inch of it visible, and it was about the circumference of three shoestrings braided together.

He dug the end out with his fingernail, then drew it out further and further until he had enough to grab with his hand. The carpet came up, as did the steel hatch beneath.

The hatch covered a hollow about as deep as the distance between the tips of his fingers and his elbow. He tapped a small LED disc light stuck on the inside of the compartment. It illuminated all the things that DJ didn't want sitting out in the open where other eyes might easily find them.

Beside a brick of pesos and a half-full mason jar of weed and magic mushrooms sat a Glock-branded hard case. He took the case out, set it on the floor beside the compartment, then pulled up the latches and opened the top.

His compact Glock 19 and three extra magazines waited inside. A good friend for these troubled times.

DJ pulled the slide back to make sure a round was in the chamber, then shoved the handgun in its holster, and clipped the holster to the inside of his waistband, behind his back. He stuffed a spare magazine in each pocket.

He closed the hard case, returned it to the hidden compartment, then felt around the sides of the compartment in *Reel Fun's* floor until his fingers came across something small and boxy. Another kit, about the size of a large smartphone.

When he got his fingers under it, he yanked it, making the Velcro attached to the kit hiss.

DJ put the slim, plastic kit in his back pocket. Then he placed the lid back on the compartment in *Reel Fun's* floor, tucked the string under the laminate, making sure to leave just enough to grasp, and then tamped the lid down with his real foot.

The weight of his new friend tugging on the waist of his jeans, DJ walked out of the salon, locking it behind him. He hopped across the gap between *Reel Fun's* stern and the floating dock, then made his way toward the marina office on shore.

Southern Cross Marina looked to be turning good business. There were yachts and cats and fishing charters of just about every size and configuration. Three or four dozen boats in total, if DJ had to guess, scattered around the various docks in no apparent order. A lot of decent folk probably owned those vessels, which made it no wonder that Blunt hadn't insisted on inviting DJ over for a couple beers around the grill.

At this time of night, the guests' boats were all buttoned up, so he had to be careful about making too much noise. The office sat at least fifty yards back from the shore, but sound carried better at night.

After tugging on the mirror-polished handrail to help himself up the few stairs leading to shore, DJ paused and peered at the office's darkened windows, though calling the building an office stretched the definition of the term.

Apparently, Blunt ran the Southern Cross out of a converted garage attached to a meager bungalow. Looked like a low-rent operation, but judging by all the boats on his docks, there were plenty of people without hang-ups about a guy running a marina out of his house. People were more relaxed around the islands. On the mainland, a neighborhood association or zoning board would have a kitten about the white banner hanging from the gutters, stretching halfway across the house. DJ imagined that most days, when the humidity was low and given a clear line of sight through all the masts and bows, one could spot the words MARINA OPEN from the shores of Cayo Pirata. As he got closer to the house, he noticed a flicker of blue light coming from a window mostly obscured by the sign. The light played through the long-ignored bushes under the window's bottom edge. DJ checked left, then checked right. The coast was clear.

He moved quietly around the front, then up the side of Blunt's house, walking through weeds and over uneven paver stones. He peered around the back corner before going forward.

A small, dirty patio lay before him. A pair of gnarled wires hung where a light should be, their copper ends reflecting the moonlight. He crossed the patio to a door beside a couple steel trash cans and a stack of old lawn chairs.

DJ took the slim case out of his back pocket, snapped open the case's latch, and without looking, his fingers knew exactly where to go. They pulled out a small penlight, which DJ clicked on as he eased down to his knee.

Pointing the light at the door handle revealed a Weiser-brand lock. He shined the light into the keyhole, having a look at the cylinder before getting down to business. The thing was dirty as all hell. The pins were probably covered in grime, and the springs were likely half-stuck.

But a little graphite would take care of that. He took a small tube of graphite powder from his kit and squeezed two or three puffs into the lock. Then he dropped the tube and popped the light between his teeth, keeping it pointed at the keyhole.

One of his tension tools fit snugly into the top of the key slot. DJ held it in place by pressing the end of it up and to the right with his thumb.

He pulled out a pick especially designed for Weiser locks and with a couple scrapes, all the pins were out of the way, and the tension tool twisted the tumbler, unlocking the door. DJ put his tools back into his kit, then stepped into Blunt's garage-office.

The inside of the garage was pitch dark, and it stunk like flavored pipe tobacco and good weed—the surest sign that Bobby the Blunt had been around. The smell followed him wherever he went. It was amazing the guy ever had anybody coming into his marina, but the sea air probably did the work of covering up the smell.

Up a step to the right, DJ opened the kitchen door.

Inside, the curtains were drawn. A pendant light over the sink glowed like a waning harvest moon, casting an inviting glow on frozen-dinner boxes scattered on the counters. The kitchen cabinets were in dire need of a paint job, and even though he probably lived alone, it was bad practice for Blunt to leave his digital scale out on the counter—with a handful of stems lying on the countertop next to it, no less.

A few plastic boxes with air-tight lids were stacked in the corner. The biggest ones, about a foot deep by two feet long by a foot wide, were filled most of the way with marijuana. Some gallon-sized kitchen baggies on a spice rack screwed into the wall held about a quarter pound of weed each.

Blunt earned his name, that was for sure. DJ shook his head and walked by. If Nick Garner saw how cavalier Blunt was being with his supply, he'd be none too happy about it. Didn't Blunt know there were men with lock pick sets visiting Culebra tonight?

As he passed the weed rack on the wall, something small and white behind the baggies drew DJ's eye.

Sniffing it out in the dim light, his fingers pinched a thin sheet of plastic and pulled it out.

Another baggie. Now, what was this? DJ laid his lock pick set on the counter and fished out his penlight, then shined it on this new discovery.

Inside this new baggie were a couple dozen smaller baggies, containing what looked like small crystals. DJ recognized the meth. It was subdivided into varying amounts—a size for any mood or type of buyer. Blunt really had himself a head full of trouble, didn't he?

But that's the way he was. Some dead nineteenth-century author would've called him a rapscallion. In modern times, people would say he was a criminal and a lowlife. DJ wondered if Garner knew Blunt was selling harder stuff now. Hell, maybe it was Garner's idea.

Whoever came up with the idea, it didn't matter. Blunt was what he was. No point in trying to change him, and as things stood right now, that criminally stupid part of Blunt was gonna come in real handy for cutting through his usual crap.

On the other hand, a semi-automatic, polymer and steel, nine-millimeter compact Glock 19 usually did a damned fine job of cutting to the heart of things. He tossed the baggie back on the counter. Hard not to drop that junk down Blunt's garbage disposal to save him from himself. Blunt had a successful marina, and a decent side-hustle selling weed. Why mess it up with something that'd get him thrown in federal prison for at least five years, but probably more? Couldn't have been worth the risk.

Then again, anything was worth risking if a man didn't feel like he had what he needed. And a guy like Blunt always had needs.

Maybe in some possible future when the DEA was cracking in Blunt's front door with a battering ram, he might cry out that his belly was full, and he couldn't pick out any clothes that he didn't own, and he'd have to sink two boats just to have a spot for a third.

Of course, once the cue-balled psychos of the DEA got his address, they'd be too jacked up to listen.

DJ clicked off his penlight, put it back in the kit, and stuck the kit in his back pocket once more. He brought out his Glock, took one last look at the baggies, and sighed.

He turned left, through a dining room centered around an old, brown card table and ahead, DJ saw the living room. A TV droned on, talking to the overflowing ashtrays, empty beer cans, and handful of .45 rounds on Blunt's coffee table. Blunt's recliner was at the end of the coffee table, blocking the front door in such a way that if you were to throw it open, you'd split Blunt's scalp over his left ear as he slept.

He snored hard. Beneath his T-shirt of the Doors, his belly inflated Jim Morrison's face every time Blunt inhaled. One dirty flip flop clung to his toes; the other was on the floor, leaning against a coffee table leg.

"Blunt," DJ said, in a voice that would've gotten most people to jump up with a start. "Hey, Blunt, wake your ass up."

One hairy arm unfolded from its resting place on Blunt's chest. He scratched at a chin hidden beneath a long gray beard streaked with black.

DJ knew it would come to this. It was a sad state of affairs, but the truth was his buddy Blunt had become such a layabout, he only ever responded when his life was threatened. How the man ran two successful businesses was a wonder.

Not wanting to waste any more time, DJ did the needful. He trudged beside Blunt's chair, his titanium leg thumping on the tile floor, hoping that'd be enough to get him up and moving. It wasn't, of course.

At least shoving a gun in Blunt's face was funny. DJ rubbed his forehead, then placed the muzzle of his Glock against the tip of Blunt's nose. Blunt didn't react, so DJ pushed, twisting the end of Blunt's nose almost a full ninety degrees before he sputtered, and his eyes flashed open.

He jerked his head back. The top half of Blunt's easy chair reclined until his feet were elevated above his head, so a fat vein in his forehead swelled as all the blood rushed upward—or downward, depending on your point of view.

A sharp breath cut through the TV's babbling.

"Jesus! DJ!"

"Morning, beautiful." DJ relaxed his arm, letting the Glock down near his hip. This wasn't the first time the two of them had greeted each other this way. These sorts of jokes kept their relationship lively, and sometimes, like now, a Glock on the nose was good for a laugh.

"I'll pay you back, I promise, DJ! I got money! I got it!" Blunt began to shiver and moan. That vein in his forehead engorged. "Please, man, we don't have to do this!"

"Do what? You think I'm gonna kill you with this thing? Come on, son, if I was gonna kill you, you'd have earned something a hell of a lot worse than a bullet through your nose." DJ looked at his handgun. "Unless there's something you did you think I'd be upset about?"

Like sell meth or rent a boat to a murderer.

"No, no—man, you know me. Same old, same old. Wouldn't do nothing to endanger our friendship. You just, uh, seem upset." Blunt couldn't take his eyes off the Glock.

"Do I?"

Blunt nodded. His jaw muscles jittered.

"So," Blunt's eyes crossed at the Glock, then darted back to DJ's, "what's got you in a bad mood, DJ?"

DJ sighed and headed to the couch to his left. Brushing aside an old pizza box and some crumbs, he sat down, resting his wrist on his knee, the Glock pointed in Blunt's general direction.

"Lately, a whole hell of a lot." He thought about going into Jerry and the mess with Garner, but that seemed like lesser business now. "A man in my condition shouldn't have to put up with this much. You know what I'm saying?"

"Anything, uh, specific?" A bead of sweat rolled off his fore-head. "What brought you here?"

"You did. I always thought you were some small-time weed dealer, Blunt. Slinging a little pot to tourists looking for a good time, and that, combined with the boat rentals and slip fees, was enough to get you through life comfortably."

"You're right, man." Blunt's jaw quivered again. Pretty bad tell for a man who should've been a practiced liar. "It's enough—it's totally enough!"

"Then what's with the meth in the kitchen?"

Blunt pressed his eyelids together, holding them there for a moment while his eyes bounced in his head. He was spinning up some kind of lie.

DJ tapped the Glock's muzzle on the table. "Don't think too hard now, Blunt. I don't like it when my friends start thinking too hard while I'm sitting down for a nice chat. Makes me wonder if I'm being lied to."

But Blunt didn't hear him. His munching jaw muttered out mushy words, giving form to the cocoon being spun up, fiber by fiber for whatever big lie he was going to push on DJ. Whatever was on his mind, he lost it when DJ pulled the trigger.

Bam!

Drywall particles and fuzzy pieces of insulation came down from the ceiling to rest on Blunt's T-shirt—right across the bridge of Jim Morrison's nose. The 9mm round left a neat hole.

Blunt hardly noticed the dust. He was too busy giving DJ a wide-eyed stare.

"I don't appreciate the lies," DJ said. "You lied to me."

"When?" Blunt whispered through his astonishment.

"You're dealing meth."

"I—well, things are different now. It's what people want! If I'm gonna run a business, I gotta listen to my customers!"

"When did Bobby the Blunt ever care about what other people wanted him to do?" DJ asked. He didn't wait for an answer. "Money's got you making bad choices."

"That ice ain't hardly nothing!" Blunt yanked the lever on his chair, making the footrest collapse. He began to roll forward, probably to get up and go to the kitchen to show DJ that all he had was that tiny stash divided out into those little baggies—it wasn't like he was playing Heisenberg.

Then, his eyes met the Glock in DJ's hand, now leveled at his face.

"You might be dealing a teeny-tiny little bit of something, but it's indicative of a pattern of behavior that I can't let slide," DJ said.

"There's no pattern! It's just the one thing—an ounce that a new connection offered me. I took it, because I'm trying to get out, okay? I needed some quick cash because I don't want this business to ruin me. I swear! Please don't tell Garner what you saw."

"I ain't working for that dude."

Blunt nodded so hard his forehead jiggled. "Right! Why would you? You've got all the money you need, right? Well, I don't. I'm just trying to turn it all around, but I need cash."

"Hmm." DJ wiped a piece of insulation fuzz off his forehead. "That why one of your boats was caught speeding away from a murder scene a few hours ago?"

Blunt cracked a smile. He must've thought DJ was telling one of his sick jokes, but DJ's expression turned Blunt's grin upside down.

"You're serious?" Even in a room lit by just the TV, Blunt's skin went visibly whiter. "Which one?"

"*Purple Daze.* You ain't sold it, have you?"

"Sold it?" Blunt's eyes searched the space in front of him. He combed his long, shaped fingernails through his mat of gray-black hair. "No, no, man, I didn't sell that one. I just had—"

He trailed off. Then he hopped up out of his chair, a lost expression shadowing his face.

No sense in stopping him now. DJ had already put the fear of God in him—which was all he needed to do from the start. The ground rules were established. Blunt wasn't going to lie to him now.

"You just had what?" DJ asked, as Blunt slipped past him, heading in the direction DJ had just come from. DJ turned and followed him.

Blunt didn't stop to answer. That is, until DJ grabbed him by the shoulder and forced him to spin on his heel. Blunt lost his balance, then caught himself on his card table in the dining room.

He gave DJ a low, guilty look, his head down and his eyes slanted at DJ sideways. He looked like he'd be sick any moment.

DJ rested a firm hand on his shoulder. He took a step closer to Blunt, so that the two of them were barely a hand's width apart.

"Listen to me, man," DJ said. "You got some trouble coming your way—I know. Whether you were in on it or not, somebody broke the law in your boat. They killed two people, and set fire to a doctor's house over in PR."

Blunt's face twisted into a pained expression. He was taking it pretty hard. DJ reassured him with another squeeze to his shoulder.

"Bud, I know things sound real bad. And I know it ain't like you to participate in things quite as serious as murder. But the fact is, that boat is registered to you. The cops probably ain't found it yet, but, loath as I am to admit it, they're going to. Maybe tomorrow, maybe in a week, maybe longer. But they *will* find it.

"You can be sure they're gonna come without knocking. They're gonna bring a search warrant with them, and they might even have a dog or two." DJ swung his head in the direction of the kitchen. "They ain't gonna be too pleased when their dogs get a whiff of this place.

"Might be those two or three officers pull each other aside for a little powwow, where they say, 'Hell, we got this sumbitch's boat with two bodies on it. He's probably a firebug too. And the dog says he's been having all kinds of parties and not inviting us—why don't we put two in his head and say he lunged at us?'"

DJ took his hand off Blunt's shoulder and looked down at the poor, pot-bellied bastard. The daylights were scared clean out of him.

"What am I gonna do, DJ?"

"Long-term? That's the question that might save your hide— but I don't know the answer," DJ said. "Short-term? All I know is what I can do for you. But you gotta tell me who rented that boat."

CHAPTER TWENTY-FIVE

Blunt considered DJ's question. One could almost see the wheels turning as the man tried to figure out why DJ wanted to know about one of his rentals. What would DJ care about a murder? Blunt didn't know about Armstrong. DJ was tight-lipped like that; nobody knew his business unless he wanted them to know. Blunt probably couldn't say whether or not DJ had a job or where his money came from.

"She was some corporate lady," Blunt said.

"Corporate lady?" DJ asked. "How in the hell would you know something like that? She drop off her resume?"

"It's an educated guess, man. Working in this business," he motioned toward the weed in the kitchen, "I gotta be good at reading folks. You know how it is. Gotta watch for the wrong type. She carried herself real tight, nice clothes, good hair, no problem paying for something, spoke real clearly—like somebody in charge. Know what I mean?"

DJ furrowed his brow. The islands were sinking under the weight of the free, crazy sort, but plenty of business types hung around too. "Did you take her ID when you rented the boat out?"

Suddenly the jitter disappeared from Blunt's face, replaced with a sudden confidence. Blunt understood he had something DJ wanted. *Here comes the bullshit*, DJ thought.

"I can show you her file, but you can't expect me to do that just for the asking. That's a bad trade, and like I said, I'm trying to go legit."

DJ glanced down at his Glock. "I don't remember this being a negotiation, man. But how about I make a counteroffer?" He raised the handgun, pointing it in Blunt's face. "How about we *don't* trade your nose for a bullet hole, and you give me that lady's info so I can catch a murderer?"

Blunt's eyes went wide.

"So, we got a deal?" DJ asked.

"Sure, we do. Yeah. We got a deal."

Blunt froze in place, testing DJ, seeing if he was kidding around again.

"Now ain't the time, friend."

"I've got client privilege," Blunt said as he stepped into the kitchen. "And by showing you this file, I'm breaking the sacred bond of trust between me and my client. You realize that, right?"

"I realize that's a load," DJ said, following behind Blunt. "You got rental records in the garage?"

"Yeah."

He didn't sound too thrilled about sharing them. As Blunt hit the door out to the garage, DJ remembered there was still one thing he wanted to do.

DJ snatched up the baggie of meth lying on the counter. He tossed it into the sink, turned the faucet on full blast, and smacked the switch to the left of it.

The garbage disposal growled and gurgled, struggling to chew all the baggies for a few seconds, then hit its stride. DJ peered down the drain and didn't see anything in the blackness. He listened for a couple seconds more, then flipped the switch off and the disposal fell silent. After he shut off the faucet, he turned to see Blunt gawking at him.

"Aw, come on, DJ!"

"That's some nasty, nasty stuff. It's nothing but a bag of misery, man. I'm just doing what I can to help you get rid of it."

"I gotta pay for that now."

DJ shrugged. "I'll pay you back when we get to the boat."

"What boat?"

"My boat—*Reel Fun*," he replied. "You didn't think you were going to ride out of here in one of yours, did you?"

Blunt set his jaw and grumbled, then turned his back on DJ and opened the door to the garage. "You know I'm trying to get *out* of messes."

"Complain all you like, *hombre*. You know I just did you a solid," DJ told him as he walked across the kitchen. "What's got you so dead set on going clean, anyway?"

The light came on inside the garage. For a place that he used as an office during the day, it was a real pit. Spilling from the shelves on the far wall was a plastic knot of bins, bags, and boxes. In front of the knot, a half-finished wood dining table rested on a bed of newspapers. Matching chairs were up in the unfinished rafters, new upholstery draped over the beams, as if Blunt tanned the leather himself.

Against the back wall rested an old fridge with its door hanging open, rusted cans of paint inside. Next to it, closer to DJ, was a wooden entertainment center with a small TV on the center shelf and junk on the other shelves. A pair of rusted Beachcomber bikes leaned against the front of the entertainment center, which must've been great for TV watching.

"Annie's pregnant," he said. "I want to see my granddaughter."

Blunt moved off to the right. He stood at a kitchen counter in the center of the garage that looked like he'd found it in a junk heap somewhere. A dusty computer monitor and matching keyboard occupied the countertop, along with some neatly stacked papers and a sea-green ash tray nearly filled to overflowing.

DJ was vaguely aware of Blunt's daughter, Annie. She'd come up once or twice after the two of them knocked back enough beers to choke a bull shark. All DJ remembered was that Blunt had met her mother in the mid-eighties, knocked her up, and blew her off. Despite all that, the torch Blunt carried for his daughter's mother only burned hotter as time went on.

"You still angling for Annie's mother?"

"It ain't about that." A flare of anger skimmed over Blunt's face. One of the few times DJ had ever seen him angry.

"Then what's it about? You got some patriarchal urges kicking in in your old age?"

He grumbled something indecipherable at DJ.

"I'm just busting your balls, man," DJ said. "You wanna be with your grandkid, that's A-OK with me. I'm just surprised to see you jumping out of the weed game. Does Garner know?"

"Garner don't care," Blunt said. "All he cares about is getting back at that reporter who almost burnt down his Shangri-La. He'd torch the whole place himself if he thought he'd catch that guy in the flames."

DJ's ears perked up. Maybe there was something to the Garner theory after all. "You think he would?"

"He said as much. We split a bag and a couple of his women hopped on our laps. You know how he gets when he's relaxed—he talks."

And Nick Garner was the kind of guy who followed through on his talk. How many people had dreams of starting up a little hippie sex cult on the islands but never got it off the ground? Garner walked the walk.

He had the money to hire somebody to do his work, too. DJ knew his glitzy little tourist-trap fairy land barely generated a dime in profit, but with one of the biggest grow operations in the Northern Caribbean, he was a player in the weed market. Blunt might not have thought it, but Garner wouldn't let him go easily.

"Do believe I found our lady," Blunt said.

DJ came out of his head, then looked up at Blunt. "You sure?"

"I can run a business, my man. I ain't got much, but I got that."

"Sure. Listen, man, I'm sorry for hassling you. I'll get you some tax for your troubles—whatever you need to buy your way out of Garner's thing. You shouldn't have to miss out on time with your grandbaby."

Blunt held eye contact with DJ for a moment, probably wondering if this was another of his jokes, but when he realized it wasn't, a grin swelled beneath his whiskers. "I won't go tellin' nobody about your heart, DJ. I know you'd hate that."

Before DJ could tell him to shut his face, the garage door rattled. Somebody knocking.

"Who the hell is that?" DJ whispered to Blunt as he tucked his

Glock into the holster inside the back of his pants. "Were you expecting somebody?"

"No, I'm not expecting anyone," Blunt replied. "But I think I should answer—it's probably somebody looking for crystal."

Shadows played over a small gap between the garage door and the concrete floor. "Tell 'em to buzz off. You're too busy to mess with it right now."

"You don't know how persistent these meth heads can get. Now go duck down somewhere. I'll shoo 'em off."

DJ looked around the garage, eyeing all the clutter. There should be a good spot to hide with all the junk around, but nowhere made itself immediately obvious.

He walked toward the back door, thinking that maybe his best bet would be to hunker down on the patio and keep an eye on Blunt by keeping the door cracked, but he stopped just short.

To his right, behind the fridge full of paint cans, there was just enough of a gap for DJ's slim frame to slip through.

So, he did just that. Beyond the fridge, he found that there was a wider spot back behind the entertainment center. It was a couple of feet deep and was blocked by cardboard backing behind the TV. A perfect hiding spot.

A sliver of light squeezed between a stack of wood stain and varnish cans. DJ sunk down until he was on all fours and looked through.

The view wasn't perfect, but with Blunt's legs and feet visible, DJ could piece together what was going on.

The garage door rumbled open. A thin black line of grime marked where the door met the ground when it was closed, and the nearest of three men who'd come calling stood half a step beyond it.

"Robert Blount?" a voice with a smooth Puerto Rican accent asked. The lead man's weight shifted on his legs.

"That's me. What can I do for you guys?" Blunt's voice was free of all the nervousness he'd exhibited just moments before. Amazing how the man could change his mood like turning a knob.

"We're with the Puerto Rican Police Force," the leader said.

Damn. Were they here to bust him for dealing? DJ felt better than ever about putting the meth down the drain.

"Well, I'm pleased to meet you gentlemen," Blunt said. "And thank you for keeping our streets safe, but, man, I gotta get back—"

"There's been a noise complaint," the same man said.

"Couldn't have been me, sir. I've been—"

The zap and hiss of a stun gun scratched the air. Blunt's feet shuffled, and his knees locked. He hit the concrete floor like a rotten tree caught in a windstorm, and it was a miracle he didn't bust into a million pieces.

With him lying on the floor, DJ caught a good look at his face. His eyes whirled back in their sockets, and a trickle of spit ran from his mouth.

Instinctively, DJ ripped the Glock out from his jeans. They were here for a shakedown. Probably to rob Blunt. He fingered the trigger, but his better senses took hold—shooting at the three men who were now coming into the garage was the same as shooting himself. Each man had a handgun holstered on his hip. Three-to-one odds weren't in DJ's favor.

A better opportunity would come whistling past. Maybe one or two of them would split off. They had to know what Blunt kept in the house, so they'd want to go hunting around for his stash.

Splitting from each other would be the last mistake the three of them ever made.

The leader snapped his fingers, and the other two guys sprang into action. Both were in jeans, one with long legs like a spider's, and the other with short, powerful legs more like DJ's—except this guy still had every bit of both of his.

They lifted Blunt off the floor by his arms. A finger of blood cast out from his mouth like a fishing line as they got him to his feet and held him up between them. Then they walked Blunt from right to left while he muttered. Their leader yanked the garage door down.

"Better hold onto your breath, *muchacho*. You're gonna need it," one of the cops holding Blunt said as they sat him down beside a stack of window air conditioning units in the corner. He went along with it, putting an arm around one of the units to better hold himself up.

Blunt's docility surprised DJ. He was probably dazed from the shock, but he should be fighting like hell. If DJ were getting roughed up by these jokers, they'd have to chop off his other leg and rip his arms out of their sockets before they'd get him down to a manageable level.

In his moment of fantasizing about maiming the bad guys, DJ lost track of the leader cop. The other two remained near Blunt on the left side of the garage, standing over him like a vague threat, but the leader was where?

The only logical place was the computer. DJ slid back, careful not to knock down the walls of his makeshift spider hole. The gap behind the fridge was only wide enough for him to slip through sideways, so he leaned on his right elbow, putting it to the ground and lying on his right side.

Peering around the corner of the fridge, he saw the back of the leader cop, standing at the counter with the computer. He was a white guy with slicked-back brown hair, average height and build, wearing a faded T-shirt and jeans.

"Hey, Bobby, where do you keep the rest of your files?"

When Blunt didn't answer quickly enough, DJ heard a sound like a slab of meat getting slapped onto a counter by the butcher. Blunt sputtered.

"The officer asked you a question, *acho*." This second cop had a thick Puerto Rican accent—not that the leader didn't have one—but this second cop might as well have been talking through a mouthful of *mofongo*.

"Computer," Blunt coughed out.

"Figured that." The leader cop moved to his left, following Blunt's rental counter until he was on the other side, showing DJ his face.

DJ's nerves froze. He knew this man.

Back at Jerry's house, Gabriela talked about the murderer who'd killed the Markels and burnt their home down. She'd said he looked like Christian Bale from *American Psycho*—and DJ took it as kind of a joke. An assessment of the guy's mental state.

Gabriela hadn't been joking.

The leader cop had his hair combed back on his head, a chiseled jaw and—lending some truth to Gabriela's impression of him—a face dressed with the kind of cruel indifference found in guys like Ted Bundy or Charles Manson.

"You don't keep no paper records? Nothing in a filing cabinet? Nothing like that?" Christian Bale patted the top of the machine.

"No, man," Blunt said. "I'm trying to save paper."

"What a good guy," Christian said. "Saving the trees." He locked eyes with his subordinates, then nodded.

A struggle kicked off on the other side of the garage.

Carefully but quickly, DJ skittered to his spot behind the entertainment center. The other two cops had pulled Blunt off the stack of AC units and to his feet again. One of the air conditioners tumbled off, but nobody seemed concerned. They were all kicking and shuffling their feet, jockeying for position.

A length of rope hit the floor. Not a coil of it, or a tangle, but one bitter end.

They were tying Blunt up—no, they were doing worse. Spider slipped a hangman's noose over Blunt's neck, and the third cop tossed the other end of the rope over the bare rafters in the garage, then, worked the line down, hand over hand, until it was almost tight as a violin string.

DJ kept his eyes glued to the other men. As soon as somebody split off, he had to make his move.

"I ain't worth it, man, I ain't!" Blunt pleaded. "Please, you boys take what you like, and I won't give you an ounce of trouble. I'll keep my mouth shut—I won't talk to a soul."

"You're a kind soul, Mr. Blount," Christian said. "You have our appreciation."

Spider Legs picked up the end of the rope. He took a couple steps around Blunt, stopping behind him. DJ couldn't see what his hands were doing.

"Ready," one of the cops said.

"Fellas, if you want money, I'll tell you where I keep my stash. You take it and you go. Never gonna see me again. Nope. Not ever. If I'm not paying my taxes or if somebody wants my territory—they can have it. I'm out. I'm done. Scout's honor."

Christian dragged a chair across the floor. The legs howled like a pair of stuck warthogs running through the brush, until the guy stopped, setting the chair next to Blunt.

"Bobby, all three of us appreciate the offer, but we're not here for scratch. We're making plenty as it is, and frankly, getting too greedy is a risk as real as any today. A lot of people could save themselves a lot of heartache if they simply lived within their means. Understand?"

Christian Bale waited for an answer. Blunt's heavy breaths choked away the silence in the garage.

"Sure," Blunt finally said.

"You don't really understand, I know. Not enough people do." He patted the seat of the chair. "Why don't you step up here, Bobby?"

Sweat trickled down DJ's back as he watched Blount look between Christian and the chair. Fight, Bobby. Fight like hell. You got nothing to lose.

But, slowly, Blunt put one foot on the chair. Then, with the help of the two cops who put the noose around his neck, he stepped the other foot up. Now, DJ only saw Bobby from the belt down.

"That's good, Bobby." Christian twirled his fingers, signaling the other two men to pull the rope tighter. "I want you to know that none of this is personal. If I could let you off for good behavior, I would—because you've been as good as they come, Bobby. But, man, the lady paying us says you gotta go, so you *gotta* go.

"Pull him!" Christian bellowed.

His two cronies pulled the rope tight as it'd go. Bobby wheezed, and his heels lifted off the chair, but he kicked off a flip flop while his toes tried desperately to keep contact with it.

"He's a ballerina!" Spider laughed. Christian chuckled.

"I'll save your dignity, Bobby." Christian kicked the chair over. It clattered to the ground. "Hold him up, boys."

While the third cop held tight to the rope, Spider grabbed the slack from the floor, found a sturdy-looking pipe running up the wall, and tied the rope on.

"Alright," Spider said. The third cop let go of the rope.

Blunt's feet dangled where the chair had been, kicking furiously.

His heavy breathing twisted into a strained noise. Not a grunt, or a yelp, but a mixture of the two. Then no sound came from Bobby's throat, just the swish of clothes and popping of joints over the echoes of all three men laughing.

"Look at him go! Look at him kick!" One of the cops howled. "Keep fighting boy, keep fighting!"

They were killing DJ's friend. He was half a dozen steps away, and even with a gun in his hand, there wasn't a thing he could do about it.

Before long, the noises coming from Blunt grew more distant and less urgent, until they were not the sounds of a man fighting for his life, but of a man accepting his death and of a body turning off the last few switches before the door was barred and locked forever. The long silence was louder than the thundering of DJ's heart.

"Man, what a dancer!" Spider broke into a laughing fit.

DJ would've kicked over the press-board entertainment center and charged at them headlong, but the soldier in him knew that would be a tactical mistake commensurate with suicide. He swore to himself, in that dusty space between Blunt's broken fridge and the moldy garage wall, that he would do this right. He would take his time; he would find these bastards one by one—catch one sleeping off a hangover and another lying in bed with his girlfriend—and he'd blow their heads off.

"Get the computer," Christian barked.

The third cop walked toward Blunt's rental counter. DJ lost sight of him somewhere off to the right.

"Is the body good?" Spider asked.

"It'll be fine," Christian responded. "Nobody's gonna look too hard into it, once they find the drugs and cash."

And with that business handled, the two of them walked across the garage to join the third cop with the computer.

Their footsteps came closer to DJ. He turned toward the fridge, waiting for them to pass the gap, offering any goodwill he still had with God for a chance, just one chance, to get a good look at all three of them.

The back door that led out to the patio—the door DJ had picked to get in here—opened and two of the three men slipped out. He caught a look at one of them and committed the man's face to memory. They had started joking with each other, laughing about something that DJ didn't catch.

Until Christian hissed at them, "Officer Dos Santos, shut your mouth!"

Christian walked out behind them, quietly pulling the door shut.

Dos Santos—two saints. Maybe God was listening, after all.

Now DJ was left in the garage, but not alone. Blunt was there, a memory that would always burn in quiet moments until, like a salve, the blood of three evil men was spread across it.

When he felt he'd waited long enough, DJ slipped through

the gap between the fridge and the wall. His feet were heavier, like Blunt's ghost clung to his shoes.

Death was nothing new to DJ Martin. He had killed. He had seen men killed. He had helped other men kill and tried to keep men from dying who were beyond hope.

But none of those men were Robert Blount.

When he came around the fridge, he wasn't prepared for what he'd find. If he ever managed to clean the greater part of the memory formed here, in Blunt's garage, he would never lose the memory of his friend's face as he saw it right now.

And DJ would never forget the name Dos Santos.

CHAPTER TWENTY-SIX

When I called Collat from *Wayward's* flybridge, his replies were clipped, and he seemed a little eager to drag me to the end of the conversation. To say he sounded busy would have been an understatement. But he spared the time to meet up at the Puerto Del Rey marina in Fajardo—a region on the central east coast of Puerto Rico.

Puerto Del Rey had long been on my list of places to sail. But, with my work for Armstrong getting in the way of my lessons, I hadn't gotten around to visiting. When *Wayward* motored us within sight of the place, I thought I'd be more excited to catch a glimpse of one of the largest marinas in the Caribbean.

My fear for Gabriela eclipsed any excitement I might've felt. Frankly, she looked guilty. She was the only person found at the scene of an arson and double murder. The boat DJ chased counted for something, but to some cops, simply having a person in-hand to take all the blame was enough, guilty or innocent. I hoped Collat wasn't one of them.

We pulled up to the dock. The smell of coffee had awakened Alicia more than an hour ago, and she jumped out to help me drop fenders and secure *Wayward* after I'd backed in. I was just tying down the last line when I looked up and caught a glimpse into the salon.

Gabriela and Flor sat on the couch, their heads next to each other. I couldn't begin to imagine what they were saying, and I had to wrestle with the fact that I was tearing them apart.

My sat phone rang in my pocket.

"This is Jerry."

"Mr. Snyder, you're late," Collat said. "We agreed to meet at the marina office at eight a.m. sharp. Now, I'm here, pacing around like an idiot while you're—where are you?"

I was on one knee, working on tying the last line, trying to reassure myself that I was making the smart move.

"Marina traffic was worse than I thought. I'll be up in a couple of minutes."

"And you have Miss Ramos in your custody?"

"Yessir."

"Good." Collat hung up.

Already off to a fantastic start. I walked aft on the dock, and caught Alicia tossing a spare coil of dock line into one of the cockpit compartments.

"Collat called."

She looked up at me expectantly.

"He's in a real cheery mood. I might have to punch him in the nose for his own good."

"I'll untie the lines." She was only half-joking.

"Thanks. Keep Gabriela and Flor here," I said. "But let Gabbie know I'm heading up to the marina office now. She'll need to be ready to go on Collat's schedule."

Alicia smiled at me with no small amount of pity. I didn't ever have to say a word about the things in my head when she was around—she read me better than anyone I knew. The day I asked her to marry me, she'd figured out I was proposing before we even set foot on the beach in Big Sur.

"I'll convince him to let us keep Gabbie in our custody," I said. "I have to."

"You don't sound convinced."

"My hope is that Collat interviews Gabriela about last night, I tell him about Dr. Markel's connection with Luc Baptiste, and the police re-open the investigation into Luc's murder with Collat in charge. If they do that, we sail off into the sunset with Gabbie and Flor no worse for the wear."

"And what're you hoping against?" Alicia asked.

"Revenge," I said. "Collat was close with Luc Baptiste. He wants someone to blame, and Gabriela might prove too tempting to pass up."

Alicia shook her head. "He wouldn't do that, would he?"

"I wish I could rule it out," I said. "All I can say for sure is I'm going to do my best."

She smiled, taking pity on me.

"You are. You always have, and you always will. Don't forget that." Her fingers played with the zipper at the bottom of her coat. She looked back at the salon—at Gabriela and Flor. "We know you'll come through—they know it."

I nodded. I stepped on *Wayward's* swim platform and took my sat phone out of my coat pocket.

"I'll call you from the marina office when it's time to bring her out."

Alicia's hand slowly brushed over mine as she took the phone. For a half-second, my spirit was buoyant—none of the things weighing on me could keep me down forever. Not with her at my side.

"You're a good man, Jerry."

Wayward bounced slightly after I stepped from the swim platform onto the dock. I stuffed my hands into my coat pockets and turned to my left.

This meeting with Collat would take massaging. After nearly forty-eight hours of work, I didn't have anything that would satisfy him, except Gabriela.

Up the hill in front of the marina, I crossed over a short drive leading to a boat ramp, then went around the south side of the building. Here, I came to the main entrance—a set of double-wide glass doors with boat anchors for handles.

Inside, a girl about ten years younger than me smiled from behind the front desk. Her hair was jet black, shining and straight as a boom line. Even for a Puerto Rican, she had a rich tan.

"Are you the captain of *Wayward?*" she asked.

"I am." I approached the desk, reaching for my wallet in my back pocket. To my right sat a couple of shelves with boating utilities—spare lines, oil, filters, spark plugs, and other items.

I spotted Collat to the left, seated in a lounge chair near a window overlooking the marina, one hand holding a small cup of coffee, the other pressing his thumb and forefinger against his eyes.

"How long will you be staying?" the girl at the counter asked me.

"Only need a day pass," I said. "Guess I'd like a refuel too."

"Of course. Do you know how many gallons?"

I looked at *Wayward's* mast gently rocking with the current.

"Honestly, it's a brand-new boat. I shouldn't have taken it

out, except my wife and I couldn't stand it anymore."

She cracked a smile and a laugh tumbled out.

"We get that a lot. If you'd like to give me a credit or debit card, I'll have one of our dock attendants fill up the tank."

I slipped her my AmEx Black Card. After she swiped the card, then handed it back to me, I veered to my left. Collat still had one hand around his cup of coffee, the other to his eyes.

"Are you always late to a meeting, Mr. Snyder?" he said without moving.

"Only when it's inconvenient." I pulled up a chair to face him, then sat down. The scent of bacon wafted in the air. Behind the detective, a hostess standing at a podium was talking to a young family.

A stack of plates clinked somewhere farther down.

"You look fresh," I said.

He lowered his hands from his eyes and stared at me. "Where's Gabriela Ramos?

"Before I bring her in, I want you to know she's innocent," I said. "I was there last night."

"So was I," Collat said. "If she's innocent, she's got a lot to answer for."

"My partner and I saw a boat fleeing the scene. The house that burnt down belonged to a doctor. A guy named Markel. She says she was going there to talk about a drug trial for her daughter. But I'm not sure he's as legit as Gabriela thought. Another contact told me Dr. Markel had been pushing some kind of phony cancer cure. I have strong suspicions there is a connection between Dr. Markel and Luc."

"Do you?" He seemed less enthusiastic than I hoped. "Before we go there, let's talk about Gabriela first. Do you have any evidence to back up her innocence? Because what I've seen makes her look guilty as sin."

"She's not a killer," I said. "I've seen killers."

"You saw this mystery man set the house on fire and kill the Markels?"

"No, I—"

"What's your alternate theory? The doctor saw her coming, and rather than talk to her, he set his place on fire, shot his wife in the head, and then shot himself in the gut? Do you know how long it takes a man to die of a gunshot wound to the abdomen?"

"Has an artery been struck?" I was already tired of Collat's attitude. "She's innocent. Her daughter is sick, she wanted to talk to Markel about a drug trial."

"I don't know much about drug trials, but I don't imagine you go to a doctor's house to participate in one," he said.

A marina employee turned a corner behind Collat and came in our direction. I shut my mouth and watched him while he went past, waiting until he was out of ear shot.

"I know how it looks, but the fact is Gabriela is innocent. Do you think she killed Luc too?" I asked, scooting forward in my chair.

"Frankly, I'm not sure of a connection between Luc and Dr. Markel. The things I *am* sure of point to me taking Gabriela into custody."

"Wait a minute, I'm telling you someone else was there. A man."

The muscles below his temples bulged and flattened, and on the tips of his fingers, his dark brown skin turned almost as white as mine as he gripped his coffee cup. "Did this man have a face?"

I tried to think of that actor Gabriela said he resembled. His name wasn't coming to me.

"Did he have a body?" Collat asked.

"She said he looked like some Hollywood guy."

"Who said? Gabriela? Funny that she'd come up with some-one else to blame."

"If she's lying, let me keep her with me so I can find out."

Collat rolled his eyes.

"This is all connected to Luc, Detective. The only reason DJ and I were there at all was because we think Luc had a meeting with the doctor before he wound up dead. He was—"

Collat's hands went up, cutting me off. He seemed to consider something, his hands now clasped, and his eyes skimming from place to place.

"You were a detective in Newport Beach, were you not?"

I nodded.

"Then you're aware that it is best not to entangle ourselves with speculation, which I've let you do far too long already."

"Detective, this isn't speculation. I spoke to a man who Luc interviewed about Dr. Markel. Gabriela Ramos is a witness to Markel's murder, and she was able to give me a precise descrip-tion of a man at the scene. She saw him do it."

"But she's also the most convincing suspect we have. And until you or I produce another suspect, letting Gabriela out of my custody is the biggest mistake I could make."

"You can't."

"Find me a more compelling suspect, and you can take Ga-briela."

The game became clearer. Gabriela was a bargaining chip for Collat. He wanted me to do the work of finding the man on the boat, either because he couldn't or he didn't care to.

"Tell me about the boat used to flee the scene. Were you able to gather any information about it?"

"My partner is following that up."

"DJ?" Collat smirked. "You couldn't have let him do this while you looked into the boat?"

"He's what I've got."

"He seems to have an agenda."

"Just an attitude problem. We aren't marrying each other any time soon; all we have to do is work together."

Collat laughed. "Yes, that sounds strikingly familiar."

"Things aren't so great at your department?"

"Sometimes," Collat squared himself in his chair, crossing his thin legs at the knees, "I don't find myself buying as deeply into the culture as my superiors would like. Maybe that's my problem, maybe that's their problem, but either way, a job remains."

My reading of Collat's political answer was that he wasn't into all the thin-blue-line, us-versus-the-world machismo that seemed to have poisoned the minds of too many good cops.

"Mr. Snyder, are you ready to bring her up to me?" Collat steepled his fingers.

I looked to *Wayward*. I didn't imagine Gabriela and Flor had left each other's sides, and they would never be ready to separate from each other, even if it were only for a short while.

"I need you to promise me you'll watch after her. I don't know if the man she saw is working alone, on his own behalf, or on the behalf of someone else, but you said yourself that your department didn't put its full effort behind solving Luc's murder."

He raised his eyebrows. "Are you positing that someone in the Puerto Rican Police Force is working with the man who killed the Markels?"

I had my suspicions. Nick Garner looked like a guy who could pull some strings with the cops if he had to. I wasn't sure if he was connected to the Markel murders or not, but his connection to Luc Baptiste was undeniable. In any case, I was sure Gabriela had done nothing wrong.

"All I'm saying is Gabriela Ramos is a good woman—a mother with a very sick little girl—and God help all of us if we forget that."

CHAPTER TWENTY-SEVEN

The emailed announcement of an emergency meeting came at 6:14 a.m., addressed to all board members. When Tamara Price walked into Hildon's principal board room, six minutes before the meeting's scheduled start time of 10:30, the place was already crowded with gray-haired, balding, suited men, burning caffeine to stay on their feet.

Tamara found a narrow gap between Tom Hall and Nick Fields—two members who held a combined four percent ownership share of Hildon. The men whispered to each other. Sounded like they had to cancel an early tee time in Miami to fly down.

Across the room, in front of windows overlooking the Atlantic, Arlen Burkhart joked with the men gathered near him. They hung on his every word. Having him there turned out to be better timing than Tamara had anticipated, because even in times of crisis, Mr. Burkhart radiated strength and confidence into the room. Given the news about to hit them—news Tamara Price was already clued into—Hildon needed every ray of confidence they could find.

Burkhart was an asset. He'd been ranked among Forbes' top business minds for years, and it was clear why.

The doors on the opposite end of the room opened. Rachel Little marched in, flanked by her assistant, Grace, clutching a stack of papers close to her chest. Everyone went quiet. All eyes turned to Rachel, who now stood at the head of the long, glass table, with her hands planted on it, her head bowed.

"Gentlemen, I know rumors are already starting to fly, so I won't waste your time with a preamble. One of our contractors has been murdered, and a Hildon employee is suspected of having done it."

A scandalized murmur bubbled through the room. Even these old masters of the universe chittered like a barbershop parlor.

"Order," Rachel said. "Order, please. I didn't call this meeting to gossip."

They didn't listen well. The talk turned to groans and mutterings about earning calls, derailed stock buybacks, and bank executives knocking on the door. Until one man's voice cut above the rest.

"Who was killed?" Mr. Burkhart asked in a way that didn't suggest he was worried, more than he was running numbers through his head. "And by whom?"

Rachel straightened up at the end of the table, one hand holding onto the other's fist. She didn't want to say it but holding too much back from the men in this room would send Hildon into financial freefall.

"An employee named Gabriela Ramos is suspected of murdering a long-time contractor," she said, clearing her throat to give her a moment to gauge the room. "Dr. James Markel."

The room almost burst at the seams.

"Jesus!" Tom Hall called out from Tamara's left. "It's actually true!"

Dr. Markel was known to most of the men in the room. Their outburst was not because the doctor was a top mind in his field; they only worried about the loss of his productivity and Hildon's potentially tarnished reputation affecting their bottom line.

Rachel waved her hands and said something at the front of the room, lost in all the noise.

"The police found—" Rachel shouted, her body pushing to get the words above the rest. "The police visited Dr. Markel's home—and I shouldn't have to say this, but this information is privileged and doesn't leave this room—they found a car at the scene yesterday, registered to Gabriela Ramos. I'm told by a contact that they'll have her in custody by lunch time."

"She was at his house?" a man shouted.

"Why would she kill him?" Jack Tremble, a round, red-faced Midwesterner, who kept a hideaway from his wife and teenage daughters on a private cay near St. Maarten, asked.

"Once the police talk to her, they'll find out."

"Are we sure he didn't leak internal documents?" somebody shouted. "Didn't he try to do that once before?"

The tenor in the room was approaching unhinged. The men were acting as if they were ready to start gnawing each other's windpipes if it got any worse.

"There's no sign that Dr. Markel's murder is connected to his past behavior," Rachel responded. "But if he slipped out anything damaging, we'll know, and we'll sue his estate for breach of contract."

Reminding them of the NDA Markel signed didn't seem to

ease any minds. A non-disclosure agreement only gave Hildon recourse once the cat was out of the bag. It couldn't physically prevent someone talking, though Dr. Markel wouldn't *physically* speak to anyone else now.

"I'm not losing my shirt over this!" someone shouted.

The meeting was almost beyond salvaging. Tamara saw panic gathering behind members' eyes, calculating acceptable losses, which vacation house to sell first, and which mistress to dump if Hildon went under. Thank God the board room was on the second floor, or these panicky babies might try opening a window and taking the short way out.

"Sit down and shut up!" Rachel screamed back. Her tone was like that of a lioness chasing a pesky male off a gazelle carcass. "Nobody's losing their shirt. Nobody's even going to lose their lunch money. Markel is *dead*. And dead men don't talk." Her eyes stalked the room, daring challengers to step up.

"I don't know about some of you, but I'm not going to chicken out because a squealer like Markel is dead. Good riddance." She mimed clapping dirt off her hands. "We need to keep our eyes on the prize, gentlemen. We need to look forward. We should be concerned about Gabriela Ramos. She's twenty-eight, and she's been an employee here for six years. Whether he told her anything or not, we need to remind her that Hildon is the hand that feeds her. Give her a reason to stay in line."

No one said anything as Rachel looked through the room, meeting eyes. Goosebumps prickled on Tamara's neck when she looked her way.

"That's a sound strategy, Ms. Little," Arlen Burkhart spoke up. "Remind your employee that a loyal hand is repaid in kind. But the girl is out of hand—she's being held by the state. How, then, do we reward her virtue?"

Rachel nodded at Tamara. Her signal to step up.

"Mr. Burkhart, she worked under me," Tamara said. "Gabriela Ramos has a sick daughter. The cost of her medical care is an extreme burden. Frankly, she needs money. We'll take care of that and get her daughter the best care she could ever ask for. And, more directly to Ms. Ramos's current problem, we can hire the best defense team money can buy. With Dr. Markel gone, I suggest we send Ms. Ramos a bouquet to show her our appreciation."

That got a few laughs from the room. Neckties and three-piece suits loosened up. Red faces returned a more natural color, and the men exchanged congratulatory glances, as if Tamara's ideas had spilled from their mouths.

"We will handle this, gentlemen," Rachel said. "Give it time. I've seen Hildon through eight of its most profitable years, and I promise, despite my planned exit, I will lay the groundwork for eight more." Rachel looked directly at Tamara, then dismissed the room with a quick nod. The board members began filtering toward the exit, their delicate nerves soothed.

"And gentlemen," Rachel's voice had shed every trace of fury. "We *do not* talk about any of this outside this room. Not Markel's death, not Gabriela Ramos, and certainly not the doctor's NDA. If I see an article citing anonymous sources in *The Wall Street Journal* this week, I *will* find out who leaked, and I'll do everything in my power to ensure your grandchildren are left picking scraps from a gutter by the time they graduate high school."

A tickle spread across Tamara's stomach. She couldn't stop herself from smiling while she watched those miserable old men turn their backs, trying hard not to react. They'd practically left their balls in Rachel Little's desk drawer.

Except one. An amused look played in Arlen Burkhart's eyes. He cracked a smile at Tamara. She returned the gesture.

Back in her office, Tamara sank into the couch opposite her desk, gin and tonic in her hand. Her neck went limp, her head on the back of the couch. Her brain replayed the highlights of the meeting as she sipped her drink and watched clouds roll through the Puerto Rican sky.

There was a knock at her door. She hopped up, went to her desk, and pushed the intercom button.

"Collin," she said to her secretary, "why didn't you buzz me?"

"Sorry, Ms. Price," he said. "Mr. Burkhart knocked before I had the chance."

Rachel looked at her door, seeing two narrow shadows through the gap at the bottom. Her pulse quickened in her belly. She stashed the drink in a desk drawer, swiped down her hair, jerked the collar of her blouse, and, snapping her shoulders back and her chin up, went for the door.

"Mr. Burkhart? What a pleasant surprise."

He returned her smile with one of his own. God, his teeth were flawless. The first step he took into her office felt like the star quarterback strutting into his girlfriend's bedroom after a homecoming victory. His perfectly trimmed black hair shone under the crystalline light coming from the windows behind her.

"I hope I'm not imposing," he said, as if she'd want to turn him away. The man was a power player. The closer she got to him, the better for her career.

"I would never be bothered by you. How can I help?"

For a moment, he stopped and eyeballed the bottle of gin sitting on the table in the corner. She'd forgotten to put it away.

"We've all had a morning, haven't we?" he asked. "Rachel Little seemed especially fired up."

"I don't normally indulge during work hours."

He laughed. "You should, dear. After what's happened, the next few days are going to be hell. You're going to need something stronger than gin."

Arlen closed the door behind him and hooked a left for her couch. Then, he bent forward, opened the small door beneath the corner table, and took out a glass for himself.

"You don't terribly mind if I have a sip, do you?" He motioned toward the bottle.

"Of course not, Mr. Burkhart." Tamara slid behind her desk, then brought her glass out of the drawer, marched over to the table, and grabbed the bottle.

Standing in front of him, she held it at her waist while she worked the cap off. A bemused smile crossed his lips. His eyes danced over the pearl silk blouse covering her chest, then down to her merlot skirt, which clutched tightly to her wine-bottle hips. She felt the heat of his eyes slipping southward, skimming across the skin above her Louboutin pumps.

He was welcome to stare—she worked for this body seven days a week, and it wasn't all for her health. Power was power, however given, however taken, and the power her body gave her over some men and women was as effective as the power granted her by diplomas and C-suite titles.

When she took his glass from him, she let his fingertips caress the back of her hand. Skin-to-skin contact, whether a handshake, knuckles to a jaw, or something much more intimate, was a powerful driver of human emotion. She wanted him imprinted by her touch, her smell, her emotions. Keeping her hand wrapped in his, she poured the gin into his glass slowly, commanding his eyes to linger on her.

A corner of his mouth turned upward, and beneath his lips, he licked his teeth.

"Did you come here for a quick drink?" She took her hand out of his, then stepped back.

He laughed, then drank.

"Mmm." He held the glass up and looked through it, at Tamara. "I didn't think it was possible to find such a bold, full-bodied drink down here. I take pity on the folks who've had this under their nose the whole time. These people don't know what they're missing."

"The gin doesn't come out for just anyone. Only for the people I think deserve a taste."

"I'm humbled to be held among an elite few," he said with a roguish grin. He leaned back against the couch and took another sip. "I have to come clean with you, Tamara—I'm not here for the drinks. Truth is, I've been wanting to meet you for some time, ever since I read about this intelligent, ambitious girl from Atlanta, I knew she was something special. When I saw your picture, I knew you'd be unstoppable. And now, you're next in line when Rachel is gone. You're an extremely impressive woman."

"I appreciate the compliments, Mr. Burkhart." She grabbed the gin and refilled his glass.

"They're meant sincerely, I assure you. But my reading habits aren't what I came here to talk to you about either." He wafted the glass under his nose before setting the drink on the table and straightening up.

"I don't know what's got Rachel Little wound so tight, but I can tell Hildon has got a hell of a scandal waiting in the wings. Something that'll bring on a changing of the guard as soon as it goes public—and despite any threats, you can rest assured that any juicy little secret will squirm its way out into the wild eventually."

Tamara shrugged. "Ms. Little runs a tight ship. I will too."

"Darling, I've been in business long enough to know that only dead men keep secrets. Markel might not talk anymore, but there simply isn't a person in the world who can convince me he hadn't talked before his untimely death. Which is why I want to know your thoughts on an insurance policy, of sorts."

Arlen's eyes settled on her. Was he testing her, or was he being genuine? To his credit, he did have a considerable sum tied up in Hildon. Still, Tamara had learned never to do anything for free.

"I think I owe Ms. Little some amount of loyalty," Tamara said.

"Oh, I wouldn't want to question your loyalties. I meant what I said back in that boardroom. But are you for the name on the back of the jersey or the one on the front?"

Tamara knitted her eyebrows. "I don't know what you mean."

"Be loyal to Hildon, not Rachel. She'll be gone soon, and you'll be captain of this ship."

That's what this was about. He was offering advice—he wanted to get in Tamara's good graces early. She kept her face blank.

"Rachel's making a mistake if she thinks she can play this

cleanly. A good leader knows when it's time to fight dirty. Word's already out there. Yesterday it was Markel, tomorrow it might be someone else. You gotta watch out for your flock, understand?"

His point couldn't be argued. Months ago, Tamara knew this thing with Markel might sink the entire company if Rachel didn't play it right.

"I appreciate the advice, Arlen."

Burkhart rose, walked toward the door, then stopped in front of her desk. He picked up the lone picture frame sitting there and cut a bemused smile at the photo of Tamara and her niece, who everyone said resembled her more than her brother, Andre. Burkhart stared at the picture, seeming to get lost in it.

He grimaced at the photo before returning it to her desk. Even then, he seemed to dote on it until he turned his back.

"One more thing, Tamara," he said, walking toward the door. "I suggest you pay a visit to Gabriela Ramos. See how she's holding up."

CHAPTER
TWENTY-EIGHT

I was sacked out in *Wayward's* master when my sat phone buzzed on the desk near the foot of my bed. I sprung up, startled, and before I blinked the sleep out of my eyes, my hand latched onto the phone and pulled it to my ear.

"This is Jerry."

"Jerry! Jesus Christ man, I've been trying to call you all morning!" DJ shouted over blaring trop rock music. I figured he was at the helm of *Reel Fun*, skipping over the waves while he ran from one ass-kicking to the next. Most guys on a rampage preferred heavy metal, but not DJ.

"I'm here now." I slid out of bed and glanced into the salon. The door out to the cockpit was closed. I left it that way—I didn't want Alicia and Flor to overhear me.

"Where were you four hours ago when I called the first time?"

I checked my watch. It was just after 2 p.m. "I was in a meeting with Collat. Or sleeping." Alicia had caught me as I boarded *Wayward* and ordered me to get some rest. Arguing with her never worked.

"Sleeping? Nobody's got time for you to sleep, man."

"I'll sleep when I have to. And this morning, I had to." I flexed my fist until my knuckles popped. "I was up all night with Gabriela and her daughter making sure they were safe. I was doing our job."

"No, *I* was doing our job," DJ barked. "I found our guys."

My ears perked up. I was fully awake.

"Who is he?"

A few seconds passed before DJ finally said, "There's more than one. And I don't know all their names."

"*More* than one? That doesn't follow what Gabriela told us."

"I saw that guy," DJ said. "Same slicked-back brown hair, chiseled face—all that Hollywood crap. That boat I chased outside the doc's house last night came from a marina owned by a friend of mine." DJ's voice hitched. "So, I went and visited him, but he—they—"

Was he getting choked up?

Thoughts ricocheted back and forth in my brain—should I comfort him? Tease him for crying? Remind him that if he'd listened last night, things would be different now?

"DJ?"

"They killed him in his own house," DJ said. "They flashed their badges, marched into the garage and strung him up from the rafters."

"Who?"

"Blunt!" DJ hissed. "The cops hanged him!"

I heard the unmistakable clatter of dirty glasses being plopped into a bar sink. Then a woman's laughter.

"Are you at a bar? How much have you had to drink?" I bounced up the stairs from the starboard hull and came into the salon.

He didn't answer.

"The job doesn't get done if you're drunk off your ass, DJ."

"Get over yourself," DJ said. "Mr. Boy Scout! I bet if you saw one of the few friends you had left on this Earth get strung up in his garage, you'd be quivering like a pile of spat-up baby food."

My jaw clenched tightly. "Tell me where you are. I'm going to get you. We have a job to finish."

"And I'm gonna finish it." DJ sucked in a loogie and spat. With the phone up against Jerry's ear, the sound was unmistakable. "Keep babysitting those girls on your boat."

He hung up.

Everything in front of me flashed red. Before I knew what I was doing, I hurled the sat phone into *Wayward's* bulkhead. It shattered into a dozen pieces.

CHAPTER TWENTY-NINE

In all her twenty-eight years, Gabriela Ramos had never seen the inside of a jail. On TV they were always shadowy, skittering places, every actors' footsteps ping-ponging off the tall, cold walls, with prisoners leaning against the bars like starving beggars intent on ripping the flesh off the guards.

The jailhouse in Bayamón was not that. It was small. Just small. No steel bars, no inky corners, nothing cold. It was unbearably hot; in fact, the air was thick with body odor like salted onions.

Time was hard to gauge, but Gabriela assumed that, for at least two hours, she'd been stuck in a shared cell with half a dozen other women. All waited to move on to some other place while the police did whatever they had to do. In her case, Detective Collat was almost certainly poring over the conversation he'd had with Gabriela in a debriefing room in another wing of the building.

"Ramos, Gabriela!" a man's voice boomed from somewhere down the hall. The cell door clicked as a pair of guards arrived, then it slid open.

"On your feet, Ramos."

Gabriela's eyes met another woman's. A woman she didn't know, hadn't said a word to, but was drawn to by an intelligent spark behind the honey-brown flecks in her eyes. Gabriela had always thought the people in jail were criminals, but this woman reminded her of her sister, Maria.

"Pick it up," the guard repeated.

She looked away from her cellmate and stepped through the open door. The guard slapped a pair of restraints on her wrists. To her right, standing just beyond a steel door at the end of the hall, Detective Collat watched Gabriela, his eyes scanning her from toes up, then back down again.

The guard brought her to Collat. And he, in keeping with the precedent he'd set since she'd been put in his custody early that morning, said nothing. He took her from the block of holding cells, down labyrinthian cinder block hallways painted gutter gray, past more steel doors, more bars, more glass crisscrossed with steel wire, until he finally spoke.

He pointed at a white line painted across the colorless tiles. "Stand here, ma'am. Feet on the line."

Gabriela did as instructed, keeping her heels together and her hands down in front of her.

A pair of heavy double doors blocked the way. A small box clung to the wall to the right, at about chest height. Collat pushed the only button on the box. It bleated.

"Detective Antoine Collat, dropping off one detainee," he said toward a camera hanging from the ceiling to the right. He pulled his badge out of his pants pocket and held it up.

The doors clicked.

Collat grabbed her by the handcuffs, pulling Gabriela forward before she had a chance to pick up her feet. She stumbled but caught her balance.

Ahead of them, a man in a gray uniform sat behind a large, circular desk encased in glass, like the checkout counter at a gas station. His silver badge flashed under the oppressive lights as Gabriela and Collat approached.

"Stand there." Collat motioned at another white line on the floor.

While she stayed put, he stepped to the desk, then leaned his shoulder against the glass, hunching forward to talk quietly with the desk officer, never leaving her unwatched for too long.

Sweat slithered across her upper lip. Her heart tapped against her ribs. What was Collat saying? What did he want to do with Gabriela?

Before her mind went too far down that road, a lock snapped open, then a motor hummed beyond the desk, off to the left. A door opened somewhere Gabriela couldn't see, and a pair of hard-soled shoes clicked against the floor.

Ahead of her, Collat mouthed the word "thanks" and nodded at the man behind the desk, who returned the gesture. He pushed off from the glass and came to her, wrapping his fingers about the chain between her wrists.

"Nervous?" he asked.

She kept her chin high. She wanted to slap him.

"Don't do anything regrettable, and you'll come out of this just fine." Thin, red veins spiderwebbed across the whites of his eyes, and wetness clung to the corners of his mouth. She wasn't sure she could take his advice for anything.

The footsteps to her left belonged to a tall man with a shaved head, his shoulders stretching the shirt of his guard's uniform.

The way he carried himself reminded Gabriela of a boy she used to know back in Santo Domingo, a head taller than the others. He used to push the other boys around.

"Antoine!" His voice was the sound of a baseball bat breaking in a backdoor. His hard mouth stretched into a big, warm smile.

"Good afternoon, Miguel." Detective Collat shook his hand.

The two men stood face-to-face for a moment before Collat spoke up.

"You have my sincerest thanks for doing this for me. These last few weeks have been..." Collat's voice faltered. "They've been very challenging."

Miguel folded his arms and averted his eyes. Gabriela never understood why it seemed impossible for one man to look at another when emotions were shown. How hard was it to share someone else's grief—because whatever weighed on Detective Collat's mind brought along a good helping of sorrow.

"I know you were close with him," Miguel said. "But he's the lucky one—he's in the Kingdom of Heaven. The rest of us here."

Someone Collat knew had passed away. That's the best Gabriela could figure.

Collat swallowed down a lump and nodded. Then he brought his eyes up to Gabriela.

"This is Officer Oliveria." He jerked his head toward Miguel. "I'll ask you to please not cause this man any trouble. He'll take care of you."

With those parting words, he walked past Gabriela—or tried to. She grabbed him by the arm. "What about Jerry?" she asked quietly.

Collat gave her a stare that could've put a chill in the devil.

"You're very skilled at manipulating people into taking pity on you, Miss Ramos."

The chill dragged its fingers over Gabriela's back. "I've only told the truth."

"You convinced Mr. Snyder with your ghost story about a hidden murderer who managed to erase any evidence of himself. Despite all evidence to the contrary, Snyder said he'll find something to clear your name. We'll see."

Gabriela straightened her spine. *We'll see.* Didn't matter one bit if he thought she was innocent, or if she'd wiped Dr. Markel's blood across her cheek, and howled her throat ragged at the moon, because God wouldn't have brought her this far to drop her off here.

"Have you asked Christ into your heart, Detective?"

He narrowed his eyes. Collat wasn't a man of faith. The way he looked, the way he listened impassively, sunk back in his chair, while she'd laid her whole life out for him this morning had made that patently clear.

Were she convicted of the Markels' murders, Gabriela wouldn't hate Collat. She would only ever pity him.

"Someday, I hope you do," she said. "If not for your sake, or mine, do it for the next person you bring in."

He opened his mouth to say something but chewed his tongue instead. Then, he ripped his arm out of her hand, and walked away. Gabriela watched, hoping he'd say she was right or curse her for being so wrong—hinting at an ember in his cold, dead heart.

As the security door closed behind him, he did neither.

"Come on." Miguel—Officer Oliveria—engulfed her little wrist with a single baseball mitt of a hand, but unlike Collat, he didn't tug her along. He waited for Gabriela to take the first step, then he took a big stride, keeping in front of her.

They walked through another set of steel doors, her heart pounding, and her knee bones like her grandmother's starfruit jam. Another hallway stretched out before them. Same off-white wallpaper, same gray and beige tiles.

"Heard you killed a doctor and his wife," Officer Oliveria said, like he was impressed.

"I didn't."

"Of course not. But he died while you were at his house, no? Did you try calling an ambulance?"

"I couldn't." Her mouth almost felt too dry to answer. She knew she didn't sound convincing.

"Yeah? How about the doctor's house being on fire? You didn't think about calling the fire department?"

"Another man was there," she said.

Officer Oliveria's whiskered cheeks spread apart for his wide grin. "Funny. From what I heard, nobody found anything that says another man was there. But they did find your wrecked car."

"Where did you hear all these things?"

"Do you think I escort everybody who comes to Bayamón?"

She didn't understand his question. He must've read the confusion on her face.

"You listen to me and do what you're told, you'll be fine. First thing: don't go talking about how innocent you are. It makes you look guilty," he said. "Second thing is I'm going to put you in your own cell block. For your protection."

"Protection from what?"

He shrugged.

They marched toward another set of gray double-doors, which opened without Officer Oliveria having to break his stride or lift a finger.

Behind the doors a path branched three ways. She heard women's voices down the right-most, chattering like some of the busier Bible study groups she'd been to.

She followed Officer Oliveria's lead, going left. The voices grew fainter the further down the hall they went, disappearing entirely when they passed through another set of automatic doors.

In this new area, rows of steel doors ran along either wall, spaced five or six feet apart. There must have been two dozen, each painted dark as a hurricane wall.

"How long am I going to be here?" Gabriela asked.

"That depends on you," Officer Oliveria said. "You want to cooperate? You'll be outta here a lot quicker than if you lie to us or cause trouble."

He motioned to the first door on the right. A rectangular slit of glass started a few inches below the top edge, then stopped around the middle somewhere. Through it, she saw unpainted walls, a bare mattress with linens neatly folded on top. The bedframe's steel legs were bolted into the floor. On the wall opposite, a small desk.

"You're lucky," Oliveria said. "This is Bayamón's newest wing. The girls who lived here before you had to spend their last three months in knee-deep water."

The door slid open. The concrete under Gabriela's feet, clad in drab gray jailhouse-issued shoes, vibrated like a big rig was rumbling past. She approached the open door slowly. Once she crossed the threshold into a cell with two walls just a foot or so further apart than her outstretched arms, she might never come out again. Collat didn't believe she was innocent. He seemed to be a friend of Officer Oliveria, who also didn't believe her.

But Gabriela Ramos didn't wilt. Shaky knees or not, she walked into the cell, rested her right hand on the top of the steel desk, and let it cool her sweaty palm. God would protect her. This was a test of her faith.

Through a small window ahead of her she saw another squat building, lined with the same kind of narrow windows as the one she looked through now.

"Is that more cells?"

"That's Block B," Officer Oliveria answered. "You won't see them much. You won't see much of anyone, aside from me and maybe a couple other guys working here. That's the way it's gotta be for now."

"I didn't kill anyone." She turned around to face him. He barely fit inside the room. "Even if you don't believe me, I never had a trial. No judge put me here."

He pursed his lips, thinking.

"You aren't wrong about that. Collat asked me to make sure you were safe," he finally said. "Best way to do that is to keep you away from everybody else. You'll have some books brought to you here and you'll get half-an-hour a day to walk the yard."

"Can't I get more than that?"

"Probably not," he said. "Got a lawyer?"

"I don't have money for one."

Her answer gave him pause. He hooked his thumbs into his belt loops and shifted his weight. "It's probably better that way. What we're doing isn't how this is supposed to work. But my friend asks me to make sure you're out of danger, so that's what I'm going to do."

"Why would I be in danger?"

"You wasted a doctor working for a big company. You played with their money. They don't like that." He said it as if that were some kind of explanation.

Hildon wouldn't be after her. She was a good employee of the company; she'd put her best years and her best work into making Hildon Pharmaceuticals richer and better. Even when Flor was at her worst, she'd never called out of work more than she absolutely had to. So many of her co-workers and her bosses were more than just that—they were practically family. Lord's sake, since neither of them had family in Puerto Rico, she'd gone to Tamara Price's condo last Thanksgiving.

"You don't know what you're talking about. You're just a prison guard."

"Got me there," he said with a laugh. "But you think I do favors for anybody who asks me? Collat told me about you. Told me everything. He took you to a holding room this morning, right? And you told him about your girl and your debts and everything else?"

The thought of Flor sent her head spinning, but she regained herself. "That has nothing to do with my job."

"Hildon's lawyers called up Collat's local station." He paused and looked at her like that should've meant something more to her than the words he said. "You gotta understand that nobody calls up the station houses. They shouldn't have known he was working on the case, but Hildon is a big company, and probably somebody owes them favors."

"You mean you're taking bribes. I hope the money spends well." She almost spat at his feet but thought better of it.

"No one cares about paying off a prison guard," he said with a grin. "And nobody's dropping off bags of cash to precinct captains, so if you think that's happening, think again. They're just being extra nice to cops. Giving them extra work for some extra dough at a competitive rate—like running security at that big party they're about to have."

The kickoff for the new campus.

"You know how much guys are getting for that?" Officer Oliveria asked.

"No."

"Twenty-five hundred. For one night of work. And that's just the grunts I've talked to. I'm sure the sergeants handing out the extra work to their most loyal guys are getting at least twice as much. Probably one of them squealed to Hildon when they saw Collat bringing you in. Nobody wants to piss off Hildon before they get paid."

The room spun around her. She couldn't stop it this time. She plopped down on the bed in a daze.

"They didn't even like Dr. Markel," Gabriela said to herself in disbelief. "They settled a lawsuit with him. I was a good employee. I didn't kill him."

"Maybe they didn't like you as much as you thought. Maybe it's nothing personal, and they just want to shove through this whole mess as quickly as they can. An employee killing a contractor can't be good for business. Gotta be hurting their bottom line." He shrugged. "Anyway, I'm going to get you some lunch. How do you feel about bologna and mustard?"

She didn't answer.

"Well, that's what you're getting." He unlatched her handcuffs, then turned his back to walk out of the cell but stopped short. "By the way, I'll have someone from the infirmary come take a look at those filthy bandages on your arms."

He walked out. A motor in the wall whined, and then the door banged shut.

She'd almost forgotten about the wraps on her arms. Now, with nothing else to focus on in her bare, gray cell, she couldn't stop her fingers from picking at them.

Contacting Dr. Markel was a mistake, Lord help her. And she'd like to say she never would have called him had she known this would have happened, but she couldn't lie to herself. Flor was too important.

An employee murdering a researcher wasn't a good look for Hildon. She knew that. Pharma corporations like Hildon worked tirelessly to keep a benevolent face. Their business models revolved around convincing the public that they were working toward cures and bettering mankind and whatever else they could say to keep people from digging too deep.

A majority of the drugs "researched" by Hildon and companies like it were actually researched by smaller, independent labs like Dr. Markel's. Those labs then turned around and sold the rights to Hildon, who then handled production and marketing.

Getting the patent was the most important thing. A patent granted a small monopoly over a treatment for a disease, and as long as companies like Hildon followed the rules, they were perfectly within their rights to set the price to whatever they felt the market owed them for "innovating."

The drug Markel had developed to treat Li-Fraumeni syndrome, the drug Hildon bought the rights to, Anthradone, had an extenuating set of rules. Li-Fraumeni syndrome was a special disease—a rare disease—and treatments for rare diseases were given legal exceptions to normal drug pricing controls.

In the end, Anthradone would probably get sold to patients

for tens of thousands of dollars a treatment, maybe more than a hundred thousand. Faced with the prospect of putting down a home's worth of money on a drug treatment would've put most people into a tailspin.

Gabriela was already so far in debt, what did an extra zero or two added onto the bill really matter?

Those extra digits only mattered to Hildon, really. They inflated the company's value, which added to their stock price, which kept the real money coming—the money that came from investors.

Officer Oliveria was right: this was all about protecting an image for the business. Investors didn't like any kind of legal entanglement. The quicker Hildon sewed up this mess with Dr. Markel, the less of a threat it became to their revenue stream.

Hildon may have been in pharmaceutical research when they started out, but they'd left it as soon as their name became an abbreviation sliding across a stock ticker. They were little more than a highly specialized bank now. One focused entirely on extracting as much money as they could from medicine.

Gabriela Ramos's life was nothing more than a cost-benefit analysis now. Would putting her in jail lower the company's overhead, regardless of whether she committed a crime? Answering that question was everything now.

Her blood boiled as her fingernails dug deeper into her palms. She had only just noticed the drop of blood that fell onto the top of her pale sneakers. She unclenched her hands, and stared at her wet, red palms.

The Lord would guide her. The Lord would save her. He could not let the unrighteous destroy Flor like this.

Angel of God, my guardian dear.

CHAPTER THIRTY

"I'm going up to the marina," I said as I came through the salon door and onto the cockpit. Alicia looked up at me from her spot on the couch, Flor's eyes glanced in my direction, then scurried away.

"Are you going for a run?" Alicia's ability to read me outmatched my own. A run sounded good. A run was what I needed.

I pulled my sneakers out of the compartment next to the swim platform gate, put them on, then hopped off the swim platform and onto the dock. "I'll be back."

A jog would cool me off. Exercise usually did. I spent most of my free time jogging or swimming or snorkeling. I was always a three-sports kid growing up. Football in the fall, wrestling in the winter, lacrosse in the spring. It kept me even. Kept me focused.

I leaned up against the nearest post, stretched one quad, got too impatient to stretch the other, then took off at a trot. My body slowed and focused on doing a job, shedding the jitters like a drunk steadying his hand to toss back his first nip of the day.

The dock pilings vibrated as I cleared them, one after another after another. A colony of gulls wheeled overhead, as if worried about the trouble they smelled coming off me. I ignored them, letting them disappear in the soupy air as I ran up the dock steps, then through the marina parking lot.

While my legs carried me, my mind wandered. It replayed my phone call with DJ, wondered what Gabriela was doing at this moment, and visited the ghosts of six men who were behind everything I did now. My strides lengthened, my pace intensified and before I knew it, I found myself running full bore along the shoulder of a road I didn't recognize, my pulse driving up and down my body like a sonar sweep.

I stopped. I wasn't aware how long I'd been running. My T-shirt stuck to me from collarbone to navel, my legs throbbed, and my feet hummed. I planted my hands on my knees, fighting to catch my breath for the first time since DJ'd hung up on me.

When I brought my eyes up and surveyed the craggy green hills taken hostage by stretches of flat scrubland, the liar in me said running up those hills and hiding in another of Puerto Rico's low, concrete houses would be easy. I was healthy, just this side of thirty, with a bank account that could tend my physical needs until I died decades from now.

Meanwhile, I'd spend the next fifty or so years locked in the worst agony I could possibly experience. I wasn't cast as a hermit. I owed too many people. So, I turned around and ran back.

At the marina office, I threw open the front door, then turned right and grabbed the first cell to catch my attention. I didn't notice the brand or care about the features. I just needed something that could make calls, take pictures, and wasn't in pieces across our bedroom. I'd order a new sat phone and have it shipped from the States. Maybe a few of them, the way I went through them.

The same girl from before worked the register. I approached, then dropped the phone on the counter between us.

"How was the run, Mr. Snyder?"

"Therapeutic." I was still out of breath, but my head was clearer.

New phone in hand, I made for the door. No matter how far I ran, this wasn't going away, and work waited for me on *Wayward*.

I walked down to my boat, thinking about my next move. DJ was out of the picture now. All I could do was let him disappear. Collat might be some help, but I had to take care not to go back to that well too soon, or I was sure, as Bob Marley said, "the bottom a-go drop out."

Why had that song sprung into my consciousness? When I lived in California, I assumed his music was primarily Jamaican, but all through the Caribbean, people seemed to see him as a mystic of some kind. And lately, some of his words had taken on new meaning. In that particular song, the sheriff had harassed Bob over and over, as habitual as going to the well each morning. Then one day, he'd had enough—the bottom fell out of the bucket—and he shot the sheriff.

Who did that leave me? Stockwell? I didn't want him involved. Not this early into my work with Armstrong. If I gained a reputation of incompetence, I was as good as done.

Gabriela? What was she going to do for me?

I looked up to see my wife standing in *Wayward's* cockpit, waiting for me. "Good to have you back."

"You can't get rid of me that easily." I handed her the package with the cell phone, then came aboard the swim platform.

"Where's Flor?"

"Tired." A spark of anguish played across her face.

"What's wrong?"

"I knew you weren't feeling right when you woke up, so I didn't want to put this on you…" Her words trailed off.

I wrapped my arms around my wife and pulled her close. She didn't care about my sweaty shirt. Her little hands rubbed my shoulder blades, and she kissed my neck, then I let my arms slacken. The tension was like pebbles under her skin.

"What if we don't bring Gabriela out again?" Alicia's jaw trembled.

The only response I had was wrapping my arms around her shoulders and pulling her close again. Between the straps of her tank top, Alicia's flesh was smooth and firm and her ribs trembled against my waist. Her hand clutched the top of my shoulder, and she buried her face against my neck.

A string of heat unfurled down my chest. One of her tears. I stroked her silky blond hair.

"I don't quit until Gabriela is out of jail," I finally said. "That's a promise."

"Flor's not eating. She misses her mother." Alicia kept her cheek against me. "She's already so little. She said the doctors told her she was done with chemo and radiation, but what if her nerves get her now?"

"I shouldn't have asked you to do this," I said. "It's too much."

Alicia pulled away from me. My arms were still locked around her, but there was space between us. Her eyes locked on mine. "I'm here because I want to be here."

I kissed her on the forehead. "You're right," I said, then kissed her again.

"This hasn't been easy on you, either."

"This is new for all of us."

Alicia laughed. "Is that doubt I hear?"

This time, I backed away and stared at her.

"It's just funny," she said. "All that training you did? The guy who used to tell me," she took a step back from me and swelled out her chest and arms, "'I'm Special Forces. I'm a Jack-of-all-trades, master of none. I can jump out of airplanes, run a swift boat, survive outdoors as long as I want, do surgery with a couple sticks, and shoot a hole in a dime.'"

She'd deepened her voice, too.

"That's not a brag," I said. "I *can* do all those things. And more."

"And you, Jeremiah Arlen Giuseppe Snyder the Third, can do this too." She tapped my chest.

I knew she was right.

"You didn't have to say my middle names out loud."

She rolled her eyes. Then she put her arms around my shoulders and kissed me. "Giuseppe is a cute name."

"That's not the one I don't like."

"I had to annoy you just the right amount to snap you out of whatever funk you're in," she said. "And don't tell me you aren't. I saw you run up that dock."

Why bother denying it? She'd get it out of me eventually, anyway.

"It's DJ," I said. "He's the human equivalent of stepping on the neighbor's dog's turd."

She laughed. "At least he's good for a surprise. Keeps life interesting."

I nodded. "He said he found the man who burnt down the Markels' house."

Alicia wrinkled her brow and blinked at me. "Shouldn't we go help him, then?"

"I'd like to, but he's drunk, Alicia. He's been at a bar all day."

"With the guy he arrested?"

"We don't have the power to arrest."

She rolled her eyes at me. "Detain, hold for the police, whatever."

I grinned. "I don't think he's *arrested* him yet—I don't know if he's even seen the guy." I stepped past my wife, toward the steps up to the flybridge. "I can't count on DJ's help. We've got a little girl in there," I motioned toward the salon, "with her mother in jail, and the man I need to arrest in order to prove she's innocent and get her out is—"

I shook my head, ending my thought.

"Out there somewhere?" She leaned against the stairs, and a corner of her mouth slid toward her ear. "You did this job before DJ. We can do it without him."

We *had* to. If DJ wanted to drown himself, that was his choice. Man-to-man, I wouldn't intervene. It'd be hard, and I had a sense that fixing this whole mess would take a miracle, but I'd do it.

I came off the steps, then flopped down into the cockpit couch, my arms and legs suddenly heavy.

"Things are different from what we thought they'd be, aren't they?" Alicia turned her chin up, her eyes studying the underside of the cockpit awning. "Guess that's the way it's always been."

She brought her eyes to mine and grinned at me.

I chuckled and smiled right back at her. "Sticking to a plan isn't really my thing."

Which reminded me of Arlen. I hadn't told Alicia that he'd called me. The moment that realization popped into my head, my smile faded.

"What?" Alicia asked.

"There's something else I need to tell you."

She broke contact with the stairs and took a slow step toward me.

"Arlen called me yesterday." I didn't want to let the words out. As if not saying it would keep it from being true. "He's in Puerto Rico."

Alicia's mouth flexed into a thin line. "Why?"

I spat out a bitter laugh. "Why does Arlen ever do anything? He's got a business interest in Hildon Pharmaceuticals."

The tension in Alicia's lips spread across her face. Then she took a breath through her nose, puffed her cheeks up and blew out the air. "That's okay," she said. "What's another curve ball? We don't need to worry about him right now. We can keep clear of Arlen. No matter what he thinks or says, he doesn't get a say in your life, Jerry. He never has, right?"

I knew that. But so did he. It never stopped him from trying.

"Jerry?"

I brought my face up, meeting Alicia a step in front of me. She put her hands on my shoulders.

"Maybe you should take a minute, and—"

"No, I've already taken a whole day. We need to get going."

I didn't know exactly where we needed to go, but it had to be somewhere away from here. I started to rise to my feet when Alicia's hands clamped onto me, keeping me on the couch.

"Maybe you should take a minute," she repeated, "and call Gene."

I tilted my head. "Gene? Why?"

Alicia ran her fingers through my hair. "It's okay to ask for help when you're lost."

CHAPTER THIRTY-ONE

I sank onto the couch in *Wayward's* salon, my legs throbbing from the run, but my head cleared. Without DJ's cooperation, I had to figure out my own way forward. Getting Gabriela out of jail was my first priority, meaning I had to prove her innocence, which I would do even if I had to nab our suspect out from under DJ.

A knife sat on the counter to my right. I grabbed it, then sliced open the package with our new cell phone and its charger. No sooner did I have it open than I realized I needed a SIM card before I could call Gene. I went down to the master stateroom.

The sat phone lay in pieces on the bed like little rips in the image I had of myself. I gathered the pieces together, laying them on the foot of the bed, and wondered where I got off warning DJ about flying off the handle when I did something like this?

I dug my old cell phone out of a drawer. Most of my contacts would be on it, but it had gotten wet and I'd replaced it with the sat phone. The SIM card was still locked in its slot. I slipped it out.

On my way up to the salon, something else grabbed my attention. A black rectangle about the size of a file folder sitting on my desk. In all the troubles I'd stumbled through today, Dr. Markel's laptop had completely disappeared into a misty corner of my mind.

I tucked it under my arm and brought it, and the new cell phone and charger, with me to the flybridge. I put the SIM card in the phone, then plugged the charger into a USB port near the helm. After turning the phone on and doing a couple things for the initial setup, it was ready to dial.

All of Gene's numbers had been committed to memory a long time ago. On my first deployment, I had problems getting a region-free phone to work in Afghanistan, so I always ended up buying one from a local and dialing numbers from memory. I put in the number for her office and hit send.

"Snyder Commercial Real Estate Group," her secretary, Olivia, answered.

I remembered Olivia well. She'd come on when Dad still ran the show. Whenever I was deployed, she sent me a care package about halfway through each tour, like clockwork. Always stuffed with homemade cookies and instant coffee that came with self-heating pouches.

God, I loved those instant coffees. I always kept one on me, in a little pocket on the upper arm of my cammies. That way, I always had one when I was sure to get an undisturbed half hour. I'd sit back in whatever FOB dug into an Afghan hill I'd been stationed in, dump that stuff in a spare canteen, and savor it. Or eat the granules of coffee straight-up when I needed a boost of energy on the move.

Thinking about the grit of those freeze-dried grounds between my teeth made the hair on my arms stand on end as I sat down in the helmsman's chair.

"Olivia? It's Jerry."

"Jerry!" she squealed. "How are you! I haven't heard from you in so long! How's married life? How's the Caribbean? When are you coming back to visit?"

I smiled. Olivia's enthusiasm was infectious. It would not be denied.

"Married life is good; the Caribbean is beautiful as ever. Things here are great. Couldn't be better. Hey, is Gene in? I had a couple things I needed to ask her."

"Oh, sure!" Olivia said. "I'm gonna put you on hold. And tell Alicia I said hi!"

"I will."

The phone clicked. Jazz fusion music played over the earpiece for a few seconds, then it clicked again.

"Jerry?" My sister, Gene, sounded perplexed, like I'd been launched to the moon and left behind, alive, and forever unreachable.

From her end of the call, I heard laughing. Not polite laughter like a dinner party or a group of friends—it was the rude, combative howling of old men in suits with their shirt collars buttoned up so tight, they had to force the air through their throats like a jackhammer.

Cigar smoke and scotch practically leached from my phone.

I pictured my sister with them. She was tall, like me, with the same runner's build Dad had given both of us. But where I had Dad's hair with Mom's face, she was the opposite. She looked like our father—sharp chin, long nose, an intelligent, but empathetic quality when she looked you in the eyes, paired with our mother's dark, straight, Italian hair.

She stood apart from all the old businessmen I'd ever seen her with—even when Dad was still around—and they wouldn't let her forget that she *was* different, not for too long. But Gene was never intimidated by them. She got that from Dad too.

We both did.

"I've been meaning to call you," I said.

"You better have," she said with a big laugh. "Living it up in the Caribbean. So, what's new down there? Any cults try to kill you lately?"

"Not lately," I said. "But I'm nibbling at the edges of something."

"If you get in too much trouble, I'm only a plane ticket away. I'll be down there as soon as you need me, ready to kick the ass of whoever's bugging my baby brother."

"They wouldn't know what to do if you came down this way."

Another round of laughter rattled out somewhere near Gene. Somebody shouted her name.

"These guys are animals, Jerry. Every time I lie down, my liver feels like a bowling ball pushing on my spine. I think you did the right thing by choosing to go live your own life down there."

"Sometimes I wonder," I said.

"I thought you had it all figured out—is that oceanography job not working the way you thought it would? What could go wrong with it? Sunburn? Eat the wrong kind of oyster? A pod of dolphins break some of your stuff in half?" She paused for a second, then followed up with, "That's what you call a group of dolphins, right? A pod?"

"I wouldn't know," I said.

"Some scientist you turned out to be."

"I'm not a scientist, Gene. I wouldn't know the first thing

about doing oceanographic research. Look, I gotta get this out right now: I'm not sure what oceanography even is. If somebody from NOAA came down here and put a gun to my head, I couldn't tell them which way the wind usually blows around St. Thomas."

She said nothing. I heard her name being called by a gravelly, male voice, but she didn't answer it. She couldn't answer it. The pieces were coming together in her head. The little brother who'd bowed out from the family business, the jock, the veteran, the ex-cop, the guy who'd had his life threatened on his honeymoon, but, somehow, *didn't* find that threat compelling enough to turn around and never come back to the Caribbean—he was up to something.

"Jesus," she finally said. "I thought those army ads about getting a job after leaving were all bullshit. Anybody with their head on straight knows being in the army doesn't make you qualified to run a bank—but here you are. Working for an oceanography company. They really *are* hiring ex-army guys just because, aren't they?"

"Not exactly." And she knew that—she had to know that. Gene was doing her Gene thing, teasing me. "I was Air Force, Gene."

She laughed.

"My job isn't what I told you," I said.

"Of course, it's not. And just so you can keep your cover story straight, Jerry: oceanography is exactly what it sounds like. The study of the ocean. Of all the plants and animals and everything else inside it. It's an interesting job. Even a guy as addicted to adrenaline as you might want to give it a legitimate shot."

I snorted and shook my head.

"Come on," she said. "Did you think I believed you were going to give it all up to live the quiet life on a boat? That's not you. I know you're keeping your blood pumping. Whatever Arlen has you doing, you know you can always come back here to be safe."

My back snapped upright. "You think I'm working for *Arlen?*"

"Jerry, you can drop the—" then she went quiet. "Are you saying you're not?"

"That's exactly what I'm saying. Why would I work for Arlen?"

"Well, I assumed," she said. "You had that meeting with him after you came back from your honeymoon—what was that about?"

"I was telling him off, Gene. Just like I told you I did." I threw my head back against the top of the chair and stared at the bottom of the Bimini. "But that didn't do a whole lot of good."

A pregnant pause came across the phone. She knew more than she let on—Gene always did. "Has he stopped by in person yet?"

"You knew he was out here? Are *you* working with him now?"

"No, no, I would never risk my reputation. A Snyder working with Arlen Burkhart brings bad memories for a lot more people than you, me, and Mom."

"Even ten years after the big breakup?" I asked. I hadn't kept up with the family business since my enlistment. Partly because I had too much to handle, partly because I didn't want anything to do with Snyder-Burkhart Holdings. The more completely I removed myself from it, the better.

"Old men have long memories. Most of the developers I've met are still living like it's the 80s. More than a few are surprised they have to shake my hand. A couple of the senile ones still ask me how Dad's doing. I've told them that they won't have to wait much longer to find out for themselves."

I laughed. My sister's caustic wit always got me.

"You didn't," I said.

"Of course, I did. These people are a captive audience. They want my money. I can insult them for days on end, but so long as I sign the checks, all is forgiven." She chuckled softly. "It's sad, really, what they'll take for the chance at a buck."

"Anyway, what do they have you doing there?" Gene asked. "Fighting terrorists? Blowing up cars in Cuba? Waiting offshore for the Venezuelans to invade?"

"Christ, no. It's nothing like that. I'm an investigator. I'm working with another guy out here, and we've been trying to help the Puerto Rican Police solve a murder."

"So, you're a cop again?"

"As close to one as I'll ever be. And that's why I called. I need a sounding board, Gene."

"Well, Jerry, I'm—I'm honored that you'd think of me. But what about Alicia?"

"We talk," I said. "She's the one who recommended I call you."

"She did?" I could practically hear Gene thinking through the phone. *What can I do to help?*

"I'm not a detective or anything," she said. "I don't even like those cop TV shows about forensics or whatever."

"That makes you an even better candidate," I said. "You've always been good at seeing all the moving pieces, like Dad."

"Please. As if you're somehow worse?"

"I do okay. Anyway, wanna hear it?"

She waited a moment to answer. Thinking more, which surprised me. Gene always ran on instincts, always had a decision conjured at the snap of her fingers. Maybe she was trying to think of a polite way to say no.

"Well, Jerry, I don't have all day. Lay it on me," she said.

That's what I did. I laid it on her. As much of it as I could, starting with our initial meeting with Detective Collat, to my visit to Luc's boat and Nick Garner's free-love paradise, to the VA, the double murder, then turning in Gabriela, to now.

I tried to include everything—including the inaccessible laptop sitting within my reach.

"Have somebody crack it," she offered, instantly.

"Have somebody what?"

"Crack the laptop. Get into it without using the password. Hack it."

I scratched my eyebrow, feeling the skin pucker next to it. "You can do that?"

"I did. And you would've seen it happen if you hadn't already flown off. Which was probably better, because everyone knows you're a squealer and the kid who did it charged me an embarrassing amount of money."

"A *kid* did it?"

"He was a teenager, I guess, but you know how it is, Jerry. The next generation is always better with technology than the last. For him, getting through a computer password was no sweat."

"How'd you find him?"

"Olivia."

Her secretary, Olivia. Instant coffee, Olivia. *That* Olivia knew a kid who could break into computers, no sweat.

"I don't think he can help you. He's Olivia's nephew from Calabasas, so getting him out to Newport Beach was a little bit of a deal. St. Thomas seems like a big ask."

"That's fine. I think I've got someone who can cover it for me." Armstrong had to have *somebody* on staff, or at least know of a person who could crack Dr. Markel's laptop.

"Well, Alicia was right again. You're a hell of a sounding board, Gene."

"Glad I could help." A new voice bled into the call. *"Christ, Snyder, what're you talking to your secret boyfriend back here?"* one of the businessmen groused.

"Why?" Gene replied. "Jealous I've got a boyfriend and you're still looking?"

He let out a long, cigar-stained laugh.

"All right, are we square here?"

Took me a second to realize she was addressing me.

"Yeah," I said. "Thanks for the help, Gene."

"Any time, baby brother. And can you *not* wait three months to call me next time? I know you're busy, but come on, Jerry, you're breaking my heart. I want to hear about island life—about catching dinner, drinking rum out of coconuts, and hot, bronze natives. Invite me to the next luau."

"That's Hawaii."

"All right, well whatever they do there, invite me?"

"Sure," I said. "Love you."

"Love you too." She hung up.

The phone number for Jack Armstrong's boat, *Ambrosia*, buzzed in the back of my head.

I went straight into my next call.

CHAPTER THIRTY-TWO

Set on getting into Dr. Markel's computer, my phone call to Jack Armstrong's boat, *Ambrosia*, was all business. An operator named Chip directed me to a freelancer out of Vieques, Puerto Rico: a woman named Macy Lane with some kind of cybersecurity background who had worked with Armstrong in the past.

Her name sounded fake, but I didn't care for details. Her name could have been the Hacker Formerly Known as Macy Lane. Armstrong's endorsement was good enough for me.

Once I got her number, I sent her a text—per Chip's instructions—and we got the ball rolling.

She gave me coordinates for a public mooring field in a bay near the town of Isabel Segunda on Vieques. *Wayward's* GPS said the trip was about sixteen miles, including a small bend in our course around the South Chinchorro Shoal.

We covered the distance in less than two hours. Alicia tended to Flor on the way, and I kept to the helm, motoring us toward a mooring ball rolling with the gentle waves. I'd already rigged two dock lines to the forward cleat on both bows but would need help.

I called out to Alicia.

"Just steer where I point with this," I said, holding the boat hook. "You might have to shift in and out of gear to keep us steady until I get the lines tied. Ready?"

She nodded and I went forward on the starboard side. We'd talked about this maneuver before but had never really done it yet.

When I reached the bow, I chose one of the buoys right in front of us. The mooring line coming off it was trailing at an angle to our approach.

"Turn right," I yelled back. "We need to line up with it in the current."

Alicia did as I said, and I pointed toward the ball with the hook. "Back to the left now," I shouted.

We were coming up to the line and I got into position, pointing the hook in the direction for Alicia to steer. I reached for the line near the ball and yelled over my shoulder. "Neutral!"

I quickly tied the two dock lines through the loop at the end of the mooring line with a bowline knot and tossed the slimy mooring line over the front of the trampoline. The current was light, and it took a few seconds for the lines to become taut.

We'd done it.

Once Alicia shut down the engines, she went into the salon to check on Flor, while I worked on getting *Wayward's* dinghy ready to take us to shore. I stepped onto the swim platform and worked at the dinghy's stern line. I'd never launched a dinghy before, but the salesman said all I had to do was take off the line, hit the button, and let the hydraulic arms lay the dinghy in the water.

Before I had the line untied, I heard Alicia opening the door to the salon. I looked over my shoulder to see my wife coming out, wearing a loose, light dress, with matching sunhat, holding onto a blue and white striped bag, ready to depart.

"Are we doing a little shore excursion?" I asked.

"It'd be smart to look like it."

She had me there. "What about Flor?"

"She's fine," Alicia said with a knowing smile.

"We can't leave her here alone."

"I've been monitoring her. She's been eating well; she's been moving around on her own. We won't be gone too long, right?" Alicia said.

"I'm not sure. Hopefully no longer than an hour, but I don't want to leave her on *Wayward* alone."

"She'll be fine, Jerry, really. Just look at her."

From my position on the steps leading to *Wayward's* stern, I turned back and looked through the salon door. I could just make out the upper-half of Flor's head, a paisley bandanna holding back the last scraps of her dark hair. Her eyes turned down, studying something in her lap.

"What am I looking at?"

Alicia opened up a compartment under the cockpit couch and pulled out a pair of sandals. She slipped them on.

"You're looking at a beautiful thing. A kid just being a kid."

As soon as she said it, I caught a glimpse of the top edge of Alicia's laptop screen. The computer rested on Flor's lap. Light played across Flor's face, and she smiled. My stomach untangled. It wasn't until I felt my gut soften that I realized how on edge I'd been in—I couldn't begin to guess how long.

The brief tour I'd had of Gabriela's apartment spoke of an existence of subsistence. In the living room, only a couch, a TV and Flor's hospital bed. Now that I thought about it, Gabriela had only packed two bags between herself and her daughter that night, and one carried solely medicine.

On the couch in the salon, Flor smiled for the first time I'd ever seen.

"What if something happens while we're gone?"

"She's been walking on her own this morning. She has plenty of food, plenty to do. The boat is quiet, she can sleep if she's tired. She can stay up if she's not. Jerry, she asked me if she could stay here alone."

"She did?"

Alicia nodded. "She just wants some time to be alone and relax. I left my phone for her, and told her how to find your number, just in case. We can give her an hour, right?"

"I can't even imagine the things that kid's been through already," I said with a heavy sigh. "What's she going to do without her mother?"

Alicia reached out and put her hand on my shoulder. "We'll never know."

"Yeah." My fingers pulled at a knot on the dinghy's stern tie-down line. "You got the laptop?"

"I wouldn't leave home without it."

"Where would I be without you?" I hopped up from the swim platform, found the controls for the lift, then lowered it down. It wafted into the calm, warm waters without a hitch. Once I had the cover off, I turned back to my wife.

"Ladies first." I helped steady Alicia as she went aboard. When she settled in, I took her bag with the laptop, made sure the button was fastened, then handed it over. I jumped in and lowered the engine, pumped the little ball valve like the salesman had shown us, then turned the key. The motor came instantly to life and I untied the line.

Compared to something as big and lumbering as *Wayward*, handling the dinghy was a breeze. It carried us through traffic and moored boats like a sparrow zipping between branches. I felt sure enough in the dinghy that I let myself look right, toward a boxy lighthouse, gray as a thunderhead pouring over the rocky, northern bluffs of Vieques.

At the dinghy dock, I tied us on before helping Alicia disembark, then I followed her. We didn't have to wait long before I spotted our contact.

Macy Lane didn't send me a description or a picture, but the instant I laid eyes on the short, fair-skinned, dark-haired woman wearing an old T-shirt and a pair of jeans that fit her like she'd traded a carton of cigarettes for them, I knew it was her. She wore the clothes of somebody too wrapped up in pursuing an interest to care about much else.

And, from twenty paces off, she didn't look like a tourist or a native to Vieques. The charming Spanish architecture didn't draw her eyes off her phone, and she wasn't rushing to sell the tourists anything.

"Macy?" I asked as I got closer.

"Snyder," she answered, in a noticeably thick Eastern European accent. She pulled her eyes from her phone, ran them up me, then down Alicia. "And you must be Alicia? Let's go."

Alicia and I exchanged a look after Macy turned around. She set off toward the same kind of buildings you'd find in quaint downtown areas in smaller cities across America. They were two-story, shoulder-to-shoulder, losing paint like gray hairs.

"You're shorter than you looked online," Macy said.

"You found pictures of me online?" I wasn't active on social media. Hadn't had an account anywhere in at least a decade.

"It wasn't hard. You have several photographs available, and an old profile."

"From what? And how old?" I thought back through the years but couldn't pin down anything concrete. Maybe an update for some of my old friends when I went into PJ school? Could have been one of Dad and Arlen's charity things. They always liked having photographers at their baseball games, and blackjack nights, or…

"Nine years, roughly," Macy said. "Nine years, six months, and a handful of days. I don't remember the exact timestamp. It's not important. The photograph I saw came from a fundraiser dinner for Meg Whitman's run at governor of California in 2010. She's a business friend of your father's, I assume?"

"Are you trying to impress me?" I was annoyed that she'd snooped on me. And I vaguely remembered that dinner.

That time in my life was clearer in my mind. Echoes remained of my dissatisfaction with the tracks laid out in front of me—carefully staked down by Dad since before I'd wet a diaper. Much the same way Grandfather did for him. The distaste for the Snyder family lifestyle had become too strong to deny, though I wouldn't talk to anyone in my family about it for years.

"I wouldn't dare try to impress the very impressive Jerry Snyder," Macy continued as we side-stepped a local selling dozens of flooring tiles painted with sunsets over the water. "I want you to be aware of the fact that once something gets on the internet, it's never getting off."

"Thanks for the tip."

"It was so easy to find you online, Snyder," she said with a smile. She eyeballed Alicia, giving her another up-and-down.

"But you were much, much more difficult. So difficult, all I managed to dig up was your wedding announcement with one of your engagement photos. You're practically a digital ghost."

"I am?" Alicia elbowed me, grinning. I pretended not to notice.

"Have you considered going into the security business?" Macy asked her. "I know a wonderful man in Abu Dhabi looking for someone who fits your description."

"Not a chance in hell," I said.

"I'm a nurse by trade," Alicia said more diplomatically. "Oncology first, then physical therapy. I'm past my prime when it comes to learning something new."

"Nonsense. You'd be a natural. I have an eye for these things. You can work for me. I've also got more contacts than I can handle at any one time, and I'd be happy to throw them to you. I usually have to make people wait for weeks before I'll see them."

"You didn't make me wait except for the time it took to get over here."

She smiled at me and cocked her eyebrows. "For you, I made a special exception. Isn't that nice of me? Besides that, I'll have the job done before you know I've done it. Cracking a password is child's play—everyone knows that."

Almost everyone.

"Did you bring the machine with you?" she asked.

"Right here." Alicia lifted the bag a few inches, then let it gently fall back to her side.

"Good. We're nearly at my office."

Passing a convenience store, we hooked a left around a wire carousel packed with novelty T-shirts, after which we faced a dirty, cramped alleyway. A rat the size of a terrier scurried from a trashcan, dashing for a sewer grate ahead and to our right. It managed to squeeze through the bars and slip into the darkness just as I was close enough to tug its tail—not that I did that kind of thing.

"That's Asimov," Macy said. "Best not to pay attention to him. He's a drama queen."

"You're friends with the alley rat? Very cool."

"I hoped I was wrong, but I knew you'd be a patronizing person, Snyder," she retorted. "You barely know me, but I'm sure you're certain you're better than me. I care for animals, so what? You didn't have horses back at Keystone Manor?"

How in the hell did she know the name of my grandfather's old mansion? I pretended not to care. Macy winked at me, not breaking her stride. She started up a set of rusty steel steps going up the back of a building. Alicia and I followed.

On the third floor—the top floor—she put a key into a dead-bolt, then turned it open. She stepped aside, and motioned for us to go in.

I'm not sure what I expected from a supposed computer security expert with a distinctly eastern European accent, but before I stepped one foot into Macy Lane's office, I got the impression there was more to her than what I'd gleaned from my first... impression. Maybe she had some kind of foreign backing. A Russian oligarch was possible, or maybe she was some kind of double-blind in Armstrong's pocket.

Or maybe she was as independent as she claimed. If she had half as much business as she boasted, I expected an office packed with high-tech computers and screens and all that crap. Something out of *The Matrix*.

Imagine my surprise when I turned the corner and found an

empty room no bigger than *Wayward's* salon. And it was truly empty. Nothing on the walls, nothing on the floor, not even carpet. We stood on bare subflooring, which bowed toward the middle of the room. Actually, there were a couple of things in the room; a cracked banquet table that Macy was pulling off the wall to our right, and a pair of folding chairs.

"Let me help you with that." I reached for her and the table.

She looked at me like I'd grabbed her ass.

"I don't need your help." She let the table smack on the floor, belly up. "I have made it this far without a big, strong man to set up my table." She flipped each pair of legs up, then struggled to get the table upright. She couldn't quite turn it over without the legs catching against the floor.

"Here." Alicia handed me the bag as she walked past, then helped Macy set the table right without catching a single word of flak.

"Alicia, so helpful!" Macy said earnestly.

If that wasn't an attempt to get my goat, I didn't know what was. Lucky for Macy, I had lots of practice ducking verbal jabs.

She and Alicia each took a folding chair and set them out next to each other. My wife sat down, then patted the other chair, beckoning me over.

"Only if it's the egalitarian thing to do," I said to Macy.

"Stand on your head for all I care, Snyder. All I want to have from you is that laptop in your bag."

I guess I wanted her to have it, too. So, I walked over, set the bag on the table, took the laptop out and put it in Macy's waiting hands.

"Do you have the power supply?" She set it down and lifted the lid.

"Nope."

"Just as well," she said. "I should have something in the back."

She went through a door on the opposite side of the room. I caught a glimpse of monitors filled with code, computers sitting in racks below, cables hanging off neatly organized pegboards, along with tools and spare parts.

A minute later, she returned, laptop in hand. "Why does this laptop smell like…" Her nose twitched. "…smoke?"

"Long story." I motioned at the laptop. "Did you crack the password?"

"Of course," she said. "You know, I can do more than run a script to unlock a machine."

"Whatever we're willing to pay for, I'm sure."

"I am running a business."

"Maybe she can find us the formula for Anthradone," Alicia said.

It took me a second to place that word, Anthradone. Then, I remembered what Gabriela had told me the night DJ and I took her in.

"You misunderstand," Macy said. "I was talking more about malware, keyloggers, self-replicating worms. Have you ever seen one of those in action? Hook an infected machine up to a network, and watch the real fun happen." She sat the laptop on the table and typed, the glow of the screen reflecting off her pale skin.

"Thanks for the offer, comrade, but we'll pass," I said.

"I'm not Russian. I'm American. Not that it matters." Macy turned the laptop around until it faced us. "Your machine is unlocked."

On the laptop's screen, I saw a picture of Dr. Markel and his wife—the first I'd seen. Her hair was like ink ribbons, his short and silver. Dr. Markel must've been past retirement age. They looked happy, sharing a deck chair, holding hands, probably planning for a future of rest and relaxation on the Puerto Rican coast. I held in a sigh.

The next thing that caught my eye was a small yellow folder on the system's desktop labeled BAPTISTE. Inside, I saw hundreds upon hundreds of documents. I clicked one, the laptop's hard drive whirred to life, and a white sheet of paper crammed with tiny, black lettering appeared. I saw pie charts, graphs. Some kind of test summary.

Summaries from tests weren't going to help us. Gabriela had said the laptop had a formula for the drug Flor needed.

The next document was the same as the last: tiny letters, numbers, data tables. I scrolled through the folder, paying attention to the file names, seeing if any one stuck out.

At the end of the folder, nothing grabbed me. If Dr. Markel had prepared information for Luc, it wouldn't necessarily have the formula for the drug Flor needed. Luc was a journalist, not a doctor. Over the next few minutes, I dissected more folders, searching for the word Anthradone.

Nothing.

I put my hands on my hips, let my head fall back, then blew out my cheeks. How in the hell were we going to comb through everything on this machine to find what we needed? It'd take weeks, at least. Meanwhile, Gabriela Ramos sat in jail.

"We'll find it." Alicia put her hands on the small of my back. "I know we will. Those reports could have had useful information."

"There could be thousands of them on this machine. Maybe a million." I said.

"I can get through them," Alicia said.

I faced her.

"I'm a nurse, Jerry." She held her hand toward the laptop. "I wrote and filed hundreds of reports like this when I worked for Dr. Branson. I must've read a half-a-million—you learn to digest them pretty quick, or you're buried under a yard of printer paper before you know it."

Alicia had a point but getting her more involved in this whole mess didn't seem like the right thing to do.

"No, I'll figure it out," I said. "Somebody at Armstrong has to know somebody else. They have analysts that can handle something like this. You can't—"

"I can," she said firmly. "Whether or not there's a formula for whatever treatment Flor needs in there, that information could very well be the reason that Luc guy was killed."

She side-stepped me, moving to the laptop, then set her hands on either side of it, and hunched over it like a bomb ticking down to zero.

"I don't know about you, but I wouldn't think somebody would go through all the trouble of killing Luc and Dr. Markel unless the information on this laptop was very… sensitive," Alicia said.

"I'd kill anyone who took one of my machines," Macy said. "Out of principle."

"Let me take a look at this, Jerry. I know you want to protect me, but I'm already involved."

Alicia had a look in her eyes that I hadn't seen since we'd left California. Sure, she'd been a good sport about the move, and she played like her life on St. Thomas was okay, but I knew this was coming, especially since she'd left her job.

All that mental energy and nowhere to spend it. She needed this badly, maybe worse than I did, and that might've been what scared me the most. But keeping this task from her would create resentment.

"All right," I said.

She almost held in a tiny squeak of excitement. She kissed me, scooped up the laptop and the charger, and then put them in her bag.

"What a good husband," Macy said with a crooked smile.

"I know I am. How much do I owe you?"

"Nothing," she said. "You call me next time you have a job that needs doing."

"I'm not one for charity," I said. "I can pay whatever you like—"

Macy's eyebrow arched.

"—within reason," I quickly added.

"Then pay me with a favor. Tell Mr. Armstrong what I did for you, and that I'm interested in heavier work if he's got it."

"I thought business was booming."

"It is," she said, "but I want to do something *fun*."

CHAPTER THIRTY-THREE

G abriela's first night in the Bayamón Correctional Women's block was cold and quiet. She lay in bed, but if she slept, she didn't know it. God was her only companion, and prayers meekly recited to the ceiling were her lullaby.

Officer Oliveria came to her door shortly after dawn broke into her cell. With a few words, he guided her through the gray labyrinth of prison hallways to the cafeteria for morning chow. She wore the same formless shift Collat had given her yesterday. Loose as it was, it pinched and clung awkwardly to her skin as she slid through the chow line, collecting a slurry of different breakfast foods.

Before she had a chance to sit down and pick through scrambled eggs, a guard she didn't know approached her. She was Dominican too, her crimpy hair pulled back in a tight bun. She was a few years older than Gabriela, with high cheekbones and eyes hardened with scrutiny.

"Ramos," the guard said.

"Yes, ma'am?"

"Put your tray down. Come with me."

Gabriela looked down at her food. It wasn't appetizing, but that didn't stop her stomach from wanting it.

"Are you soft, Ramos? I said leave the food behind." She slapped the tray out of Gabriela's hand. The rattle it made reverberated through the cafeteria, cutting off all conversation, and drawing every eye.

A shiver rattled up Gabriela's throat.

"Back to your meals, inmates!" a large, bearded man bellowed from across the room. "And somebody clean that up before I have to ask twice."

Most of the other girls went back to their food, picking up their conversations where they'd left off. An old woman with skin the color of wet sand and hair as light seafoam doddered over with a bucket of murky water and a dishrag. She went to work on the mess.

"What do you want with me?" Gabriela asked the guard.

"I want you to let me do my job before I lose my temper." She grabbed Gabriela's arm and slapped a pair of handcuffs on her. "Let's go, Ramos." The guard dragged her through the cafeteria, then out the exit.

They went down another maze of indistinct hallways until they came to a dead-end. Almost. A door waited on the left wall with a guard posted in front of it. Gabriela's guard stopped her and unlatched the handcuffs.

"Visitation is ten minutes. Kindergarten rules: no touching, no kissing, no hugging. Keep your hands visible at all times. I will be watching you."

She pulled the door open and shoved Gabriela through.

Gabriela found herself in a brightly lit, brightly colored room with half a dozen small, square tables with about as many people hunching over a couple of them, talking softly. Some wore pale gray inmates' uniforms, others were in regular street clothes which, since she'd been locked in a gray smear, almost hurt Gabriela's eyes. The high windows reinforced with steel wire dispelled any illusion she might have had about being free of Bayamón.

"Hi…Gabriela," a familiar voice said, haltingly.

At the centermost table in the room sat Tamara Price. Gabriela's skin puckered as a chill crawled over her scalp. What was she doing here?

Ms. Price rose to her feet. She looked at Gabriela as if the guards had resurrected her from the floor of her cell. Ms. Price stepped forward, then stopped. Her arms came up from her sides, then went back down, her fingers becoming a tangle while a tear rolled down her cheek.

"I'd hug you," she said as she swiped at her eye. "But the guards told me not to."

Gabriela approached slowly. This was wrong. She shouldn't be here. Inside her mind, a shard of primordial instinct slipped into her consciousness—should she run? Scream? Fight? Why was Tamara Price here? How did she know where Gabriela was? What did she want?

"Gabbie? What's the matter?" Tamara didn't move, and, somehow, that drew Gabriela closer. "What happened to your arms? Were you hurt?"

Gabriela struggled to pick an answer. Her head was a jumble of truths and lies and questions. Then, one thought snuck past the rest. "I was."

"Did that happen when—"

"My arms are the least of my problems." Gabriela managed

to keep her voice low.

"Your last twenty-four hours would've flattened me." Tamara's voice was fragile, yet in control of itself, despite the tears wandering down her face. "I have so many questions."

"Me too."

"Did you sleep?" Tamara asked. "Are they feeding you? Did you want—"

"Why is Hildon blaming me?" The words came out of Gabriela before she knew they were there. This wasn't her. She was possessed. The sleeplessness or the fear—something had taken hold of her. She was so far from her meek center, she was out of her body.

An inmate's face turned Gabriela's way. She moved closer to Tamara to keep their conversation out of other peoples' ears.

"Blame you for what?" Tamara's eyes grew wide. "You don't think Hildon is trying to convict you for what happened?"

"Murder is rough on business. Hits the stock price in a bad way. My whole person reflects on the company, right?" Gabriela stopped at the table. She laid her hands on the back of the chair opposite Ms. Price. "A judge may take my person out of this jumpsuit, but in a lot of eyes, I'm wearing it the rest of my life."

"Honey, you're tired. You're not making any sense. Would you please sit down for a minute and talk with me?" Tamara motioned at the chair Gabriela rested her hands on. "I'm worried about you, Gabbie. You're not made for a place like this. You're acting paranoid."

Gabriela sat, though she didn't want to. "There aren't people in that boardroom of yours who want this over as quickly as possible?"

"They want you back. Humanity was robbed of a brilliant

man and they want justice for him. Gabriela, you haven't slept, you're in a new place—"

"I'm in jail."

Tamara's lips puckered. "You think Hildon is out to get you?"

"It makes sense. I don't know." She shrugged.

"Be clear-headed, Gabbie. Think for a second. None of this makes sense. The way you're talking right now makes the least sense of all." Tamara's eyes darted side to side, then she reached across the table, letting the smallest part of her fingertips brush against Gabriela's balled-up knuckles. "Are the guards telling you things?"

Gabriela *was* being paranoid. God in Heaven, what was she doing? Why would she be so rough with Tamara?

She combed her hair back from her face and bit her lip to keep herself from crying. All these emotions swirling inside her were going to tear her apart. Tamara Price was the only person at Hildon to have a relationship with Gabriela outside of work; the only one to meet Flor. What about the Thanksgiving they'd spent together? Would the woman who made candied yams and a turkey just for the three of them turn on Gabriela?

Across the table, Tamara's expression forced Gabriela to avert her eyes.

This was all wrong. "They said someone at Hildon contacted the detective working my case. Why would anyone do that?"

"That's why you're upset? Honey, the person who contacted Detective Collat was me." Tamara let out a ragged breath and relaxed her body. "After the meeting at work, I had to find you. The police hadn't processed you yet, Gabbie, so I called a contact, who called someone else, who got me in touch with

Detective Collat, who told me you were here."

God help her, how had Gabriela become so lost she couldn't tell her friends from her enemies? Tingles played under her eyes. Before she knew it, she was crying. She wiped them away with the sleeve of her jumper.

"No one at Hildon is out to get you," Tamara said. "I'm here, meeting you, with Rachel Little's blessing. She knows how much you mean to me, and I'm doing my best to get you a great lawyer on Hildon's behalf. We take care of ours. You'll get out of here, and you'll be with Flor before you know it."

The tears stopped, but the ruts they'd cleared across Gabriela's skin remained hot and sharp. She was out of her mind. "I'm so sorry. I'm sorry."

"Shhhh..." Tamara reached for her but pulled her hands back. "One of the cops told you Hildon was coming after you. Am I right?"

Gabriela nodded.

With a sigh, Tamara pushed her hair back from her face. "They're all the same everywhere, aren't they? Just looking to blame somebody and move on.

"You know, back when I was a kid, growing up in East Point, my brother was taken in for something one of his dumb friends did."

Gabriela picked her head up. Tamara Price had always kept her past at a distance—that much had become obvious to Gabriela at the Thanksgiving dinner at Tamara's. Since she wasn't spending the holidays with family, Gabriela was certain of some past trauma. Maybe a relative with bad habits or an abusive parent. At least, that's why Gabriela never visited family. She'd left them in the Dominican Republic so as not to see her father again. He'd kicked her out at seventeen.

"Don't get me wrong; my older brother had a juvie rap sheet as thick as a Bible, and he was taken in later, on his eighteenth birthday, but this particular time, he was clean. That didn't stop the police from trying to trick him into believing things that didn't happen. Saying his friends gave him up, or they had tape of him, or somebody saw him. There's no lie they won't tell just so they can get you to confess to something you didn't do and make their conviction rates .01 percent better. They're going to play on every fear of yours they can find."

Officer Oliveria had done just that, hadn't he?

"Then what am I supposed to do?"

"Be fearless." Tamara laughed.

She couldn't say what was funny about that, but Gabriela laughed too. Then an uncertain feeling settled between them.

"I'm sorry I came at you the way I did," Gabriela finally said. "The truth is I'm scared like I've never been. I'm scared for Flor. But more scared that when I get back to her, I won't be able to trust anymore, and I won't be the same person."

"You can trust me." Tamara leveled her eyes on Gabriela. "You know you can."

"I know." That might've been the only thing Gabriela felt certain about since she'd been dragged into Bayamón.

Tamara's eyes shifted away from her. "There is one thing I have to know about the night before last. They found your car totaled at the Markel's house. How did you get home? Did you walk?"

Gabriela should've known she'd have to discuss some part of what happened. And, considering the vulnerable position she'd placed herself in by coming here, Tamara deserved to know the truth. Not only that, but she also had to tell someone about Jerry, someone she could trust to keep an eye on him.

"A man took me home," she said. "Someone I'd never met before. He showed up at the Markels' that night, pulled me out of my car, took me back to his boat, patched up my arms, and he's been helping me ever since. He and his wife took me on their boat to San Juan so I could pick up Flor."

"Sounds like you found a good Samaritan."

"God has a hand in it all. Jerry was there by chance, investigating the murder of that journalist, Luc Baptiste."

Tamara's eyes went wide. "The guy Ms. Little hates? The one that tried to dig into her ex-husband's finances?"

Gabriela nodded. She'd never mentioned the bad blood between Luc Baptiste and Rachel Little to Jerry. Just didn't seem important. Rachel Little had nothing to do with the journalist being killed.

"What's his name?" Tamara asked.

"Jerry Snyder."

"And he's a cop."

"I don't think so. At least he's not *La Uniformada*."

"Private eye?"

"I don't know," Gabriela said. "He has money. And a partner, I think. They're crazy enough to do what they do for fun. I'm not sure. They both used to be in the military."

"And Flor is with this man now?"

"She is," Gabriela said.

"Do you want me to check on her? How do I find this man?"

Gabriela couldn't answer. She didn't have Jerry's number, or his address. She'd only ever been to his house in the dark and couldn't pick it out—she wasn't entirely clear what part of St.

Thomas he lived in. Suddenly, she felt much less assured about leaving her daughter with the Snyders.

Then, she realized how Tamara could find them.

"Collat," she said. "Detective Collat knows how to reach him."

CHAPTER THIRTY-FOUR

After a night spent banging around the inside of *Reel Fun,* The Club Nautico de San Juan felt downright cavernous. At least, it had the prettiest bar DJ Martin had ever seen in a marina. Sitting at it made him feel like a wart on Mona Lisa's nose.

His sweaty, bare arms stuck to the polished ebony wood bar top. A dribble of Medalla Light rolled down his goatee, until it let go and swan-dived on the spit-shined brass rail, dead-center between his crusty New Balance shoes.

The big window behind the bartender let in a stirring western view of San Juan Bay past the marina docks, where *Reel Fun,* bathed in the pure mid-morning light, fit in a helluva lot better than DJ did at the bar.

That was the problem with San Juan: he didn't know where the good dives were, so he had to settle on whatever he could find through the internet, which wasn't much.

"Another one, sir?" the bartender asked. DJ was fairly sure the bartender had on the same outfit DJ had worn as a grooms-man in his brother's wedding a few years back.

"Yeah, man. Hit me with a fresh pair." Stuffy as the place might be, the beer was cold. Took the edge off just as well as the cans opened in fishy dives.

The bartender slid the cans to DJ just as a lady in a floppy-brimmed sun hat came up on his right and ordered a mojito. She looked clean as a bird colonel's boots. That pretty hat alone probably cost twice as much as DJ's wardrobe.

DJ gave her a smile and nod, just like he'd do to any other woman he met at a bar. She responded by pretending not to notice, even if he was close enough to crank his arm around her liposuctioned waist. As the bartender put a napkin under her glass and slipped it across the bar to her, she gave him a side eye.

"I don't smell that bad, do I?" Self-deprecation always broke the ice.

Except she wasn't having it. She walked back to her booth, where a few yuppie-types in pastel shirts and fresh-out-of-the-box deck shoes were yukking it up all afternoon.

DJ sniffed his armpit. It wasn't the worst, but it wouldn't get turned into a scented candle. He guzzled down the rest of his open beer.

"Mr. Martin, would you care to look at our menu?" the bartender asked, as he took DJ's empty can and tossed it in the trash. A nice way of saying DJ was stinking drunk and on the verge of running business off. Either sober up or get out.

"Coupla' brews is all my body needs right now, my man, but I thank you for your concern."

"Would you care for a complimentary bottle of Perrier, then?" As he asked, the bartender dipped his hand into the cooler, twisted the cap off the sparkling water and set it in front of DJ before he could say no.

"Appreciate the hospitality." DJ tilted a beer can toward the bartender, cracked it open, then took a deep drink. Without thinking, he closed his eyes. By God, they were shut a half-second longer than a blink when he saw Blunt's face puckered up and blue, his eyes receding into his flesh, like old buckshot stuck in a tree trunk, sinking deeper every season.

DJ slammed the can down and hid his eyes under his hands.

What the hell was he gonna do? DJ had never been a spiritual man. Maybe there was something out there, a God, or a Spirit, or a big mass of fire and dust out in space from which all things were spat—but what was he going *to do*? Pray to it? That'd be like a termite praying to him, rolling on its back, and beseeching an indifferent God who would just as soon ignore it as inadvertently squash its little body and send it reeling into oblivion.

Nothing would exorcise the flashes of Blunt zipping around behind his eyelids. If a man could leave behind a ghost, or a psychic impression, or whatever some yahoo with a few nice-sounding prayers believed, Blunt's manifestation was within DJ, feeding on him.

And Blunt's spirit would keep coming back, keep tearing off the edges of DJ's mind until he fed it the offering it craved—blood.

Prayers were wind. Prayers could not pool in your hand. Prayers would never run through a man's fingers. Prayers would never feed the Earth, or run sticky down your legs, furiously pumping out of you while you begged your brothers for help.

On the bar, next to DJ's hand, his satellite phone rang. He inhaled sharply, like he'd cried without tears, then picked up the phone and answered.

"Make this worth my time," he said.

345

"It's Chip." The analyst from Armstrong. Same guy who'd traced *Purple Haze* back to Blunt's marina on Culebra. DJ's hand tightened on his beer.

"What did you get?"

"The address you asked for. I just... are you with Jerry Snyder? Because you told me you two are normally partnered together for assignments, and he just called me, asking for a cybersecurity contractor—and now you want this San Juan address, and..."

The kid was getting too nosy for his own good. He knew something was off. He'd probably report any irregularities to the higher-ups at Armstrong unless DJ threw him off the scent.

"It's all right if you're suspicious. You're just doing your job, but keep it on the hush, alright?"

"Alright," Chip said.

"Normally Jerry and I are together," DJ said, careful not to raise his voice loud enough for the bartender to hear. "But he and I had a sit-down last night. There's a lot of ground to cover with this one, and not enough time for us to do it all together. We both know it's counter to the way Colonel Stockwell wants to run the show, but it'll all come out in the wash. He'll be okay with it as long as we catch the bad guys."

"I guess that makes sense."

"Trust Jerry, son. He may be new to Armstrong, but he's a real sleuth," DJ said. "Now, you got that address for me?"

"Yessir." Keyboard keys clacking came through Chip's end of the call. "Are you ready?"

"Go ahead."

"99 Calle B, Dorado, Puerto Rico."

DJ repeated the address in his head. "You're sure that's the right place?"

"Ninety-percent confidence," Chip said. "Since our call last night, I was able to get a few pieces of information about PRP officers with the last name Dos Santos. From my research, the name Dos Santos traces back to three officers in the Puerto Rican Police Force. One, a captain that worked in the force around 2002—I found him through a news article that quoted him as a newly minted FOP regional manager working a charity soccer tournament. So, I counted him out.

"The second was a woman who worked as a parole officer in 2015. I was able to figure all that out by chasing down her LinkedIn profile. She moved to Florida in late 2016 and started work for a private prison corporation.

"That left the man I believe to be your guy: Adrian Dos Santos. He gave a statement to the media three months ago when he was part of a PRP-DEA joint raid. His picture matched the description you gave me, so it's my belief that he's your guy."

DJ straightened up in his chair. *Got you, you son of a bitch.*

"So that's 99 Calle B, Dorado, Puerto Rico," DJ said.

"DJ, I want to stress my ninety-percent confidence level: could be there's another Officer Dos Santos out there, so please bear that in mind as you proceed."

"You know I will. I just want to talk to this fella, and I'm not about to say anything stupid before I know who he is."

"Why'd you want his home address anyway? Can't you meet him at his station?"

"No, that's too risky," DJ said. "Keep this on the hush, but Jerry and I believe somebody in his department killed the victim we've been looking into. I don't want nobody to see me talking to him. Understand?"

"Yessir, I understand."

"You've done a good thing, man. Thanks for all your help." DJ ended the call before Chip had a chance to respond.

No time to waste. DJ hopped off his barstool. The floor rolled under his feet, but he grabbed onto the edge and kept from going ass-up and embarrassing himself.

"I wanna settle up," he announced as he got his legs under him.

"Please drink your water before you leave, Mr. Martin." The bartender slid a bowl of pre-packaged crackers to DJ. "And would you consider some crackers? Are you planning on driving or boating anywhere?"

Normally, DJ would have scarfed down as many crackers as he could stand. But there wasn't a normal thing that had happened to DJ Martin in the last three days. Still, he could use a little food in his belly. He put a few packages in his pockets for later.

"Yeah, man—but how about my tab?"

"I'll get it right away, Mr. Martin."

Once the bartender returned with a receipt, DJ signed it, gave the man a hundred bucks for a tip, and decided to get out of Dodge. Those yuppies at the booth eyeballed him as he wobbled to the exit.

"Don't mind me," he said, knocking his prosthesis into the wooden corner of their booth. "I usually walk like this."

They didn't say anything. Too busy being mad that somebody like DJ would have the nerve to not sit quietly.

DJ spilled out of the front door into the piercing sunlight. Once he remembered where he'd left her, he meandered toward *Reel Fun,* and was back in the salon, digging in a floor compartment for a tool bag. This particular bag was a surplus GI duffle bag he'd picked up from an Army/Navy store in Fort Myers, Florida.

The straps felt like an old friend's hands clapped on his shoulders, though the pack was much lighter than what he'd gotten used to in the service.

After he had what he needed, DJ disembarked *Reel Fun*, making his way toward land, ignoring blondes giving him looks and pesky kids skipping all around the dock. Eventually, he was street side. With his sat phone, he called for a cab, which arrived about five minutes later—just as the sun was reaching its apex in the sky, scouring him with its harshest glare. He blinked and saw Blunt, then got in the cab.

The cabbie yelled something at him. Or maybe he hadn't? The world was turning like a capsizing boat.

"I said 99 Calle B, Dorado, *Puerto Rico*," DJ heard himself grumble.

Jesus. Did that bartender spike his beer? How many did he have anyway?

Later, the car stopped in a rough-looking neighborhood in a small suburb on the western edge of San Juan, about a mile inland from the north coast.

He opened the door, stood, and took in a lungful of the fresh sea air, laced with burning rubber and frying grease. He stepped onto the sidewalk in front of a little bar and grill, then turned around and slipped the cabbie a fifty for the ride and a tip.

"I'll keep your number," DJ said.

"Okay." The cabbie waved him off.

DJ closed the door and the cab rumbled away. Now, all he had to do was get his head on straight while he waited for the sun to go down.

CHAPTER THIRTY-FIVE

The water in Bahia de Mulas, cupped by land to the east and west, was as serene as a grandmother's smile. The wind teased ribbons of Alicia's blond hair, one of her hands clamped to the crown of her hat, the other cradling Dr. Markel's laptop in her bag.

Good life I was living, all things considered.

Then, my phone rang in my pocket. I was pulled out of my swaddle of good vibrations. I let go of the dinghy's throttle to answer. Caller ID showed a number I didn't recognize, but it was local, so I answered anyway.

"This is Snyder."

"Hello, Mr. Snyder, how are you?" A young woman's voice asked. She had an American accent, very proper, like she'd paid for coaching, and it wasn't cheap.

"Things were going good a few seconds ago."

Alicia looked at me, bottling up a laugh.

"I'm pleased to hear that. Mr. Snyder, you don't know me, but my name is Tamara Price. Detective Collat from the PRPB gave me your number."

Great. Collat was giving my number out. Did he think I needed more work?

"If you're in a bind, I'm sorry, but I can't do anything for you right now."

"I know. You've been assisting my friend, Gabriela. I'm sorry to call with bad news, but she doesn't seem to be adjusting to life in Bayamón."

My stomach sank. "Is Bayamón a prison here?"

"That's correct." Tamara paused a moment. She said part of a word, stopped, then went back to the board and plotted out a new thought. "I know she didn't murder anyone."

"That makes two of us." Actually, five of us, at last count.

"I know who did."

"Unless you're calling me to confess, I'm going to have a hard time believing that."

"Are you familiar with an investigative journalist named Luc Baptiste?"

I tipped to the side, then braced myself against the dinghy's gunwales. If she knew how Baptiste tied into this, she was closer to answers than I assumed.

"I am," I said, trying not to give everything away.

"Mr. Baptiste was tapped to help Dr. Markel blow the whistle on some malfeasance at Hildon. I'm not at privilege to give specifics, but the information the two of them planned to reveal would've been extremely damaging to certain people in the company."

"Like who?"

"Rachel Little, the CEO."

"She killed Luc Baptiste and the Markels?" I asked.

"Not herself," Tamara answered. "I believe she hired hitmen

to do it."

"Do you have evidence of this?" I found this difficult to believe, but certainly not outside the realm of possibility. The idea of Hildon's CEO being the guilty party was worth entertaining, at least for a few minutes.

"I do, but I can't share it with you at this time. Not until you do something for me."

"So, your help is conditional? Do you think this makes me want to work with you?"

"It poses some difficulty, I'm sure," she said. "However, I'm part of the management team at Hildon. Unlike Dr. Markel, I have an ethos that precludes me from openly sharing sensitive information. I'm of the opinion that this is best dealt with inhouse."

"Yet you called me."

"My opinion is you are the right man, in the right place, at the right time, Mr. Snyder. You're helping my dear friend, Gabriela, and there's nothing I want more than justice to be done."

Good God. I could smell it blowing through the phone. I thought people like Tamara Price were trapped in my rearview mirror.

"Let's be honest. You also want your boss's job," I said.

"I won't try to mislead you. Yes, I want to be CEO of Hildon Pharmaceuticals. Who, in my position, with my pedigree, and my aspirations, wouldn't?"

"And what aspiration would that be?"

"To be the youngest CEO of a Fortune 500 company."

I silently retched. Alicia gave me a puzzled look.

"You've got the chops for it," I said.

"Thank you," she said. "Gabriela told me she took a laptop from Dr. Markel's house. That machine is considered property of Hildon, and contains documents not meant for public consumption. I'll expect you to return it to me now."

"Sorry, I don't know what you're talking about."

"I don't want this to become an adversarial relationship, Mr. Snyder. We can work together."

"What relationship? I could be looking at you right now, and I wouldn't know it."

"I want to get my friend out of prison. She didn't murder anyone, but so long as that laptop is out of Hildon's possession, you can be assured they'll do everything in their power to prosecute her."

"Now you're not part of Hildon?"

"I'm not part of legal."

These people always deflected. Never around to eat the blame, but happy to suck up the credit.

"You remind me of someone I grew up with," I said. "I didn't like him."

She sighed. More for my sake than hers.

"I'll be in contact, Mr. Snyder. For Gabriela's sake."

After Tamara ended the call, Alicia gave me a curious stare.

"Telemarketer," I said.

"Seemed like an aggressive sales pitch."

"Some lady named Tamara Price. Said she was a friend of Gabriela's, but I got the impression she didn't have Gabriela's best interests at heart."

"Think we should tell DJ?"

I shrugged and turned the throttle. The dinghy puttered toward *Wayward*.

CHAPTER THIRTY-SIX

The sun went down over DJ's right shoulder, but he didn't notice. The sweat on his T-shirt channeled the cool, evening air to his skin, but it didn't make him comfortable. He sipped his beer in a chair outside the bar, but it didn't quench his thirst. The chair was probably meant for the bouncer. In the empty lot across the street, a gecko streaked from a sun-bleached plastic toy car to a wooden box. Birdsong rang out. Wouldn't be long before one swooped down and snatched the gecko for dinner.

He took another sip of his beer. His duffle slumped over against his leg, and his thigh muscle twitched, ready to get on the move. So, DJ gulped down the rest of his beer. He held the last sip in his mouth, letting the slight aluminum tang settle over his taste buds, then spat it out.

He picked up the duffle bag, slung it over his shoulder and turned his eyes to the empty lot across the road.

"You're on borrowed time, friend," he said to the gecko, though he couldn't see it. "Make the most of it, while it lasts."

DJ started down Calle B, walking over the cracked, grassspackled sidewalk. To all outward appearances he looked like a bum hunting for a good tree to sleep under. The houses he passed were built like shoeboxes and painted like birds of paradise.

He hardly saw a soul. Sure, a pack of kids played soccer in the street, and a plump woman beat the dust out of a rug draped over a fence, but no one gave him a second look. Bums probably weren't out of place on Calle B.

The street was cracked worse than the sidewalk. More than one house looked abandoned, and more than one car parked street side was up on cinder blocks or a rusted-out jack, waiting for somebody to get a bug up their ass and finish the repairs.

Every boxy house had a security fence—some taller than DJ, most made from wrought iron. A handful were chain link, but others had concrete bases thick enough to shrug off a head-on with an '84 Chrysler. Front yards were mostly sand, with palm trees providing sparse shade. Gardens popped up in raggedy patches where there was no shade at all.

DJ only noticed the houses because he was scoping the yards for good hiding spots, and at the same time, checking for house 99, which he found about a dozen lots from the intersection at the north end of the street where the bar was.

Like the others, 99 Calle B was a boxy house with a gravel driveway and a picture window on the front of the building, trapped behind steel bars.

Nobody was home. At least to DJ's eyes. The front window was a black rectangle, and the set of four divots in the gravel said a car would be parked there. Or would be, whenever the right honorable Officer Adrian Dos Santos decided he'd had his fill of hanging fat hippies in their garages.

An image of the rope they'd used to kill Blunt, its strands

coming off like split ends, swung through DJ's head. He blinked it away as he stepped off the sidewalk in front of 99 Calle B and hunted for a place where he could observe the house without being seen.

A single lot northward, he spotted a place that looked abandoned. There was a rusty car in the yard, which was being overtaken by reedy grass. Broken windows. Rusty lock and chain hanging on the front gate. But most promising of all was a thicket of overgrown bushes around an old tree in the abandoned house's front yard. From there, DJ would have a clear line of sight into Dos Santos's driveway. All he had to do was get inside the security fence.

As he shuffled slowly northward, DJ kept his eyes ahead and his pace steady. He didn't want to draw the attention of the kids down the street. The abandoned house's front gate looked awfully suspect. One good push, and he might snap the chain apart. He had to walk up to it without any kind of cover or concealment and try his luck.

When he came to the house's front gate, he checked to make sure nobody was looking his way. Satisfied, DJ examined the lock and chain. Now that he'd had a closer look at it, something jumped out at him; the chain rested on a horizontal cross-member at eye level, and there was nothing to stop him from shimmying the chain up the wrought-iron fence and slipping it off the top.

So, working quickly and quietly, he did just that. After he passed through the gate, sure that he was undetected, he put the chain back where it was.

DJ moved about halfway up the driveway, watching the house for any signs of movement inside. Darkness was quickly settling in. All the freaks would be out soon, and he didn't want to get ambushed by some junkie squatter with a rusty needle.

After giving the place a once-over from the front yard, he went to the southeastern corner of the lot, to the old tree and the overgrown bushes. The bushes were prickly little things, snagging on his jeans and T-shirt, but so long as he protected his eyes, he'd be fine.

Once inside the heaviest part of the thicket, DJ noticed he couldn't see a damned thing except a wall of green leaves and the dust under his shoes. Unless Dos Santos shouted out his name when he pulled into his driveway, DJ would never know he was there.

The lowest branch of the tree was about six feet from the ground, behind and above DJ. It stretched out over the fence and had plenty of leaves. In the darkness, it'd be hard to spot him, so long as he stayed low. DJ pulled himself up until he was sitting on the branch.

Chin-ups were a damned joke when a guy didn't have to contend with the weight of half a leg. The titanium prosthetic, even with a sneaker on, didn't weigh four pounds.

Straddling the tree branch, he could peer through the leaves well enough to see the entry to Dos Santos's driveway. All he had to do was make sure he didn't fall out and break his neck.

For the next three hours, DJ sat on that tree branch and sweated out the day's beer in the dark, watching cars and stray dogs go by. Nobody looked up.

It wasn't the first time DJ had sat perched in a tree to watch. Most people thought very linearly. They surveyed their surroundings at eye-level or looked down at the ground. So, rooftops and trees made for great observation posts.

Around 9 p.m., a car's headlights slowed in front of Dos Santos's house. They lit the front entrance as an electric motor kicked to life, and the gate moved out of the way.

A grim anticipation came over DJ. There was nothing like catching an enemy unaware—especially one who had tormented you.

The headlights disappeared up the driveway. The engine stopped as the gate moved back into place. A single car door slammed. Good. He was probably alone. Dos Santos was humming a little tune to himself, and his footsteps sounded uneven. Apparently, he'd been out drinking. DJ smiled.

When the front door slammed shut, and DJ saw a tattered square of light shining through the leaves, he checked the duffle bag's strap on his shoulder, then scooted forward on the branch until he'd passed the fence beneath him. Then, he lowered himself down.

Not a soul up or down the street. Perfect.

DJ crouched low and scrambled to the nearest cover—the rear-passenger side of an old Chevy truck with a flat tire. He crouched on the sidewalk, then scouted Dos Santos's front window once more. Satisfied, he hid again, then slipped the bag off his shoulder and opened the drawstring.

Aside from the money he kept in an outer pocket, a few entry tools, and a single MRE, there was a knit hat, a pair of latex gloves, a box of double-aught buckshot, and a short-barreled Mossberg 500. He brought the gloves and hat out, putting them on. Next came the shotgun and shells. The gun felt good in his hands, like justice waiting to bark out its judgment. He quietly opened the receiver, slipped a shell in, then inserted five more into the tube magazine.

He closed the box of shells, returned it to his bag, then tossed the duffle into the bed of the truck. If the truck's owner came back, fixed the tire, and took off before DJ could get back to it, oh well. Lucky enough to find the cash, lucky enough to keep it.

Holding the shotgun, he stayed hunched over and went to the back of the truck. Nothing to see through the living room window of Dos Santos's house. The light had been turned off, which raised the hair on the back of DJ's neck. He needed eyes on his target. He needed to know if Dos Santos was cracking beers in his kitchen or pulling something out of his gun safe.

Lingering at the back of the truck, DJ watched for movement. No cars had passed for some time. He heard nothing except the tick of the car's cooling engine across the street, and the faint sound of salsa music shaking through the muggy night air.

A concrete post at the corner of Dos Santos's neighbor's yard looked like the perfect entry point for DJ to hop the fence, so he darted across the street, staying low.

He leaned his left shoulder against the post, keeping his shotgun ready to snap upward and fire. Before he brought his eyes around and exposed himself to enemy fire, he listened. Bugs chirped a block or two away, a night bird cackled, and a dog barked far down the street, toward the bar.

When he darted a look around the post, he saw Dos Santos through the wrought iron fence. He stood at the kitchen window on the north side of the house, staring across his driveway at the neighbor's wall, an empty shot glass in his hand.

Dos Santos couldn't have been more than twenty yards off. An easy shot, even with the short barrel and the wide choke on DJ's Mossberg. Might not kill the guy, but he'd have a hell of a lot to think about when shards of his kitchen window went flying into his face.

Of course, that'd make it impossible to get information out of him. DJ had a few questions burning in the back of his head.

Unaware that a violent death was just outside his window, Dos Santos boogied away from it, swinging his shoulders, and bobbing his head to music DJ could just hear coming from the house.

DJ couldn't lose sight of him. He slipped his shotgun through the iron bars of the fence, into Dos Santos's yard. Then he pulled himself on top of the short concrete post. From there, he had no trouble swinging his legs over and sliding down the vertical bars of the fence.

Once he had his feet under him, DJ picked up his Mossberg and hurried toward Dos Santos's car—a very nicely kept late model BMW i5.

Snuggled up against the front left tire, D. J. was suddenly aware that the skin under his goatee itched like hell. As he scratched it and smacked his lips, the air took on a copper flavor, and the low thuds of salsa music bleeding through concrete seemed to knock around inside his ears. In that moment, DJ felt his eyes could pierce the darkness, that he could see the birds sleeping in trees and he'd be quick enough to catch a possum with his bare hands.

Been a while since he'd felt like that. Maybe since he'd helped McDermitt pick off those acid-brained cultists. No, there had to be a couple times since then. Maybe Port-Au-Prince.

Mark Antony's famous phrase popped into his head: "Cry 'Havoc!' and let slip the dogs of war." It felt good to be let off the lead. To be the invader. To not have somebody wagging a finger at him while he did the things that took courage to do. It wasn't

DJ's fault that the world was a violent, chaotic pit full of folks eager to shove their fingers in somebody else's eye. The only thing that might be his fault was ensuring that anybody who tried to poke his eyes out instead pulled back a bloody stump.

DJ focused himself. He had to stay on the mission. He got down on his hands and knees, peering under the car and across the backside of the house. He saw the patio table lit from a yellow glow spilling through a frosted window.

Dos Santos was in the bathroom.

Not wasting a second, DJ sprang up. He ran around the front of the car, but as soon as he did, something else caught his eye. A length of rope. The same kind of rope they'd used to kill Blunt. It lay on the car's dash, for anyone to see. The son of a bitch had balls the size of Jupiter, DJ had to give him that.

Instead of running to the back door, DJ made a short detour. He walked over to the passenger side of the car and checked the handle. The door opened.

How could anybody leave their car unlocked at night in a neighborhood like this? Then again, DJ would bet that everybody on the block knew Adrian Dos Santos was the kind of cop that'd cuff you before he bashed your head into the wall.

He grabbed the rope off the dash. Must've been ten feet of it. DJ coiled it around his chest so that it ran from his left shoulder to the opposite hip.

That done, he aimed himself toward the back door. Seeing it there, knowing what he was going to do, made his nerves hum and his lungs gulp for air.

DJ was a door kicker again. Just like every other time, this might be the last time ever. He felt charged, energized.

He stopped a few feet from the door, then pivoted so that his left shoulder propped against the wall closest to the knob. He held the Mossberg out from his body, left hand on top of the barrel, right hand gripped tightly to the pistol grip, fingertip on the forward part of the trigger guard. He aimed where the door met the frame, just beside the doorknob, and his finger moved to the trigger.

The shotgun roared and swung backward in his arms like a battering ram on the rebound. Buckshot hammered the door, the sound bouncing off the neighbors' houses and cars, startling a yappy dog next door. The door stubbornly held fast. DJ pumped the shotgun, then adjusted his grip on it once more, and squeezed the trigger. This time, the door reared back and the knob cracked clean off.

Salsa music blared out louder than the last Megadeth concert DJ had gone to in Fort Lauderdale. He wondered if Dos Santos even heard the gunshot, but it was smarter to work on the assumption he had.

Before entering, DJ glanced around the corner. Ahead was a small kitchen, and beyond it the front of the house. To the left, a doorway to another room. No Dos Santos. Every moment DJ hesitated gave advantage to his enemy. So, he rushed in, took the doorway left, and found himself in a small hallway. The only light came from a door to his left. He opened it up.

Dos Santos was naked, leaning halfway out of the shower. He'd been caught completely unaware and unprepared. Probably the music inside the house was so loud, he either didn't hear the shotgun blasts, or mistook it for something else.

But now that he and DJ were eye to eye, Dos Santos put it together.

"En serio?" His lip curled at DJ.

"Oh, I'm serious, man. Believe that." DJ motioned with the shotgun, signaling him to step out of the shower.

He did. One heavy leg at a time, his eyes transfixed by DJ's shotgun, as if he'd spot the buckshot flashing out and sidestep it in the same instant. He raised his hands until they were even with shoulders the size of cannonballs.

Funny, as big of a guy as he was, having him stand there completely naked, alone, and dripping with water, he looked more like a scared kid caught out in the rain.

"That's a good start," DJ said. "Now, I want you to take this rope, and put it around your neck."

Dos Santos shook his head. "You're making a mistake, *acho*. I'm not some nobody you can roll up on and rob. I'm connected."

DJ smiled at him.

"What a small world it is. Turns out I'm connected too, *acho*. I'm connected to the guy you strung up last night." DJ tossed the rope at his feet.

It didn't take long for Dos Santos to connect the dots.

"Wait a minute." He backed into the wall. "That wasn't my idea. I'm a working stiff, bro, and your buddy was unlucky, and I was doing what I was told—man, you don't know the whole story."

"Tell it to me," DJ said. "Let me hear the whole story, and maybe I won't blow your ass through that wall behind you, and you can get back to getting squeaky clean."

The color blanched out of Dos Santos. He looked like he was going to throw up.

"Go on, friend. Tell me your story. You asked me to wait a minute, and I'm waiting."

"I'm sorry about your buddy, okay? I never wanted to hurt nobody. But man, I got a job that needs to be done. All right? It's nothing personal. I'm just trying to survive like everybody else— like you, right?" He kept his hands up, but Dos Santos would've gotten down on his knees, kissed DJ's rings and paid for an indulgence if he thought it'd get him out of his bathroom alive.

"I got bills to pay. I got alimony, child support—I gotta think about retirement. I gotta hustle and do everything I can do to make ends meet. Okay, man? I'm sorry about your friend, I truly, deeply am, but he was in the wrong place at the wrong time, and I had business to do. Plus, you know he wasn't clean. We knew that too. He's with Garner's people. He knew the risks."

"Garner?" DJ's hand squeezed the shotgun's stock. "Did he put you up to this?"

By his expression, Dos Santos knew he wasn't getting his point across to DJ.

"There's all kinds of madness in this world, man," Dos Santos said. "I know I'm a bad person. But you ain't clean either, right? What's the difference between what I did and what you're doing? You don't think I got friends that'll miss me?"

DJ only stared at him.

"We were just gonna shake your boy down—keep a felony over his head to make sure he stayed quiet—that was the plan from the start, but she said she didn't—"

"Who said?" DJ said, as softly as he could over the salsa music.

The tips of Dos Santos's fingers nervously bobbed in the air. He'd blurted out too much, and he knew it.

"Let me go, and I'll tell you," he said.

DJ laughed. "You know I got a few double-aught shells in this thing, right? And they're pointed right at your gut. How about you tie yourself a noose and put that thing on, then we'll talk."

The dynamic of their negotiation must've finally hit home with Dos Santos. Because he slowly bent over, checking with DJ whether or not he was moving too quickly, then picked up the rope at his feet, and tied it into a perfect hangman's noose.

When that was done, Dos Santos seemed to have lost the inches of nerve he'd built up. He looked at DJ, silently begging for him to stop.

"Did you have something you wanted to ask me, Officer?"

"Man, we don't have to go this far. You got a problem? Let me pay you for your troubles, okay? Nobody has to know—"

DJ squeezed the trigger of his sawed-off. Buckshot turned a handful of white tiles on the wall behind Dos Santos into ringlets of dust, and the man's entire body clenched up. Having never shot at a naked man, DJ had never seen how the muscles from a man's feet to his neck rippled and tightened when they were energized with fear.

"I won't miss next time!" DJ roared. "Count on that." He racked another round into the chamber. The spent shell fell into the open toilet. "Now put that rope around your neck."

Dos Santos clenched his eyes shut as he brought the rope over his head. He let it rest on his shoulders.

"Good boy. Now tell me about that lady you mentioned."

Conversation wasn't coming so easily to Officer Dos Santos now. His eyes were wide and his chest was heaving like a dying buck. DJ had never seen a naked man piss himself, but he might yet.

"What do you want to know?" Dos Santos barked.

"Who is she?"

He shook his head. "I don't know her name, man. I swear to Christ I don't know it. She pays good, that's all I need to know. Names stay out of my head."

"Then who in your crew knows her name? The leader? The white guy with the slicked-back hair?"

Dos Santos's muscles tightened across his body as soon as DJ asked about the leader—he was right on the money. Questioning a naked man apparently had its advantages.

"Okay, so he's the point man," DJ said. "How do you know he was dealing with a woman?"

Dos Santos hesitated. He thought he could get away with teasing DJ with tidbits of information—like DJ would let him go without finding the things worth knowing. So, he aimed the gun at Dos Santos's foot and pulled the trigger.

The man collapsed to the floor, writhing silently. DJ walked closer to him.

"I didn't come to your house for the tunes," DJ said as he racked the shotgun again. "Tell me who wanted my friend dead."

"Some executive!" Dos Santos hissed. "I don't know her name, man, I swear to God! She's a CEO or something! She works at Hildon!"

Hildon.

That word put DJ's brain in a chokehold. A pharma company wanted Markel dead. They used one of Blunt's boats to get to Markel's house, then, after the deed was done, they snipped Blunt to cut off any loose ends. He shut his eyes and saw Blunt's purpled face, the corners of his mouth stretched back in mute horror, eyes bulging from their sockets.

Before he realized it, his emotions had roped him. They'd pulled him forward until he could see the broken vessels in the end of Dos Santos's nose—until DJ was standing over him with the shotgun inches from the back of Dos Santos's hand, cradling his head in fear.

"Did you kill the doctor?" One word had put DJ into a frenzy. Spittle came off his mouth, leaping onto Dos Santos's forehead. "Who else did they pay you to kill?"

"I had nothing—"

DJ jammed the gun against Dos Santos's head.

"Don't lie to me! Don't you lie to me, I'll blow your brains out, I'll kill you right here, and I won't—"

A hand clapped across DJ's chin. He'd let his emotions get the better of him, and they'd led him into making a fatal mistake by getting too close—why did he need to be this close to Dos Santos? He had a shotgun; he should be across the room. What was he thinking?

Nothing.

And that left him open to getting this whole thing turned around on him.

When Dos Santos struck him, DJ's body tensed in shock. Including his finger on the trigger of his shotgun.

That was the end of Officer Adrian Dos Santos. He would not have an open casket.

DJ stumbled back, nearly falling, except for the sink and cabinet behind him.

Whatever information Dos Santos had in his head was now spread across his bathroom wall.

While DJ stood with the Mossberg in his hands, his brain struggled to take in all the carnage.

Then one neuron connected with another, and he pumped the shotgun in a daze, ejecting the last shell. He bent and picked it up, dropping it in his pocket. He picked up the empty shells too, even the one in the toilet, and put them all in his pocket.

The shotgun itself was unregistered; serial numbers scratched off with a Dremel tool. Bought from a guy who knew a guy for about ten times its value. He left the shotgun on the bathroom floor.

DJ retraced his steps through the house. When he stepped out to Dos Santos's backyard, he scanned to his left and then his right. None of the neighbors were outside. Either they didn't hear the shots or didn't want to get involved. Possibly they knew who the shot was for and didn't want to stop a good thing from happening.

DJ stooped and picked up two more shell casings before moving quickly to the corner of the yard. There, he climbed the fence, bracing his good foot on the concrete post. He ran back to the truck across the street and grabbed his sea bag, removing the shells from his pocket and dropping them inside. Then he pulled the string and put the strap over his shoulder. He'd call a cab from the bar he'd hung out in this afternoon.

Then, he'd find Hildon Pharmaceutical's CEO.

CHAPTER THIRTY-SEVEN

Wayward floated sedately in the mooring field near Vieques.
As soon as we got back, Alicia parked herself at the built-in desk in the starboard hull, popped her earbuds in and started in on the files on Dr. Markel's laptop.

My part was to keep an eye on Flor. I wasn't used to being the nurse, and I think Flor understood that. She went easy on me and by early in the afternoon, she dozed off. While she slept, I took the dinghy back to shore and picked up some supplies. Mostly groceries.

When I got back, everything was the same as when I left, except for Alicia's cup of tea. I put another kettle on for her, letting it heat up while I loaded the supplies, including some fresh-caught shrimp and a pair of red snappers I bought straight off the docks.

After slipping a fresh cup of Alicia's preferred brand of tea—Tazo Passion Fruit—next to her on the desk, I seasoned the shrimp and put them on the cockpit grill along with some fruits and veggies.

I took a plate back to my wife as soon as dinner was ready.

Then, I woke Flor. She sat on the cockpit couch while I plated her fish and shrimp straight from the grill. Outside the awning, the afternoon sunlight glared down on the light chop stirred up by other vessels coming in and out of the bay. A breeze blew out of the southeast, crossing Vieques, before it swept over *Wayward*, and straight on to Puerto Rico.

I set her plate, with half a snapper fillet, an equivalent amount of shrimp, and some grilled vegetables, on the cockpit dinette. She looked at it like she didn't know what to do.

"That's red snapper," I said. "Good protein, low fat. Lots of B12 and omega-3 in that. Should be safe to eat since you're done with chemo."

Flor picked up a shrimp and absent-mindedly nibbled on it, her attention more focused on a superyacht lumbering into the bay than on me.

"I picked that fish up especially for you," I said. "No need to thank me."

She sighed, her sunken eyes sprawling over the bay. "So, this is life for you?"

Hearing something that blunt escape the lips of a twelve-year-old girl made me stop short. I knew what she meant. The crystal blue waters, the boats, the luxury of idle moments. What she didn't consider was the dull moments being cleaved in two by absolute chaos and murder.

"Cooking shrimp and chasing murderers?" I shrugged. "Sometimes I switch it up. I prefer to catch crab near the beach behind my house."

Flor smirked at her shrimp. "Must be a fun job."

"I'm certainly not in it for the money," I replied.

She snorted.

As she worked on another shrimp, I noticed her fingernails. The polish she and Alicia had applied yesterday looked like the slats of an abandoned house. I'd been with Alicia long enough to know that a coat of good polish stayed for three or four days before it started to chip.

I remembered my father's fingernails when he went through chemo. The way they flaked and cracked.

"You know, B12 is good for your nails."

Flor pursed her lips and glared at me as if I'd threatened to leave her mother to rot in jail. I wasn't sure where all this static was coming from. Maybe it was typical of a pre-teen girl, maybe it was something else. In either case, I didn't deserve flak.

"Is there a problem?" I put on my best Dad voice.

Her eyes widened, but she kept her attention on her shrimp.

"No, sir," she said. "This is all perfect. Not a problem in the world. I'm on the back of some rich guy's boat, eating grilled shrimp on a perfect day, talking about B12."

Before I gave her a piece of my mind, I looked away from Flor, watching a racing cat lift one of its hulls out of the water as the vessel turned toward Puerto Rico.

What the hell did she know, anyway? She was just a kid. When I was twelve, I didn't give much thought to anything outside of surfing, soccer, and keeping Gene out of my room.

"Sure, it's a perfect day, kid. Remember it. Because when you're older, you'll look back and thank your lucky stars I came along."

She looked past the stern to her right, at the same superyacht. She quickly wiped a tear out of the corner of her eye. Part of the nail on her index finger was simply not there.

Flor needed a wide berth. She could have been bathing in

champagne, and she wouldn't be feeling right. For God's sake, her mother was in jail, and I'd helped put her there. What in the hell was I getting so worked up about? I needed sleep.

"Look, I know things are sideways, but I'm going to right the ship. I'm not going to quit until your mom is back. I'll get the both of you squared away, and I won't quit until I do."

Tears flowed freely out of Flor's eyes now.

"Don't worry about it. Don't worry about me at all. Okay? I'm out of here. I'll just—" She sat up and searched the cockpit for a way out, like a mouse trapped in a bucket. "Please take me home."

"I'm not doing that."

"You can't keep me here—I don't want to be here."

"You may not want to be here, but I *can* keep you here."

She turned around on the cockpit settee, got on her knees, and cupped her hands around her mouth. "Help!" she screamed. "Help me! I'm being kidnapped!"

Alicia rushed out to the cockpit. "Jerry, what's going on?"

"Flor's having a teenager moment," I said, barely keeping myself from rolling my eyes. "She forgot how lucky she is to be here."

"I'm *lucky?*" Flor asked. "I didn't want any of this, Jerry."

Her paisley headband had slipped downward, resting on her bony shoulders. I saw the patches of naked skin in her scalp, her uneven hairline, the hurt in her tear-filled eyes.

She was right to be mad. Life had not been kind or fair to her, and, thoughtlessly, I wrote her problems off. I was ashamed of how callous I'd been.

"I'd like to go lie down in my room for a little while."

I wished I could've apologized. Instead, I took her outstretched hand, helped her stand up, and supported her as we went down into the port hull. There, I helped her onto the big bed in the forward guest stateroom.

The room was stifling—the air somehow heavier than I remembered it ever being. After pulling the comforter over her, I opened the porthole across from the foot of the bed.

"Do you want the rest of your dinner?"

She'd turned away from me in the bed and said nothing.

"I'll keep it in the fridge for you."

I went back out to the cockpit and sat down.

"Don't take it so hard, Jerry," Alicia scooted next to me.

"In taking in Flor, and trying my best to help Gabriela, I knew I was doing a good thing," I said. "All my life all I'd ever wanted to do was try to save lives and try to right wrongs. That's why I'd become a PJ. Sometimes I feel like trying isn't enough. No matter how hard I try, or how long I prepare, whether or not I succeed feels like a coin toss. The wrong breeze could change our fates for better or for worse."

Alicia rested her head on my shoulder. Her fingers entwined with my own.

"You're in one of your moods again."

"I guess I am."

"This is hard for all of us. You don't have to beat yourself up, Jerry."

"I know I don't."

"But you still do."

I took a deep breath, then squeezed the back of my wife's hand. She did the same back to me.

My episodes had become less frequent over the time I'd known Alicia—and she'd become better at taking them steadily, helping me navigate around my bigger, more dangerous emotions. I wasn't a religious man, but I thanked God for sending her to me.

"I liked the dinner you made," she said.

"I'm glad."

Her arm hardened. A wave of tension seized Alicia's body, and I knew she hadn't come out here to hold my hand and compliment dinner.

"Jerry," she said, my name resonating through her cheek bone and into my shoulder, "things are going to get more complicated. I know who had the Markels killed."

CHAPTER THIRTY-EIGHT

A ll the blood went to my head. I sat up and faced Alicia.
"I found a compressed file on Dr. Markel's laptop. White papers and abstracts. I think they were meant for Luc Baptiste."

"White papers and abstracts? Dumb it down a little."

Alicia tucked her hair behind her ear and smiled patiently at me. "Papers explaining the research Markel's lab did. They were meant to be shared with the executives at Hildon."

"That would follow," I said.

"Remember what Gabriela said about Markel's laptop? That he told her something important was on it? I think she was hoping for Flor's cure."

"Anthradone."

"I don't think it's here. At least I haven't found it yet. And the papers meant for Luc Baptiste had nothing to do with Anthradone."

"How does that tip you off to who killed them? He probably worked on more than one medication."

"Of course, he did," Alicia said. "What tipped me off was—

well, have you ever heard of something called pleiotropy?"

I gave her a look, and she knew the answer. Alicia rubbed her forehead, clearly struggling to come up with a way to explain this to me.

"It's when one gene has control over several unrelated phenotypic traits."

I didn't move, except to raise my eyebrows.

"Let me rephrase that. Pleiotropy is—" she stopped herself and reconsidered. "So, you know what genes are, right?" She took a shrimp off Flor's plate.

"Yeah." I *did* graduate high school.

"Gene editing is the new big frontier for pharma companies. CRISPR is a buzzword all the big money junkies won't keep out of their mouths—it's a technique for gene editing. Naturally, a whole rash of research labs have sprung up to meet demand. They're all researching the newest methods of gene editing." She finally popped the shrimp into her mouth. "Did I tell you I can't get enough of this shrimp?"

"I know, my baby," I said. "But anyway, gene editing is a new field, and there's a lot of money in it. I assume that means people are playing fast and loose, and paid in accordance?"

"Right. But with that reward comes a big risk. There's a lot we don't know about the human genome."

I nodded. "That probably doesn't stop many people from getting in there and turning knobs."

"Exactly," Alicia said. "That's where pleiotropy comes in. Imagine a gene that has control over your eye color. One of those research labs comes up with a new therapy that interacts with that gene, and only that gene, to change your eye color from brown to green.

"They kick the therapy up to a big company like Hildon, who does all the paperwork and marketing, and after some number of years, you, Jerry Snyder, can go to a cosmetic surgeon and get an inert virus injected into you."

I tilted my head. "Why would I want a viral injection?"

"That's how this works, most of the time. A harmless virus is used to carry the genes for green eyes into your body. The virus goes into your healthy cells, deposits the green eyes gene, and before you know it, everybody calls you Paddy Murphy."

"Can they really do that now?" I asked.

"Changing your eye color with therapy?" She shrugged. "Probably there's a lab working on vanity pills. But that's beside the point. Gene editing exists now."

A finger of wind lifted a tuft of Alicia's hair. She brushed it behind her ear, then picked up another shrimp.

"Let's take the example of the eye color therapy," she said. "I mentioned it takes years to go from the research phase to an actual therapy a patient can use. Those years are spent testing and re-testing the therapy on as many people as possible.

"In our hypothetical, the eye color therapy has been tested exhaustively. It has gone through about 10,000 people, a hundred testing groups, and all the side effects present in those testing groups are meticulously recorded and cataloged. Even if somebody has a cold, or gas, or any other thing that probably wasn't caused by eye color therapy, it is recorded, just to be thorough. The FDA looks at the tests and approves the eye color drug for sale.

"When the eye color therapy hits the streets, it's a big success. People love changing their eye color, and some big pharma company is making a mint." She raised her eyebrows at me.

The other shoe was about to drop.

"Except for one tiny little detail." She held up the shrimp. "Some people experience a side effect that wasn't seen in the tests. Those people still have the eye color change, but at the same time, the roots of their teeth get thinner and their teeth fall out. After more research, it's found out that the eye color gene that everyone has been switching around also has an effect on the thickness of tooth enamel. That's pleiotropy."

I shook my head slowly. "So, one gene controlled two unrelated things."

"Exactly!"

"What does this have to do with Flor's drug? Does that mean the cure Markel developed doesn't work?"

"No, that's not it." She checked left, into the salon. "The info drop for Luc Baptiste was all about a discontinued Hildon Pharmaceutical gene therapy called Poraxim."

My gut told me where this was going, but I let her continue.

"Poraxim was used to treat chronic indigestion. It turned off a gene that sometimes led the body to create too much stomach acid. Poraxim was groundbreaking in that it was one of the very first widely available gene therapies.

"For most people it worked. But, according to the information Dr. Markel was going to hand off to Luc Baptiste, about one in ten thousand patients experienced a serious side effect.

"How serious?"

Alicia tossed the shrimp back onto Flor's plate.

"According to Markel's research, for these people, the stomach acid gene happened to be the same gene that inhibited the growth of cancer. When Poraxim interacted with that gene, it shut off both functions."

Her eyes came to me, gleaming like hailstones. "Poraxim gave those people Li-Fraumeni Syndrome, and I think Luc Baptiste and Dr. Markel were going to tell the world."

"Which would have done serious damage to Hildon." I leaned against the stairwell going up to the flybridge. Luc Baptiste had made it his business to step in everything he could, but never in my wildest dreams did I think his murder involved one of the most powerful multi-national corporations in the world.

A company the size of Hildon Pharmaceuticals wielded immeasurable political clout. Name a first-world country, and Hildon likely had influence with someone at every level of government, whether through campaign donations, community grants, or outright bribery. That's how Dad and Arlen did things, anyhow.

What had I stumbled into?

I had to call this whole thing off before it spun out of control—if that was possible. Hand it off to Armstrong, if they'd take it, then sail *Wayward* to Cuba or Venezuela. We needed a place to bug out. A place where a western corporation wouldn't be able to throw cash around and get what it wanted.

But what about Flor? And Gabriela?

"Jerry?" My wife looked at me with enough gravity to pull me out of my spiral.

"Poraxim is what gave Flor all her tumors," I said. "Right?"

"Gabriela had the Poraxim therapy done three years ago," she said. "Four months after that, Flor was taken to the hospital and diagnosed with soft tissue sarcoma in her abdomen."

I clenched my teeth. I couldn't have forced myself to talk if I wanted to. What sort of insight could I add?

"Dr. Markel included some memos from high up in Hildon,

too," Alicia said. "I think to prove they knew exactly what was going on with Poraxim long before they yanked it out of pharmacies across the country."

"Bastards."

"It gets better," Alicia said. "Li-Fraumeni is considered an orphan disease."

"Does that mean something?"

"Means it's rare. And it means Hildon has the FDA's blessing to charge whatever the hell they want, which, in this case, is two hundred thousand dollars for a single dose of Dr. Markel's cure—Anthradone."

All I could do was shake my head. "Two hundred grand or a short, painful life with cancer. Hell of a choice."

"Now," Alicia said, "what do we do with this information?"

I glanced toward the door to the salon. "First things first. We might not be able to hide from trouble, but we need to make sure Flor can."

Alicia looked around the anchorage. "We can see anyone coming for quite a way."

"No," I said, feeling the wind on the side of my face. "Vieques is still too close, we're going back to St. Thomas tonight."

CHAPTER THIRTY-NINE

D J whiled away the early morning hours with slivers of
broken sleep. First, in his unbearably quiet stateroom, the
walls acting as a cast for the stale air, then on *Reel Fun's* flybridge,
where his heavy eyelids were lifted by the sounds of cars grinding
over the bridge between San Juan Island and the mainland.

After the sun rose, he gave up. The day would not wait for
him to be rested and ready, nor would it wait for DJ to sweep his
mind clean of all the fragments of Officer Dos Santos's final
moments.

Showered, he pulled out a pair of work khakis—pants he
hadn't worn since he'd first visited the cay he'd bought outside
Antigua, intent on clearing out a spot in some of the brush for a
shack that he hadn't built yet. Instead, he'd spent the days fishing
and poking around the neighboring islands, watching pairs of
white-cheeked pintails slip around mangrove roots and loiter in
brackish inlets.

DJ pulled the pants on. He put on a decent T-shirt, then
grabbed a Day-Glo orange vest out of the stateroom closet.

The vest was critical. Wearing one was like becoming a skeleton key. It let a man get behind the scenes; into sub-basements, parking garages, and dig sites. The average person rarely questioned a man in a safety vest, content to follow his directions in traffic, or let him poke around a backyard, despite the fact that the thing could've been bought at a thousand different places, by as many different people with as many different motivations.

Digging through the compartment beneath his bed, DJ found an old box of Winchester double-aught buckshot. In it, he'd stashed away a couple things; a dummy wallet and a GPS tracking device, which, like the orange safety vest, could be bought at an alarming number of places, granting a person the ability to prick the balloon of privacy everyone believed they lived in.

He put the wallet in his pocket, then dropped the GPS in a backpack on the floor, which he'd packed with tools like latex gloves, dark clothes, and his lockpick set. On his way through *Reel Fun's* salon, he rummaged in his fridge, grabbing a couple beers, some leftovers locked in a plastic container and a loaded S&W 640—a snub-nosed .38 caliber wheel gun that he kept behind the milk. He stuck all of it in his backpack, save for one beer, which he opened as he disembarked.

Street side, DJ called for a cab, then sat on a bollard, watching the cars pass by while he sipped his beer. Within a few minutes, the cab arrived. Its front passenger side window rolled down, revealing an older black guy with straight, white teeth and wet eyes. He'd probably been up all night working.

"Cosgrove?" he asked in a Haitian accent.

"You're looking at him." DJ took the last sip of his beer, then tossed it in the flowers behind him. He told the cabbie to take him to the Hildon building, then took the phone out of his pocket, then pulled up the web browser and searched for "woman CEO Hildon."

Her smiling face found him within seconds. DJ followed the link.

Hildon's CEO was a stuffy-looking blonde named Rachel Little. She seemed the type that would curl her hair before walking to the mailbox, and she probably sucked alcohol like an E85 pump.

DJ found her headshot on Hildon's website, right below an announcement for a big party the company was having in a couple days. He studied her face carefully. The inflammation cupping her cheekbones, the stiffness of her upper lip, the unnatural smoothness of her brow. It didn't seem at all unreasonable that she would hire hitmen to murder anyone who dared to tarnish the image of the company she helmed.

Before long, the car slowed as the cabbie guided it to the shoulder of the road. DJ hadn't noticed they were in the shadow of a tall, glass building across the street, with the word HILDON barnacled above the main entrance.

"What do I owe you?"

"$13.02."

DJ pulled a fifty out of his wallet and slipped it into the cabbie's waiting hand. "Thanks brother."

He grabbed his backpack off the seat, got out of the car and hurried across the street.

The morning sun was glinting between the high-rises, reflecting off the tops of a scattering of cars, as he approached Hildon's parking lot. He checked his watch—seven o'clock. He had gotten there plenty early.

Using his phone as a prop, he walked the perimeter of the

parking lot, pretending to take measurements, while keeping one eye on the working stiffs rolling in to start the day. His bright orange vest was perfect camouflage. Men in their off-the-rack suits and ladies in solid-colored dresses never gave him a glance as he watched them exit their economy cars and lope into the front door of Hildon's cubicle farm.

At 8:28, a sleek Mercedes-Benz SL convertible approached the entrance to the parking lot. The automatic barrier gate rose up, and the Benz slinked inside. A ribbon of blond hair flapped in the muggy San Juan breeze as the car moved toward the building.

A hundred meters off, DJ recognized Rachel Little when she got out of her car. She was taller than he'd imagined. As she came around the front of her car, stepping onto the sidewalk that ran across the front of the building, her eyes fixed on him.

Might be that a lesser man would feel a chill settle into his gut, but not DJ. He smiled politely and nodded, then turned to inspect a downspout nearby.

After he'd silently counted to thirty, DJ made his move. Trying not to appear in a hurry, he moved toward Rachel Little's car, stopping at a lamp post in the parking lot to peruse its wiring. He opened his backpack, took out the GPS tracker and held it up to the light post like it was a voltmeter. Then, keeping it in his hand, he moved on.

At the back of the Benz, he dropped to a knee, pretending to tie the shoe on his prosthesis. After checking left, then right, and seeing no one watching him, he pulled a plastic film off an adhesive pad on the back of the tracker, then slapped it on the underside of the car. His thumb flicked a toggle, and he walked away.

Once DJ was an appreciable distance from Rachel Little's car, he pulled out the smart phone and checked that the tracker app was getting a signal. A green dot appeared on a map, along with a serial number corresponding to the tracker.

Done.

He headed for the exit and would've clicked his heels if it were possible.

As he crossed the street, moving away from the Hildon building, his phone rang. He checked the screen. Jerry.

"Morning, sweetie pie. I'm a little busy bringing home the bacon in San Juan, so I don't have much time to talk."

"I need to meet you face-to-face," Jerry said. "It's important."

"You got my ear right now."

"Face-to-face," he insisted. "This doesn't work over the phone."

"Sorry, Dep, I don't have the time to sit on your back porch and look at the water."

"Neither of us has time for games, DJ. Cut it out and get back here."

"Well, looky there! I think that's the first thing the two of us actually agree on—I don't have time for *your* games, amigo. I'm not giving up a lead to sail my happy ass back to Charlotte Amalie, so if you got something to say, best say it while you can."

A long silence fed into DJ's ear like a roofing nail. He should've known Jerry wasn't serious about solving problems. He was just a rich kid trying to make a name for himself by bringing peace to the Middle East.

DJ didn't owe him a minute of his time.

"Last chance, Dep. Say it now or forever hold your peace."

"I'm your damned partner, DJ," Jerry said. "Hildon Pharmaceuticals is connected to this. They killed Luc Baptiste, and they killed Dr. Markel and his wife. They're in the process of killing Flor and will kill us once they realize we have the information Markel died trying to get out. We have to hang together on this. Get me?"

DJ laughed. "Man, I'm way ahead of you. They aren't gonna do nobody harm now. I'm seeing to that."

"You're seeing to that?"

"You did all that preaching about keeping a steady hand, about not giving into my…" DJ looked down the street and saw a guy hanging out of a food truck window, within earshot. He lowered his voice. "…need to get things done the way they gotta be done, because you thought I'd get checked. But guess what? Doing things my way, I scouted your urgent news last night. I already saw all the pieces moving on the board. I already knew whose hand was on the queen. You're playing two moves behind me, partner."

"You can still get hurt," he said.

DJ bit the inside of his cheek and laughed. God help him, Jerry couldn't admit when he was wrong.

"Spare me the bullshit about my mortality. I got that rubbed in my face by a Taliban IED years ago. And you know what I learned from that? I got no problem giving my life up, so long as I'm doing it for something right."

"This isn't what you think it is. You're not helpless, DJ." But the way Jerry said it, DJ practically smelled the lie through the phone.

"So, you look at my leg and talk about how we all gotta play it cool and not let things get out of hand, because some of us can't hold our own and that's—what? A nervous tic?"

"I never did that," Jerry said.

"Using that half-hearted tone, you know you said it," DJ continued. "You don't call me a cripple and kick my leg out from under me, but, damn man, you treat me about as bad with that polite *I'm worried about you* look in your eyes.

"Whether you want to believe it or not, I've been handling my business for years, Jerry. I climbed up on a boulder with McDermitt to save your ass. You remember that night you and Alicia got paraded to the edge of a cliff and held at gunpoint by all those drugged-out cult people? They were going to toss your ass to the sharks, and if it weren't for me, you'd be chum."

"I don't remember it that way," Jerry said.

"Then you don't remember it the way it happened."

Jerry didn't answer. Only the wind came to his defense, and it offered nothing of substance. He must've been on *Wayward.* Must've been nice to stand on the flybridge of his luxury catamaran, chastising the guy on the street.

DJ remembered the day after he'd finished Armstrong's orientation. He'd never pictured himself working hand in hand with anybody—much less that same blond surfer-boy he'd saved months earlier—but that was exactly who Stockwell had sitting on the deck of *Ambrosia* when DJ came aboard to get his first assignment.

If DJ had known he'd get mothered by Jerry Snyder, he never would have shook the man's hand that day. He would've told Stockwell to stick his papers in his craw.

"Look, DJ—you're right." The jarring shift in Jerry's voice caught DJ off guard. He almost tripped over a broken piece of sidewalk, but he caught himself against a mural of two dogs nipping each other's legs. Was Jerry being sincere or was this a trick they taught all the kids who went through cotillion?

"I hear what you're telling me," Jerry said. "You're a man. I didn't mean to treat you like you couldn't handle yourself, but I did. You don't need me to be your mother."

"Damned right I don't." He should've put that a gentler way, but the collar of DJ's T-shirt still felt a touch warm.

"But DJ, just hear me out before you go forward. I've got things I don't feel comfortable discussing over the phone. Please don't do whatever you're about to do."

DJ felt the clench of Blunt's neck, gasping for air, as if it were his own. Adrian Dos Santos was laughing at him.

"It's too late for that, man," DJ said. "Too many pieces are moving."

"It's never too late. You can still stop yourself."

Stop himself? The ache suppurating in DJ's guts squirmed. It would not sleep until it had been fed.

"Do you know what it's like to see a man's eyes ripped with fear one second, then glassy as a doll's the next? You know what it's like to see that in your friend's eyes?

Jerry began to say something, then hesitated. He cleared his throat. "I do."

"Then you know why I can't stop."

"I stopped," he answered.

"Then you've got no heart."

CHAPTER FORTY

D J hung up on me.

A chill rolled down the back of my neck. It'd been almost midnight when we'd gotten *Wayward* back to her own slip. I was tired, stressed, and dangling by a thread DJ was trying to cut.

Standing near the port side of *Wayward's* flybridge, I rested my hands on top of the bulkhead and watched the mast of the twenty-seven-foot sailboat in the next slip over sway with the gentle waves in Long Bay.

I didn't want DJ running headlong into a fight. Facts were facts, and the fact at hand was DJ only had one leg. Whether he wanted to accept it or not, it was a liability. But it wasn't my place to stop him. He was his own man, playing his own game.

"Jerry!" Alicia's voice came up from the docks at *Wayward's* stern. Her smile dropped away as soon as she laid eyes on me. "DJ isn't coming along, is he?"

I shook my head.

"I don't know why I got my hopes up." Alicia pinched her nose and sighed. "Working with the only guy on the planet more stubborn than you must be hard, huh?"

I pushed away from the rail and stood up straight. "For most people, it probably would be. But I've had lots of practice with the world's most stubborn woman."

She stuck her tongue out at me. I returned the gesture, then walked over to the helm to gather my sunglasses and this morning's coffee cup. I couldn't let DJ drag me down. I had to keep a brave face. This enterprise with DJ seemed to be drifting apart for good and dwelling on it did nobody any favors.

I climbed down the steps from the flybridge, turned to make sure the salon door was locked, then stepped onto the swim platform and hopped onto the dock.

Alicia linked her arm in mine, then laid her head on my shoulder for a moment. I kissed her, then we walked up the quay.

"Once DJ gets his head out of his ass, I'm going to shove it back in," she said. "Did you talk to Armstrong about him?"

"I thought about it, but I'm not a snitch."

She laughed lightly. "Snitch? Does that make me your moll?"

"Stoolie, tattler, informer, whatever. DJ's mess is self-made, and I don't want any credit for it."

"He'll come back around. He has to," Alicia said.

On the way up, we made a quick stop at the Yacht Haven Grande office. I told the guy at the counter to fill up Wayward's fuel and water tanks at his first opportunity. The future wasn't clear at this point, and I wanted her gassed up and ready to depart as soon as possible.

After that, Alicia and I walked out front. Our second-hand Wrangler was idling curbside, with Flor already sitting in the backseat, her head leaning against the rollbar with a pillow.

"How're you feeling this morning, kid?" I asked.

She smiled weakly, her eyes regarding me with shame. She opened her mouth to say something, but I spoke before she could.

"I owe you an apology," I said.

She knitted her brow. Something told me Flor Ramos wasn't used to seeing men offering apologies.

"What you're going through—I can't begin to imagine how hard it is, and you don't need me making it harder. Instead of grabbing you, I should've shut my mouth and listened to what you had to say."

"That would've been better," she said with a thin smile.

I reached over the side of the Jeep and planted a kiss on her bandana.

"Flor, I promise you we're going to get through this. All of us."

She nodded, but I could tell she was holding something back.

"Talk to me, kid. I want to know what's going on inside that head."

Flor inhaled deeply through her nose, then let her breath go. "I know you mean well, but a lot of men have made a lot of promises to my mother and me. None of them have ever lived up to it. My whole life, it's only been her and me relying on each other."

The two of them alone against the world. I tried to imagine how close they must've been, and now Flor was apart from her mother, left in the hands of strangers.

"It's hard to trust someone new," I said.

She nodded.

"I hear what you're saying. And to that, I say this: you don't have to trust me. All you have to do is let me try."

She searched my face for any hint of a lie. She wouldn't find one. "Okay, Jerry."

I got behind the wheel. Alicia smiled at me, her eyes misting before she quickly hid them behind her sunglasses. She put her hand on my thigh and kept it there as I drove us a half mile down Frenchman Bay Road, toward our house on Havensight Point.

Once we were in the driveway, I helped Flor out of the Jeep, then carried her up the steps to the back door.

We didn't get any farther than that.

The sliding glass door had been shattered. My heart jumped around inside my rib cage. I looked at Alicia behind me—she'd seen it too.

"Jerry—"

"Back to the car!" I hurried down the steps, right on Alicia's heels. We got Flor into the backseat, then I turned my attention to Alicia.

"Take the keys." I clapped them into her hand.

"But Jerry—"

"There's no time to argue," I said, closing her fingers around the keys. "Get back to the marina. Make sure they've got *Wayward* filled up—we might have to make a quick getaway."

I turned toward the house and started forward but stopped when Alicia snagged my arm. She pulled me toward her, her eyes like morning sky. I didn't want to leave her.

"Be careful, Jerry."

I kissed her. "You can't get rid of me that easily."

She was too worried to laugh. Alicia sank into the driver's seat of the Jeep and started it. As she backed out, instead of going to the back door, I made for the beach.

I stayed low, weaving between the tree trunks and the brush, heading toward a sandy ridge to the southeast. The crest of the ridge was somewhere about four or five feet above sea level, dropping down a thirty or forty degree grade where it then flattened into beach, closer to the water.

Once I'd gotten over it, I dropped to my belly and faced the house, which was about twenty yards off.

Except for the broken glass in the sliding door, nothing else struck me as suspicious. The drapes behind the door flitted, but I assumed that was only the wind.

We'd been gone all of two days—whoever broke in had had plenty of time to do the job, and the sounds of the waves killed nearly every other noise around, unless you were a lot closer to the source of it than our neighbors would have been. I was sure they couldn't say for sure when it had happened, or whether anyone had come or gone. I had to proceed like someone was still in the house.

Hildon might have known about Markel's laptop. In the case of a high-profile contractor being murdered, it wasn't completely out of the question for a company with Hildon's clout to hire a private eye to do their own investigation. That person may have interviewed Gabriela already, and they might've traced her back to my house.

On my elbows, I crawled to my left, sure to keep my head below the top of the ridge. One of the first things I'd done after buying this place was to set up a couple of insurance policies around the property. I found an old stump with a dark gray rock about the size of a bowling ball next to it—both were just inside the tree line.

I rolled the rock aside. Below it was a small hole in the stump, about the size of my fist. The tide had brought in sand to fill it, even after I dug it out, so I had to scoop it all out again until the tip of my middle finger brushed against a sheet of plastic. I grabbed it and pulled.

Out came a Beretta 92F handgun—almost the same as the M9A1 sidearm I'd used throughout my time in the service. Both layers of the plastic bags I'd wrapped it in seemed to have held up okay. I opened the first and found the second one to be as clean as the day it was buried.

Inside that second bag, my Beretta was wrapped in clean linen, lightly sprayed with gun oil. It didn't have so much as a grain of sand on it, nor a hint of rust. I pulled back the slide, inspected the chamber, and saw nothing that gave me pause. When I let go of the slide, it clicked back into place. Two magazines the gun was wrapped with also passed the eye test as well.

I fed one into the handgun, then loaded a round into the chamber. Ready to go.

Armed, I set my eyes on my house and lay on my belly, perfectly still, except for my slow, shallow breaths. I tuned out the waves hitting the shore behind me and tried to pick up any odd noises coming from the direction of the house. I watched the curtain dance near the back door.

After a time, I decided to get closer.

I hopped up, my back hunched low, knees bent, and my sidearm leveled and ready to fire.

My thighs burned as I came down the other side of the ridge and flattened myself against a tree trunk. Adrenaline coursed through me, making my fingers tingle around the grip of the handgun. I came off my cover and pushed forward.

Slipping underneath my back deck, I leaned my shoulder against the foundation of my house. The concrete felt cool to the touch, a world apart from the hot, sunny beach just out of sight. I looked up through the slats of the deck and listened.

Any kind of sound would've set me off. Footsteps, a coffee mug placed on the living room table, the AC unit under the deck kicking on. But I heard nothing.

So, I tiptoed out from beneath the deck, then stopped at the bottom of the wooden steps leading up. I kept my eyes on the curtain at the back door. They fluttered, and I pulled the trigger, making the curtain ripple when the bullet cut through it and sent it wafting to the floor.

My nerves arcing, I rushed up the steps, keeping the smoking mouth of the Beretta ahead of me and at the ready. When my sneakers crunched over the broken glass on the tiles inside the back door, I realized there was no one there—all I'd managed to do was ruin the curtain and put a hole in the ceiling.

But that was the least of the damage—my house had been ransacked. The couch cushions sliced up, the bookcases cleared, the cabinets emptied, so I went room to room, checking corners and closets, until I was satisfied that Hildon hadn't paid someone to kill us too.

I returned to the ripped sectional in the living room and plopped down. Somewhere deep in my gut, I felt a burning, like I'd swallowed hot coals and was roasting from the inside out, but I knew it was this whole mess finally catching up to me as the tide of adrenaline pulled back.

I put the Beretta on the coffee table, then slowly looked around the room. The hutch near the dining room table was completely empty, our wedding photos pulled from their album and strewn around the floor. Alicia's good silverware was, likewise, spread around the dining room, along with various knickknacks and keepsakes.

But nothing valuable was taken. The TV was here. And I seemed to remember Alicia's jewelry box in our bedroom, disorganized, but still holding her things.

It had to have been Hildon. Probably looking for Dr. Markel's laptop, which was back on *Wayward*, tucked into a locked hold underneath our berth in the master stateroom.

A chill fell over me. *Wayward*—if they knew where I lived, they had to have known about our boat too. For all I knew, we might've passed whoever did this on the way out. They might be on our boat now. They might have taken Alicia.

I jumped up, dug my phone from my pocket, hurried outside, and called Alicia as I ran toward the marina down the road.

She answered on the first ring.

"Jerry?" she said. "Oh my God, Jerry, are you all right?"

"Are you back on the boat?"

"Yeah, the guy at the marina is just finishing with the fuel tank—is something wrong? Are you hurt? Why are you breathing like that?"

"No, I'm fine. Everything at the house was fine," I said. "Listen carefully, baby—you've checked all over the boat? Did you see anyone?"

"No, I came in and just put Flor back on the guest bed. Do you think there's someone here?"

"Nobody was at the house."

"What? Do you think someone is on *Wayward?*"

"You can handle this until I get there," I said. "Do you remember where the revolver is?"

"In the compartment under the wheel, up on the flybridge," Alicia whispered.

"Go get it. I'm coming to you now." I said "I'll be there in four minutes. Get the revolver. I love you."

"I love you too." She hung up.

I would've stayed on the phone with her the entire way to the marina if she wanted. Instead, I kept the phone in my hand as I pumped my arms and sprinted down the middle of Frenchman Bay Road. I only had to cover half a mile.

Was telling Alicia to get the little S&W Shield the best thing to do? I should have told her to leave. Grab Flor, get off the boat, and get the hell out of there. Stay in the marina office, call the police.

No, not the police. They'd ask too many questions and explaining why we thought someone was hiding on the boat, intending to kill us, would mean having to explain why we had a laptop stolen from a murder scene, and that we had illegally accessed Hildon's private documents.

We were outside the Armstrong organization, doing this without a net. Getting the gun was the right call.

I came down the big hill and kept my speed as I passed the cruise ship dock and bounded onto the sidewalk. Ahead, a throng of tourists extruded through the gate from their boat, and I side-stepped a pair of teenagers, then spun past a bald man with a long white beard and came out the other side of the thickest part of the crowd.

Yacht Haven Grande sat on the water to my left. Through a forest of masts, I spotted *Wayward's*. An image of Alicia, gritting her teeth and pointing a handgun passed through my head. My feet moved like wildfire.

Then, I hit the intersection of Frenchman Bay Road and Long Bay Road. The crossing signal on my left told me to stop, but I ran harder. In the street, a sedan zipped past me, the driver laying on the horn. A guy behind the wheel of a truck stomped on the brakes and swerved to miss me. I kept going.

I crossed through the entrance of the black iron fence around Yacht Haven Grande, got through the parking lot, then took the stairs down two at a time.

My heart was butting up against the backs of my teeth when I came to the dock and looked up at *Wayward's* cockpit. I saw nothing, heard nothing, but moved like Alicia was being strung up before my eyes.

I jumped onto the swim platform and hurtled into the cockpit.

"Alicia!" I screamed, then burst into the salon.

"Jerry?" she answered. I saw her peer up from the port hull, her cheeks flushed, her eyes wide and the black revolver in her hand. Flor's little face peeked out from behind her.

I ran to them and wrapped my arms around them.

CHAPTER FORTY-ONE

The pinkened sky in Santurce, a metropolitan neighborhood in San Juan, painted the high-rises and the streets with fading glory. DJ walked toward the sun.

A car in need of a new muffler rattled past. A street vendor worked over a steaming griddle, calling out *"Bacalaitos! Bacalaitos! Two dollars!"*

The GPS app said Rachel Little's car had been stopped in a neighborhood almost due west of Santurce for the last six minutes. With that woman, Rose, likely to pop out of the bar behind DJ, now seemed a fine time to get a cab and get the hell out.

Leaning up against a mural of crowned skeletons with eyes like kaleidoscopes, DJ Googled the address where Rachel stopped. It was a three-story, Spanish-style house in Dorado about a half-hour's drive west of San Juan.

He pushed off the mural, moved toward the street, and raised his hand at a cab coming his way. Inside, the vehicle smelled like incense, and the driver, a plump, balding man with dark brown skin, smiled at DJ.

"Can you take me here?" DJ held up his phone, showing the driver Rachel's address.

"Okay," the driver said. He flipped on the meter. They were off.

Thirty minutes later, the cab zipped down a road cut through the jungle. According to DJ's phone, they weren't far from Rachel Little. When the cab slowed to make the final turn into a neighborhood of stucco villas with clay-tile roofs, DJ tapped the back of the driver's headrest.

"Let me out here, *compadre.*"

The driver pulled to the shoulder. DJ slipped a hundred-dollar bill over the cabby's seat. "Mr. Franklin thanks you for your hard work."

"My pleasure, *acho,*" he said in a thick Puerto Rican accent. DJ climbed out, his shoes settling into the bare sand between the shoulder of the road and a high stone wall marking the boundary of a front yard.

When DJ shut the door and swung his backpack over his shoulders, the cabby rolled down his window. He handed a slip of paper out. "Call me next time. I'll drive you."

A phone number was written on the paper in marker.

"I don't think you want to see me again, man. Better for you if we go our separate ways."

"I'll see you," the driver insisted. Probably hoped DJ would tip him another seventy-odd bucks. "Are you staying here?"

"Eagerness isn't something I can handle right now, okay, friend?" DJ turned to walk away, but the cabby honked his horn.

In a flash, DJ was leaning through the guy's window. He grabbed him by the front of his shirt and was a breath away from punching his nose backward, when DJ saw a picture of a little girl stuck halfway over his speedometer. She was beaming, despite missing a front tooth, and her straight, dark hair was capped with a white headband. She wore a matching white dress—probably for her first communion.

DJ let go of the old man's shirt.

"My granddaughter," he said gently. "I give her mother money. Cute, yes?"

"She's adorable." DJ wouldn't throttle her grandpa. "You need some cash for her?" He pulled out the Mark Cosgrove wallet from his back pocket. As a matter of good habit, he always kept a thousand in various bills inside—mostly hundreds. He pinched off two and held them out to the cabby. "Make sure she's got nice clothes. Does she like to read?"

"Books? Yes," the man replied.

DJ took another hundred from his wallet. "Get her some good ones." He dropped the money in the driver's lap.

"Okay," he said. "I will wait for you."

"No, man, I don't—" DJ stopped himself. No point in arguing with the man. DJ nodded at him, just to get the guy out of his hair. He probably could use a ride when this was all done, but who the hell knew when that would be?

"Don't hang here while I'm gone. Drive around but stay close."

"I will do that, sir." He picked up the money and stuffed it into his shoe. Then he rolled his window up and drove off, the tiny four-cylinder coughing and sputtering down the road. DJ watched until the taillights disappeared around a corner.

Getting his bearings, DJ surveyed the road ahead. Big walls hemmed every lot—some stone, some iron. He walked along the left shoulder, seeing what he could see. Where rooflines rose over the fortifications, he noticed red clay tiles and stucco. The houses were of a similar type, but each had its own architectural fingerprints. One had turrets over the driveway, another, an arched entry, and a big fountain in the front yard. The assholes who lived here must've pictured themselves as noblemen tucked in private villas. If you put a picture of this neighborhood next to one of Officer Dos Santos's, DJ would've assumed they were from different countries.

Even in the dead of night, in its quietest moments, Dos Santos's neighborhood had a heartbeat kept by barking dogs, night insects, and rattling cars zipping down the road.

Here, the air was still. Bugs were kept at bay by chemicals sprayed on the lavish lawns. To DJ, this place felt wrong.

Before giving in to his nerves, DJ slung one of the straps of his backpack off his shoulder, then worked the zippers apart and slipped his hand inside. Touching the clammy steel of his .38, his body felt surer.

He zipped up the backpack again and slung the free strap over his shoulder.

After squeezing his hand into a fist until his knuckles cracked, he got his phone out to check the GPS app again. It said Rachel Little's car was parked nine hundred feet ahead, and about fifty feet south of the road. Looking down the pavement, he judged the distance, about half of a quarter-mile dragstrip. Three driveways.

Before long, he came to an arched, black iron gate about one-and-a-half times his height. Beyond it ran a driveway, flanked by dozens of twenty-foot-tall Puerto Rican hibiscus trees—maga trees, their branches sagging with blood-red flowers about half the size of DJ's hand. They were the state flower of Puerto Rico.

He couldn't see much beyond them—only vague points of light that hinted at a house beyond. Checking his phone one last time, DJ made sure he had the right place.

The GPS app indicated Rachel Little's car was parked due south, and unless the lot was much smaller than it appeared from the road, and it looked like she had at least three acres of land, this had to be it.

DJ stepped back, examining the stone walls on either side of the gate for a handhold. They were rocky, with a decorative cap that gave an inch overhang. Chances were good the marble cap hung an inch over the other side of the wall as well. If he could get a decent start, he could swing his arms over top and latch on.

Taking two large steps backward, DJ shook his arms out. He cracked his knuckles, and breathed through his nose, then exhaled through his mouth. Whether from the breathing, or the beers he'd been feeding himself all day, he felt limber enough to get over the top. He took one last breath.

Go.

DJ exploded forward. He'd shocked more than one person with his footspeed when he had to but going more than a few steps usually led to disaster. The prosthetic under his right knee would wobble like a top, eventually slipping the cup off what remained of his leg.

He planted his right leg and jumped up. The toe of his left shoe hit the stones, caught, and boosted him up. When he threw his arms over the top, his fingers caught on the back of the marble cap stones as his chest bashed against the front.

Something popped inside his torso. He cringed at the impact, then gritted his teeth and sucked air, but didn't let go. Ignoring the pain, he pulled himself up with help from his left foot, which scrambled against the front of the wall.

As quickly as he'd mounted the wall, he pushed himself off the other side, and landed in the yard. The prosthetic held, allowing him to duck behind a hibiscus tree. Through one of the house's large windows, he spotted an athletic, blond woman riding a stationary bike in the living room.

Rachel Little.

Coals settled in his gut. Blunt's face flashed through his mind. Now the real work began.

Dropping to one knee, he slung the bag off his back and unzipped it. From an inside pocket, he took out a pair of latex gloves and two shoe covers, all rolled up with a hair band holding them together. He slipped the hair tie off, sliding it around his wrist, then laid the gloves and the booties on the ground next to him.

Reaching inside again, he pulled out a dark, long-sleeved shirt. He put it on over his T-shirt, then found a beat-up ball cap stuffed in the bottom of the backpack. He combed his hands through his hair a few times, making sure to gather up every loose strand in his left hand, then slipped the hair tie off his wrist with his right and bundled it together.

With the hat on his head, and his hair tucked inside it, DJ pulled the latex gloves on, blowing into each to get a good fit. He took the .38 out and tucked it in the back of his pants, then slipped on the shoe covers and leaned his bag against the tree.

Hunching low, DJ darted from tree to tree, working his way up the driveway with the unwavering nerve of a combat veteran.

When he reached the front of the house, he crouched low under the window, mashing down the flowers and staying clear of the light spilling out from inside. Inside lights were his ally, as long as they didn't fall on him. Anyone inside would see nothing but blackness outside.

DJ took the .38 out of the back of his pants, opened the cylinder and checked that it was ready to fire. The brass reflected the shine coming through the window, turning it into a twisted reflection of the world outside. DJ saw his own figure, dark and featureless, and felt Death lay a hand on his shoulder.

Then, like an angel on his other shoulder, Jerry's disembodied voice came to DJ. "You're not a cold-blooded killer."

But his partner's voice was wrong: this wasn't killing in cold blood. This was retribution. Sliding a bead on the cosmic abacus from one side to another.

"This is murder."

Call it what you want, he thought. *Maybe we're both right.*

DJ heard the thin sound of pop music reverberating through the glass above him. From his position, he saw the top of Rachel's head, bobbing along with the bass. It looked like a melon on a fence post, begging to catch some lead.

Maybe it'd be best to shoot her from here. The front door was probably locked. Likely alarmed. If he kicked it in—if he even managed to kick it in—there'd be a hell of a calamity. Pretty risky.

He squeezed the grip of his snub-nosed Smith & Wesson. Best to shoot her from here, no question.

On one knee, DJ leaned back, thumbed the hammer back, and slowly lined the shot up with the side of her head. With all the movement from her peddling, this wasn't as simple as he'd hoped it would be. He had to fish around for a moment, find the space where some part of her head would be, then he had to feel the rhythm of her movements.

Soon, he had it. He coiled his finger around the trigger. The steel was warm to the touch, as comfortable as holding the hand of an old girlfriend. Rachel Little had no clue. Her chest heaved as she pedaled faster, her shoulders rippled as she leaned forward on the bike. A bead of sweat trickled down DJ's ear.

"You're an evil man," Jerry's voice said.

Not as evil as her. The trigger pressed back against his flesh. The compact .38 had a ten-pound trigger pull that he knew very well. Blunt's purple, bloated face suddenly bloomed in his mind's eye.

DJ flinched. He blinked. He lowered his weapon.

Jerry was right.

"Hands up!"

DJ spun right and saw the darkened figure of a large man. A light at the corner of the house outlined his body. His feet were spread shoulder-width apart, his arms lost to the light glaring behind him, but DJ knew he was looking down the barrel of the other man's handgun.

CHAPTER FORTY-TWO

"**P**ut your hands up or I'll blow your head off," the other man bellowed at DJ.

DJ didn't doubt the man's ability to follow through, but the way he locked and unlocked his elbow and adjusted his feet like he had ants in his shoes seemed to suggest there might be some wiggle room here. If DJ could talk him down or scare him off.

"I don't have a fight with you, friend. The only person I got a quarrel with is your boss." DJ slowly raised his hands, letting his S&W 640 dangle off his finger by its trigger guard. "Now, you seem like an observant man, so I'm going to step a little off my path, and not attempt to lie to you, because I know it wouldn't work. So here it is. Your boss is a bad person."

The other man's ears perked. He lifted his chin. DJ had piqued his curiosity, it seemed.

"I know that sounds funny but let me explain. When I say *bad*, I don't mean she takes a penny from the gas station tray, even when she don't need it. Partner, she's *real* bad, like paying-the-cops-to-hang-a-man-from-the-rafters-in-his-garage *bad*. Get me? The man she had killed wasn't an angel by anyone's standard, but he was my friend, and he never hurt a soul. And he didn't deserve to die just because he had the rotten luck of renting a boat to the wrong person."

Did the other guy get it? Who the hell knew? At least he was letting DJ talk, which counted for something.

"In short, I intend to kill your boss. And rest assured, I *will* do it. But it was never my plan, nor is it my desire, to hurt anyone else, least of all a working man trying to earn a wage."

When DJ expected the man to answer, he stayed silent. Muggy as the air was, strands of vapor rose off the top of the man's bald head. Was he deaf, or simply paralyzed by fear? Of course, the third option was that DJ had presented him with a difficult decision for most folks to make. More time to decide seemed prudent.

Behind DJ, the front door clicked open. He didn't dare take his eyes off the man pointing the gun at him, but Rachel Little surely had come out of her house after noticing DJ in her flower bed with his hands up.

"Ramon, who is this man?" Her voice needled through DJ's ears. She seemed comfortable using the sort of tone that only demanded, never asked; that expected perfect service from anyone she deigned worthy enough to be a servant.

Upon hearing Rachel Little speak, DJ liked her even less.

"He's a trespasser, ma'am," Ramon, the guard, said. A fresh bead of sweat dripped off his earlobe. Rachel Little might've scared him more than an armed man crouched in the bushes.

"There's a sign by the front gate. What does that sign say?"

"Trespassers will be shot," he answered. He took one hand off his pistol, then wiped his arm across his brow.

"I didn't read your sign," DJ said.

"It's impossible to ignore," Rachel answered. "You can't go past the front gate without seeing it. That's why we put it there, isn't it, Ramon?"

"Yes, ma'am. That's why the sign is there."

"I jumped the wall," DJ said.

"Aren't you impressive?" Rachel said. "Ramon, please shoot the trespasser."

DJ felt Ramon's eyes shift from Rachel's face to his. Ramon hadn't pulled the trigger yet, but he was damned close, and if DJ couldn't remind him of why that ran counter to his interests, DJ Martin's guts were going to become a permanent art exhibit all over the porch behind him.

"Ramon," DJ said slowly, "remember what I told you: I ain't here to hurt you. I'm here to avenge a friend, and so long as you don't make yourself part of it, we're square. Understand?

"So, before you pull that trigger, I want you to reconsider what I told you before she walked out. I am a killer. I was trained and re-trained by the United States federal government over a period of years, with a particular focus on infantry combat—of the science behind killing other armed men. This woman wants you to kill me. For what? Forty thousand a year? Fifty? What kind of benefits does she offer?"

"Don't answer that," Rachel snapped.

"I get two weeks off a year," Ramon said anyhow.

DJ clicked his teeth. "Poor compensation for murdering in defense of a murderer."

"I am *not* a murderer. Ramon, shoot the trespasser now."

Ramon didn't move a muscle. DJ considered that a victory—a small one, as Ramon hadn't taken the gun off him, but at least he wasn't dead yet.

"I'm asking a lot of you," DJ said. "I know I am, but she ordered the death of a dear friend of mine. Have you ever had a friend killed, Ramon?"

"I did no such thing!" Rachel protested.

And that about settled things for DJ. Quick as he'd ever been, he twisted around, letting his pistol's grip slide back into the palm of his hand. He pointed the business end square at Rachel Little's forehead.

"Hey!" Ramon shouted. "Drop the—drop it!"

His piece rattled so hard, it was a wonder Ramon's finger hadn't tripped the trigger by accident.

"I'm sure a lady like you has made a real nasty habit out of lying to people. Even you don't know what's true and what you made up," DJ said. "But I know what I saw. I saw my friend, strung up in his garage by three plain-clothes cops from San Juan. I saw him kicking and screaming, I heard them laughing. And one of them swore up and down you ordered it before he got his head blown off in his bathroom."

A thin sheet of light cast through the front door fell across Rachel Little's bony shoulders and shone across the harder points of her face. DJ watched her eyes stretch open.

"Officer Dos Santos?" she whispered, just loud enough for DJ to hear. "I just heard from SJPD."

"Yup."

"I did no such thing—I would never ask a person to do something like that. *This* man is the murderer," she said to Ramon. "He killed a uniformed police officer."

"He wasn't in uniform when I got him. He was naked as a bad gambler—and I already told Ramon what I am.

"We're getting off subject, anyhow. I asked Ramon a question. You ever had a friend get killed?" DJ kept his eyes buried behind the S&W 640, making sure the sights stayed on Rachel.

When Ramon didn't answer, DJ glanced at him. "Hey, Ramon, *habla Inglés?*"

"Yeah," Ramon said, almost inaudibly against the sounds of coquis chirping behind the house. "A friend got shot when I was in middle school."

"Ramon!" Rachel whined. Pretty clear that she did not enjoy being out of control of a situation.

"Made you mad as hell, didn't it?" DJ asked. "Made you want to find the guy who did it and beat his brains out through the back of his head."

Ramon said nothing. But DJ knew he was right.

"This is an armed man on my property! What clearer violation of my safety do you need?" Rachel's voice reached a new, whistling pitch. "If you don't shoot him, you're fired!"

"I've got no quarrel with you," DJ restated.

"Think of your daughter, Ramon!" Rachel said. "How can you take care of her without a job? How will you feed her? How will you pay for a place to live? What about those braces she needs?"

"I find that argument as disgusting as it is manipulative," DJ said. "How're you going to invoke a man's daughter as a motivator to get him to kill?"

As it turned out, Ramon disagreed with DJ's perspective. He squeezed the trigger.

Whether Ramon intended the shot to be a warning, or if he was too nervous to hold his weapon steady was unclear. What was clear was the bullet that whizzed past DJ's ear as he turned in shock to Ramon. He'd genuinely thought Rachel Little's hold on

Ramon was a lot weaker than she imagined it.

After he turned, something struck DJ in his shoulder blade, like a crazy man had darted out of the bushes with a claw hammer and whacked him. He doubled forward, dropping his snub-nosed S&W.

When DJ brought his eyes up, he saw Ramon standing motionless, a finger of smoke lifting from the end of his pistol, which he now held at his side, muzzle down.

"Oh man, bro." Ramon sounded deeper in disbelief than DJ felt. "I'm really sorry."

Not that it really mattered. DJ had no desire to stop and talk about it.

He made a break for the wall and ran as fast as his prosthetic leg would let him, forgetting his promise to kill Ramon if he got involved.

"Shoot him!" Rachel screamed as DJ escaped through the yard.

Ramon held his fire.

"I said shoot him!"

DJ sprinted for the hibiscus tree where he'd left his backpack. A pair of shots cracked through the air—one over his head, one thumping into the grass. When DJ looked over his shoulder, he was surprised to see Rachel Little aiming his own Smith and Wesson 640 at his back.

A bullet bored into one of the trees to DJ's right, and a wash of splinters hit the seam of his work pants. A follow-up shot rang out, and DJ's prosthesis flipped up, kicking him in his own ribs.

DJ rolled to the ground. He landed on his belly, and another shot hissed through the air over his head. He crawled to the nearest tree as quickly as he could, his prosthetic leg flopping behind him—must've been quite a confusing sight for Rachel Little and her security guard.

At the tree, DJ sat up, putting his back against the trunk. His prosthetic hung loosely inside his pants. He pulled it out by the shoe, and immediately noticed a new dent in its shaft, unmistakably left by a .38 caliber bullet. He worked the leg back on, rolling up his pants, fitting his stump into the cup, then rolling an elastic sleeve over that to keep everything in place.

Intending to stand up, he planted his hand down, and realized he was pushing against the backpack he'd left behind the tree earlier. He slipped it over his shoulders.

Another bullet zipped past, hitting the perimeter wall a few paces from DJ. The shot had a new timbre to it, sounding slightly heavier. She must've run through all five rounds in DJ's 640, and taken Ramon's handgun from him.

Dust popped from the wall again, almost directly in front of DJ. She had a good bead on his position, which he tried not to think about too hard when he pushed himself up to his feet.

DJ ran to his one o'clock, trying to keep the trees between him and Rachel as best he could. He jumped up the wall with his left foot—just as he'd done on the way in—but this time, when he tried to latch his arms over the marble cap, pain radiated from his upper back like a hot poker.

His hands lost their grip, and he fell on his ass.

With his back throbbing, he knew something was wrong. He remembered that sensation of being whacked with a hammer in front of the house, and realized it was probably a ricochet. When Ramon fired, the bullet, or a shard of it, must've bounced off the wall of Rachel's porch, then struck him.

Which meant getting out the way he came in would be impossible.

DJ remembered the gate. It must be to his right somewhere. He hunched low, and hurried forward, keeping the front wall to his left. Off to the right, closer to the house, he heard the sound of Rachel's voice barking commands at Ramon. He hoped they'd lost sight of him.

Within a few yards, DJ came to the gate. He pushed a button on a nearby post, and the gate's motor hummed, lifting it out of the way. He sprinted away as soon as he could, escaping with his life. But then, so did Rachel Little.

CHAPTER
FORTY-THREE

The human spirit is a funny thing. A kid who has every reason to give up keeps going, and a man who has half a dozen reasons to keep going can't shake it off.

As I untied *Wayward* from the dock, then motored her out of Long Bay, I pretended to have nothing on my mind. But the thought of losing my wife and Flor haunted me—and feeling so bothered by it made me feel guilty. What right did I have to be upset? Why did I feel entitled to sulk? When I was in the service, one of my commanding officers, Captain Evans, wouldn't have sulked if he were in my shoes. When others depended on him, he did his job, and as lofty a goal as it was, I had to live up to him.

We anchored about half a nautical mile southwest of Havensight Point, where I had a clear line of sight to the shattered back door of my house. On *Wayward's* flybridge with a pair of binoculars, I maintained watch on my house. I ate breakfast, lunch, and supper on the flybridge settee, then took a cup of coffee and a kiss from Alicia in the helmsman's chair after sundown. All the while, the names of the fallen men I'd served with bumped around my head.

Sleep didn't come that night. Not that sleep had come easily to me at any point in the last six years. Regardless, I had to keep watch.

I stayed on the flybridge, maintaining light discipline, with only the required anchor light on the masthead turned on. I left my post only when I couldn't relieve myself over the side of the boat, or to grab a stack of protein bars around three a.m., when I got too hungry to concentrate. Other than that, I never looked up at the blanket of stars, or laid my head back in the helmsman's chair and listened to the waves passing beneath our hull to fall upon the shore. I didn't let my mind wander into the misty darkness.

I had to stay ready. My lack of readiness had almost cost Alicia and Flor their lives. I wouldn't be caught unaware again.

When the sun came up over the eastern edge of the ocean that morning, I barely paid it any attention. My eyes were dry and weak, but still, I watched my house.

Around seven that morning, I saw a man wobbling up the deck stairs. My eyes had trouble picking out the details at first, but when he approached the back door, I noticed the blood on the back of his T-shirt. A big, crimson drape clung to his body, revealing the wiry muscles beneath.

It was DJ. I was still pissed at him, but that didn't stop the cold finger running down my spine.

I spun my chair back to the helm console, then picked up my phone and mashed my finger on DJ's entry in my contacts.

Through the binos, I saw him fumble around his hip until he got his phone out of his pocket.

"Yeah?" DJ didn't sound himself. That one word sounded like it took the better part of his energy to form and spit out.

"It's Jerry. Stay where you are." I jumped up from the chair and hurried for the steps down to the cockpit. "I'm coming to get you."

"You what? I'm at your house." He laughed, half-crazy. "It's been a hell of a night, man. For both of us, I guess." Glass crunched in the background.

"We're on *Wayward*, just off-shore," I said. "Sit tight. I'm coming to evac you." I hung up. I practically leapt to the aft settee, then unfastened *Wayward's* dinghy like we were taking on water.

"Alicia!" My voice echoed off the trees on shore. "Alicia! Get up!"

Once I had the dinghy in the water, I turned around and ran into the salon, then hooked a hard right, and jumped down the stairs into the starboard hull.

My wife was sitting up in our bed, rubbing her eyes.

"Were you up all night, Jer?"

That wasn't important.

"DJ's at our house," I said.

She blinked hard. "He's what?"

"He's hurt." I grabbed her by an ankle, and tugged, trying to get her out of bed faster. "I need an IFAK and the advanced trauma kit."

Alicia's eyes went wide. The individual first aid kit was one thing, but the advanced trauma kit wouldn't come out unless something serious happened. We kept it packed with the kind of stuff used to tackle a variety of more serious medical emergencies like broken bones, puncture wounds, births—the kind of stuff that, if we were hours away from land, couldn't wait.

"Where is he?"

"At our back door," I replied.

We kept a pair of IFAKs and the advanced trauma kit in my hanging locker since I had fewer clothes. Our advanced trauma first aid kit was a medium-sized duffle bag packed to bursting. The smaller, more transportable IFAK was about the size and thickness of a small laptop and included a Velcro strap that wrapped around a thigh or hooked into a tac vest. I wrapped it around my thigh.

"What did he do? How bad is he?" Alicia lugged the advanced trauma kit over the lip of the hanging locker, letting it thump onto the floor.

"I'm not sure, but he's bled a lot. The back of his shirt is covered. He said he had a wild night."

"Then he's responsive."

"He's slurring," I said. "I don't know how much blood he's lost."

She nodded. I didn't have to tell her this was going to be a dicey one.

"Where do you want me to set up?" she asked.

"Cockpit," I answered. I turned to leave, then stopped myself, circled back to Alicia and pecked her lips. "I love you."

"I love you too." She slung the advanced trauma kit's strap over her shoulder, and almost fell sideways. I reached out to help her get it through the door. "I got this," she said. "You go get DJ."

"I will." I spun on my heel, then took all three steps into the salon with one stride.

"Jerry," Alicia called.

I stopped. "Yeah?"

"Slap him once for worrying me."

"If he doesn't come willingly, I'll have no choice but to knock his ass out," I said.

"Don't do it too gently," she said, the advanced trauma kit audibly dragging on the starboard hull's floor.

I ran out of the salon door and leapt to the swim platform. Within seconds, I was in the dinghy, twisting the outboard's throttle, cutting for my house, not thinking about how I felt both tired and wired, not realizing I heard Captain Evans's voice telling me I wasn't responsible.

All I thought about was DJ.

I hit the shore, jumped out, and ran. Looking up through the trees toward the back door, I couldn't see DJ. Except in my mind's eye, where he'd collapsed on the deck, lying on shards of broken glass.

When I came sprinting up the stairs, I was relieved to be wrong.

DJ sat on one of our Adirondack chairs, one hand tucked behind his head, his face turned to the sunlight, his eyes closed. His skin was the color of bar soap left in a gas station bathroom.

"DJ?"

One eye peeled open, a hint of a smile crossing his features. A drop of blood plopped to the deck.

"Look who came crawling back." His lips had trouble keeping up with his words.

I unstrapped the IFAK from my thigh, dropped to a knee beside him, opened the kit on the wood decking, and pulled out a pair of nitrile gloves.

"Jesus, DJ," I said as I snapped them on. "What the hell happened to you?"

"Hey, man, no cavity search, all right?"

I frowned at him. He reeked of alcohol. "Can you lean forward?"

"When the mood strikes me." I noticed his right hand clamped to the arm of the chair and his fingers let go, so I assumed he tried to raise his arm, but a grimace arced across his face. "Suppose I'm not feeling it right now."

"How about I help?"

He looked up at me, then looked away. Normally, I would've let him be. If DJ wanted to be a pain in the ass, it wasn't my place to stop him. Luckily for him, this wasn't normal.

So, I moved my hands behind his shoulders, trying to lay them flat on his shoulder blades to help roll him forward, but as soon as I got my left hand in place, DJ yowled like a tomcat.

"Jesus, Joseph and Mary, Jerry!" He bowled over, rocking forward in the chair, and I caught a glimpse of the dime-sized hole in his shirt over his right shoulder blade.

"If you had just told me—"

He shot an angry look at me. "Not exactly in the talking mood, man!" A cord of slobber dripped down his goatee.

"If you stay hunched over just like you are, we're good." I got down on a knee and fished through my pack, then pulled out a pair of trauma shears. I cut down the back of his T-shirt, from neck to waist, getting the fabric clear of the wound. "Who shot you?"

"Nobody important," he said through his teeth. "I didn't know him. A bodyguard, I guess. I told him I didn't have any beef with him—I just came to see his boss, but I guess everybody's so damned worried about keeping their paychecks."

"Or they're worried about the strange guy with a gun."

With his shirt out of the way, I saw the wound clearly; a crescent-shaped break in his skin, about an inch long. At first blush, it didn't look deadly serious. My assessment was that the wound was too wide for his body to clot. Combine that with the alcohol in his system, and all the blood on DJ's shirt must've slowly leaked out over a period of hours.

Wind shook the tree branches, and a dapple of sunlight skimmed across DJ's back, revealing a lead shard in the wound. Once I had that out, Alicia could stitch him up, and that'd be the worst of it.

"Any idea what the bodyguard got you with?"

"Handgun of some kind. Probably a nine," DJ said. "I think it was a ricochet."

The wound did look smaller than what I had seen from 9mm or .38 caliber bullets. Too small to be anything bigger than that. Maybe a .22, but it didn't seem to me like a professional body-guard would carry a .22 caliber handgun. A ricochet seemed likely.

I put the shears back in the IFAK, then slid out a packet of sterile combat gauze and an antiseptic towelette. I opened the towelette's package and snapped out the sheet.

"Grit your teeth, buddy. I'm gonna clean you off a little, then pack your wound and put pressure on. It's gonna hurt, but it'll feel rather good compared to what we'll have to do on the boat."

"Jesus, Jerry, your bedside manner is piss poor. You know that?"

"That's why The Snyder Clinic is free."

"Just do it already."

"You got it." A lot of the blood on his skin was already dry, but with a few strokes, and minimal wincing from DJ, I had a good, clean ring around the wound. I packed the wound with a single packet gauze, watching for a moment to see if the blood soaked through.

"How much have you had to drink?" I asked.

"Don't come down on me about booze, man. Not right now."

"You'd be a lot less bloody if you hadn't drunk so much."

"I'd be in a lot more pain, too."

Fair point. Didn't seem to matter anyway. DJ's blood hadn't come through the gauze, which was a good sign.

"You're patched up for now," I said as I Velcroed my IFAK shut. "How do you feel about getting to the dinghy on shore? Think you can walk it?"

DJ creaked upright, his lips twitching and fresh beads of sweat running down his face.

"I can walk it," he said, sitting tall.

"Let's see." I motioned for him to stand with me. He gave me a glare that would've scared off a less determined man. "Don't give me a dirty look, Dudley James—on your feet."

His glare deepened. "Where in the hell did you find out my name?"

I grinned at him. "I think we've got more important things to worry about, don't you?"

"That's a family name, all right? And I didn't have a say in picking it." DJ scooted to the edge of the Adirondack and planted his left hand on his left knee, his right arm hanging loose. He pushed, trying to lift his butt off the wood slats, but never rising more than a fraction of an inch.

Rather than let him struggle, I reached down. He looked up at me and shook his head. So, I dropped my hand and let him try to stand up on his own again. No progress. In fact, he might've sunk a little lower in the chair.

I put my hand out again. "Come on, DJ."

He pursed his lips at me. If he spat on my hand, it wouldn't have caught me unaware. At least I was wearing a pair of nitrile gloves.

This wasn't about offering a hand to help him walk. It wasn't even about me being overly concerned with DJ's safety. Our problems were deeper than that. When I looked into his sunken eyes, I saw a man stuck on shore, cursing the ocean, and kicking the sea foam. A raving mad bastard daring the water to take him into oblivion, fully aware that his mortal flesh and bone could never hold back the sea.

The waters took his dare. He held to his soggy piece of land. As if we were the same person, I felt the seafoam rise past our knees, smelled the brine in our nostrils as it crawled over our upturned face, coming together an inch beyond our lips. Our hair wafted in the current like seaweed.

We shared those feelings because he and I both knew what it meant to keep our feet firmly dug under the muck. The same tides that swallowed him swallowed me.

Looking back on it, we both sensed that about each other, I think. Since Stockwell's meeting on *Ambrosia*, sure, or before that, when the Onayans wanted to force-feed Alicia and me to a swirling school of hammerheads.

The exact moment didn't matter. What mattered was that we'd never acknowledged it, we'd never treated each other honestly. Was it both of our faults? Probably. I don't know. I couldn't control DJ; I could only control myself. I could only make myself do the right thing.

I crouched down and scooped my arm across DJ's back, getting his left arm to rest on my shoulders.

"All right, partner," I said. "We've got a long road ahead of us. You ready to get the hell out of here?"

DJ squinted at me. I wondered if the gulf between us was too deep to be bridged. Then he nodded, and I knew we had a chance.

"On three?" I asked.

"Let's do it, man."

I got in a squat position, my feet under me. DJ's pulse tapped my shoulder.

"One, two, three!" I lifted off. DJ was much lighter than I'd expected, and the two of us got him standing without much trouble.

We negotiated our way down the steps and across the yard. On the beach, I lowered DJ onto the floor of the dinghy. We had just enough space to lay his head on the inflated bow, with his legs going under the single bench. I shoved us into the water, then hopped in, started the motor, and guided us back toward *Wayward's* swim platform.

Alicia came down from the flybridge, looking at me as if I'd pronounced DJ dead on the scene.

"He'll be fine," I called out to her. "He's lost some blood, and he drank himself stupid, but his wound is not life-threatening. I've got it packed with a small amount of gauze."

She combed her hair back from her face and blew out her cheeks. I tossed the line to her and she pulled the dinghy in. With her help, I got DJ onto a settee in the cockpit.

He and I had a lot to talk about.

CHAPTER FORTY-FOUR

We stayed anchored off Havensight Point through the day and into the evening. The currents moved gently and the wind tiptoed past, letting DJ and Flor rest. Even I got some rest in, after Alicia begged me to sack out in our stateroom, promising me she'd keep watch.

Sleep came quickly, but I woke at least twice. The first time, I calmed myself and rolled back into sleep. The second time, my hand whipped out before I was fully awake, looking for the dream journal I kept in my nightstand back at the house. All it found was *Wayward's* starboard bulkhead and a nasty ache that hung around as I got out of bed, got dressed and walked out to the cockpit.

I'd slept longer than I thought. The sun was going down over the waters to my left. DJ was lying awake on the port settee, looking up at the pink sky.

He had on my T-shirt from the SDCCU marathon. Specifically, the year I finished a hair under three hours. I treasured that thing.

"You're not going to get blood all over that, are you?" I sat down a few inches from his foot.

"The thought occurred to me, but I hadn't got around to it yet."

On the built-in cooler in front of me sat a plate with the remains of a peanut butter and jelly sandwich, a mostly-finished glass of orange juice and a banana peel—Alicia had tried to get some blood back in him.

I scraped the folds of my brain to figure out what to say next. Nothing felt sufficient. Nothing felt right. What had happened on the back porch of my house? I'd patched DJ up. He was shot. I was proven right.

I didn't feel vindicated. Shouldn't I feel pissed, at least? I'd warned him not to do what he did, and look at him now, laid up on my couch. But I couldn't muster up any anger toward him. I was glad to see him alive.

"What?" DJ sat up on his left elbow. I noticed his right arm was in a sling.

I waved him off. "It's nothing."

"Oh, come on now, man. You can say, 'I told you so.' I won't be mad. I jumped out of the frying pan, and you pulled my ass from the fire. Ain't that the very thing you've been warning me about from the beginning? False modesty hurts worse than just owning up to the fact you were right."

"Yeah, I was right." I shrugged at him. "I'm just glad you're okay."

He studied my face for a moment. Then his eyebrows went up. "Man, Jerry. You actually *are* glad I'm okay." His fingers combed through his goatee.

It was impossible to know what he was thinking, but we must've been close to the same mind. We hated each other. We did. No point in lying about it. In the couple of months DJ and I had been partnered together, the things we'd agreed on didn't stack up anywhere close to the stuff we argued about. Our relationship seemed destined to blow up, and probably one of us would be killed, to the other's indifference.

But now, our arguments, our fights—they seemed like childhood quarrels being left behind by boys who had grown into young men.

"Can't believe I just said that out loud," I said after a moment. Then I chuckled. "Two days ago, I would've shot you myself."

"A sobering thought, ain't it, *compadre?*" DJ said with a grin.

I noticed Alicia in the salon. She was rummaging around the kitchen, then winked at me.

"You were in a bad way this morning," I said to DJ. "Glad you haven't seemed to have lost as much blood as I thought."

"I'm gonna miss being a cheap date. Might let some of my blood out next time I want to get ripped."

"Then you show up at somebody else's back door next time," I kidded. "Fact is, DJ, I'm not your dad, and I shouldn't have acted like I was. You're capable of a lot—I know that—but I can't help myself." I took a slow breath, steadying my shivering hands.

"My service re-wired me," I began. "Things happened for me that shouldn't have. Everything fell my way. I passed all the tests, I got all the certifications, put in all the training hours, got the good assignments that other guys were breaking their backs trying to get—" My face pinched. I sounded like an asshole. Like I was bragging, which made me want to stomp myself into a hole.

"I shouldn't have come back from the Sandbox," I said. "And

I know that sounds crazy, but it's the truth. We left behind better guys, guys more capable, guys with more to offer the world, and more to live for. But I came back. For the life of me, I can't square why."

DJ stayed silent. And it helped, like he was giving me a blank canvas to color with all the rotten junk I'd been bottling up for years.

"I think about those guys every day. They're behind everything I do. I have to live for them, I have to do well in their memories, I have to fill in the blank spaces where their lives would've been. Understand?"

He nodded at me.

"Before I joined up, I wanted to test myself, but I wanted to do something good, too. I wanted to save people, and being a PJ gave me a chance to do that. When I got out, I didn't know what I wanted to do. So, I started doing what *they* said they wanted me to do."

"The men you lost." DJ knew without me having to say it.

I nodded.

"Dad and everybody else expected me to take over Snyder & Burkhart. Instead, I became a cop. I wasn't sure if that's what I wanted to do. Hell, the only thing I've been sure about since I left the service was marrying Alicia."

"Are you sure about Armstrong?" DJ asked.

I scratched my head. "Armstrong hasn't gone the way I pictured."

DJ clicked his teeth and nodded. "Man, I know that feeling. When I lost ole' righty and picked up this bad boy…" He tapped the cuff of his prosthetic, which stood at attention on the floor between the settee and the cooler. "…I thought, 'well, DJ, here it is, the thing you've been crying for since you found out you kicked in the wrong door, so put it on and get your ass in gear.'"

DJ leaned forward a bit. "My ass is in gear, but I still got problems. Some days I wake up wondering why I bothered to wake up at all." He sat up higher. "But, Jerry, I learned the important thing is that I wake up. From there on, things happen as they happen."

Movement in the salon grabbed my attention. Flor was awake, walking over to Alicia, then sitting next to her and resting her head on my wife's shoulder.

DJ noticed me looking and turned to look as well.

"That's Gabriela's kid?"

"The one and only."

"How's she holding up?"

"She's a strong kid, but she misses her mother."

"I would too," DJ said. "How about we do something about that?"

CHAPTER FORTY-FIVE

I helped DJ get to his feet after he put his leg on. He moved into *Wayward's* salon under his own power, while I walked behind him, ready to catch him if he stumbled. We sat down on the big settee with Flor while Alicia got up and threw together some pasta with marinara sauce and the last of the shrimp from Vieques.

After we all ate, Flor cuddled her head onto my wife's lap while she, DJ and I split a twelve-pack of beers. Despite the messes around us, it felt good to sit and talk with them, to laugh like friends enjoying a nice evening on a boat together.

I was hesitant to break the mood, but every time I looked at Flor, I was reminded of what had brought us here.

So, I told DJ what we'd learned from Dr. Markel's notes. About Hildon's botched drug, Poraxim, and how it had given Flor, and God-only-knows how many others Li-Fraumeni syndrome. And about Hildon's plans to double-dip on their own mistake by selling the cure for Li-Fraumeni for more than most people made in a year.

Outwardly, he took the news calmly, but I could see the motors kicking to life in DJ's head. I heard the fires popping and smelled the smoke. Things were going to get dicey. I just had to make sure DJ remembered I had his back, and that if we were going to take on Hildon, we had to do it together.

He shared the information he'd learned and told me about tracking Dos Santos. I excused myself from the table and finished what was left of my beer while I walked toward the fridge to grab another.

"How'd you know the cops were hired by Hildon?" I asked DJ as I reached into the fridge and pulled a beer out.

"Wasn't hard to figure out." DJ's eyes danced toward Flor. He was concerned about sharing all the details with a kid around.

"Flor, why don't you go sack out in your stateroom for a little while?" I asked.

She lifted her head. "I've been lying down all day."

"How about a shower, honey?" Alicia asked. "It's been a couple days."

She grimaced at Alicia. "You can talk around me. I'm not scared to hear what you guys are saying to each other. I deserve to know."

Alicia and I exchanged an uncomfortable look. Flor wasn't oblivious. She'd gained a lot of perspective in her short time on Earth—more than most people twice her age.

"I'll help you walk down to the head." Alicia slid out behind her, then wrapped an arm around Flor's waist and kissed her on the cheek.

After she and Alicia disappeared down the port hull, I grabbed a second beer from the fridge, and slid it across a corner of the table to DJ.

"Thanks, boss." DJ cracked it open and drank.

"So... the cops and Hildon?"

He finished his sip and smirked. "A man finds the truth real easy to tell when he's staring down a sawed-off."

"You got a confession under duress?"

He shrugged with his eyebrows. "I wasn't gonna get it any other way."

"Getting information that way is no good, DJ. You can point a gun at a man and he'll confess to kidnapping the Lindbergh baby. Did you get some other source to back up Officer Dos Santos's claims?"

"Hell, Jerry, the boys at the station and I weren't really on speaking terms."

Still, information gained under duress was flimsy.

"What about that computer from the doc's house?" he asked. "Doesn't that back up somebody at Hildon being behind all this? Who else but the lady at the top?"

"Rachel Little?" I asked. "I'm sure she didn't like Dr. Markel, but does that mean she'd hire the police to kill four people? If she wanted to get at Markel and Baptiste, she could have had Hildon sue both of them into oblivion."

"Sue them? Come on, Jerry," DJ said. "You think that'd stop a professional muck-raker like Luc Baptiste from going to press? If I'm running a big company, I'm not taking the chance that it would. Once Luc writes about the stuff Markel had, it's over. People aren't going to forget seeing Hildon's dirty laundry waving from a flagpole."

He had a good point. Dead men told no secrets.

"Even if Rachel Little weren't behind the murders, a drug her company made gave a little girl cancer." He looked pointedly at me. "We can't let this get away from us, Jerry. Was I wrong to try and kill her? Maybe. But you read those papers from the doc."

Another good point.

In either case, we had to act. The time to drop the laptop in the ocean and forget about this whole thing had come and gone. Gabriela was in jail, Flor needed help, and I couldn't live with myself knowing I'd walked away from this.

"We can't kill her," I said. "We can't go to the local police, either. Stockwell or Armstrong has to know somebody in the FBI. So, we get Rachel, turn her in to Armstrong, and let them hand her off to the feds."

"Sure. We'll turn her in." DJ rolled his eyes as he turned away from me.

I kicked him in the shin. "I'm not helping you, or anyone else, kill this woman out of revenge."

"Fine."

"Did I just hear you two promise not to kill someone?" Alicia came up the steps from the port hull, looking a shade paler.

"Just the boys talking," DJ said.

"No reason to get worried, honey," I said.

"Good. If you were seriously considering it, I'd take Flor and leave."

I believed her.

She opened the refrigerator and took out a fresh beer. After cracking it open, she rested her elbows on the counter behind me. "I suppose your little Boy Scout troop doesn't have a place for a girl, huh?"

"Alicia, darling," DJ began, "I'm all for women doing their part in things, but—"

"Jerry, I want in. I want to help."

DJ's eyes pleaded for help from me. What the hell did he

want me to do? Snap my fingers at her?

"Alicia—"

She held her hand up at me. Whatever I was going to say, I forgot it. Then, she slowly brought her beer to her lips and took a long, loud sip.

"Actually, I don't know why I'm asking, because I'm already in this with you two," she said. "Or did you think I was still on the outside?" She looked at me, then at DJ, waiting for one of us to open our mouths.

Neither of us dared.

"When you brought Gabriela to my home, I was in. When you needed someone to take care of Flor, I was in. And when we both agreed, Jerry, that I was the best person to read over Dr. Markel's notes, you better believe I was in."

She stood up straight and sauntered to the salon table, spreading her fingers on it. My wife's nails, which were normally immaculate, were chipped in places, chewed in others. Alicia raised her eyebrows at me. "Do I need to say more?"

DJ's toe tapped into mine. His head shook almost imperceptibly—a clear no. She was not *in*.

Too bad for DJ. He didn't have to live with her.

"You're in," I said.

"All right!" Alicia clapped her hands and bounced. "So, what's the plan?"

"We already decided we're not blowing away Hildon's people, right?" I said, with a nod toward DJ. "It's pointless to shoot anybody. They'd have someone else come in and keep things running the way they've always run. That doesn't help anyone. And I'm not so sure Armstrong would look kindly on us for killing business people."

"Even scumbags getting people sick, then charging their first-born for the drugs they need?" DJ asked.

"Even them," I said. "There's a fate worse than death for them. I know."

"What's that?" DJ asked.

I grinned at my partner. "Losing their money. If we can get Markel's info out to the press, Hildon's sunk."

"Dr. Markel already tried that," Alicia said. "God rest him."

"There's another way," DJ said.

My ears perked up.

"They got this thing coming up," he said. "I remember seeing it on their website when I was scoping out Rachel Little." DJ pulled out his phone, turned it on and poked around. "They got a new campus opening up. Some big party to celebrate—I'm willing to bet all kinds of reporters and cameras will be there, and anybody who's got money in Hildon will be there."

Alicia took the phone from him and looked it over. "He's right, Jer. With the right eyeballs there, we could do a lot of damage."

"You wanna get them good, you do it right in front of their friends," DJ agreed. "Pull their pants down while the whole class is watching."

Then, I noticed my wife's expression darken.

"This happens tomorrow." Alicia turned the phone around to show us.

"Tomorrow night," I said. "That gives us less than twenty-four hours to prepare."

"You guys can't go in there with less than a day to plan what you're going to do," Alicia said. "They'll have security there, and you'll be outsiders—it's not like paying a cover and walking in the door. You'll be lucky if they even let you walk up without arresting you." The portside head door came open out of view, drawing Alicia's attention for a moment. Flor was out of the shower, and within earshot.

"You're both right about what has to be done," she said quietly. "Hildon has to be exposed, publicly, but this might not be the time to do it."

"It's the only time to do it." DJ took another swig from his beer. "You ain't wrong about the problems it poses. Planning a mission is ninety percent of the job, and planning takes time, but sometimes the only choice is to go in with what you got."

"Assuming you can get in at all," Alicia said.

The air soured. We all went quiet, listening to waves splashing against *Wayward's* hull. I shuddered to think Gabriela and Flor might not see justice done against the people who'd caused them so much hardship. And that Gabriela would stay locked up until we figured out a way to call out Hildon.

Then, my hands went cold. "I might have a way in." I slid out from the couch.

"Where are you going?" DJ asked.

"I need my phone." I grabbed it off the counter and headed for the salon door.

"Jerry?" Alicia asked as I stepped into the cockpit. "What's going on?"

"Gimme a minute. I'll be right back." I bounded up the steps to the flybridge. Night had settled around St. Thomas. Out of habit, I picked up my binos, and looked at my back porch. The light was on, and except for a couple bloodstains on one of the Adirondack chairs, it looked the same as it had at dawn.

I let my eyes linger on the house a little longer. After I made this phone call, I might have to sell the place.

Putting the binos down near the helm, I unlocked the phone and opened my contacts list. There were a hundred old numbers in it. Numbers I hadn't called in years. I should have cleaned it out a long time ago, but every time I went to do it, I figured out a different use of my time, or Alicia needed something, or I went free diving off the beach outside my house.

Arlen's name was near the top of the list. I tapped it before I could convince myself otherwise.

It rang once.

"Well, Jerry! What an unexpected pleasure," Arlen said. "I was just thinking about you. I hated leaving our conversation the way we did the other day—just didn't seem right to say goodbye like that to someone I've long considered a surrogate son."

My fingers went numb. I switched the phone to my other hand. I had to do this for Flor.

"Arlen," I said. "I need a favor."

CHAPTER FORTY-SIX

Arlen rented an Amels 180 custom superyacht anchored in Long Bay. The coincidence of him being that close to my house was too much to swallow, but I had to bite back my misgivings. Gabriela and Flor's lives depended on it. Besides, Long Bay was called Long Bay for a reason. And it was a popular anchorage.

A couple hours after I hung up with him, we motored *Wayward* around Havensight Point, turned northward into Long Bay, and arrived at a set of coordinates provided by Arlen. His rented boat, *Heart and Soul,* was anchored exactly halfway between Hassel Island and Frederiksberg Point. The yacht sat both high and low on the water, the hull sleek as a shark's fin, the boat's four decks towering over the calm, black waters like an oil platform. Lights ran the length of *Heart and Soul,* illuminating her as an aspiration for all people.

Wayward came within a hundred feet of *Heart and Soul's* stern. I saw a man's figure break away from beside a woman, both dark against the lights of Charlotte Amalie. He stalked along the boat's sundeck, moving with singular focus, practically shoving aside the rented crew, trying to get as near to us as possible.

I'd recognize Arlen anywhere.

DJ hailed *Heart and Soul* over the VHF. An answer came right away. Her captain invited us aboard, asking that we maneuver *Wayward* thirty feet off *Heart and Soul's* stern. A dinghy with a tie line would come out to meet us. The captain welcomed us as Mr. Burkhart's family.

Under most circumstances, I would've forgiven the assumption we were family as a mix-up. Not with Arlen. He demanded all things carried out with machine precision. Woe to the man in Arlen Burkhart's patronage who couldn't tie a Windsor knot as crisp as a fresh twenty-dollar bill. There was no oxygen for accidents.

We slowed behind *Heart and Soul*. A good current flowed, judging by the discharge ports on either side of her stern. Using a crane, crew members lowered her tender into the water, which then moved toward *Wayward*.

Alicia went down to the guest stateroom to make sure Flor had something to eat while DJ and I tied a bridle to the forward deck cleats on both bows. A bridle was usually for anchoring to take the stress off the windlass. It was basically two dock lines with regular loops at one end to attach to the boat's cleats and thimbles at the other end, with the rope braided around it. The two thimbles were connected to a shackle that was then attached to the anchor chain.

One of the tender's crew saw what we were doing and carried *Heart and Soul's* stern line to the tender's bow. A large swivel and carabiner-type snap hook had been fixed on the end for just such a docking. With practiced precision, the helmsman brought the tender's bow to ours, where the crewman with the heavy stern line quickly clipped it onto the snubber's shackle. The snubber would keep any wave shock from being transferred to the windlass.

The helmsman backed away from us, as the guy on the bow paid out the rest of the line and dropped it in the water. I shifted to neutral and killed the engines.

Wayward was attached to Arlen's boat.

Arlen's eyes never left me. Even when I couldn't see him, a needling discomfort prodded the back of my neck. He was always a step behind me.

"Honey," Alicia said softly. She didn't finish her thought, but instead laid her hand on my wrist, and gazed at me like she'd found me alone at the bus station, clutching a teddy bear to my chest.

"I'll be all right," I whispered to her.

When the boat came alongside *Wayward's* stern, we all boarded, including Flor, who I carried in my arms. The tender, a sleek, dual console of about twenty-six feet, with rich woodwork and plush seating, took us to *Heart and Soul's* stern, where a pair of crewmen caught the line thrown from the boat and pulled us in.

Arlen's superyacht looked big from thirty yards off, but now, as we were drawn closer to it, I realized the swim platform was wider than half of *Wayward's* length.

Heart and Soul's builders were aware of their boat's size, too. When Alicia and I went shopping for a vessel, I'd been hard pressed to find anything that let me spread my arms out without whacking into a grill or a staircase or a kitchen cabinet. Not here. The swim platform comfortably accommodated all of us.

"Welcome aboard, sir." A clean-cut, middle-aged man in a captain's hat extended his hand to me. "Are you Mr. Snyder?"

I put Flor down. DJ gave her his free arm to lean into.

"I am," I said, shaking the captain's hand.

"Excellent." He reached his toward Alicia and shook, smiling politely. "We're excited to have some of Mr. Burkhart's family aboard *Heart and Soul* tonight. It's a real treat getting to know our clients, and an added bonus to meet the people closest to them."

"Thank you, Captain," Alicia said. "This is our friend, DJ Martin. And with him is Flor Ramos."

The captain's gaze switched to DJ and Flor. "Wonderful! Just wonderful." He clapped his hand into DJ's and shook. "Mr. Burkhart is entertaining a guest on the sundeck, with an after-dinner drink. Would you care to—"

"Actually, Captain Higgins, there's no need to send these folks all the way up there." Arlen appeared at the top of the spiral staircase that led down to the swim platform. His smile was as bold as a knockoff watch, with his combed-back hair like crude, smothering dead coral. A loose-fitting button-up shirt covered in tiny neon palm trees was opened down to his breastbone. Linen pants swished around his legs as he came down the steps.

Arlen always presented himself like a cocktail of Hugh Hefner, Sean Connery, and a retired Confederate colonel, but his lack of spontaneity diluted the effect. Every gesture he practiced, every word he picked out days ahead of time, loaded into tubes and ready to fire when the moment was right. Arlen said he was born and raised in West Texas, but I'd never met any of his extended family, or anyone who'd known him longer than Dad.

"Jerry," he breathed, his smile opening wider as he came toward me. "Great God Almighty, you don't know how much it warms my heart to have you standing right here in front of me again." He wrapped me in a hug.

I clenched my teeth. He pretended not to notice.

"You don't look a day older than the last time I saw you. Must be all that island living," he said, clapping me on the back with a hearty laugh. "I can see the draw. A few days here, and I'm already looking at properties, half thinking about staying and half wondering about all the development we could do. Have you seen the prices that people are willing to pay for bare islands out here? Think what could happen if two sharks like us got loose in these waters. We—"

"Snyder Holdings isn't my company," I reminded him. "It's Gene's company. She's running it."

"I know that," he said, with a bewildered smile. "I was thinking out loud, that's all, Jerry. Don't take these things coming out of my mouth too seriously. You know how my brain is. I got all sorts of thoughts rattling around in here."

He let go of me and brushed a bit of nothing from my shoulder. "There's a lot of money to be made out here is all I'm saying. Every man needs money. Every man needs land, too. And that land needs to be developed. The right partnership could take care of that."

I didn't break eye contact with Arlen. The only way to get him to back off was to come at him like you'd come at a bear. You had to present yourself without fear, like you didn't know how to give an inch of ground. The main difference between Arlen and a black bear was you could shout the bear off.

"Just an idea," he smiled at me. "No harm meant."

Sure.

"Is this Alicia?" He turned to my wife, putting his hands on the outsides of her elbows, inspecting her. "Heaven and Earth, isn't she beautiful? I can see why you fell for her. You know," he said, leaning closer to her, "he used to have this girlfriend back when he was in high school—he and my son, Jefferson, both went after her—but what woman could resist Jerry? My boy didn't stand a chance." He cocked his head toward me and winked.

"I'm a very lucky woman." Alicia was trying to be polite. but she knew how I felt about Arlen.

Arlen brushed a hair out of Alicia's face. "If I were twenty years younger…"

Then, as if coming out of hypnosis, his neck twitched. He let Alicia go and set himself to DJ and Flor.

"Who's this, Jerry? Your boat captain? And his daughter?" He motioned at DJ's sling. "Is it hard to man the helm with one arm?"

"Flor ain't mine, sir, and I'm his business associate, DJ Martin," DJ said, with a barely contained glare. "We're in oceanography together."

Arlen turned to me. "I thought you were doing charity work down here?"

"I don't know why you thought that."

"Well," he said, shaking DJ's left hand. "It's good to meet you, son. If you're partnered up with Jerry, I'm sure you've got a good, steady head on your shoulders. How'd you get into oceanography anyway?"

I exchanged a glance with DJ. We'd never discussed a cover story. Not in detail.

"I went to school for it," DJ answered.

"Of course, you did." Arlen laughed as he turned his back on DJ, heading for the staircase. "Would you fine people care to join me for a drink?"

"We're here on business."

"Oh, come now, Jerry. You're not imposing on me. A drink won't kill you, will it?"

"Jerry," Flor said. She sounded out of breath.

"Do you want to go lay down?" I asked.

She nodded.

"Captain," Arlen snapped his fingers. "Take care of little Flor, would you? Let her pick out her own room below decks." He winked at Flor, who mustered a smile.

Captain Higgins extended an arm to her. "Can you make it down a few stairs, darling?"

She nodded.

"We'll be here, Flor," Alicia added as Flor and Captain Higgins left the swim platform and went into *Heart and Soul's* interior.

That done, Arlen started up the stairs. Alicia went first, I came behind her, and DJ followed me.

At the top of the stairs, we entered a cockpit with expensive-looking hickory chairs, arranged around a gas fire pit filled with glass beads. Arlen stood behind a chair, beaming at us.

"Like it? Stick around a little while, and I can have the crew get a fire going. Alicia, I'll tell you all about little Jerry running around, raising hell with my boy. We can roast hotdogs, like when you were little, Jerry. Wasn't that fun? Remember that camping trip up to Yosemite you took with me, Jefferson, and your dad?"

Of course, I remembered. But I wouldn't allow Arlen to slip under the cover of memories from happier times. Not that any of my memories of Arlen weren't tainted by the things I realized he'd done. The money, the shady deals with men whose names he never dared mention when Dad was in the room.

"Can't say I recall that one."

"That's too bad. You had the time of your life, to my memory of events. I think we went to Big Sur, too, where you and Jeff tried to surf."

Arlen stepped away from the chair, turning his back while massaging his forehead. "In any case, I can see that you're a busy man. Let's go inside and talk shop." He slid open a tinted glass door, revealing an expansive salon.

I pulled Alicia closer to me. "If he brings out a photo album, I'm jumping over the side."

"He's lonely, Jerry."

"Lonely? He said he had a guest up top, which I'm almost certain will be a hooker. He was practically sniffing your hair."

"Be nice." She gave me a look before she went into the salon herself. I followed a couple steps behind.

The salon on most boats would have a small seating area, a table, and a compact galley. Larger vessels like *Wayward* included a little more; a desk, full-sized countertops, a large refrigerator, and cabinets. *Heart and Soul's* salon included all that, more, and a bone-white baby grand piano.

DJ walked in behind me. Decorative molding hid the strand lights in the ceiling, and the floor, with its wood tiles and gold inlays, reminded me of the ballroom floor in a country club where Dad had held his first fundraiser. The wood paneling on all the drawers and cabinets in the salon were like velvet. Every handle, hinge, sconce, and lamp was clad in brass.

Nearer the bow, beyond a dining table with seating for eight and ample room for the crew to move around and serve dinner, a TV the size of one of *Wayward's* bunks droned from the wall.

"Look at this piano!" Alicia tapped a key, then her eyes shot to me, full of surprise. "It actually works!"

"Why else would it be here?" Arlen asked. "There's plenty of room onboard. She's got another salon above us, on the bridge deck. An exercise room just beyond that wall," He pointed forward, "al fresco dining on the sundeck, which includes a jacuzzi, a small theater, and a full bar. Most of the cabins and the crew quarters are on the lower deck—but they won't let me go down there to visit. I'm quartered in the master, which is on this deck. She sleeps twenty-three, including the thirteen crew members."

"This would be one hell of a place for an orgy," DJ said.

I cupped my head in my hands.

"Must'a been quite a pile of money you sank into renting this boat," he added.

"It's just money," Arlen said with a smirk. "And what hope does money have against desire?"

I swallowed back the bile rising in my throat. "That's bull-shit."

Alicia elbowed me. "Jerry!"

"No, it's all right. Your husband knows me as the person I used to be. I was a showoff, and old habits die hard." He smiled a practiced smile. His embarrassed smile. "At this point in my life, the only habits I have left are the old ones. But there is one new thing I've learned: time is precious, and I'm wasting yours. Please, sit with me."

He walked to the oval table at the center of the salon, then pulled out a chair, beckoning Alicia forward with the subtle movement of his eyes. She obliged. I was sure to pull out the chair next to her, and DJ took the chair across from me.

Arlen sat next to DJ. "So, Jerry, what can I do for you? You mentioned something about Hildon over the phone?"

A blond woman appeared, dressed in the same white uniform as the men who'd helped us aboard. She carried a silver tray holding flutes of bubbling champagne and she looked strangely familiar. Under the table, I felt someone tapping my toe. DJ gave me a knowing look—gently signaling toward the blond woman with his eyes. I wasn't sure what he wanted.

"You're a board member at Hildon," I said to Arlen.

The woman with the champagne came up beside him. He turned and took a glass by the stem, thanking her with a quick smile.

"I am," he said. "But my involvement with Hildon is very... passive."

The blonde came around to our side, and placed glasses in front of me and Alicia. I left mine where it was, but Alicia picked hers up and took a sip.

"You said you came to help them with their problems," I said.

"They wanted to ask me, as an informal adviser, some awfully specific... questions they were facing. Being one of the biggest pharmaceutical companies in the world..." He waved his hand and shook his head. "They're a leader in their industry, and their industry has had record-breaking quarters. Hildon is doing very well. The problems they have are at an exceedingly high level, if you get my meaning, and what wisdom could a neophyte offer them?"

Arlen sipped his champagne, pinkie out, then stared into the glass. "Just among us at this table, I think they brought me out to woo me into pressing more money into their palms. Some people can't get enough."

I laughed.

"Is that why you came here, Jerry? Are you thinking about shifting some of your portfolio their way?"

"No."

"Are you seeking employment?"

"Why would I?"

He inclined his head and scrunched his brow. "Pardon the questions, but I'm unclear as to why you're so interested in Hildon. Does your oceanography venture have some kind of proposal for them? Do you want me to help you pitch them?"

I met DJ's eyes, looking for his approval. He nodded once. The blonde who'd served us the champagne was hanging around near the baby grand, behind me on the right.

"This is sensitive," I said to Arlen. "It runs... counter to Hildon's business interests."

Arlen sat up straighter, folding his arms and asking me a question with his furrowed brow. Before I started, he addressed the blond woman behind me.

"Christy, dear, would you please go and get the bar ready on the sundeck?"

"Right away, Mr. Burkhart." Her voice tapped that cognitive nerve of having met her before.

She went around the table, crossing behind DJ and Arlen, giving me a strange glance on the way. Though she looked and sounded familiar, I still couldn't quite figure out where I knew her from. She collected her tray and disappeared up the spiral staircase behind me.

I leveled my eyes with Arlen. "There's more going on here than I've let on. The oceanography thing is a front. In reality, DJ and I are working for a group of like-minded people."

Arlen put his knuckles to his chin.

"We're law enforcement," I said. "That's the best way to describe it."

"Are you federal agents?" Arlen asked. "FBI? CIA? Homeland Security?"

"No, we're not officially with the government. We're private," I added. "It's hard to explain."

"Go on." Keeping his eyes down, he swirled the champagne in his glass. He kept a cool exterior, but I knew Arlen must have dreamt of the day I'd come back to him with my hat in my hand. My stomach murmured, but it was too late to back out now.

"As I mentioned, we need a favor."

"What kind of favor are we talking about? Because you know I can't do anything that breaks the law."

I almost scoffed. "Get us into Hildon's party. The one tomorrow."

Arlen shifted in his chair, bringing his eyes to mine. "You mean to say you're acting this squirrelly because you want me to invite you to a party?"

"More or less."

Arlen's lower lip jutted out while he thought on that. He lifted his wrist, the sleeve of his shirt pulling back to reveal a watch encrusted with diamonds sparkling like fresh snow. "That party is eighteen hours away."

"Can you get us in?"

"That depends," he said.

I didn't like this. He knew I needed the invite, and he was going to make me pay to get it. "On what?"

He nodded at Alicia. "Does she know of anyone who can get her a suitable dress?"

My brain hitched.

"There's a strict dress code at Hildon's kickoff celebration. I know someone in Puerto Rico, so I can get you and DJ tuxes by tomorrow afternoon. But the dress?" He tapped his chin. "Not so easy."

"I've got some at home," Alicia answered.

"Have you worn them before?"

She knotted her fingers together. "Yeah."

"That won't do. Has to be something new." Arlen popped out of his chair, fiddling with the buttons on his shirt. Striding to a curio cabinet on the left, he opened a drawer and took out a smartphone. "My tailor referred me to a man in San Juan. Being a local, I assume he might know someone. If he does, then, yes, I'll take you."

"All of us," I said. "To Hildon's event."

"Of course, Jerry." He turned to me, beaming like I'd just signed over my soul. "There's nothing I wouldn't do to have you back at my side."

I was afraid he'd say that, but I couldn't let my idiotic fears get a hold on me. Gabriela and Flor both needed this done. They needed Hildon to go down. While Arlen made a couple of phone calls, I kept that in mind. Alicia picked up on my nerves silently going haywire, but she didn't get a chance to ask about it before Arlen hung up the phone and clapped his hands.

"He can get us a few dresses," he said beaming. "He'll bring them aboard *Heart and Soul* when he comes tomorrow, and you'll pick out the one you like best, sweetheart. Now, how's about we all head up to the sundeck, and have a couple drinks in celebration of reuniting old family?"

Refusal wasn't an option. For one, we couldn't risk Arlen taking the invites back. For two, he grabbed Alicia by the hand

and led her out of the chair before I got a chance to tell him to buzz off. DJ didn't put up much resistance, either.

"Last one up's a rotten egg!" He hop-skipped in Arlen and Alicia's trail.

We took a set of spiral stairs to *Heart and Soul's* sundeck. Yet again, the sundeck had a table with chairs, and beyond it a semi-circular bar staffed by the same blond crew member with the champagne glasses, now mixing a drink for a woman sitting at the bar. Must be Arlen's guest.

First glance, I could tell she probably wasn't a hooker. Her dress looked too new, her makeup too light, and even at the bar, she had a way of sitting as if her spine were reinforced with a confidence I had never encountered in the few prostitutes I'd met while working for the Newport Beach PD. She was a light-skinned black girl, slender, pretty hair with wavy, loose curls. She wouldn't have to turn tricks to get men to give up their cash. There was a quality in her bearing that told me she didn't *need* their cash.

"Mr. Snyder." She looked right at me.

I recognized her voice. "I didn't expect to meet you here, Tamara."

CHAPTER FORTY-SEVEN

"That another long-lost family member from back home, Dep?" DJ said quietly to me as we walked toward the bar.

"Nope, she can't even try to claim me. She's a new one. Watch yourself around her."

I sidled up next to her, DJ next to me.

"As I recall, you owe me a laptop, Mr. Snyder," she said, as I pulled in my bar stool. "I'm assuming you have it on your catamaran. Beautiful boat, by the way."

"Thanks," I said. "And I still don't know what laptop you're talking about."

"*Jerry.*" She tilted her head toward me. She didn't like my answer, but what was she going to do about it?

I shrugged.

"I don't see why you want to keep playing this game. I'm on your side. We both want Gabriela out of jail."

"True. That's something we both want. Except you also want to take over Hildon—even after you knew your company poisoned Flor. Or did you forget to mention Poraxim when we talked?"

Tamara's eyes opened wide. If it were possible, I'm betting her hair would've stood on end. Instead, her posture sagged, as the smug self-assurance fizzled out of her. I enjoyed seeing it.

"That's—no. That couldn't have—" Tamara Price didn't strike me as a woman who often had trouble expressing herself. "Where did you hear that?"

"Read about it on the laptop I don't have," I said. "A few internal memos passed around Hildon."

She pressed her fingers to her eyelids, hiding her face, playing guilty. She was putting me on. These big corporate types were unfeeling automatons, powered by tax evasion and the wails of the small folk. Did she care that her company gave a little girl a deadly disease?

I couldn't be sure. But I know I saw a teardrop hit her knee.

"I didn't know about it," she said, almost too quietly to understand. "I never would have gone along with them if I did. Excuse me, I should go."

She hopped off her barstool and hurried past Arlen, who looked her way, then looked off when he saw she was upset. She disappeared down the steps, and the sense that I'd been a complete asshole lingered on.

"Good thing you're already married." DJ slapped my back and laughed.

I ignored him.

"Now that you two have finished charming the room," Christy, the bartender said, "how about a couple of drinks?"

"Gimme a little charity. What kinda drink is in style?" DJ turned and gave me a knowing look.

Then, realization whacked me like a jibing boom to the head.

Christy was with Armstrong Research. I couldn't remember her real name, but I was sure I had seen her on *Ambrosia*, talking with Stockwell. What the hell was she doing on Arlen's boat?

I looked toward the stern. Arlen had his back to us, his arm draped over my wife's shoulder, pointing at Bluebeard's Castle up the hills in Charlotte Amalie.

"Is Armstrong investigating Arlen?"

"I'm working, sir."

DJ punched my elbow. "The hell's wrong with you?"

I couldn't say. I don't know why I bothered asking. Guess the whole thing with Tamara had scrambled my brains. If I needed to know why "Christy" was here, Stockwell would've told me. I needed to keep my cool.

"Yeah." Then I turned to DJ. "Take it easy on the booze. You lost a lot of blood."

"Don't that mean I need to give my body some fuel to make more?" He winked at me, then motioned at his sling. "I'm only looking to take some of the pain off my shoulder. I'll keep myself neat."

"We've got a long day tomorrow."

"I could shoot a bird's beak with a pint in me. But don't worry, you're not the only one with skin in this game, man. My head stays on my shoulders."

Christy, or whatever her name was, slid a drink to DJ. The smell of alcohol peeled off it like paint fumes. DJ toasted me, then sipped. His eyes rolled into his head, white as cue balls.

"A beak, huh? Must be a big bird."

He shrugged and laughed. "Good rum's worth more than the fuel it takes to ship it. Can't waste it now, Dep."

He nodded his head toward the aft rail and pushed away

from the bar. I followed him.

When he reached the rail, he turned toward me, careful to keep his voice low. "The bartender—her name's Charity Styles. She joined Armstrong the same day me and McDermitt did."

"Is she checking up on us?"

"Doubt it," DJ replied, seeming suddenly more sober. "Big Daddy Arlen might have some dirty laundry and she's here for a totally unrelated reason. Remember, our assignment's across in Puerto Rico."

I couldn't forget if I tried. The fact that I lived on St. Thomas didn't preclude other Armstrong investigators from working there. We returned to our barstools, where I nodded at Charity.

Arlen's hand landed on my shoulder.

"She's a hell of a catch, Jerry," he said, referring to Alicia. "That's the kind of woman you have to keep an eye on. Know what I mean?"

I knew what he meant, but he didn't know a thing about my wife. Alicia leaned her elbows on the port side gunwale, the lights of Charlotte Amalie twinkling around her shoulders and the wind playing in her soft hair. She was as beautiful and unaware of me as the moment we'd met.

"I don't have the problems with Alicia that you had with your wives. I can trust her." His fingers constricted on my shoulder as if he wanted to rip my collar bone free. I slid away from him.

"Jerry, men who insult me find themselves pushing against the boundaries of their own mortality." His eyes coated with a vicious sheen. I didn't doubt what he said, but I wasn't afraid of him.

"Too bad for them."

For a moment, it seemed his muzzle would slip, and he'd try

to come at me, snapping his teeth and howling for his rented crew to boot me off his rented ship. Instead, he threw his head back and laughed, clapping my shoulder.

"Oh, come on now. You know me better than those rumor-mongers out there. Hell, you know me well enough to see I was never good at picking my women. I sorely missed a straight talker like you, Jerry. Took me until my late forties to accept I was deficient with women—all the money certainly didn't fish up the honest ones."

He put his hands in his pockets and sighed. I wasn't sure if he was gawking at Alicia or at Charlotte Amalie.

"What about Tamara Price?" I asked.

"You two know each other?" he answered. "Isn't that a funny thing?"

"Don't act surprised."

He chuckled. "You were asking me a lot of questions about Hildon over the phone, and I thought we might benefit from a true insider's perspective—she's next in line for the big job."

"CEO?" I asked.

"The papers are all but signed, once Rachel Little is out, Tamara is in," he said. "Where did she run off to anyway?"

"She needed a moment. I told her some upsetting news."

"It's not easy to do the hard things, is it?" He nodded sagely. "You know, I'm glad you called me."

I grunted. I'd be second-guessing myself about that phone call for a long time to come.

"I'm a changed man. At the time, you were right to walk away, and I'm glad of it." He set his eyes on me, earnest as a beggar's. "When you left Orange County, I got my first wake-up call since Jeff. I realized that if I stayed on the path of self-interest, not only would I lose everyone I cared about, but I'd also lose myself too. So, I got right with God."

I stared at him. Arlen was a man who loved his vices, and judging by *Heart and Soul*, he hadn't abandoned them. There was the time, when, after learning of his son's death, Arlen had gotten blind, stinking drunk. When my mother called him to extend her sympathies, she suggested her church as a venue for the funeral— knowing that Arlen didn't belong to a religious organization of any kind. He declined, saying an old man in a robe would not restore his only son to life, and letting one mutter over Jeff's lifeless body would be a betrayal. Reciting nonsense from a book of magical stories would do nothing to ease the pain he felt. Arlen ended the conversation after calling my mother a papist wop bitch.

"You don't believe me—I can read it in your eyes," he said. "But I want you to know that since you left, I've had time to think. I've re-evaluated what's important to me, and what I want people to say about me when I'm gone for good. Legacy is what matters to me, Jerry. And I'm using the last of my time to repair the damage I've caused. Why, I even started my own charity."

Charity? Legacy? When I was ten, Arlen had told me that when a man dies, he doesn't care about the worms gnawing holes in him. A nihilist doesn't pull substance from a void. Arlen hadn't changed.

"You started a charity?"

"Mostly housing for low-income families. I've also funded a scattering of non-denominational churches, both in SoCal and West Texas. But you know what? When I've been on shore around here in these Virgin Islands, I've seen downtrodden people of a sort I cannot ignore. Their bellies are empty of substance, their faces don't shine with the light of God's love, and I ask myself, what is faith without works?"

"You're just the guy to help out," I said. "How many churches could you have built for the cost of renting this boat?"

"I can't help that God chose to bless me with more money than I could possibly spend in two lifetimes," he said.

"You sound defensive." I faced him and inclined my chin, looking down my nose. "Why's that, I wonder?"

Fissures began to pop beneath his mask. He maintained his affable smile, his well-meaning body language, but I knew what was going on inside. I wish he would have lost his temper, if only for half a second. I wish Alicia and DJ could've glimpsed the rage I'd seen from Arlen Burkhart.

Instead, he rubbed a vein in his forehead, calming himself, and then came closer to me.

"I'm a changed man. You've got to believe that."

"That's great," I said flatly. "I'm happy to see you've reformed yourself, Arlen. All of your churches are going to change a lot of lives."

His eyes scoured over me, anger hissing through like steam in old pipes, until he clamped his emotions off with a quick laugh, and a swat on my back.

"That's the plan, Jerry. I've got a lot of things to atone for, and I'm gonna give it my level best," he said. "Now, how about you sit and have a beer with me? We can talk about tomorrow."

Good. The sooner we were out of here, the better. I took the barstool next to DJ.

"Hey, sweetness?" Arlen called out to Alicia. She turned around; brow furrowed. "How about you come over this way and help us boys put our party plans together?"

My wife looked to me as if I'd told him to say that. I shrugged with my eyebrows, and she grimaced, but took the stool on DJ's right.

Arlen's eyes met the bartender's. "Say, Christy, the four of us have another round of personal matters to discuss. I hate to send a beautiful woman away, but would you please see yourself out?"

"Of course, Mr. Burkhart." She picked up a tote full of ice, then turned for the exit when Arlen stopped her with a wave of his hand.

"Just a minute, sweetie." He looked at us. "Anyone care for another drink before little Christy leaves us?"

"I'll take another one of these," DJ said, holding up his glass, apparently intent on getting ripped. Charity put down the ice and got to work.

"Jerry?" Arlen asked. I shook my head. "Alicia?"

"Something fruity."

"Painkiller, coming up," Charity said, as she refilled DJ's rum.

Within a minute, Charity had Alicia's painkiller made, and she poured a glass of rum for Arlen—the same stuff as DJ had. Her work done, she took the tote full of ice and disappeared down the aft staircase.

The three of them sipped their drinks. I closed my eyes and concentrated on my breathing while a familiar mix of sensations settled into my belly. Mute anticipation flowed between the crevices of my mind as I tried to blend drips of the past with what I thought might happen tomorrow, when the mission would envelop us all, and our only choice would be to follow the steps of what we were about to plan.

"So." Arlen set his tumbler down and smacked his lips. "Now that we're no longer in mixed company, I need to address a curiosity that's been burning in the back of my head all night. You actually haven't told me what about this party with Hildon has you so eager to attend. Are you investigating some kind of securities fraud?"

Alicia, DJ, and I all looked at each other in turn. We hadn't told him everything. That wasn't an accident. None of us wanted to—me least of all, but we'd made Arlen a key component in our investigation. Without him, nothing happened.

"We believe an executive at Hildon has ordered the murder of at least three people," I said.

"Rachel Little," Arlen said, without missing a beat. "What do you intend to do about her? Surely you don't think marching into the party and arresting her is going to produce any kind of meaningful justice."

"I don't. Experience has taught me better," I said. "We're going to sink the company."

He smirked behind his drink. "I've got three billion in Hildon Pharmaceuticals. A two percent share of the company."

"Consider the loss a donation to a worthy cause."

Arlen chuckled, then put his drink down. He stretched out his fingers and slowly rotated the glass between his palms, thinking. "What kind of evidence have you got?"

"A confession from a co-conspirator," DJ said. "One of the cops she hired to do the job."

"The police?" Arlen laughed. "Isn't that a hoot? I guess they're willing to do a little extra work for what she's paying them."

DJ looked at me, as if Arlen had made the point for him.

"Is this why they've got that woman locked up for killing that doctor?" Arlen asked. "Because Rachel had him killed?"

"James Markel," I said. "He contacted an investigative journalist named Luc Baptiste. We think Dr. Markel wanted to pass on information about a bad therapy manufactured by Hildon that made people sick."

"Makes sense," Arlen said before he took a gulp of rum. "Rachel Little's been jumpy as hell."

"We think she knew that the drug, Poraxim, was giving people Li-Fraumeni syndrome," I said. "People like Gabriela Ramos's daughter, Flor."

"She has cancer," Alicia added. "This is her third diagnosis in as many years. And she'll have recurrent soft-tissue tumors for the rest of her life, unless we can get her the treatment that Markel was supposedly working on."

"So Hildon has a cure, and you want to put them under? Why don't you just offer your silence for the cure?" Arlen asked. "Is this about saving a little girl, or is it about retribution, Jerry?"

"It's not just Hildon," I said. "It's everyone like them. You know what these big corporations get up to, where their priorities are. They'd dump mercury in a school yard if it meant posting a good quarter—and as soon as the next quarter rolled around, they'd twist the arms of their former and future employees in Congress until they agreed to pass a law protecting any company that dumped heavy metals on a fifth-grade jungle gym.

"These people have to be stopped, Arlen," I said. "They'll kill us all for a salary bonus."

Arlen considered my point with a long stare into his glass. The lights on the sundeck reflected on the rum, twirling, and trembling across his drink like a soul trapped in a glass. He savored each sip.

"You always did care a great deal about strangers," he said.

"But can you figure out a way to make strangers care about what Hildon did?"

"There has to be a way."

"Most of the people at Hildon's party will be insiders. Many of them have a considerable amount of resources tied up in Hildon's continued successful operation. Their livelihoods are at stake," Arlen said. "When you bust into the party screaming about murders and little girls with cancer, they might simply have their off-duty cops shoot you, then toss your bodies into the ocean."

"There'll be media there," Alicia said. "A company like Hildon has to toot their own horn."

Arlen scratched his chin. "A lot of them will be in Hildon's pocket. They'll let themselves be convinced y'all are rabble-rousers."

"Nobody's gonna defend giving a sweet little girl like Flor cancer," DJ said. "Ain't a person alive who's that raw."

"You better believe there are, son. There'll be a couple in the building that night, and they'll be right on your heels, talking about the cost of innovation, market forces, and all the talking points the pharma industry has honed over decades of silencing their critics. In all those minds you're trying to change, the idea of a little Puerto Rican girl with cancer will morph into a nameless, faceless statistic," Arlen said.

"Big American companies eat up little girls every day by pinching the pockets of schools through sheltering their taxes overseas, by mucking around in drinking water because dumping industrial runoff correctly cuts a half a percent off their bottom line, by pricing families out of their neighborhoods in the name of bigger returns, and we're all a part of it." Arlen paused and took a sip of rum. "You ever used a smartphone, or watched football on a big, flatscreen TV? Little girls in Malaysia put together the smallest pieces of those things. The most you'll ever hear about them would be a page-nine column about factory abuses in some place with a name you couldn't spell to save your own hide. And if that name somehow beats the odds and sticks in the burger-wrapper minds of mainstream America, the bosses in that factory will sell to a company they created yesterday, changing the name.

"The system belongs to corporate America, and there isn't an argument in all of God's green Earth compelling enough to make them give up control."

Arlen's broader point was hard to swallow, but he was right. No amount of bad news would make a certain type of investor question what their money enabled, so long as the returns came. That kind of person would be everywhere in the room at Hildon's party, arriving in a limo, and dressed to the nines.

We would be deep in enemy territory, alone. My specialty.

"Suppose we should quit now and be content with drinking our misery away until we croak, then?" DJ swigged his rum.

"Three people can't change a system as big and as en-trenched as the one Hildon serves—which is what you folks are talking about. Burning down Hildon is a romantic idea, but too many people get too much out of it. They'll do everything they can to turn your little Flor into an acceptable loss in the margins of a spreadsheet."

"Not if we don't let them," Alicia said.

"Well, isn't that my point? No way you can do that, sugar. I think the best approach for you bunch is to get rid of any notion that you're going to change the world. Best you can do is trade information for Flor's cure—you can't upend Hildon at a party."

"Not with pictures, or by saying a name out loud," she insisted. "An idea can be manipulated, you're right, but the truth is the truth. People at that party can't explain the truth away."

Alicia met each of our eyes in turn, pulling us toward a conclusion we could not sidestep, no matter the mortal danger it would inflict on an innocent life.

"We need to bring Flor."

CHAPTER FORTY-EIGHT

After plans were made, Alicia collapsed into bed on *Wayward*. Moving off the bed seemed impossible, even to put on pajamas and brush her teeth. Instead, she watched Jerry, pacing up and down the corridor in the port hull, his fingers mashing the screen of his phone.

"What's Macy saying?"

"She thinks we're grossly misusing her skillset." He looked up from his screen. "But she'll make the presentation for us."

"We're sure there'll be a projector or something at the party for us to use?"

"Arlen's sure. The man doesn't mix up details. Besides, if he's wrong, there are other ways we can get everyone's attention at the party."

Still, Alicia wondered if their plan would work.

"When are you going to meet Macy tomorrow?"

"Tonight. At four."

"In the morning?"

"That's what she wants. She says she's got a chartered helicopter arriving at Cyril King at 4:05."

The clock Velcroed to the wall read 1:00 a.m. "That's not a lot of sleep, Jerry."

"Not a lot of time for Macy to do what we're asking. And don't worry, I'll sleep when I'm dead."

Alicia gave him a long, hard stare.

"That's not happening any time soon," he said. He came toward her, crawled up over the foot of the bed, and planted a kiss on her forehead. "I'm pretty sure."

When he started to move away, Alicia grabbed him by the wrist. "Nuh-uh, buddy. Get in this bed."

He smiled at her, then laid his head on the pillow next to hers, and threw his long, lean arm over her body. She traced the veins in his forearm with her eyes until she fell asleep.

She woke again at 3:15, when Jerry slipped out of bed, and cracked open an eyelid to watch him pull on a light jacket, then bound up the stairs into the salon. A few minutes later, the dinghy's motor puttered to life. Alicia fell asleep again.

———

The next morning, Arlen had the tailor and his assistant flown out to Charlotte Amalie. He, DJ, and I did a fitting onboard *Heart and Soul* while Flor and Alicia ate breakfast and critiqued our modeling skills. The tailor brought a couple of tuxes, which he fit to DJ and me, as well as a half-dozen dresses for Alicia and Flor to choose from when we were done. I didn't see Tamara.

Flor had never worn anything like this before. She seemed giddy to the point that I worried about her overwhelming her own frail body, but she pulled through, alternating between sitting and standing when she had to. Flor's glowing face lifted everyone's spirits.

After picking out our evening wear, the tailor and his assistant got to work on alterations. Alicia and Flor went back to *Wayward* to see what hair and makeup products they could scrounge together, while Arlen, DJ and I ate lunch at the sundeck bar and discussed some of the details of our plan for that night.

Alicia and Flor returned an hour later with a bag that smelled like rubbing alcohol and fruit. Arlen had three of his crew sail *Wayward* back to Long Bay Marina. When they returned in *Heart and Soul's* tender, we were off for San Juan. The voyage would take about three hours, giving us time to kill before we had to get dressed and ready to ruin a party.

I caught Flor on *Heart and Soul's* lowest deck, in her own state-room. As she sat at a built-in vanity, pinning her hair high on her head, she spotted me in the mirror.

"You're looking awful sad for a man about to take on the whole world."

"It's a bittersweet time." I leaned against the open door and smiled at her. "Whatever happens tonight, Flor, I'm glad to have met you. You're a hell of a kid."

"Whatever happens?" She put down her bobby pin and turned on the vanity stool to face me. The hollows around her eyes seemed to deepen. "These people did this to me—you caught them trying to bury it. They're sunk."

I was caught off-guard by the blind optimism of youth.

"You're right," I said. "I'm just having pre-game jitters. We'll knock their teeth out. You're the star of the show, so you better think about what you're going to tell your mom when you see her."

She grinned at me, then turned back to the mirror. I hoped

that shine never wore off her.

I turned to my left and was heading toward *Heart and Soul's* aft when Tamara Price appeared in the hall. Her hair was done, and she wore a robe, her eyes cherry red. When I stopped, she sniffled at me.

"You're good with her." Her voice faltered.

"It wasn't easy at first, but I'm a quick learner." I kept my voice low—Flor's door hung open about ten feet behind me.

"I'm sorry for causing a scene last night," Tamara said. "I care deeply about her. And her mother."

"What I said wasn't easy news to take. And I didn't sugarcoat it."

She nodded, her chin wrinkling like she had to bite back tears. I started to walk away when Tamara grabbed my hand. A wet sheen guarded her eyes as they pierced mine.

"Jerry, I want you to know that whatever you and Arlen are doing tonight, I'm all in. Rachel has to be stopped."

I wasn't surprised she'd figured it out. She knew we had Markel's laptop and all the incriminating information it held. Why wouldn't we throw that in Rachel Little's face?

"All right," I said. "When things get hairy, I'll be looking for your help."

She smiled. "You can count on me." She slipped back into her room and shut the door.

I went deeper into the belly of *Heart and Soul*, to the fore stateroom, where my tux had been laid on a queen-sized bed next to Alicia's emerald green gown. I had glimpsed her trying that dress on earlier in the day. It left her shoulders bare and cut her figure in a way that got my heart popping. Tonight, when she put it on with her hair and makeup done, I hoped I'd be able to breathe.

Once dressed, I went topside, and spotted a stranger in a tux at the bar. From the aft staircase, I thought he was another of Arlen's surprise guests, who had come aboard when we'd docked a few minutes ago.

I was halfway across the deck when the man at the bar bellowed, "Don't look at me like that, Dep."

"DJ?"

His hair was buzzed, and his goatee had been trimmed like the green at the Riviera Club. I walked over to him, my brain searching for a way to recognize my partner. When I was within distance, I kicked him in his right shin. The titanium rang.

"It's me, wiseass," DJ scratched his goatee. "Enjoy looking at this handsome mug while you can, because after tonight, I'm growing it all back, man."

"Who cut your hair?" I asked, as I settled into the stool next to him. There was no bartender on duty, so I reached behind the bar and pulled out a pair of beer cans. One for me, one for him.

"A crewman hooked me up. It was my idea. I figured with me being face-to-face with Rachel Little not so long ago, I'd better change things up if I want to get inside."

I cracked the beer, sipped, and nodded. "Smart thinking, Dudley."

"I told you to forget that name," he grumbled.

"DJ Martin told me that. I don't know who *you* are, buddy." I passed the other can to him. He cracked it open.

"You're gonna kill me one of these days. Ain't gonna be a bullet. It's gonna be you, Dep."

"Speaking of killing you, how's that shoulder holding up without a sling?"

DJ's right hand rested in his lap. I knew that wasn't an accident. He clenched his fingers into a fist, then relaxed them.

"Hurts," he said. "But granddad's cough syrup is gonna keep me well-oiled."

We drank our beers and watched the crew use the crane near the bow to lower *Heart and Soul's* tender into the water. Shortly after, Arlen joined us on the sundeck.

"Gentlemen." He reached behind the bar and pulled out a bottle of gin. "If I knew you boys were here tailgating, I'd have come up a hell of a lot sooner." He poured himself a glass. "Actually, that's a lie. The business world waits for no man."

Over the next hour, the three of us drank quietly at the bar, and watched the sun paint San Juan red as it lowered to rest. The last streams of light were following the sun out of the sky when I heard my wife's voice behind me.

"The three of you ever coming down from your treehouse? Your ladies are waiting."

I turned on my stool, and nearly fell off when I laid eyes on Alicia. At the top of the aft stairs, she was every bit as beautiful as the day I met her. God, I wanted to walk across the deck, pick her up and take her down to our private stateroom.

"Jerry, where did you find her?" Arlen rose from his seat. "And do they make more of her somewhere?"

My wife beamed and blushed. I had to remind myself to breathe. Her smile had the power of a clear, moonless night, far out on the sea where a million pinpoints of light kissed the Earth and lifted a man's heart in his chest.

"No," I said. "She's one of a kind." I rushed to help her down the stairs, grabbed her hand and kissed her cheek. We looked deeply into each other's eyes. I had a flashback to our wedding on the beach in Nassau.

"You're looking handsome, Jer. Part of me wishes we weren't cratering a multinational organization tonight," she whispered. "Feels like I'm getting dressed up for nothing."

"The night's still young," I answered.

We headed down the stairs to *Heart and Soul's* swim platform. Tamara Price was already seated on the tender, and a pair of crewmen worked in tandem to get Flor off the swim dock and into the tender. Arlen had arranged for a wheelchair for Flor, which was neatly folded and tied down to the tender.

Charity, the other Armstrong asset, was there to see us off as well. I wondered if she planned to come along—maybe Armstrong had been onto Hildon for some time—but when our eyes met, and she smiled like a crew member wishing a guest farewell, I got the feeling she wasn't coming. She must have been there for a different mission. I didn't have time to know what it was, and I didn't need to know.

The tender—more a speedboat than anything—was big enough to accommodate all six of us, plus a crewman at the helm and one at the stern. I hopped on board after Flor was situated in the cockpit, then I held my hand out for my wife. Alicia bunched up her skirt, then stepped across, settling on one fork of the V-shaped bench in the bow. Then I helped DJ aboard. He plopped down next to Flor, the two of them exchanging big, goofy grins.

I wished Gabriela could have seen her daughter now. How beautiful and strong she was, how brave she'd been when I'd asked more of her than any child should have to give.

Arlen came aboard last, saying something to the crew that was inaudible over the tender's bubbling engine. He walked aft, taking the seat next to the helmsman. I sat where I was, next to Alicia on the front bench. Her fingers were interwoven with mine.

"Everyone settled in?" the helmsman asked.

"We're ready," Arlen answered.

The helmsman nodded and pushed gently on the throttle. We headed westward from *Heart and Soul*, leaving San Juan Marina behind us.

In open water, away from other boat traffic, the helmsman opened the throttle slightly. The wind was on our stern, and he seemed to be cognizant of Alicia's and Flor's hair, and only went fast enough to bring a gentle breeze over the bow. Still, the engine and wave noise prevented any talking unless we shouted.

Nobody did. Each of us was alone with our thoughts. I'd had an amicable time with Arlen—someone who didn't know the man the way I did might say it was pleasant. But as we went further from *Heart and Soul*, my mind cruised into a fog of darker memories, which fed my paranoia.

Or maybe it was clarity, because now, as I sped into certain danger with Arlen Burkhart, I was asking myself the one question I should've answered before I'd called him: why would I ask *him* for a favor against Hildon?

Arlen noticed me looking. He flashed his magnanimous smile, and I pretended not to see him, to be looking past him at the water.

The tender slowed. I turned, looking out in front of us. On the coast, a lone building rose over clusters of rectangular houses that seemed as emblematic of Puerto Rico's identity as coqui frogs. Hildon's logo blazed from the tower's crown, white as a full moon, shining down on the low houses sleeping on the dirt below.

Soon, we arrived at a brand-new dock, teeming with small pleasure craft.

"Welcome to the celebration, folks!" a worker on the dock said as he reached for a line being passed by the helmsman. "Once we have your craft all tied up, you're free to disembark, walk up the dock and take one of the shuttles to the new campus." He nodded over his left shoulder, toward land, where a trio of passenger vans waited in a parking lot.

The dock worker tied the tender down, then helped us disembark. I let Alicia, Tamara, and DJ go first, then helped Arlen get Flor and her wheelchair out safely before I hopped onto the dock.

I pushed Flor in her wheelchair up to the vans, where the driver helped her into the front seat. The rest of us piled in, the doors shut and the van pulled out of the parking lot.

The van carried us through residential streets, for three or four minutes until it slowed to a stop near Hildon's new building—a high-rise with their logo glowing neon blue at the top.

I got out first, helping my wife along, then went to the back, pulled Flor's wheelchair out, and carted it to the front passenger's door to get Flor.

Our group moved into the concrete courtyard. The space lacked finishing touches, but at the center of the courtyard, a fountain with a bronze family of three—mother, father and daughter holding hands, looked toward San Juan Bay. The fountain was lit but had no water.

Ahead, the lobby shimmered behind large glass windows that must have been six stories tall or more, creating an open feel. An abstract chandelier from MC Escher's fever dream hung about forty feet over the heads of a couple hundred people milling in the lobby.

As expected, the men were in black tuxedos with dabs of color on a watch or lapel. The women, in their long gowns with gems and precious metals splashed across their bodies, looked like the patrician wives of Roman senators. A string quartet, inaudible from outside, sawed at their instruments. People pecked at food on a row of tables against the glass nearest us. Reminded me of being a kid.

We entered the labyrinth of velvet rope leading to the door. As we waited for our turn to pass through the wall of off-duty cops in dark suits, I felt Flor's rib jittering against my arm.

I bent close to her and whispered. "You've got this. Whatever happens, I'll make sure you're safe."

She nodded, but her little body continued trembling.

"Evening, ladies and gentlemen." A man with dark shades and the calm speech patterns of a veteran police officer stepped in front of us. "May I have the name of the invitee?" His English was perfect, with only the barest hint of a Puerto Rican accent.

"That would be me, Arlen Burkhart. I've come with Ms. Tamara Price, whom you may know. We've brought along four exceptionally fine people as guests."

An officer to our right flipped through a few pages on his clipboard, then stopped, finding Arlen's name.

"Dos personas," he said to the officer in the shades.

"I'm sorry, Mr. Burkhart, but the list says you've only been approved for one guest, as has Ms. Price."

Arlen slipped on his billion-dollar smile. "Gentlemen, surely we can come to some kind of arrangement to allow all of my guests entry. They've all come a long way to join me here tonight, and I would be disappointed if our evening were ruined over something as inconsequential as a guest list."

"Mr. Burkhart, we were specifically told to keep to the list. I apologize, but that was Ms. Little's rule." Sunglasses motioned toward the clipboard. "You may bring one guest—the rest are free to take the shuttles back to the docks and enjoy San Juan's nightlife."

"And it is a beautiful city that you folks have kept here," Arlen said, as he reached into his pocket and approached Sunglasses. "We'd be so lucky to spend an evening out on the town for a second night in a row. But, as I said, these people are *my* guests, and I feel an obligation to see that they are allowed into a celebration for a company that is so near to my heart." He held out his hand, inviting Sunglasses for a handshake, which was accepted.

When his hand slipped out of Arlen's, it went straight into his own pocket. Arlen had paid him off.

"You've made a very strong point, Mr. Burkhart." He unlatched the velvet rope across the entrance to the lobby. "And those of us here with *La Uniformada* appreciate the respect you've paid our city. I think my fellow officer simply misspoke. The list says you're cleared for four guests—I checked it this morning, myself."

The officer with the list must've spoken a little English. He riffled through the pages, confused, as Sunglasses let us all in.

Arlen stopped at Sunglasses, again digging into his pocket as I passed with Flor.

"These things happen," he said. "I hope the language barrier doesn't keep us from working together in the future."

I looked over my shoulder to see him passing another wad of cash to Sunglasses.

"I'll make sure it doesn't," Sunglasses said, grinning amicably.

"Good man."

I stopped with Flor, waiting for Arlen to rejoin us.

"How much was that?" I asked him as I looked at Sunglasses to make sure he didn't hear me.

"Oh, it was a petty sum. Nothing to get too excited about."

"Couldn't Tamara have gotten us in?" She was ahead of me, already glad-handing with a silver-haired man and his much younger wife.

"No, I think we're asking enough of Tamara tonight, don't you?" Arlen clapped me on the back and ushered Flor and I inside. "Consider the money as a donation to the cause."

We walked alongside each other through the lobby. The upper floors were walled with glass, letting a person look down onto the lobby while they worked or sat in a waiting room.

"It is a nice piece of architecture," Arlen said. "Shame that it's all for nothing."

"You're not getting cold feet, are you?"

Arlen stopped, then put a hand on my shoulder.

"I never commit myself to a cause without intending to see it through." He looked at me with a grim expression. "You know that about me, Jerry."

I did. But what I didn't know was which cause Arlen had committed himself to.

CHAPTER FORTY-NINE

O nce more, I had to hurry up and wait.

The day on *Heart and Soul* was hard enough, but now that I was swallowed up by a sea of black neckties and bow ties, shoes, and accessories, I thought I might split open with anticipation.

Still, I forced myself to pick up a hampagne flute and clink glasses with Alicia. From the far end of the room, we watched a string quartet play on the stage, beneath a projection of Hildon advertisements about changing the future for the better and helping people improve their lives.

All the while, I hovered near Flor, who sat at a table and poked at caviar and pâté hors d'oeuvres, drawing curious glances by aristocratic men and women who probably wondered what in the hell some kid was doing at a high-society soiree.

I remembered my days of getting those looks and poking at that same food. It sucked.

Still, she held on. Then, Rachel Little, dressed in a ruby red gown, took the stage. Applause erupted around us.

I exchanged a glance with Alicia, who nodded, and separated

from me. Go time. First point in the plan was to get Alicia upstairs into the AV room. In addition to the makeup in her clutch bag, she'd packed a taser and a USB flash drive carrying the presentation Macy Lane had whipped up for us the night before.

Arlen assured us the AV room was unmanned. Hopefully, he was right. If there happened to be an underpaid sap on AV duty upstairs, he or she was about to catch a few thousand volts.

To my left, in her chair, Flor's eyes were bigger than caviar crackers.

"This isn't going to go the way we planned, okay?" I whispered in her ear. "But if you stay with me, you'll be okay. I promise."

She looked at me, confused. She'd understand soon.

"Good evening, everyone!" Rachel Little couldn't hold in her excitement. If she'd known about the bottle we were about to open, she'd be screaming like a banshee. The applause died down.

"Welcome, all, to Hildon Pharmaceuticals' new headquarters!" The applause came roaring back like a jet engine. Even I joined in, to keep up appearances.

Behind and above Rachel, an image of an old couple blowing bubbles changed to a mother holding her newborn baby, with some kind of patch stuck to her shoulder.

"Thanks to your wise investment in this company's future, we're going to use this state-of-the-art campus to bring Hildon Pharmaceuticals to new heights, and to push the pharma research industry into a new dawn of discoveries, improving the lives of people around the world."

More applause. They were like trained monkeys.

"Before I go any further, I would like to extend a special thank you to Tamara Price."

The mother and newborn were replaced by a blue screen.

"Without her tireless effort, leadership, and vision, we wouldn't be standing here today."

Black text on a white background appeared over Rachel's head. Macy had put up the most damning memo first—the one in which Rachel had acknowledged that Poraxim had given Li-Fraumeni Syndrome to "some test subjects" in later clinical trials, but that it was too late, and too costly to pull the therapy now. A year later, she would reverse course, and Hildon would discontinue Poraxim without explanation.

I looked at a balding man to my right, the screen reflected in the lenses of his glasses, his mouth agape as he read.

Rachel said something, but no one heard.

"Excuse me?" she raised her voice. She turned and looked up at the screen in time for the next slide—a doctored version of her corporate headshot, blood oozing from her mouth and eyes. "What on earth is that? Who's in the AV room?"

She spun around, squinting at the beam of light coming from the projector.

"Turn that off!" she screamed into the mic. "Turn that off now!"

The next slide came up. Another memo from Rachel. A short one. Macy had blown up the words and underlined them for emphasis: WHAT INVESTORS DON'T KNOW WON'T HURT THEM.

A murmur rolled through the crowd. Killing children was one thing but lying to investors was an unforgivable sin.

"That's taken out of context!" Rachel yelled. "Please! You

have to understand! I didn't—"

All the bluebloods in front of the stage had started booing her. She gave up trying to explain herself and left the stage in a huff.

That was my cue.

"Ready?" I said to Flor, as I scooped her in my arms.

"I'm scared, Jerry."

"I know, kid. Me too. But we'll get through this."

She cinched her thin arms around my neck, burying her face against my shoulder. I hurried to the stage.

Every eye turned to me. In the dim room, I saw the confusion, felt the panic simmering. No one knew who I was or why I was here.

"Lift your head up, sweetie," I said to Flor. "Let them see you."

She did. The audience's attention shifted from me to her, as if they knew something was wrong with Flor.

"This little girl was given Poraxim at the age of eight," I said into the microphone. "Her name is Flor Ramos. She has Li-Fraumeni syndrome, and she's had cancer three times."

The room went silent. I'd sucked all the air out.

"Hildon knew what their drug—"

A scream cut me off. It came from the AV room.

I deposited Flor on the stage, whispering to her to stay put, jumped down, and elbowed my way through the crowd.

"DJ!" I'd lost sight of my partner. "DJ, it's Alicia!"

When I reached the edge of the crowd, I saw DJ running into the hall, ahead of me. He hit the door for the stairs first, and I came right behind him.

"I told you I shoulda been security for Alicia," he said as we ran up the steps.

"You were right," I said. "Now help me save my wife."

We cleared the stairs faster than I thought possible. I rammed through the third-floor door, then spilled into a half-finished hallway. Based on the projector in the window overlooking the lobby, I knew the AV room had to be to my right. I cut around a corner, and saw an open door, the projector sitting on a stack of boxes.

I sprinted toward it.

Two steps into the room, I saw Alicia wasn't there. Before I could turn around, I heard a pop like a circuit breaker blowing and an electric hiss, when something bit me in the neck. My body tightened, the popping stopped, and my knees turned to jelly.

No sooner had I collapsed to the floor than I felt a knee against my spine. On my belly, I tried to fight against it, but the shock had taken everything out of me. A cord tightened around my wrists, binding them behind my back.

"Don't struggle too much. You're gonna hurt yourself."

I didn't recognize the man's raspy, accented voice. His hand pulled at the cord around my wrists, forcing me to either break my shoulders, or get to my knees.

"Where's Alicia?"

"Is that your woman, bro?" He clicked his teeth. "That dress she's wearing is killer. Know what I mean?"

"Where is she?"

"Don't worry about that now. You got bigger problems." He pulled me up. My feet were uncooperative, but I got them under control by the time DJ was marched in, also with his hands behind his back, escorted by security. Blood clung to DJ's lips.

The guy holding me laughed. "What happened to your neck?" he asked DJ's guy.

"Crazy bastard bit me," he said. "Can you believe that? I hit him square with the stun gun."

"I'm impressed."

The guy holding DJ grunted and pushed him toward a door in the AV room opposite from where we entered. I was forced to follow.

We entered another hallway, then were taken to the right, then left around another corner, and right again. It appeared we were zigzagging toward the building's corner. We hit a fire exit door, and walked the stairs down, coming out of the side of the building.

Two SUVs idled in the alleyway, guarded by three or four men dressed in black suits.

DJ was stuffed into the first car and my guy took me to the backseat of the rear car. He buckled me in on the passenger side.

"Where's my wife?"

He shook his head. "You're getting worked up over nothing." He slammed the door.

I watched him, as well as the guy who'd restrained DJ, go back into the building through the fire exit. My heart pounded in my ears, and my veins throbbed in my wrists. By the time they came out with Arlen, in handcuffs, and Flor, who was carried out and handcuffed, my hands were numb.

As she was carried to the seat in front of me, I saw the tears streaking down Flor's cheeks.

"It's all right, honey," I said after she was loaded in. I tried to lean forward to put my chin on her shoulder but couldn't reach. "Just stay with me, okay?"

She nodded.

"We'll get through this."

To my left, the door ripped open, and the officers loaded Arlen in.

"Now, Jerry," he said, as a seatbelt was looped over his lap, "remind me. Was this part of the plan we discussed last night? Because I don't seem to recall this coming up."

"This wasn't part of the plan we discussed," I confirmed. "Sit tight."

"I'm not excited by the prospect of fighting off a jail sentence for a second time."

I said nothing.

The officer who arrested me opened the driver's door and got behind the wheel.

"What's your name, son?" Arlen asked him.

"Officer Abalos."

"Officer Abalos, do you know who I am?"

"I don't care, Grandpa. Shut your mouth and keep it shut."

Arlen looked at me, exasperated.

"Officer, you should—"

"Don't tell me what I should and shouldn't do." The muscles in his hands rippled as he grabbed the wheel and held on.

"That little stunt you all pulled is for nothing, you people realize that?" The faux leather on the steering wheel squealed as his hands clamped and twisted. "Hildon is evil? They're all evil. Every single big corporation out there. So, what do you care? What's the difference?"

"It has to stop somewhere," I said.

Abalos's head whipped around. He glared at me from the driver's seat. I thought he was going to say something else, instead his knuckles cracked squarely into the bridge of my nose. For a moment I saw nothing. The only sensation came when his next shot popped my lip open, then I heard Flor screaming.

"You're out of your mind!" Arlen growled.

"You want it next, Grandpa?"

I opened my stinging eyes. Blood flowed from my mouth into my lap.

"Jerry?" Arlen asked. "Jerry, can you hear me?"

I nodded at him.

"He's fine." Abalos ripped the shifter, and we started moving.

Getting my bearings was challenging, but through the windshield I saw the taillights of the car holding DJ and now I could see that Alicia was in there too, thank God. We meandered deeper into the neighborhood around the Hildon building, going past crumbling houses and empty lots. Within a few minutes, we turned into a driveway and Abalos put the car in park. He got out, walked to Flor's door, and pulled her out.

While he carried her into the house, I hoped against hope that I could figure a way out of this, and Flor would be all right. But with the building in front of us being a rundown house and not a police station, I was having a hard time keeping that thought.

Arlen was more concerned about other things. "Bad news," he said. "There's a backhoe in the front yard."

"Thanks for the warning," I said.

"Maybe you aren't considering the subtext, but in my experience, Jerry, being abducted and taken to a construction site has never ended well for the abductee. Typically, it's an outstanding place to hide a few bodies." He set his gravest glare on me. "They mean to kill us."

CHAPTER FIFTY

Abalos came back for Arlen first. Then, it was my turn.
He undid my seat belt, grabbed me by the neck, and pulled me out. I tumbled to the muddy ruts that served as a driveway, landing on my ass.

"Come on, I gotta get home to my family soon." He forced me to my feet and marched me through the front door.

Inside, the house was dark. I could see well enough to know I was in an entrance hall of some kind. The walls were decorated with framed pictures and crosses, as if whoever lived here had only run out to grab a gallon of milk. But I knew that wasn't true. Straight ahead, at the back of the house, I saw kitchen counters and part of a table.

Abalos led me to the left, into a large room. His accomplice stood in the near corner, pointing his handgun in the direction of my wife, DJ, Flor, and Arlen, who all knelt in front of a large, rectangular hole dug through the floor. They turned and looked at me. Alicia's face twisted in horror.

"Jerry, what happened to you?"

"He tripped and fell," Abalos answered. "No more questions."

I was marched beside Arlen.

"On your knees."

The floor was muddy and cold, and the chill lanced up from my knees, threatening to freeze out my brain. I had to keep it back. I needed my wits now, more than ever.

To my right, past Arlen, I heard Flor quietly sobbing.

"It's okay," Alicia whispered. "I promise we'll be okay."

I'd heard that phrase out of her mouth more times than I'd like to admit. I hoped Flor took it to heart as much as I did in my darkest hours.

"Why don't y'all quit dicking around and bring your boss out here?" DJ asked. "Where's Rachel Little? Has she even got the guts to see us off, or are you two gonna do all the work, like you did with Blunt?"

Abalos and the other man looked at each other in confusion.

"What did you say, *acho*?"

"Surprise," DJ said. "I seen what you did to my friend Blunt, along with your third amigo. Too bad I painted Dos Santos's bathroom wall with his own face, but before I did, he told me all about Rachel Little, and how she put you up to all the murdering you been doing. I wish he were here now, trying to explain how he isn't some yella' coward."

Abalos stomped around the hole. He took his pistol out from under his suit jacket. I thought DJ was done for. Instead, Abalos pistol-whipped him across the jaw and blood splattered across the wall.

He grabbed DJ by the chin, forcing him to look up. "You think you're tough? You think killing cops makes you somebody?"

DJ smiled at him through a bloody mouth. "Why don't you just shoot me, *hombre?*" he mumbled. "Or do you gotta wait for Miss Little to come out and give you permission?"

Abalos threw him to the ground, then went back to his position on the other side of the hole.

"She isn't coming," I said to DJ. "Rachel Little was never part of this."

Abalos stomped to me, then grabbed me by my hair and pulled until my chin jutted out. He pressed the end of his handgun to my throat.

"Did I tell you to talk?"

"Officer Abalos, there's no need for that." Into the dark, musty living room stepped Tamara Price, her eyes settling on me. "I knew you were sharp, Jerry."

CHAPTER FIFTY-ONE

Flor was the first to react to Tamara. "*You* put my mama in jail?" she screamed. "How could you do that? You were supposed to be her friend!"

"Let him go," Tamara said to Abalos, ignoring Flor. He released my hair. "And why did you put Arlen Burkhart in handcuffs? I specifically asked you not to do that."

"I didn't know which one he was, ma'am," Abalos said. "Safer to restrain them all and figure it out later."

"Safer? And yet you beat this man?" She motioned toward me. "Does that seem like a safe thing to do? What if he were Arlen Burkhart?"

Abalos shrugged.

"Let Arlen go." Tamara said flatly. "He's the gentleman you *didn't* beat."

Abalos motioned for the other man to keep his pistol trained on me, He crossed to Arlen, then used a small knife to cut through his restraints and helped him stand.

"I tried to tell him who I was," Arlen said to Tamara. "I won't repeat exactly what he said, but he very rudely stated he didn't care to learn my name."

"Officer Abalos, we'll discuss this matter later." Tamara wasn't pleased with his on-the-job performance.

As Abalos walked to the other side of the hole, Arlen noticed me watching him.

"Is there something on your mind, Jerry?"

"So much for a Snyder and a Burkhart working together again."

Arlen frowned at me.

"He has interests that don't concern you, Jerry," Tamara said. "Did you really think Arlen would burn a fortune to keep you happy?"

"Maybe for a minute or two," I said. "But when he told me you were next in line for CEO, I knew you couldn't be trusted. So, I kept an insurance policy. Journalists around the world are going to print with stories written on the information from Dr. Markel's laptop."

Macy would keep up her end of the deal. I promised her more work from Armstrong in exchange for her help.

Tamara's brow wrinkled. "You think newspaper articles are going to help you right now?"

"Let's find out," I said. "If everyone stuck to their embargoes, the first batch of articles should have hit about an hour ago."

"Hildon has had a thousand bad articles written about it," Tamara said. "You're not scaring me. The company has more than enough money to pay out lawsuits."

I couldn't help but smile. My busted lip stung.

"Sure," I said. "But how about you? Think you've got enough to cover four counts of conspiracy to murder? Last I checked, a person can't pay out a life sentence."

Even in the darkness, I swore I saw steam coming from Tamara's ears.

"You should check The Wall Street Journal," I said. "They seem like a timely bunch."

She pulled her phone out of her pocket. The glow of the screen put a feverish color in her eyes as she searched for the article, then found it.

"No," she whispered.

"The best way to solve a murder is to answer a simple question—who benefits? If you didn't stop the Poraxim scandal from breaking, you'd take over a company headed under—your career would be over."

Suddenly, I heard the familiar sound of a helicopter's blades chopping through the air. It was low, but recognizable—a sound I learned to listen for and appreciate during my time in the service. Salvation.

Tamara pulled her eyes from her phone. "None of this changes the math in this room, Jerry." She motioned at Abalos and the other man with an open palm. "You should've turned me in yesterday."

The helicopter was louder now. Loud enough that Arlen looked through the window. I felt like I could exhale again. We'd all get through this. We were too close not to.

The deep thudding of a chopper's rotor couldn't be ignored. It made the walls shake. Abalos looked up at the ceiling. Being a cop, he must've known what was coming.

Light flooded through the front window.

"That's a bird!" Abalos said.

"A what?" Tamara moved toward the window. Not a smart move. *La Uniformada* would spot her. Abalos snatched her away before she hit the light.

Her face trembled with panic. She was cornered with nowhere to go, nothing to do. Her life was over.

"Kill them," she said looking into my face.

"What?" Abalos asked.

"I said *shoot them*, Abalos!"

For a moment, I think he understood the futility of their situation. He knew killing us would solve nothing—in fact, if he, Tamara, Arlen, and the other officer survived, they would be up against four additional counts of murder.

Still, he raised his pistol at me.

He was a desperate man with nothing to lose, a man at his most dangerous.

Arlen leapt at Abalos.

CHAPTER FIFTY-TWO

I didn't waste a split second. Before Arlen and Abalos hit the ground, I was launching myself at Abalos's partner. I didn't know his name. It didn't matter. I had to beat him into submission with my arms behind my back. Failure meant watching my wife, my partner, and a little girl getting murdered before my ticket was punched too.

Surprise was my only weapon. That, and my skull. He was too busy watching Arlen go for Abalos to notice me coming at him like a missile. I jumped like I meant to fly through the front window, leading with the top of my head, aiming it directly at his chin.

I connected. Jawbone drove into the crown of my skull as his teeth crunched together. My vision fuzzed, and I heard glass shattering and I realized I must've put his head through the front window. When I saw the dark, dirty floor again, a pistol was lying at my feet like a prize.

Only problem was, I couldn't simply bend over and pick it up.

Abalos had Arlen in a headlock near his hip, taking complete control of Arlen's body with one arm free.

With Arlen handled, his attention turned to me. Abalos pointed the pistol at my head. In the beam from the helicopter's spotlight, I saw sweat trickle down between eyes mad with desperation. He was going to kill me without a word.

Then DJ's prosthetic leg twirled through the air at Abalos. There was a sound like a metal baseball bat cracking a dinger to the upper decks. Abalos staggered and let go of Arlen.

"Get down!" I jumped, kicking my legs out in front of me, landing flat on my butt.

When I hit the ground, I think my palms slapped the grip of the handgun. The zip ties had cut off most of the circulation to my hands, so I wasn't exactly sure. Did I have the grip, or the slide? I had to work fast. Abalos was shaking his head, clearing out the cobwebs.

I thought I felt a steel loop—maybe I had a finger under the trigger guard. I went with it, awkwardly trying to get the muzzle pointed in the right direction.

Abalos raised his weapon at DJ.

Whether my aim would hit Abalos or Arlen, lying on the ground in front of him, or the floor beneath me, or even myself, I didn't know until I took a shot.

I fired.

The muzzle flash was hot against my back. In the time it took to blink, I battled against the near certainty that I'd muffed the shot. What was I thinking? I might as well have tried to hit the moon, or maybe throwing the handgun at Abalos would've worked better.

Then the cloth of Abalos's jacket rippled out from the point of impact, like the surface of a pond disturbed by the first raindrop of a hurricane. He cried out. He dropped to the floor, holding his hip. Not a great shot, but with the circulation to my fingers cut off, I'd gladly accept a shattered pelvis.

Behind me, the front door busted in.

"*Policía! Policía!*" A dozen men barked all at once.

They flooded into the room, pointing guns at Abalos, at me, and DJ. Even at Tamara Price, who remained frozen against the wall, horrified at the chaos she'd unleashed.

"Drop the weapon!" someone bellowed in English.

They'd get no argument from me. I let go of the handgun, then was pushed to the ground, and searched—never happier to have it happen.

"It's all right!" I said to whoever would listen. "We're not armed! We're hostages!"

"Let him up! He's my informant," a familiar voice said.

Detective Collat helped me to my feet. Another officer cut the zip tie off my wrists; as the blood rushed in, my hands felt like beehives at the ends of my arms. Nice to know they hadn't lost all sensation.

"How in the hell did you find us?" I asked.

"I was in position on the south end of the Hildon building, waiting for you to signal me when I saw these men stuff you and your friends into their cars," Collat said.

"Imagine that, a cop actually doing his job," DJ quipped as he pulled his leg back on. He grinned at Detective Collat.

"It's been known to happen from time to time," Collat replied.

"I guess y'all aren't all bad," DJ admitted.

Collat smiled at him—the first time I'd seen him do anything but grimace.

CHAPTER FIFTY-THREE

Two days after that night where we all faced death together in an empty house near San Juan Bay, Alicia, DJ, Flor, and I gathered at the Bayamón Correctional Complex.

With Tamara Price's capture, Gabriela had been cleared of all charges against her.

Flor eagerly waited in her wheelchair, a clear morning's sunshine gleaming on her face. The bouquet of flowers in her hand bounced on her knee. We'd been waiting in the parking lot across from the prison entrance for an hour already, and if she had to wait another minute, she might explode.

Luckily, it didn't come to that. Gabriela came through the gate, beaming. Flor squealed at the sight of her, and Gabriela ran to her daughter, wrapping her in a hug.

"Those two back together is the sweetest thing I ever saw," DJ said, leaning against the car next to me, his face bruised and his right arm back in a sling. As bad as he looked, we all agreed I was the uglier one. The bridge of my nose was black and uneven as a lump of coal, the bone broken clean across, but I was happy to have made it through our ordeal with nothing worse than that.

"You know, Dep, it's good to have someone you can rely on," DJ said.

"Agreed, Dudley."

He looked at me and laughed. "You're embarrassing me, man."

We didn't have to say it to each other, but I believed DJ and I both knew that despite our differences, we were better together. I could get used to having him as a partner.

I wrapped my arm around Alicia's shoulders and pulled her close. "When we're done here, what do you think about looking up those sailing lessons?"

"I think I need another month of doing nothing." She dropped her head back on my shoulder. I kissed her.

"Nothing but sailing," I said.

As Flor and Gabriela picked through the bouquet of flowers, my phone buzzed in my pocket.

"If that's Armstrong, tell 'em we died on the way to San Juan," DJ said.

I pulled out my phone and saw it wasn't a call at all.

"Nope, we're still alive," I said, showing DJ the screen. "It's an alert Macy helped me set up yesterday. Hildon is in the news again."

"Already?" Alicia turned to see my phone. "What did they do this time?"

"A bankruptcy court is making them file Chapter Seven. They're liquidating everything."

"They're toast?" DJ asked.

"Buttered on a plate. The next thing they'll announce is when the auction starts."

"Maybe I can get that projector they used at the party?" DJ

wondered aloud.

"But if they're auctioning all of Hildon's assets, doesn't that mean Flor won't get her cure?" Alicia asked. "The patent to Anthradone is an asset."

She was right. That dampened the mood. At least Flor and Gabriela were too busy catching up to hear us talking.

"Man." DJ said. "Who's going to tell them?"

Gabriela kissed Flor's forehead, the two of them in their own world. My stomach sank, but then a solution hit me.

"I'll bid on the patent," I said. "I've got the money. In fact, I don't care how much it costs, I'll buy it."

"But you need someone to actually make the drug," Alicia said. "Unless you know someone who can do that."

I didn't know any pharmacists, or geneticists, or whatever "ist" would be able to make Flor's treatment. "We can't give up on her. We'll find somebody out there."

My phone rang in my hand. This time, an actual call. One I especially didn't want to answer, but I did anyway.

"Arlen." I walked from the car, away from everyone else.

"How's your morning, Jerry? Did Flor's mother get released from prison?"

"Yep," I said, looking over my shoulder at her. "She's talking to Flor right now."

"Give her my regrets. I would have liked to be there when she was released," he said. "Unfortunately, it was impossible to break my prior obligations."

"Right. The island. How's it look?"

"Pretty as a postcard. God's own getaway, with white sand, thick mangroves, lots of sunshine and plenty of space for another home, if you should ever desire…"

"I'm good for now, thanks."

"Of course," he said. "Jerry, I wondered if you'd heard the news about Hildon this morning?"

"Chapter Seven—yeah."

"Couldn't happen to a finer bunch of folk."

"I'm worried about Flor's treatment, Arlen," I said. "They're going to sell off all of Hildon's patents."

"No need to worry. I took care of the Anthradone problem."

"You took care of that? Past tense?" I couldn't believe my ears. "How? There hasn't been an auction for Hildon's patents yet."

"Now, Jerry, the auction is only a formality for the official exchange of assets to pay off Hildon's debtors, so what's the difference if some things are sold before the opening bell? Money still gets to the pockets of people who are owed, and ownership is only a minor detail in the instance of a pharmaceutical product. The more important consideration is getting treatments to the people who need it, wouldn't you agree?"

"You're not answering my question."

Arlen chuckled. "You're all business, aren't you? A well-placed connection let me get the jump on things. Considering a child's life hangs in the balance, timeliness became a factor. I was able to expedite the normal process."

"Holding the Anthradone patent is only half the problem," I said.

"Creating Flor's treatment is the other half," he answered. "I know; I've got those ducks all lined up. Markel's old lab was very eager to come to a financial agreement with Burkhart & Associates. Flor's dose of Anthradone will be ready in about two weeks. I'll get it shipped to your house on Frenchman Bay Road, along with instructions on how to administer it—Alicia can handle that part, I'm sure."

"Yeah," I said, dumbfounded. "She can do it."

"Wonderful!"

"Thanks, Arlen."

"Anything for family. Now, I really must get back to this property inspection—you know how it is. Folks are always so busy."

"Sure," I said. "Bye."

I ended the call, still unsure how to process everything. Arlen had saved Flor's life. That was a good thing, wasn't it?

Then, something else surfaced from the murkiness of that conversation. How did Arlen know I lived on Frenchman Bay Road?

EPILOGUE

A rlen's new private island looked better in person than it did online. On a computer screen, though, the sun could not kiss your bare arms, and the salty ocean breeze could not press into your nostrils. A computer could not take you to the highest precipice of your island's coast any better than it could do backflips for your pleasure.

From this vantage point, on the leeward side of his new private island, Arlen saw the shimmering hot air baking across the terracotta shingles of the fourteen-bedroom, sixteen-bathroom mansion about a mile off. Between there and here, a mass of untamed greenery, rife with secrets and hidden places. Not a bad spot to call home for the foreseeable future.

At the base of the cliff, he marveled at the deep blue water fraying against the rocks a hundred feet below. The ocean was a patient, persistent thing, always working toward a greater goal of wearing down all the land, taking the whole of the world into its possession.

"Sure is pretty, Mr.—uh, Condor." Patrick Edwards, the greasy little man Arlen had paid to keep an eye on Jerry's home, grabbed the trunk of a sapling, bending it almost to the point of breaking as he pulled himself to the crest of the hill.

Didn't he know that tree didn't belong to him? Where did he get off mistreating it so?

Mr. Edwards was getting too familiar, too casual, and much too fast. Did he think of himself as a peer to Arlen Burkhart? He certainly seemed pleased as punch to step up to that line, and lift his foot over, daring his superiors to cut it off, or suffer the embarrassment of his idiocy.

"Please, call me Arlen," he said, sure to smile amicably. "There's no need for codenames or any of that clandestine nonsense now that we're communicating face-to-face—it's too impersonal."

"Right." Edwards nodded his little round head. "I was just thinking, this is such a nice place you've got here. But now that you've got it, it needs protecting, right? There's lots of dangerous people out there."

"Too true, Mr. Edwards. The world has never been a particularly kind-hearted place."

Edwards wiped sweat from his brow. For a man who lived in the Virgin Islands, he sure seemed poorly adapted to the climate.

"This is a little beneath my talents," Edwards said, "but I'd be willing to go on contract for you. I can manage a security team for you or run the kind of discreet errands you'd need from a man like me."

"That's a very generous offer, Edwards, but I wouldn't want to reduce a man of your stature to work best left to your lessers. You're a busy man, with a long client list, I'm sure."

"Well," He gulped down a breath. "I can make you my only client, Arlen. You need someone like me."

There he went, overstepping boundaries again. He was a pushy little cuss, assuming he knew what Arlen Burkhart needed.

Arlen had been around his fair share of pushy men. They had a way of pushing into things they shouldn't. Keeping Edwards around would inevitably end up with him digging into Arlen's business, rooting around for blackmail.

"We could talk about a retainer, perhaps," Arlen said. "I must admit, you did a very fine job of bringing my boy's journal back to me from Jerry Snyder's home."

"Sure, Mr. Burkhart. I can write up a proposal if you like."

The slimy little man was too eager—Edwards practically had dollar signs for pupils.

"No, I'd rather not create an unseemly paper trail. These sorts of things are best handled with as little trace as possible; don't you think?"

"A written contract is an absolute must, sir. Maybe I could sign it with a subsidiary of yours—keep your name off the deal."

Arlen lifted an eyebrow and looked at Edwards. He wasn't completely ignorant of how these things worked. Too bad the man didn't know what he didn't know, or he never would've pushed Arlen.

"Fine idea, son, fine idea. How's about we walk back to the house, and talk shop in the parlor over lunch? I can have the crew on *Heart and Soul* bring a bit of marlin steak ashore. Do you like marlin steak?"

"Yessir."

"Well, then, after you." Arlen motioned for Edwards to take the lead. When he was two steps away, Arlen reached into the pocket of his shorts, took out his snub-nosed revolver, and fired two rounds into the back of Patrick Edwards's head.

Pity the man who didn't know his place.

The End

AFTERWORD BY WAYNE STINNETT

This book has been a long time in coming. I got the first inkling for it while writing Rising Water in early 2019. At the same time, I was cowriting Vigilant Charity with Kim Bindschatel. Prior to that, I was searching for someone to take over writing the bulk of the Charity novels and mystery author, Stewart Matthews, volunteered. I'd read his books and had no doubt he could do it, but he lacked the one quality I wanted—the feminine touch.

I knew I wanted to do another spinoff even before that, and introduced several new characters in Rising Charity, who I thought would be worthy of a series of their own. One of those characters came back in Rising Water, a one legged former Ranger by the name of DJ Martin. A new couple also appeared in that book—Jerry and Alicia Snyder. The chemistry between DJ and Jerry was all wrong, which made them perfect to become a team.

I asked Stewart if he were still interested in collaborating on a new series, and he agreed. This was in the Fall of 2019. By the first of December, we had developed a working outline, then the hard work began.

Today is March 11, 2021. Stewart and I have been working on this book for eighteen months, and it will be released in less than a month. During the time it took us to write this book, we each wrote and released several more on our own. Wayward Sons was a side project. During the writing of this book, I moved my office to a new location. The view at Lady's Island Marina was spectacular, but unnecessary. People often commented on how motivational it must have been. Truth be told, when writing, I closed all the blinds in my office above the marina. It was a huge distraction.

As always, I thank my family first. The support, ideas, and guidance they provide, even when unintended, is without measure. We made it through 2020, with all its challenges, and are looking forward to a brighter 2021.

Much appreciation to a very select group of individuals, Jason Hebert, Mike Ramsey, Rick Iossi, Deg Priest, and Alan Fader, for their local knowledge and experience in helping with the details of this book.

I owe a great deal of gratitude to Samantha Williams and Ashley Lobocki, owner and manager of Aurora Publicity. Their tireless efforts have provided me with the time I need to relax and recharge. Anyone who knows me well, can attest to me being a bit of a control freak. But I think taking off several of the many hats an indie author wears and turning that work over to someone better experienced to do it, will become one of the best decisions I've made. This allows me more time to write and spend with my family. God grants each of us only a certain number of hours to fulfil our lives and I want to make the most of those I have left.

Marsha Zinberg is my editor. She has decades of experience and worked for a large publishing house in New York for many years. She now works independently and I'm fortunate to have met her at a writers conference several years ago.

Donna Rich has been the last critical eye on my manuscripts almost from the start. By the time she gets it, there's little left work left, but she always finds something to fine tune the helm. Thanks, Donna.

In recording the audiobook version of Wayward Sons, Nick Sullivan breathed life into my and Stewart's characters. Nick has been the voice behind Jesse and Charity for six years and twenty-four novels, plus my one volume of non-fiction. We've become great friends over the years and Nick co-hosts my monthly, livestreaming, video podcast, *Talk Write*. In case y'all didn't know, besides being a veteran actor of stage and screen, with hundreds of audiobooks to his credit, Nick is also an extraordinary novelist. Check out his *Deep Series*, with Boone and Emily. Thanks, Nick, for all the late hours, texts, and phone calls.

Wayward Sons is the first book in this brand new *Caribbean Mystery Series*, and I hope there will be many more to come. Thank you, my loyal readers, for taking another chance with me.

AFTERWORD BY STEWART MATTHEWS

Among some circles of authors, Wayne Stinnett is a past master of all aspects of the craft. Wayne would be embarrassed if I went too deeply into why he's a venerated figure, so allow me to cut to my point: when he asked me to co-author a new series with him, I said yes. I said it without reservation, without talking to my wife, and without asking too much about what the work actually entailed.

Wayne earned his reputation. I trusted him, implicitly. After writing a novel with him, I trust him more.

He sent me an advance copy of his 15th Jesse McDermitt novel, Rising Water. My task was to get to know two characters featured in the book (DJ Martin and Jerry Snyder) then to spin up some adventures for the both of them, which he and I would talk about.

I had no trouble. Many authors keep a collection of notes, or a file, or a notepad in their night stand, filled with unexplored plots and half-finished ideas which are nearly indistinguishable from the ravings of a lunatic. I send text messages to myself with ideas that usually come to me in the shower or while driving. If a person were to gain unimpeded access to these rambling, incoherent messages, I would be in a straitjacket.

Many of my ideas germinate from longform magazine articles. GQ, The Baffler, New Republic—I'm a junkie for them. Especially stories about people fighting back against, or suffering under, corporate abuses. The germination of Wayward Sons came from a mish-mash of articles about Big Pharma's manipulation of researchers, patent laws (if you're curious, research Allergan and the Saint Regis Mohawk tribe), and drug prices.

That last one—pricing—is a real trip. Big Pharma regularly participates in a practice the industry calls salami slicing. Briefly, salami slicing means placing diseases into smaller and more nebulous categories until the drug used to treat a particular cluster of symptoms is given orphan status. By federal law, once a drug achieves orphan status, the red tape is unwound and a drug which previously sold for twenty bucks now costs multiple thousands of dollars when used for its newly "discovered" treatment.

Salami slicing is profit-seeking of the worst kind, and is becoming increasingly popular among an industry setting new profit records every year—profits made from the desperation of the sick and dying, mind you. The practice is emblematic of an industry that cares little about its moral obligations in the face of leveraging as much gross income from people as possible.

DJ was a no-brainer for a plot that revolves around the strong exploiting the weak. He's untamed and idealistic. Getting him fired up over a little girl being poisoned by corporate malfeasance was easy. Jerry, with his backstory, was a little more complicated, but his willingness to leave behind a born-rich life to join the USAF, and later become a Newport Beach PD detective, evidenced a strong moral compass.

Given those elements, Wayward Sons sprouted in 2019 and grew over 2020.